COMPLETELY AND FOREVER

A WEDDING

Emmy's Story, Part 5

by
Kenneth Lee McGee

To My Wife and Family,
You Are Everything

I want to thank one person who has been a loyal and generous supporter of my attempts in creating this series of books. Andy Walker. Thank you for being my one-man PR team.

I want to thank the people from my church who have graciously allowed me to include fragments of their lives as inspirations.

Denise and Stephanie continue to share their expertise for which I am grateful.

Once again a special thanks to Sue Midlock for creating the cover. Check out her Facebook page 'Your Book Cover.'

I want to thank my wife Sheila for all the late nights reading my manuscripts when she could have been sleeping.

Prologue

Tony Bertucci drove his GMC Envoy to the house Emmy Colasanti shared with her best friend Kristen Keasling. He parked alongside the house, jumped out, ran around to the other side and opened the door for his mother.

"Thank you, son," she said as he helped her out of the tall vehicle.

Tony noticed the brightly colored leaves covering the yard and glanced up at the two tall trees lining the driveway.

"I love fall colors," Mama said.

"So do I, but I don't like raking all the leaves."

They walked to the front of the two-story red brick house, climbed the steps to the front door, and Tony knocked instead of walking right in.

Emmy ran down the hallway, unlocked the heavy door and opened it. "Too bad Kristen is at her parents," Emmy said as she let them in. "She loves Ciao Bella."

"Yeah, too bad." Tony put a finger under his collar and tried to stretch it out.

"I asked her to come with us, but she couldn't. Do you want to see the kitchen, Mama? We painted it."

"Maybe another time, sweetie," Mama said. "What do you think, son?"

Tony shifted his weight back and forth but didn't say anything.

"I didn't know you were going to wear a sport coat, tie and dress pants," Emmy said. "Do you want me to wear a dress?"

Tony shrugged and stuck his hand into his coat pocket, but he didn't reply.

"You look fine as you are, dear," Mama said with a smile as she noticed Emmy's jeans and white top. "Shall we go?"

"Absolutely! I'm starving." Emmy grabbed her purse and jacket.

Only when Emmy turned around, did Mama notice the braids in her hair and a piece of purple ribbon tied in a bow.

Tony dropped Mama and Emmy off at the door to Ciao

1

Bella and found a parking place only a block away. *That's a miracle.* He locked the car. *I'll take that as a sign of good fortune later. Thank you, Lord.* He hustled back to the restaurant and stood next to Emmy.

She reached for his hand and squeezed it. "Did you abandon the car?"

"You'd never believe where I parked," he said.

"Mrs. Bertucci, it's such a pleasure to see you again," Mr. Sabatino said as he kissed her hand. "I have a very special table for you tonight, Maria."

"Thank you, Enrico. How is Florentina tonight?"

"She is very busy, but I will tell her you are here. I'm sure she will want to talk to you."

He escorted them to a table right in the middle of his restaurant.

Tony looked around the crowded room and felt every eye in the place focus on him. Beads of sweat dotted his forehead.

Mama ran her hand along the burgundy tablecloth.

"The place is packed tonight," Emmy said as she placed the matching burgundy cloth napkin in her lap. "And Tony found a spot less than a block away. That's like a miracle for a Friday night in The Hill district."

"We were very fortunate." Mama caught a whiff of freshly baked focaccia bread as a waiter hurried out of the kitchen carrying a tray of several loaves.

Tony reached into his coat pocket. He could feel the small gift box containing the engagement ring. His collar tightened until he thought he would choke.

"Do you have a taste for anything special, Tony?" Emmy asked as she perused the leather-bound menu.

Tony drained his glass of water as soon as the waiter filled it. "I'll probably just order some chicken."

Mama listened to the subdued conversations of the surrounding tables. Tony checked his fingernails for the fifteenth time. Emmy listened to the piano player in the far corner. *Hey! That's a Fridays At Five tune.* She hummed along to the melody.

Several times Tony started to pull out the ring, but

something always stopped him. First, a waiter came by to take their drink order. Tony used a napkin to wipe the sweat off of his forehead. Another time the server brought their salads. Tony wiped his sweaty hands on his pant legs. Two more times Tony was interrupted as he attempted to pull the gift box out of his pocket. Tony stuck his finger in his collar as it tightened even more. Finally, they finished eating dinner. Tony waved for the check, picked up his water glass and took a sip.

"Are you all right, Tony? You look like you're about to be sentenced to life in jail," Emmy joked.

Tony nearly choked on a sip of water. "I'm okay. I want to ask you something important, really important."

"Okay. What is it, Tony?"

"Emmy, would you..."

Just then a waiter stopped by to collect the empty plates. Emmy smiled at Tony while Tony glared at the waiter.

"What do you want to ask me, Tony?" Emmy wiped a piece of tiramasu from his cheek.

Tony asked, "Would you..." He looked around to spot the waiter.

The waiter walked into the kitchen.

Tony turned back to Emmy. "Would you be..." He stopped as another waiter picked up the check.

"Yes, Tony. Would I what?"

Tony felt beads of sweat roll down his forehead and face.

Emmy smiled.

Tony's throat became as dry as the Sahara desert.

Mama nodded.

Tony's heart raced.

Emmy licked her lips.

Mama closed her eyes and prayed.

Tony blurted out, "Did you like the ravioli tonight?"

"Yes, I love the way they make their ravioli," Emmy answered.

Mama sighed. *This isn't going to work.*

"That's good. I liked the chicken tonight." He tried to coax a few drops of water from his glass.

Mama tapped Tony's arm. She realized what was supposed to happen would not happen in the restaurant. "We should be going, Tony. I want to stop at Emmy's before you take me home. I want to see how the kitchen looks."

"Okay, Mama." Tony sighed with relief as he wiped the sweat off of his brow.

Tony took Mama and Emmy back to her house.

"Kristen picked the color," Emmy explained. "I didn't want a yellow kitchen at first, but I kinda like it now."

"It looks very bright and almost like sunshine," Mama said as she touched the wall.

"Should we go sit down?" Emmy asked.

Tony nodded.

They went into the living room and Mama and Emmy sat on the couch. Tony paced back and forth while wringing his hands.

"What is wrong, Tony?" Emmy reached out to grab his arm as he walked past her. "You're acting like there's something on your mind. Did you have a bad day at practice?"

"No, practice went all right, and we actually got out early." Tony paused his pacing.

Mama smiled at Tony, nodded and whispered, "Go ahead, son."

Tony took a deep breath, looked at Mama and then reached into his pocket as he dropped to one knee. He pulled out the red velvet gift box and opened it. Emmy gasped and then held her breath. He looked at Emmy. She looked at the ring, and then at Tony. An image of a three-year-old boy flashed into her mind. Tony gazed into Emmy's blue eyes as they glistened and sparkled. Emmy covered her heart with her hands.

Chapter One

"Emily Olivia Colasanti, will you do me the honor of becoming my wife? I love you more than anything, and I want to marry you. Will you have me?"

"Oh, my God!" Emmy had tears rolling down her face as she looked at Tony and then at Mama. *Oh, no. What have I done?* She paused for a moment trying to think of something to say, but the right words wouldn't come.

Tony held out the ring and looked at Emmy.

Mama closed her eyes and touched her wedding band.

"I'm sorry, Tony, but I can't marry you," Emmy whispered.

Those words drifted through the air for an eternity before fading away. The only sound in the room was the ticking of the clock on the wall. No one moved, or dared to even breathe.

Emmy bit her lip and closed her eyes. *This is all my fault. I knew what happened that night was wrong, and I should have told him. I never thought he would buy a ring. Everyone is going to hate me now, and I don't blame them. How am I going to salvage our friendship? God, please help me. Tell me what to say.*

Mama felt her heart skip a beat. She knew how much this answer would hurt her son. She reached for the box of tissues on the end table. She took one and handed the box to Emmy.

Emmy opened her eyes and took a tissue, and then another, and then another. "Oh, Mama, I'm so sorry. This is all my fault."

Mama patted Emmy's hand. Emmy turned her attention back to Tony.

"I know I said something different that night in the car, but that was just the heat of the moment. I still love Kenny, and I will wait for him to marry me."

Tony lowered his head as he knelt in front of Emmy. He didn't say anything for a moment as he stared at the floor. He didn't have the strength to look up.

After what felt like hours, he raised his head. "Has he asked you to marry him, yet?"

Emmy still sat on the couch with her feet tucked under her. "Not in so many words. Not the way you just did. I thought he was going to before he went out to LA, but he didn't."

Tony recovered from the shock of her answer, forced a smile and said, "So, there is a chance he might never ask you. I know this sounds crazy, but maybe if you tell him I proposed, it might encourage him to do the same." He stood up and thought, *I feel as weak as Grandpa now. I must have aged fifty years in the last minute.* He gazed at the ring for a moment, snapped the jewel box shut and stuck it back in his pocket. "I guess what I mean is I want you to be happy, Em. I was hoping you had finally decided to stay with me. I know it hasn't been easy for you. We fight a lot and there is always something coming between us. I do know that when we are together, and not fighting, we are good for each other."

"I know we are. We've had a lot of good times together, but I feel we are better off just being friends. I know I used to get upset when you treated me like a little sister, or a cousin like Kristen, but now I feel that's the way it should be. We get along so much better when we are just friends. I like the way you tease me."

"Well, I guess I should have listened to Kristen. She told me I was crazy to do this..."

"No!" Emmy jumped up and stood in front of him. She took his arm and held it tenderly. "It's my fault, Tony. Would you have proposed if I hadn't said what I did in the car that night?"

Mama glanced up at Emmy.

"Not now, anyway. Maybe at some point in the future."

"It's my fault. I'm sorry about what happened that night." Emmy pulled Tony to the couch. She sat between him and Mama. "I know we both got a little excited." Emmy bit her lip, and looked at Mama before continuing. "We were in the backseat and things got a little out of control. It was totally my fault. I really screwed up."

"That sometimes happens, Emmy," Mama said without judging.

"I feel like a real... pardon my French... but a real ass now. I won't blame you if you never want to see me again. I know you won't want to still be my friend." Emmy sobbed and Tony placed an arm around her shoulders.

6

"I will still love you, and, if all we are going to be is friends, then I will be the best friend possible. If Kenny doesn't propose soon, I will tackle him and twist his arm."

Emmy looked at Tony and grinned even as tears flowed down her cheeks. "Will you make sure you don't break his arm because he needs them to play guitar? Maybe you could bust his kneecap instead."

"Whatever it takes, Em!"

Just then Kristen Keasling walked in the back door, through the kitchen and dining room and on into the living room. She took one look at Tony and Emmy and knew he had already popped the question. She looked at Mama. Mama shook her head.

Kristen started to cry as she walked over to Tony and Emmy. Tony jumped up from the couch, hugged her and said, "It's all right, Krissy. You were right. I should have listened to you."

Emmy stood up and started to cry again, too. "I'm sorry, Krissy, but I can't say yes. It wouldn't be right. You know Tony wants to have kids and since I can't, it wouldn't be right."

Tony looked at Emmy and then at Mama. "What do you mean? Why can't you have kids?"

Mama told Tony, "Emmy's doctor told her it would take a miracle for her to ever have a baby."

"Emmy, if that's the only reason you said no, then please think about it. We could always adopt kids, or maybe God will provide a miracle."

"That's not the only reason, Tony. I'm sorry I never told you about this before. Maybe if I had you would have never asked me to marry you."

"Does Kenny know?" Tony asked.

"Yes, he knows, and he feels the same way you do. He would be willing to adopt kids at some point if we weren't successful in having our own baby."

Mama used the arm of the couch to help her stand. "Maybe you should take me home now, son."

Emmy looked at Tony and asked, "What will you do with the ring? Can you take it back?"

"I don't think I can return it. I would be too embarrassed to even try. I think I'll keep it for now. Who knows? I might need it in a few years."

He managed to smile and Emmy kissed his cheek as they hugged.

"I'll walk out to the car with you, Mama." Kristen held Mama's arm as they walked outside. "I should have tried harder to stop him. I'm so sorry."

"I don't think you could have done anything, dear. He can be kinda determined once he sets out to do something."

Emmy walked to the door with Tony. "Now I know why you were so nervous at the restaurant tonight. Were you going to propose there?"

"I was trying to, but I kept getting interrupted by those pesky waiters." He recalled how four times he started to propose, but couldn't. "Maybe in a few years we will both look back at this night and appreciate the humor. Right now it just kinda hurts, Em."

Later, Emmy and Kristen sat on the couch in the living room to talk.

"Do you hate me now, Krissy?" Emmy asked as she twisted her long, dark curly hair around her fingers.

"Of course not. You have to do what your heart tells you. I tried to talk him out of buying a ring, but he seemed so determined and sure of what your answer would be."

"I feel so awful, but I can't say yes just because he asked and bought a ring."

"I know. It may take him some time, but he'll get over this. At least no one else knows. I don't think he even told John."

"I need to talk to Kenny and tell him what happened."

"Are you going to tell him because you hope it will encourage him to propose or what?" Kristen raised her voice a couple of decibels.

"No, nothing like that. I just need to talk to him, and I can't keep this a secret. I have to tell him." She closed her eyes. *I'll have to tell him about that night, too. That's what started this whole mess.*

"Maybe it will shake him up enough that he will realize he better get his act together. I thought you told me he was going to propose back in February."

"I thought he was going to, but he didn't. That doesn't mean he never will."

"I don't suppose I need to ask this, but I will anyway." Kristen paused as she looked into Emmy's eyes. "If Kenny asks, will you say yes?"

Emmy smiled. "You know I will."

Emmy knew Kenny was in the middle of a show and his cousin and guitar tech, Frankie Hanna, probably had his cell phone. Kenny always gave it to him so he could check for any important matters or emergencies while Kenny was busy entertaining the crowd. Emmy sent Kenny a text asking him to call ASAPAS—as soon as possible after show. This way Frankie knew it was not an emergency, but something important. He was on stage when the text message arrived. Frankie saw that Emmy had sent a text and opened it.

"Hi, Frankie, please ask Kenny to call ASAPAS. Have a good show."

When Frankie handed Kenny his guitar for the next song, he passed along the message.

"Call Emmy after the show. Something important, but not an emergency."

"Thanks, Frankie. Did she say what it was about?"

"Not really." Frankie was a man of few words.

Kenny finished the show and the encores and the band headed to their dressing rooms. They would have a few minutes of privacy to chill out and clean up before they met some of the fans. Kenny called Emmy right away.

"Hey, Emmy, what's up?"

"How was the show?"

"Good. We had a full house, and the crowd was really energized. I love doing shows like tonight. What's up? I know there's something on your mind."

Emmy bit her lip and decided to just tell him. "Tony proposed to me tonight. He asked me to marry him."

Kenny was stunned. His legs gave out and he fell back onto the couch. He was quiet for a few seconds.

9

"Kenny... Kenny... Are you still there?"

"Em, I don't know what to say. I'm really speechless."

"So was I! He took Mama and me out to Ciao Bella for dinner. Then we came back here because Mama wanted to see the kitchen. Krissy and I painted it. Then we went into the living room, and he started pacing back and forth. I asked him what was wrong, and he got down on his knee and proposed. It was so sweet and romantic. He had a ring and everything."

Tears filled Kenny's eyes as he told her, "That's...that's..."

"Oh, Kenny!" Now Emmy started to cry and neither of them said anything.

Finally, Emmy regained her composure enough to say, "I said no. I started crying, and I told him I couldn't marry him."

"You said no?" Kenny asked softly.

"Yes."

"I'm getting confused. Did you say yes to his proposal or yes you said no?"

Emmy giggled before saying, "I told Tony I couldn't marry him because I love you. I told him I would wait until you ask me to marry you."

"You're not gonna marry Tony?" Kenny realized and a smile gradually formed.

"No, I love *you*. I know I love Tony, too, but not the same. I want to be his friend forever, but I want to share my life with you."

"Oh, Em. I want to spend my life with you, too..."

"Don't you dare ask me to marry you over the phone. If you are going to propose, and I'm not putting any pressure on you, but if you ever propose to me... again..."

"That's right. I did ask you to marry me once before."

"Yeah, right in the middle of an argument. The next time you propose you better do it right. I want it to be romantic just the way Tony did it."

"Should I take you to dinner with Mama and Tony and..."

Emmy interrupted with a giggle. "Yes, and I want Kristen to be there and your parents and maybe our grandmothers and..."

"I get the picture, Em. Should I rent the SoHam stadium and invite the whole city?"

"Now you're just teasing me."

"How did Tony react? You didn't tell me."

"I think he was shocked because he didn't say anything at first, but then he recovered and told me he wanted me to be happy. I guess it's a good thing Tony and I never... slept together. Maybe God was watching over us even back then. I know it's weird, but I can't imagine my life without Tony as my friend."

"Did you get to see the ring? Was it nice?"

"I just saw it for a brief second. It looked nice, I guess. I hope he didn't pay a lot of money for it."

"Maybe he'll be able to sell it or return it."

"I told him I can't have a baby. I never told him that before. Maybe if I had, he never would have proposed. I know he wants to have a family."

"I want to have a family, too. Not like right now, but sometime and if that means adopting, then that's what we will do."

Emmy was quiet for a moment.

"Are you still there, Em?"

"Yeah, I was just thinking about the game on Sunday. Maybe I shouldn't go to any more of his games."

"Why not? You are still his friend and you love football."

"You won't mind if I still go?"

"I think you should go. Maybe when I get home, I can go to another game. I had fun the first time we went."

"I'm sure he could get us tickets. It is exciting to watch him play."

"I gotta go, Em. We've got to meet some fans. I'll call you later tonight or maybe tomorrow."

"Night, Kenny. I love you."

Kenny stared at his phone after Emmy hung up. He closed his eyes and prayed silently.

Thank you, Lord, for this wake up call. I know now it is truly your will that Emmy and I are together. I don't know why it's taken me so long to realize it. I'll get my act together now, I promise.

Chapter Two

"Are we still planning to go to Tony's games?" Emmy asked Kristen the next evening as they ate dinner in the TV room. "Tony might not want me to be there after last night."

"Well, I want to go. You do realize that John is still on the team, right? John Randolph. The guy I'm dating who plays tight end."

"I know who you mean, Kristen. Do you think Tony will mind if I go to the games? Kenny said I should go."

"You can be such a goof at times." Kristen pointed her fork at Emmy with a piece of chicken breast attached. "Just because you and Tony aren't going to get married doesn't mean you won't be friends. I know for a fact he wants you to come to the games."

"Did he tell you?"

"No, he wrote me a letter," Kristen teased. "I'll bet he will still like to tease you."

"Yes, and he'll try to hang me from the ceiling again."

Emmy sat quietly for a few minutes.

"Okay. Spill it. What's going on in that weird mind of yours?" Kristen asked as she finished her chicken and wiped her mouth with a napkin.

"I still feel like a total ass for what I did."

"Are you talking about that night in the backseat of his Envoy? If so, I agree with you."

"I didn't mean to let it go so far. We just kinda let our physical needs overwhelm our..."

"Brains," Kristen interrupted.

"At least we stopped before... you know."

"No, I don't know. You've never told me, and I didn't want to hear it from Tony. Why did you stop, anyway?"

"We were interrupted by campus security. It was so embarrassing. I wanted to die." Emmy shuddered as she thought about that night.

"Yeah, I can picture that." Kristen put her plate on the end table. "What on earth ever possessed you to do that in the parking lot?"

Emmy bit her lip, shrugged and said, "Hormones, I guess."

"Not funny!"

"Did he say anything about the next day?" Emmy dropped her sandwich on the floor. "Five second rule!" she hollered.

"Gross!"

"The floor's clean."

"So, what about the next day?" Kristen muted the TV and then looked at Emmy.

Emmy scooted to the other end of the couch, out of Kristen's reach. "I went over to his house..."

Kristen put her hands over her ears. "La la la," she began singing.

"Do you want to hear this or not?" Emmy dropped her sandwich again. She lunged forward, grabbed Kristen's hand and pulled it away from her ear.

"Not if it's what I think it is."

"I went over there and Mama wasn't home. Tony and I kissed a bit and then went up to his room."

"You're supposed to know better, Emmy. Did he at least use protection? Oh, probably not since you can't have any babies," Kristen said sarcastically.

"He didn't need protection since we didn't go all the way." Emmy made air quotes. "We did something else."

"La la la," Kristen sang loudly as she covered her ears.

Emmy jumped up and stepped on her sandwich. "Fine! Be that way. I'm going to bed, and I'm never talking to you again."

"Get back here. I'll listen." Kristen grabbed Emmy's arm.

Emmy picked up her sandwich. She still wanted to eat it, but didn't dare because of the look in Kristen's eyes. "After we... finished he talked about maybe getting married. I assumed he was kidding because it was kind of awkward."

Kristen glared at Emmy.

"What? Was everything perfect when you and Ryan... oh, never mind. I feel I led him on, and that's why he bought the ring."

"I think you did lead him on, and you should have known better, but we can't change the past. I wish you would have told me what you guys were doing."

13

"I'm sorry, but I just couldn't. I was too embarrassed."

"I told you about the night I spent with Ryan, but you've never confided in me about your relationship with Kenny the same way."

Emmy lowered her eyes to the floor. "I've told you some stuff."

"Oh, Em, it's all right. I still love you," Kristen said as she stretched out her arms.

Emmy embraced Kristen. "I want us to be best friends forever."

Tony Bertucci became a starter and an immediate fan favorite in his first year with the Bears. The loss to Atlanta in the second week of the season disappointed him. He felt it was a game they should have won. The Bears played the New Orleans Saints in Soldier Field the third week of the season. Emmy and Kristen brought Mama and Kristen's father, Daniel Keasling to the game. The temperature at kickoff was a balmy fifty-nine degrees with sunny skies and a light breeze from the north. This was only the second game Mama had watched in person since Tony played at Jamie McGee Junior High.

"Tony, score a touchdown," Mama yelled as she held tightly onto her rosary.

"Mama, Tony plays defense, and they don't score touchdowns as often as the offense. It is unlikely Tony will score a touchdown today," Emmy explained.

"You just need to have faith, Emmy. I'm sure he will score a touchdown today," Mama insisted.

Sure enough, late in the fourth quarter, Tony intercepted a pass and ran it in for a score to increase the Bear's lead to eleven.

Mama looked at Emmy and smiled. "I told you he would score a touchdown. I just didn't think it would take him this long."

Emmy and Kristen looked at each other and then at Mr. Keasling. They rolled their eyes and shrugged. Daniel didn't show any reaction. He knew better than to ever doubt Mama Bertucci.

After the game, which the Bears won 28-17, Mama felt emotionally drained and told Emmy and Kristen, "I am worn out. I

14

worked harder than the players. I'm too old for this much excitement. I think I should stay home in the future."

"Maybe you can watch the games on TV, Mama."

"That would be easier. I could turn off the sound and just watch the picture."

Emmy and Kristen shrugged... again.

Since Emmy and Kristen were planning to attend all the home games, they would miss church a few Sundays.

"Do you think Pastor Hillman will be upset that we are going to miss a few Sundays?" Kristen asked on Monday evening. *I have to remember that he likes to be called Chase.*

"I think he will understand. I hope he does." Emmy checked the Bear's schedule. "Hey! There is a Monday night game. That means we will only miss five weeks."

"We are going to sing on the other Sundays, right?"

"Are you sure you still want to sing?" Emmy knew the answer.

"I like singing with you, Em. I'm not sure I would do it if you quit."

"We should tell Chase at practice this Thursday." Emmy opened the fridge and pulled out some leftover mac and cheese. "You have to help me tell him."

On Wednesday evening as Emmy cleared the dishes from the dining room table, she asked Kristen for a favor. "I need to go see my parents. Would you come with me? They've always liked you, and you seem to know how to get along with my mother better than I do. Please, come with me."

"Do you mean right now?"

"Yeah, this is my only chance to go over there this week."

"Okay, I'll go, but it'll cost you," Kristen said.

Emmy hadn't been to her parents' house for almost two months—since August eleventh. Her parents had told each other in front of Emmy that they were sorry they ever had kids. It upset Emmy so much that she had gotten sick. Emmy felt she could never visit her parents without them arguing about something.

15

As they sat at a stoplight, Emmy told Kristen, "I used to fight with Mom about the silliest things. I would get so frustrated with her because she always let Diane get away with more than me. Now I don't let it bother me as much."

"You are becoming more mature about your relationship with your mother. It will become easier as you get older."

"I don't know about that." Emmy glanced at Kristen with an uncertain look on her face. "I don't know if it will ever get easier. I'm afraid we will just grow farther and farther apart. By the time I'm forty, Mom will be almost eighty."

"I get along with my mother better than ever," Kristen said.

"You and your mother are a lot closer in age. That's part of why you get along," Emmy said. "I've never told you, but sometimes I would hang out with some kids who got into trouble. Everyone always assumes I always behaved like an angel, but I didn't. I did some things that I'm not proud of."

"What kind of things did you do? I have a hard time ever imagining you as a rebellious teenager." Kristen looked up. "By the way, that light won't get any greener."

Emmy checked the rearview mirror. Thankfully there wasn't anyone behind her. "It all happened before I met you. I would sneak off with Rory Porter and some of his friends. They were into smoking and drinking... and sex."

"Please tell me you didn't smoke." Kristen poked Emmy's arm. "I know you didn't fool around. You didn't, did you?"

"No, but I did drink beer with them at times. I wanted to get back at my mom. I never drank too much. I didn't get drunk like the other kids. I certainly didn't want to end up like Daddy."

"Sorry, but I have a hard time picturing you as a bad girl."

"Sometimes the quiet ones are the worst," Emmy said as she bit her lip. "I kinda went from not knowing anything about sex to knowing a lot in a hurry."

"Stop the car and pull over there!" Kristen pointed to a spot.

"Why?" Emmy turned the corner without stopping.

"Will you pull over? I need to talk to you," Kristen yelled as she pointed to the curb.

Emmy stopped. "What?"

"Care to explain that last statement?" Kristen frowned.

"What? What did I say?"

Kristen repeated Emmy's statement.

"Did I ever tell you about the night Diane told me about her and Craig going all the way?" Emmy asked.

"Yeah, kinda."

"Well, before that I didn't know much about sex. Diane explained some stuff. I never learned anything about sex from my mother."

"So, after that you knew everything," Kristen said sarcastically.

"Not exactly." Emmy hung her head and didn't say anything for a few seconds.

"Tell me before I smack you. Just what did you 'learn' from Rory and his friends?"

"I sorta learned how to make out and stuff."

"Oh, my God! Did you make out with him? How far did it go?"

Emmy shook her head. "I didn't make out with anyone. I watched."

"You did what?" Kristen shouted.

"The other kids were all older and they would make out and... you know."

"So, you were like an observer just taking it all in so you would know what to do."

"Kinda, yeah. I always went to these parties with Rory, but I never kissed him. He had older girlfriends that he would mess around with."

"I don't even want to hear what the older kids did." Kristen closed her eyes and put her hands over her ears. Then she quickly opened her eyes and removed her hands. "Did you watch them having sex?"

"No! No way!" Emmy shook her head for emphasis. "Some of the girls might have done that later in private, but these parties were always outside."

"So, you didn't learn about sex at these parties?"

17

"No one ever touched me. I guess they were afraid because I was so young. Rory never let me drink more than two beers."

"Oh, that was mighty decent of him. Making sure a fourteen-year-old child never drank more than two beers." Kristen's sarcasm was as sharp as a razor. "I suppose everyone has some secrets. Did you ever tell Kenny about this stuff?"

"Yeah, he knows, but he still loves me. God forgave me for all this stuff, so I don't like to think about it."

"I won't bring it up again." Kristen squeezed Emmy's hand. "Now let's go face your parents." Kristen pointed down the street.

Emmy had come to love her parents more than ever since accepting Jesus—at least she became more tolerant. Today she and her mother entered into a discussion about politics. Usually, Emmy didn't care about politics, but one certain candidate upset her. Emmy paced around the living room as she ranted and raved—waving her hands all around. Finally, Kristen grabbed her hands and held them still to keep her quiet.

Kristen laughed and told Emmy's mom, "Works every time. If I want her to be quiet, all I have to do is grab her hands and she can't talk. Must be an Italian thing." Kristen pulled Emmy to the couch.

Her mom and dad laughed, but Emmy scowled at Kristen until she released her hands. Emmy looked at her mother and decided to mention Tony's proposal.

"Last Friday Tony asked me to marry him."

"He did? Why have you waited so long to tell us?" Mom sat upright in her recliner. Dad lowered his newspaper to listen.

"Mom..."

"You could have told us on the weekend. Are we the last to know?"

"Mom, will you let me..."

"Have you decided on a church yet? I saw Mrs. Sanders at St. John's a couple of days ago. It was bingo night. That would be a nice church for your wedding."

"Mom, you didn't let me finish." Emmy looked to Kristen for help.

"Do you know where you are going to have the reception? I

could check about the V.F.W. It would be pretty cheap. If you expect your father and me to pay for this wedding reception, it will have to be somewhere like the V.F.W. We can't afford much."

"I've never expected you and Daddy to pay for my wedding or reception."

"Are you pregnant, Emily? If you are, it's all right, but maybe you should move the date up."

"Mom!"

Mom couldn't shake the idea that the only reason girls got married was because they were pregnant. It was why she and her other daughter, Diane, got married. Emmy started to cry.

"It's all right, Emmy. Lots of girls are pregnant when they get married."

Emmy stopped crying. She stood up, stomped her foot and raised her voice, "I'm not pregnant, Mother. You didn't let me finish. Will you just listen for a second?"

"Fine. I'll be quiet. What else do you have to tell us?"

"I told Tony I couldn't marry him because I want to marry Kenny."

Dad finally spoke up, "Do you even know who the father is, Emily? The doctors can do a test to find out whose baby it is if you're not sure."

Emmy looked at Kristen again for help.

Kristen explained, "Emmy isn't pregnant. Tony misread the situation and proposed to her. She said no because she is in love with Kenny Colwell."

"Did he propose, too?" Mom asked. "I'm getting confused."

"Not yet, Mom."

"What if he never does? He's certainly known you long enough. Maybe he just thinks of you as a friend even if you guys sleep together."

Emmy glanced at Kristen as her mother continued.

"Maybe you should think about this some more. Do you still love Tony? I know you were in love with him before, but you guys always argued about something. Lots of couples argue. Sometimes couples need the strife." She looked at her husband.

"I still love Tony, but I can't see myself spending my life

19

with him as his wife. It would drive me crazy to be always arguing the way you guys do."

"We are getting along better now that your father isn't drinking as much."

"Have you been to see your doctor lately? You should have a checkup before you get married," Dad said.

Emmy said a quick silent prayer asking for patience as her mother and father continued to ask questions about the proposal for the better part of an hour.

"We gotta go, Mom. I'll talk to you soon, I love you. Bye, Dad."

Her father got up and slowly made his way to the front door. Emmy hugged him and whispered, "I love you, Dad, and so does Jesus."

"I love you, too, Emmy. Take care of yourself. Are you sure about this?"

"Yes, Daddy. I know I'm in love with Kenny, and it's the right choice not to marry Tony."

"And you aren't...?"

"No, Daddy, I'm not."

"Good. Getting married is hard enough. Having to deal with a baby makes it worse."

Halfway down the sidewalk Emmy stopped and grabbed Kristen's arm. "Hey, I just realized, Mom and Dad didn't argue with each other while we were here."

"You're right. They didn't. Maybe they're trying something new," Kristen said.

"I don't know. Maybe they were just waiting till after we left." Emmy seized Kristen's other arm and shook her. "Or maybe the counseling has made a difference."

"Okay, Em. Relax. You're hurting me."

Mrs. Colasanti watched Emmy and Kristen as they walked to the car. She hollered over her shoulder, "I still think she should say yes to Tony until she can figure out who the father is."

"Patricia! She said she isn't expecting." Mr. Colasanti opened the fridge. "Why can't you believe her?" He opened a beer and then walked back to the living room.

"I guess because that old cliché is true."

"What are you talking about?"

"The one about the apple never falling far from the tree."

Once in the car Kristen looked at Emmy, and they both started to laugh.

"I guess laughing is better than crying right now," Emmy said.

"I suppose so, but maybe you should see a doctor. They can run tests so you know who the father really is," Kristen said as she teased Emmy.

"Are you gonna start with that now, too?"

"It would have been easier not to mention anything at all, you know."

"Hindsight is always twenty-twenty." Emmy pulled away from the curb. "Maybe I better pee on another stick."

Kristen stared, but didn't say anything.

"I'm kidding! You know my periods are always late."

On the way home Emmy and Kristen stopped at a gas station to fill up the tank.

"I'm gonna run inside to grab a snack. Want anything?" Emmy asked.

"I'll take a Coke, I guess. Thanks, Em. Don't worry I'll figure out this pump. Eventually." Kristen found the slot for her credit card. "Oh, here it is."

As Emmy grabbed two Cokes, she saw somebody from her past.

"Hello, Mrs. Porter."

At first Mrs. Porter didn't recognize her, but then she remembered Emmy as the girl who lived down the street. "Emily, right? Emily Colasanti. I haven't seen you in so many years. Let me look at you. My, you're all grown up. I can't remember, but weren't you just a couple years younger than Amy?"

"Actually, Mrs. Porter. Oh, never mind, it doesn't matter." *I'm actually two years older than Amy.*

Kristen came inside to pay for the snacks and saw Emmy talking with a lady. She walked over and stood beside her.

"This is my friend and roommate, Kristen Keasling. This is

21

Mrs. Porter. She's Rory's mom. They lived just up the street from our house when I was a kid."

"It's nice to meet you, Mrs. Porter," Kristen said as she thought, *What a coincidence! We were just talking about Rory.*

Emmy grabbed a bag of chips despite Kristen's frown. "How are your kids? I haven't seen them for years."

"I have bad news to tell you," Mrs. Porter said and then sighed. "Owen moved to Arkansas and was killed there in a car accident two years ago."

"Oh, I'm sorry." Emmy put the chips back on the shelf and grabbed some cookies instead. "Wait! What did you say?"

Mrs. Porter repeated the news as Kristen frowned and took the cookies from Emmy.

"I am really sorry," Emmy said. She didn't know whether to hug Mrs. Porter or not.

"It was his own fault. He was drunk and hit a tree."

"What about Rory, Mrs. Porter?" Kristen asked. "Emmy used to hang out with him."

Emmy poked Kristen in the side.

"Oh, right. I forgot about that. Rory married a girl from high school 'cause he got her knocked up. He lives in Georgia and has a decent job, and he's really settled down. He loves his kid and is a good father. He even takes the family to church every Sunday. I haven't seen him for a couple of years. Not since the funeral."

Emmy whispered to Kristen, "I told you about Rory and me, but his mother never knew."

"You're lucky that didn't happen to you, Emily, since you used to sneak out to those parties with him," Mrs. Porter said.

Emmy stood still and turned bright red.

"Amy has two kids, but she's divorced. She lives with me. I moved out of that big house down the street from you and found a smaller place. Now with Amy and her kids, I wish I could have kept the big house."

Emmy felt so sorry for Mrs. Porter because her life had been rather difficult. Although she had resented the way Owen and Rory treated her when they were younger, Emmy never would have wished them any harm or misfortune. *Maybe I should try to*

22

reconnect with Rory. He really did try to protect me from the older kids.

"It was nice to see you again, Mrs. Porter. Please say hello to Amy for me, and if you ever talk to Rory, please tell him I said hi."

Kristen listened to their conversation, and back in the car Emmy told her more about Owen, Rory and Amy.

"So, Owen tried to kiss you, but you didn't let him because he smoked. Diane had an affair with him. You used to hang out with Rory who had a thing for Diane."

"I never kissed him, either." Emmy held up her hand as Kristen raised her eyebrows. "I swear I didn't. I drank beer with him, but nothing else."

"Amy was the goth girl I saw at the dance the night we first met."

"Yep! That about covers it."

Kristen laughed. "You should have seen your face when Mrs. Porter mentioned you sneaking out with Rory."

"I never thought she knew anything about that. She always appeared to be oblivious to what Owen and Rory did."

"I guess she knew more than you thought."

Kristen understood Emmy's feelings of sadness. Though Emmy didn't have any feelings of friendship for those kids, they were part of her past.

Emmy prayed silently. *Dear, Lord, would you please keep an eye on Mrs. Porter and Amy. They've kinda had a rough life and could use Your guidance. I'm so glad to hear Rory has changed and is even going to church. Although, he and I kinda did some bad things when I was a kid, he was like a protector in a way. I guess this just proves no one is ever too rotten of a person and Your love can change the hardest of hearts. Amen.* Emmy opened her eyes.

"Can we go now?" Kristen asked.

"I was praying for them," Emmy said quietly.

"I know you were. You're so good about doing that. I should try to pray more often. I guess I'm too busy with all the stuff that goes on in our daily routine."

Later that night, Kenny called and talked to Emmy for over an hour. They talked about everything under the sun except for Tony's proposal. Kenny avoided all talk about marriage or the future. Emmy wondered if he was changing his mind about her.

On Thursday evening before worship band practice, Emmy and Kristen saw Yvonne Hillman in the hall outside of the music suite.

"Hi, Yvonne, how are Anna and Jada doing?" Emmy saw the two young Hillman daughters running down the hall toward the children's classroom.

Yvonne replied, "As you can see they are full of energy. Did you run around church like that when you were that age?"

Emmy bit her lip. "We didn't really go to church when I was a kid."

Yvonne hugged Emmy. "Oh, Emmy, I'm sorry. I should have remembered that."

"Is Chase in his office?" Kristen asked. "We have some bad news for him."

"Or maybe it's good news," Emmy said. "Is he in a good mood?"

"He's in his office, and I think I know what you are going to tell him. It's about football season, right?" Yvonne moved out of the way as several more kids ran through the hall.

"Yeah, we'll talk to you later."

Emmy knocked even though the door to Chase's inner office was open.

"Come on in, ladies." He waved as he looked at his computer monitor.

"We have to talk about football," Emmy blurted out.

"I sorta guessed you might." Chase pointed to the chairs in front of his desk.

"I checked the schedule and made a list of the days we will be gone. I hope it's okay that we will miss a few Sundays." She handed Chase the list.

As he looked it over, he shook his head and muttered, "Oh, no. Oh, my."

24

"I'm sorry, Chase. Maybe we won't go to all the games," Kristen said.

He smiled, and Emmy knew they had been had. "I think we will make it through somehow. I might have to lead worship again. It will be good actually. I will be able to shake off the rust. It's been so easy to just play and not have to lead the songs. You and Kristen can go to all the games. Maybe the Bears will make it to the Super Bowl. Are you going to be here this Sunday?"

"Yes, the Bears are in Buffalo this week."

"And I see they are playing the Packers the following week. That should be a good game."

"That's a Monday night game. We won't miss church that Sunday," Emmy said.

Chase tilted his head. "All right. I won't fire you ladies for missing a few services."

"Thanks, Chase. I know John really appreciates Kristen being at the games."

"What about Tony? Does he expect you to be at the games?"

Emmy had not mentioned Tony's proposal to anyone at church. Neither had Kristen nor Tony.

"He doesn't expect it, but I think he likes the fact I'm there. I took Kenny to the opening game, and he enjoyed it."

"When will he be home?" Chase checked the calendar.

"Not until December unless he surprises me. They don't have too many nights off this fall."

"Are they playing every night?"

"Not every night. They usually have Monday and Tuesday off, but it gets expensive to fly home all the time."

Kristen laughed then said, "I think he could probably buy his own jet, Em."

"Well, I hope he has a chance to surprise you sometime soon, Emmy," Chase said.

Chapter Three

John Randolph knocked on the back door of the Bertucci house and walked on in. "Hi, Mama, is he ready?"

Mama set down her dish towel and opened her arms for a hug. "He should be ready. Did you eat?"

"Yeah, but I could always eat more." John walked over to the stove. "You're not cooking anything. What's up?"

"You guys will be gone this weekend, so I'm going over to see Carmen and Sharon."

Tony walked into the kitchen carrying his large duffel bag and a garment bag containing his suit. "I'm ready." He kissed Mama on her cheek. "I'll be back on Sunday night. Say hi to Uncle Carmen and Aunt Sharon for me."

"You guys play hard and stay safe. John, you make sure you don't miss any blocks and don't drop any passes."

"I'll try, Mama."

Mama pointed a finger at Tony. "If you guys let Doug Bledsoe stand in the pocket all day without putting any pressure on him, I will be upset."

"Yes, Mama."

"If Donte Henry gains over a hundred yards, I won't cook for you all week," Mama warned Tony but then grinned. "Emmy told me to say that."

Tony and John looked at each other.

"All week?"

"Shoo! Get going so you won't be late." Mama chased them out of the kitchen.

The guys walked out the door and got in John's old truck.

"Do you think she was serious about not cooking? I noticed there wasn't anything on the stove now," John said as he backed out of the driveway.

"I don't know, but I'm not taking any chances. I'd rather have Coach yelling at me than to have Mama be mad and not cook."

"You are so spoiled. What will you do if you ever get married?" John asked and then laughed.

26

Tony and John left on Saturday for Halas Hall, the Bears team headquarters, in Deercreek Estates. The team would be flying into Buffalo for the game on Sunday. John turned right onto Larkin Road.

Tony looked out the window at the businesses lining the busy commercial street. *I didn't know Numark's Sporting Goods closed.*

"Hey! What's on your mind? You seem kinda in another place." John poked Tony in the arm.

"Can I talk to you about something personal?"

"Duh! You've told me everything for the last three years. What is it?" John thought for a moment. "Did you talk to Brenda again? Are you trying to get back together with her?"

"No, it wasn't Brenda."

John waited. "Are you gonna make me guess?"

"It's about me and Emmy."

"Emmy! I thought you guys were getting along all right. Sorta like cousins or however you put it."

"I kinda messed that up."

"I'm listening," John said.

"A while back I met Emmy after her night class. We went for a walk and to make a long..."

"Yeah, just get to the point." John kept his eyes on the road.

"We made out in the back of my Envoy. We sorta got carried away."

"You did Emmy? Are you nuts?"

"I am nuts, but we... stopped. I don't want to say why. Anyway, she said she wanted to marry me, so I bought a ring and asked her."

"You asked her...?"

"To marry me."

"Wait a second. If you guys were engaged, I would have heard about it. No way Emmy or Kristen could keep that a secret."

"She said no. Kristen tried to talk me out of it, and I should have listened to her, but I didn't."

"Aw, crap! I'm sorry about that."

"I'll get over it. I should have known better."

27

"You're too stubborn," John said. *You actually proposed to Emmy. I thought you might propose to Brenda out of guilt, but I'm glad you didn't.*

"One of these years I'll tell you about that night."

"The night you guys did it?" John looked surprised. "You don't have to tell me all the details about you and Emmy."

"No, not that night! I'll never tell anyone everything about that night. I meant the night I proposed. It really hurt at the time, but even now I'm starting to see it in a different way."

"Is this a religious thing?"

"Not totally, but I do believe God has His hand in the whole thing. I think Emmy and I are going to be even better friends because of what happened."

"I know you really love her. I could tell as soon as we met. You were always talking about her and Kristen." John paused. "Oh, I kinda get it now. I always assumed you loved Emmy like a girlfriend, but it wasn't always like that. I've never had a female friend who was just a friend. You know what I mean?"

"Yeah, I understand."

They rode along in silence for a few minutes.

"I'm assuming you don't ever want anyone else to know, right?" John asked.

"Yeah. I'd like to keep it under wraps."

Emmy and Kristen left church as soon as they could the next day.

"I know we're gonna miss the start of the game, but if we hurry, we can catch most of the first quarter," Emmy hollered as she ran to the car.

"Should I drive?" Kristen asked. "You might get pulled over again."

"I'll keep it down to ten miles over the limit, Krissy." Emmy jumped in the car and waited while Kristen talked to one of the ladies from the church. *Come On! We have to get home.*

Kristen got in the car and Emmy took off immediately. "Will you give me a chance to buckle my seatbelt? We aren't going to miss much of the game."

Emmy zipped out of the parking lot and zoomed through a yellow light. "Who were you talking to?"

"That's Mrs. Kochanek. She said she really liked the songs we did today."

They made it home without any trouble. Emmy parked in the long driveway and jumped out. "I'm gonna turn on the TV. I'll change clothes at halftime," Emmy hollered as she sprinted inside.

Kristen got out of the car and followed at a more leisurely pace. She paused in the kitchen to grab a bottle of water.

"Come on, slowpoke." Emmy smacked the couch and hollered. "Oh, crap!"

Kristen ran into the TV room. "What is it? Did something happen to John?" Kristen sat on the couch.

"He's all right, but the Bears are losing by ten points already."

"It's early. They have plenty of time to come back."

When Emmy ran upstairs to change, the score was tied at ten apiece. The Bears scored a touchdown on their opening possession of the second half.

"I knew they would come back, Em. They just have to throw the ball to the right guy." Kristen gloated because John had caught the TD pass.

The Bears upped their lead to ten on a field goal as the third quarter ended.

Emmy couldn't sit still as she watched. "Come on, Tony. You guys can do it. You just have to get some pressure on Bledsoe."

Buffalo took the ensuing kickoff and marched down the field. The Bears could not mount any pressure on the Bills quarterback and he used a short passing game to control the clock. A draw play up the middle surprised the Bears and Buffalo scored a touchdown.

"For heaven's sake, Tony. You know the Bills like to run draw plays twice a game," Emmy said as she shook her head.

"How do you know how many times they use a certain play?" Kristen asked.

"One of the announcers said so."

"See! You don't know as much about football as you make people believe."

"One thing I know for sure is they need to run some clock," Emmy said as the Bears started the next series on their twenty-six yard line.

After two first downs, the offense stalled and the Bears punted.

"I've got a bad feeling about this, Em. The momentum has shifted to Buffalo," Kristen said.

Emmy laughed. "Do you even know what that means?"

Kristen poked Emmy is the side. "Shut up, you stinker, I know enough about football to understand what it means."

The Bills marched down the field again and scored a go-ahead touchdown with just over two minutes remaining in the game.

"There's time!" Emmy had faith in the team. "They have two time-outs and the two-minute warning."

The Bears moved steadily down the field. With one minute left, they called their first time-out.

"Way to go, John!" Kristen yelled as John Randolph caught a pass over the middle for twenty yards to give the Bears a first down at midfield.

A pass up the seam on the right fell incomplete on the next play. On the next play, Bears' quarterback Bobby McMullen was sacked for a nine yard loss and the Bears used their final time-out.

"They have to be careful now because they can't stop the clock, right?" Kristen asked.

"They can stop it if they get a first down. They just have to spike the ball." Emmy made the motion the quarterback would need to do.

"I've seen them do that before. I always wondered why. Now I know." Kristen grinned.

"You knew that. Don't mess with me."

Any chance for a Bears' victory was squashed when McMullen's next pass was tipped by a linebacker and popped into the air. The Bills free safety intercepted it and all Buffalo had to do was run out the clock.

30

"That sucked," Emmy whined.

"Oh, Em, you take it so seriously. It's a long season. Who knows? They might win all the rest of their games."

When Tony returned home later that night, Mama was in the living room.

"Hi, Mama, I'm home."

"I'm sorry you lost, but at least that running back didn't gain over a hundred yards."

"I know. I was worried you wouldn't cook, so I made sure we kept him under control," Tony said.

Emmy hurried out to her car after class at North Park College on Thursday and tossed her backpack in the backseat.

"What's the big rush, Emmy? A bunch of us are going out for pizza. Wanna join us? We're going to Beggar's," one of her classmates asked.

"Thanks for the offer, but I can't. I've got ten minutes to get to worship band practice. Chase doesn't like for people to be late."

She parked in the side lot at church, dashed inside, sprinted down the hall, into the music suite and nearly ran over Yvonne Hillman. "I'm sorry if I'm late, but I have class on Thursday nights."

"Slow down, Emmy. You're not the last one here."

Emmy looked around. "Oh, I guess I didn't have to drive like a maniac."

Practice lasted for ninety minutes. Everyone left except for Chase, Kristen and Emmy. They stayed to help organize the music folders.

Chase put away the last file and said, "Thanks for your help. I appreciate it. I need to make a few calls."

"No problem," Kristen said as she took Emmy's arm. "If you're going to be here for a while, I need to talk to Emmy. We'll be in the coffee shop thing if you need us."

"Take your time. Someone will be in the building until midnight."

Kristen tried to pull Emmy out of the music suite, but she resisted.

31

"What's up? You know the coffee club is closed, right?"

"I know. I just thought that would be a good place to talk."

"We could go home and talk. I have some homework I should start." Emmy grabbed her jacket and looked around for her backpack.

"What are you looking for?" Kristen checked the room.

"My backpack. Did I have it with me?"

"I don't think so."

"Shoot! I know I didn't leave it at school," Emmy said and then bit her lip.

"Did you leave it in the car?"

"Yeah. I was in such a hurry to get here. I just forgot. It's got my papers for class. I would be lost without them."

"Yeah, you might get a B," Kristen teased.

They walked down the hall to the foyer. In the far corner was the "Coffee Club" as it had been recently renamed. They sat on a love seat in the corner.

"Now, what is so important that we can't discuss at home?" Emmy asked.

"The Bears are playing on Monday night..."

"Duh! I know that. Are you going to tell me you can't go?"

"No! Will you just listen for a minute?" *You can be such a brat at times.*

"Sorry, my lips are sealed." Emmy made a zipping motion as she put her feet under her.

Kristen shook her head. *Such a baby.* "Tony will be at church this Sunday." Kristen waited for a response, but Emmy zipped her lips again. "You guys haven't seen much of each other since that night. Will it upset you that he's here?"

"No, why should it? We're just friends now."

"Are you sure? You did almost have..."

"That was a mistake and is never going to be repeated." *Will I ever hear the end of this. I screwed up. Almost literally. I'm not perfect.*

"I'm concerned about you, Em."

"I know you are and I appreciate it. It won't bother me to see Tony in church. Just the opposite." She waved her hands. "If he

32

wasn't here, I would wonder why."

"I should have known that's how you would feel," Kristen said. "You don't hide your emotions at all. I would have been able to tell if something was bothering you."

"Can we go now?" Emmy asked. "I have homework."

"You can leave anytime you want. We drove separately, remember?"

"See you at home." Emmy jumped up and rushed out the door. *It totally slipped my mind that Tony would be here Sunday. I wonder if I will feel kinda funny about seeing him?*

"Are you going to eat any breakfast?" Kristen asked on Sunday morning. "I'm having a bagel and yogurt."

"I'm not very hungry," Emmy said as she grabbed a bottle of water from the fridge.

Kristen watched as Emmy braided the ends of her hair. "You're nervous about something and since you're never nervous about singing anymore, it must be because of Tony."

Emmy jumped up and sat on the kitchen counter. "I didn't even think about it until you mentioned it on Thursday. Now it's got me all worried. What if he doesn't want to be my friend anymore? What will I do?"

"I guess we will know pretty quick since he just pulled into the driveway."

"You didn't tell me he was picking us up." Emmy jumped down and smoothed out her skirt. "Do I look all right?"

Friends, huh? Kristen smoothed out a wrinkle in Emmy's skirt. "You look fine."

Tony knocked on the back door but then walked on in. He saw Emmy in the kitchen. "Hey, Emmy, are you ready to go?"

"We'll be right out," Emmy said abruptly.

"Oh, should I wait outside?" Tony caught the tone of her voice. *Geez! Is she going to be upset with me because of what happened that night? Maybe she's more embarrassed about it than I figured.*

"You can come on in, Tony," Kristen said as she frowned at Emmy. "Why would you be like that?"

33

"Sorry, Tony. I didn't know you were picking us up. You can come in."

He walked into the kitchen but waited at the end of the counter closest to the door. "If you don't have any plans, Mama would like for you guys to come over for lunch."

Emmy looked around the room. "Who do you mean? Who are you talking to? Kristen, do you see any guys in here?" Emmy put her hands on her hips and glared at him.

"Oh, Emmy, don't be upset." Kristen put on her jacket and grabbed her purse.

"I know you're not a guy, Em."

"I should hope so after what you did to me."

Great! Here it comes. Kristen set her purse on the table. "All right! What's going on between you two?"

"I'm mad at him for what he did in the parking lot." Emmy frowned at Tony and jabbed a finger at him.

"Hey! You can't lay that all on me." Tony took a step forward and pointed back at Emmy. "If I remember correctly, it was your idea to get in back. You never said to stop."

Kristen looked back and forth between them. "If you guys are going to argue, we will be late for church. Can we talk about this later? I thought this was all behind you. Why is all this anger coming out now?"

Emmy kicked at a kitchen chair and looked at the floor. Tony turned and walked out of the kitchen. He slammed the back door closed.

"Oh, this is just great! Is this the way you're going to act at church? I thought we were supposed to be in a worshipful frame of mind when we go to church." Kristen glared at Emmy. "Are you coming, or will I have to explain to Chase why you aren't here?"

"I'm coming, but you have to sit in front with him. I'm sorry about getting mad, but it just came out. I guess I've been keeping it bottled up inside." Emmy grabbed her Bible and jacket. "I'll be all right by the time we get to church."

Kristen gave up trying to start a conversation between Emmy and Tony, and the ride to church was filled with silence.

Emmy spent a few minutes praying in the chapel before

34

church. By the time she walked into the music suite, she was smiling and everything appeared to be back to normal.

"Morning, Chase, how are you doing? Are there any donuts left?" Emmy checked the table with the coffee pots and grabbed the last glazed donut just before Hank, the bass player, could grab it. "I'll share if you want," Emmy said as she split the donut in half.

"You can have it, Em. I've already had two." Hank Lysenko had been playing bass at the church for over twenty years. He planned to retire from his job at Somersett Technologies by summer so he could spend more time with his grandson.

"I'll split it with you, Emmy." Steve Van Zant, the lead guitar player, took one of the halves from her. He nearly spilled his coffee on her.

"Hey, be careful there old man," John Patterson said as he slapped Steve on the back.

"Who are you calling old man? You are just as old as me." Steve swallowed half of his part of the donut.

John Patterson played acoustic guitar and was only a few months younger than Steve. He worked for the Cohen & Kliegman accounting firm in their local office as an account manager.

Emmy turned around and was nearly run over by Skip Mason, the drummer, as he rushed into the room.

"Sorry I'm late, but I stopped to talk to someone and couldn't get away." He checked the donuts and grabbed one with chocolate frosting.

"What was her name?" Chase asked. "Was it Jenara Ribiero? I saw you talking to her last Sunday."

Emmy grinned at Skip and playfully punched him in the shoulder. "She's really cute. Are you going out with her for real?"

"We've been on a few dates," Skip said as he glanced at Kristen.

Kristen smiled at Skip and then looked at Emmy. *Maybe now he won't be asking me for a date. He's too young for me.*

"It looks like we are all here," Chase said. "Let's run through that new song before we practice in the sanctuary."

Tony had saved seats for Emmy and Kristen and they joined him after the worship team finished their songs.

35

"Are you still pissed at me, Em?" Tony whispered.

"We'll talk about it after church." She poked him in the ribs. "And don't say pissed in church. It's like swearing."

He grinned at her. "I've heard you use much stronger language."

"You have not!" she insisted, but then bit her lip. "Not in church. I know I sometimes use some colorful language at times, but I'm trying to be careful here."

"Sssh!" Kristen leaned forward and scowled at them. "You have to be quiet and pay attention to Pastor Herb." *And don't you dare stick your tongue out at me.*

Mama asked me to pick up some ice cream," Tony said to Kristen as he was shaking hands with some of the other worshipers after church. "Any special flavor?"

"What flavor don't you like?" Kristen asked.

Tony rubbed his chin. "Uh, I guess I'm not particularly fond of strawberry."

"That's what I want. Strawberry."

"I'll still eat it, Kristen. All ice cream is good. Except that coffee flavored one Mama likes. I can't stand it."

"That's a nice story. Thanks for sharing," Kristen said.

"You're a stinker!" Tony said as he turned to Emmy, who was standing quietly beside him. "Can I say stinker in church?"

"Knock it off before I smack you. You know what you can say."

Tony grinned and made a big mistake. He pulled on the braid in Emmy's hair.

She smacked his arm. "Stop that, you... dork!" She started to call him something worse than dork but stopped in time.

"Stop fighting!" Kristen ordered. "I'm going to smack you both if you can't behave." *I'll be a grandmother before you ever grow up.*

"Can we leave now?" Emmy began walking toward the exit. "I want to watch some of the games even if the Bears aren't playing. Maybe there'll be a team that knows how to play defense."

Tony took a step toward her, and she laughed and started to run.

Kristen grabbed his arm and squeezed it. "Don't you act like a child and chase her."

"I wasn't going to," Tony said.

"Why do I have a difficult time believing that?"

They made a quick stop at the store and then headed to Tony's house. Emmy jumped out of his Envoy and ran into the house through the back door.

"Hi, Mama, is it all right if Kristen helps get lunch ready? I have to talk to the big dork down in the basement."

Mama laughed. "I didn't realize there was a big dork living in the basement. Is he dangerous? Should I be concerned?"

"Oh, you know who I mean." Emmy hurried through the kitchen to the door leading downstairs. "And I'm sorry I called him a dork even if he is one."

Tony and Kristen walked into the kitchen without being in a rush.

"Emmy ran through here like a tornado. Is she upset about something again?"

"I'll tell you later," Kristen said. "Did she go upstairs?"

"She's in the basement. Would you help me get lunch on the table?" Mama looked at Tony and pointed toward the door between the kitchen and dining room. "I assume you must be the big dork she needs to talk to. Go! Talk!"

"I didn't do anything." Tony protested by raising his hands in surrender.

Mama countered, "Then you don't have anything to worry about."

Tony reluctantly opened the basement door. He looked back at Mama. She shook her head and pointed down.

Emmy heard him coming down the carpeted stairs. *That step always squeaks.*

He saw her sitting on the couch watching the early game between the Steelers and the Saints. "Who's winning?" He walked up behind her, touched her hair but didn't tug on the braid. He walked around to the front of the couch.

"Saints are up by ten." She was sitting Indian-style and clutching a football in her arms.

37

"Can I watch with you?" Tony asked and then chuckled. *I live here. Why am I asking you if I can sit on the couch?*

"Duh! You live here, dork."

"That's big dork to you, brat."

Normally this wouldn't bother her, but it did today. She threw the football at him. He caught it in self-defense.

"You took advantage of me, and I'm pissed at you," she yelled.

"So, it's okay to use that word now because we aren't in church, huh?"

"Screw you, Bertucci!" She yelled even louder.

In the kitchen, Kristen looked at Mama. "That doesn't sound good. I think I'll close the basement door."

"Good idea, dear." Mama nodded. "Should we hold off on lunch? Do you think they will be fighting very long?"

"Who knows?" *I don't know why they're fighting in the first place. It's ancient history.*

"Where is this anger coming from?" Tony asked. "It happened over a month ago."

"So the statue of limitations is up, huh?"

"Statute..."

"I know the difference."

"I'm not complaining about what happened."

She glared at him. "Give me back the football."

He tossed it to her.

She instantly threw it back at him. It bounced off of his shoulder and fell to the floor "Guys never complain when they have sex."

"Hey! Do you need a refresher sex ed class?" He picked up the football. "What we did wasn't sex." *Unlike you, I do know what constitutes real sex.*

"Says who? Just because we didn't finish doesn't make it any better... or worse... whatever." Emmy's attention was drawn to the TV as the Steelers scored on a long pass. "Yes!" She raised her hands to signal a touchdown.

"You sure weren't complaining that night." *Crap! That was the wrong thing to say.*

Emmy didn't look at him as she crossed her arms over her chest. She added emphasis by giving him the finger.

"Sorry, Em. That was uncalled for." He turned to look directly at her.

She drew her knees up to her chest and put her arms around them. "Don't look at me!"

"What? Now I can't even look at you. That might make it kinda rough to be friends."

"Then maybe we shouldn't be friends," she said as her eyes filled with tears.

"Have it your way." He stood up and started for the stairs.

"No!" Emmy turned around and got on her knees. She held her arms out toward him. "No! Come back. I didn't mean that. I just said it to hurt you."

He didn't hug her, but he returned to the couch. "As far as I'm concerned we can do one of two things. We can either forget about being friends and never see each other..."

Emmy shook her head as she sat back down. She drew her knees to her chest and wrapped her arms around them.

"... or we can talk about this and work it out. I vote for the second option. I never thought we would have trouble being friends even after you shot down my proposal. Like I said that night, Em, I want you to be happy.

"Everyone says that. Doesn't mean much."

He grinned. "Fine! I want you to be miserable."

She laughed in spite of herself.

"I really mean it. How can I make you see that? Any suggestions?"

She didn't say anything.

Kristen stood by the basement door and whispered, "I don't know, Mama. It's getting rather quiet down there. Do you think they knocked each other out? Should I go check?"

"I don't think that's wise. They will come back upstairs when they finish."

"Or when they get hungry enough," Kristen said as she walked back into the kitchen.

"Can you say something?" Tony pleaded. "The silence is

39

hurting my ears."

She looked at him. "Did you tell John about that night? Or anyone else?"

"Which night do you mean? The night I proposed, or the other night?"

"Both."

"I told John about both nights."

"You didn't tell him the details, did you? I know guys talk about that stuff."

"How do you know?"

"Because I'm one of the guys, remember?" Emmy grinned "You sure didn't think I was a guy that night."

"I learned my lesson," he said. "Kristen knows and Mama knows I proposed..."

"Mama knows about the other night, too. I talked to her about it." *I could never talk to my mother or Mrs. Colwell about it.*

"Are we through fighting, Em? I'm getting hungry," Tony said as he rubbed his stomach.

"I see you still have your priorities in order," she said. "We're through fighting for now. I'm sure I will get over this. I really want you to be a part of my life."

They stood up and Tony hugged her tenderly.

"Let's go see if lunch is ready." He grabbed her around the waist and slung her over his shoulder like a slab of beef. He carried her upstairs and into the kitchen. "We're hungry!" he announced.

Kristen looked at Emmy. "You're not even trying to make him set you down. Are you all right?"

Tony set Emmy down.

She grinned at Kristen. "I was trying to remember the first time he did that. That's why I didn't struggle to get down. I would really miss it if he didn't treat me like one of the guys at times."

"So, all is well in your world now?" Kristen asked.

Emmy turned around and poked Tony in the stomach. "That's for carrying me up the stairs." Emmy giggled as she turned back to Kristen. "Yep! It is now."

Chapter Four

"What time are Christopher and Randy picking us up?" Emmy asked Kristen on the way home from work Monday.

"They said six. We can grab a quick bite and then leave."

"I want to eat at Soldier Field. I'm going to make them buy all our food and drinks. After all, they are getting in for free."

The Braun brothers were going to the game with Emmy and Kristen. Emmy and Kristen sat in the back of Christopher's 2001 Ford Escape XLT, and caught up on the events in their lives.

"How is Elena doing? Is she keeping you up all night?" Kristen asked Christopher.

Randy wondered, "How old is she now? I can't keep track."

"She will be four months on the eleventh, and she's sleeping about four hours at a time during the night. She sleeps all day. It's like she's on the night shift."

"Is Victoria nursing her?" Kristen asked.

Christopher sighed then said, "She tried, but it didn't work out. Elena's on formula."

Randy turned in the front passenger seat to face Emmy. "Christopher is disappointed because now he can feed Elena. He was hoping to get out of it."

"Hey, little brother, I like feeding her. She is the most awesome thing that's ever happened to me. It's amazing how you can learn to love someone who can't even talk to you."

Kristen looked at Emmy and whispered, "You all right with talking about the baby?"

Emmy nodded. *Just because I may never have a baby doesn't mean I can't talk about other people's babies.*

"Who you calling little brother?" Randy asked as he grinned. "You may be older, but I'm taller by a couple of inches."

"Are you and Vanni still dating?" Emmy asked. *I haven't seen her at church for a while.*"

"She's hasn't been at church because she's in Mexico City working on that mission project," Randy said as he smiled.

Emmy tilted her head and tugged on her ear lobe while gazing at Randy's earring. *I should get my ears pierced one of these days.* "I thought that was supposed to be over at the end of August. What happened?"

"The church came up with some more money and they are finishing the building. I heard someone donated fifty grand. That's what I heard, at least."

Emmy bit her lip. *I wonder if that's what Kenny was being so secretive about. I know he wrote a check for something.*

"But to answer your question, I'm not sure if we will start dating again when she returns. It's really difficult to maintain a long distance relationship."

"Yeah, tell me about it." Emmy sighed as she looked out the window.

At halftime Christopher stood up and said, "I'm buying the food and drinks this round. What does everyone want?"

"You bought the last time, Christopher," Emmy said. "They must be paying you a lot over at Liberty Manufacturing because hot dogs and beer cost a fortune here."

"Randy can buy the next round. They don't pay associate professors-in-training much more than peanuts over at North Park even if they are alumni," Christopher teased though he was proud his brother was striving toward his goal of being a full-time professor at North Park College. "Could you come with me and give me a hand, Emmy?"

By the way he said it, Emmy knew he wanted to talk to her in private. "Sure, I can help."

As they waited in line, Christopher confided to Emmy, "Things are not all sunshine and roses at home, Em. To be honest, they weren't even before Victoria became pregnant. Actually, it's been a struggle from the beginning. Sometimes I think we should have never dated, let alone gotten married."

"I'm sorry to hear that. What are you going to do?"

"I suggested counseling, but she won't have anything to do with it. I even suggested going to see Pastor Herb."

Emmy stood beside Christopher as they waited in line. *You must be serious if you even thought about Pastor Herb. Randy has told me you rebelled against the church and haven't set foot in one since high school.*

"Do you have any ideas?" Christopher asked.

"Pastor Herb would be a good place to start. He could even refer you to someone not associated with the church if you would be more comfortable. He's done that for people."

"Thanks, Em. You've always been a good friend."

"Thanks." She scooted out of the way of a man trying to carry four cups of beer. *And thank you for not mentioning that I've had a crush on you since we first met.*

"So tell me, are you dating Kenny or Tony? Or is there someone new in your life?" he asked. "You don't have to tell me if it's too personal."

"Tony and I are good friends. Maybe better friends than we've ever been. Kenny is gone so much..."

"I saw the look on your face when Randy mention long distance relationships." Christopher put a hand on her shoulder. "I know you and Randy are just friends."

"Did he ever tell you about our kiss?"

"Yeah, he said it didn't work out like he had hoped." Christopher smiled. *I know you would enjoy it if I kissed you.* "Have you met anyone special?"

"No, and I'm not really looking." *I love Kenny even if he is away so much.* "Would it be all right if I ask Pastor Herb if he would have time to talk to you? Randy knows him. I'm sure he can vouch for his character."

"I'll think about it, Em."

As they were walking back to Christopher's Escape after the game, Emmy high-fived Randy again. "Tony tipped that pass and the Bears intercepted in the end zone. What a way to end the game, huh?"

"What did you say, Em? I can't hear anything out of this ear. Someone was screaming so loud because the Bears won."

She poked Randy in the side. "I didn't scream that loud."

He retaliated by taking her Bears stocking cap and then pulling on her braids.

"Give that back! Tony gave that to me," Emmy hollered.

Randy held the cap high over his head and Emmy jumped up trying to grab it.

"Here you go, Em." Randy put the cap back on her head, but he pulled it down over her eyes.

"Creep!" she yelled as she lifted the front of the cap. "And another thing. You said something on the way up here that bothered me."

"What was it? I'm sorry if I said something I shouldn't have." He tried to recall what it could have been.

"I think there are some long distance relationships worth all the effort it takes to make them work."

Tony turned twenty-two on October tenth, and it just so happened to be the Bears week off. Emmy and Kristen came over to the house to eat dinner with Mama Bertucci. Mama took a loaf of garlic bread from the oven and said, "We can eat now. Tony won't be home until after ten."

"Are he and John watching game film again?" Kristen asked. "It's funny to observe them studying game film. They watch the same play over and over like they expect it to change."

Emmy set the kitchen table. "The mostaccioli smells different tonight. Did you change something?"

"I added a secret ingredient, but don't tell anyone."

"What is it?" Emmy bounced on her toes.

Mama held up a jar of pasta sauce.

"Mama! You used store-bought sauce? I'm shocked."

"I didn't have time to make my own. We'll see how it tastes."

During the meal, Mama announced, "I want to have a party for him here on Saturday evening since more people would be able to come. You two can help with the plans."

"Mama, you should have the party in the evening after dinner. That way you could just serve dessert, and you won't have to make a lot of food," Emmy suggested.

"You know I don't mind cooking."

"I know. You would make enough food to feed the whole Bears team if they were coming over. You could order a cake from the store and serve it with ice cream. Provide some beverages. Just have a simple party."

"It would be much simpler." Mama gave it some thought. "All right, dear. We will have dinner with just the family. I expect you to be here, too."

"I'll be here. FYI, this sauce isn't as good as yours."

"Thank you, but it is so convenient. Sometimes Tony inhales his dinner so fast I don't think he even tastes it." Mama patted Emmy's hand. "I hate to say this, but since you turned down his proposal, I think you two are getting along so much better. It's like all the doubt and uncertainty has been erased and now you can get about the business of just being friends."

Emmy glanced at Kristen. "I think you're right. I always want us to be friends. It would be terrible if we weren't, and I couldn't come and see you."

"You can always come and see me, child. Do you want to invite your parents to the party? They would be welcome."

"I'll think about it, but I'm not sure it's a good idea. I didn't tell you, but Kristen and I went to see them and I mentioned the proposal. Mom assumed I was expecting and that's why Tony proposed. It was very confusing."

"You do what you think best," Mama said.

On Saturday, Mama prepared an early dinner for eight family members, which included Emmy. Kristen invited her parents. Emmy invited her parents, but on the day of the party her mother called.

"Emmy, your father and I aren't feeling well. I don't think we should go to Tony's party."

"Are you sure? Do you need to see your doctor?"

"Maybe tomorrow. I think we will stay home."

"All right. I hope you guys feel better soon." Emmy looked at Kristen, who happened to be listening. "I wonder if they're afraid to go because I turned down Tony. Maybe they're upset or embarrassed."

"We could leave early and stop at their house," Kristen said and then chuckled. "Maybe I could talk them into coming, since they like me better than you."

"I would smack you, but you're probably right."

45

Emmy and Kristen stopped at the house on their way to Mama's, but Emmy's parents weren't home.

"Where could they have gone? I wonder if they were even sick at all."

"Would you rather they be sick?" Kristen asked.

"Of course not, but they should have told me the truth. Come on, let's get to Mama's." Emmy walked back to the car as Kristen followed. "Where could they be? Why would they lie? If they didn't want to go to Mama's house, they could have said so."

Tony and John met Emmy and Kristen at the back door.

"Would you take this, please?" Emmy asked as she handed Tony a large bowl.

"What is it?" He tried to smell it.

"It's salad, you goof. And this is bread," Emmy teased.

"You're gonna get it, Em."

John and Kristen kissed and headed to the living room.

"Hey! Aren't you gonna help in the kitchen?" Tony hollered at Kristen.

Mama smacked his arm with a wooden spoon. "Let them be. They have more important things to do. You can help Emmy set the table."

"But it's my birthday," Tony complained. "Why should I have to help her?" He bumped Emmy's hip with his.

Mama waved the spoon at him. "Shush! If you help now, you won't have to clean up later."

"The mostaccioli and ravioli smell delicious, Mama," Emmy said.

"I used homemade sauce for tonight. Karla called. They'll be here soon."

"My parents aren't coming," Emmy said as she stirred the mostaccioli with a large wooden spoon. "They claimed not to be feeling good, but I think they didn't want to come because I turned down the proposal."

"I can understand, dear. They might feel uncomfortable." Mama lifted the lids on the vegetables to check their progress.

They ate earlier than usual, around five, and were finished by six o'clock. This gave Emmy and Kristen time to clean up the

46

kitchen before the party guests started arriving.

By seven-thirty most of the guests had arrived. They were just serving cake and ice cream at the party, as planned. Mama told everyone not to bring presents, but some of them did anyway. Emmy was surprised several of Tony's teammates showed up. Tony introduced his teammates to his mother, and she told all of them to call her Mama. He introduced Emmy and Kristen to the guys.

"Kristen, isn't it amazing how seven big football players fill up the house?" Emmy asked.

"Tony is the smallest one, except for Desmond Apumalo."

"He's a cornerback, Kristen. They are smaller because they have to be quick and fast so they can cover the wide receivers."

"I do know a little about football, Emmy."

"Have you ever seen so many tattoos?" Emmy commented. "Does John have any?"

"No."

"Are you sure? Maybe he has some in places you haven't seen," Emmy said with a twinkle in her eye.

"I'm not going to answer that." Kristen shook a finger at Emmy. "You're just trying to pry into my love life."

"What would you do if he got one?"

"He is an adult, Em. If he chooses to get a tattoo, that would be his decision."

"Tony said something about getting one, but as far as I know, he hasn't yet."

"Does Kenny have any tattoos? Any you can see, I mean?" Kristen asked as she smiled at John.

Emmy grinned. "He has my name tattooed on his butt."

"That's nice, Em," Kristen said as she walked toward John.

"And I have his name on mine." Emmy rolled her eyes.

"Did you say something, Em?" Tony asked as he walked up behind her.

"Nothing important," Emmy replied.

Emmy stuck close to Tony and he introduced her to his teammates as a friend. Only John knew about the proposal.

"Emmy, this is Sterling Jeter. He plays in front of me on the d-line. Sterling, this is Emmy. She's a real singer."

Emmy looked up at Sterling. "I like those earrings."

His diamond earrings sparkled. At six and a half feet, Sterling towered over Emmy. He weighed over 320 pounds, but moved as quick as a linebacker.

"Thank you, little lady. I happen to be a singer, too. Maybe you should hear me sometime." His deep bass voice rumbled.

"Maybe I should. What kind of songs do you sing?"

"All kinds, but I sing like Barry White. The ladies love it. They find me irresistible."

"Hey, Sterling, are you makin' a move on Em?" Tony put his hands on Emmy's shoulders. "Don't pay any attention to him, Em. The only place he sings is in the showers in the locker room. He only thinks he sounds like Barry White. He usually shatters the tiles with his screeching."

Sterling's laughter filled the room as he high-fived Tony.

By ten everyone had left except for Emmy, Kristen and John. Mama put them to work straightening up the house.

"Doesn't Tony have to help?" Emmy asked.

"Not tonight because this is my birthday party." Tony touched the tip of her nose as he gloated.

Emmy swatted his hand away and stuck out her tongue at Tony. He grabbed her and threw her over his shoulder.

"Put me down you overgrown kid!"

"I think I will hang you from the ceiling," Tony said.

Mama stared at him and shook her head. "I think you are too old to be treating Emmy like this."

Tony set her down.

"Mama is right," Emmy said. "Just because I let you do that when we were kids doesn't mean I still want you to."

"I'm sorry, Em. I won't do it again."

Mama frowned and poked his arm. "Just because you can pick Emmy up like that, doesn't mean you should."

"I know, Mama. I would never drop her though. She doesn't weigh anything. I could hang Kristen up on the ceiling, too." Tony grinned as he moved toward Kristen.

"Don't you dare, Tony Bertucci, in case you haven't noticed, I *am* wearing a dress." Kristen hid behind John.

48

"I'm teasing you, Kristen. You are way too heavy to lift."

Kristen stepped out from behind John. "What do you mean? Do you think I'm fat?"

"You weigh more than Em."

"A child of ten weighs more than Em."

Everyone except Emmy laughed.

"I can't help it if I'm small. It's all I've got in my genes."

Tony and John looked at her with devilish grins. Emmy realized what they were thinking, so she turned her back to them and wiggled her bottom.

"You guys are gross. Kenny is the only one who will get into these jeans."

"Emmy! Don't talk like that." Mama pointed a finger at Emmy. "If you were living here, I would ground you for a month."

Everyone else laughed.

"Would you really ground me?" Emmy asked.

"No, but I would worry about you. Have you checked the dining room?"

"I'll check it," John said as he dragged Kristen along.

Fifteen minutes later the house was clean again.

"Is everything okay now, Mama?"

"Yes, thank you, Emmy. You girls can go home now. John and Tony can take the garbage out to the garage."

Emmy was getting ready for bed later that night when Kristen walked into Emmy's bedroom and sat on her bed.

"Are you all right? You're acting a little nervous tonight."

"It's nothing really," Kristen answered.

"Kristen Lynn Keasling, I know you well enough to know something is bothering you. Now give!"

Kristen stared at the floor before she looked at Emmy and said, "I guess I'm a little worried about my solo tomorrow."

"You don't need to worry. You'll do fine. We can pray about it if you want."

Kristen nodded, so Emmy sat beside her on the bed and they prayed together.

They woke up early the next morning and arrived at the

49

church by eight o'clock for rehearsal. Chase listened to Kristen as she practiced her solo.

"Kristen, are you a little nervous? It kinda sounds like it."

"I've been worried about it all week. I'm not sure I can go through with it," she admitted.

"Do you remember a couple of weeks ago when I screwed up the song 'Rescue Me?' I started singing the wrong verse, and then, to make it worse, I sang a C when it should have been an E. It sounded terrible."

"Are you trying to cheer me up or depress me, Chase?" Kristen asked with a grin.

"I'm trying to make you laugh and relax. Did it work?"

"Maybe. I guess we'll just have to wait and see." Kristen relaxed and sounded just right during the service.

Tony was able to be at the service and congratulated her afterward. "You sounded just perfect, Kristen. I really liked your solo. You really nailed that high C. Way to go."

Kristen looked at Tony for a few seconds. "You don't have a clue about what note I sang, do you?"

"Not a bit, but Emmy told me to tell you that," Tony said.

As Emmy, Tony and Kristen were walking out of the building, Chase stopped them.

"Hey, did you know the CD is actually on the *Billboard* chart?"

"Really? You mean like a Fridays At Five CD would be?" Emmy asked.

"Maybe not exactly like one of their CDs, but it is on the chart. I think it's number 158 and climbing."

Tony patted Emmy's back. "Do you know what this means, Em?"

Emmy expected a smart aleck comment. "No, what?"

"It means thousands of people have heard you sing. When you guys tour in March, you will be packing in the crowds."

"Yeah, right. I don't think we'll have to worry about selling out our concerts."

"Emmy, do you realize the impact the CD could have on the people who hear it?" Chase asked seriously.

Tony laughed and said, "Yeah, they will think you're a teenager if they see the photos of you."

Emmy smacked his arm.

"Will you guys behave?" Kristen scolded.

"You could have such a positive influence on the kids who listen to it," Chase said. "By the way, I met with Sondra Wojtek from Steward Music. We discussed the tour, and we have the time frame set up. We would leave on March fourth and return on Saturday night, or Sunday morning, however you look at it. We would do that for three weeks."

Emmy said, "That sounds like fun. I can use vacation time."

"The guys at Prater-Saylor are filling in the actual dates. They're trying to coordinate everything so we're not traveling all over the country."

"I'm grateful we've got these people to take care of everything. I know how difficult it is to do a Fridays At Five tour," Emmy said. "Plus, Mr. Robertson agreed to let me have the time away from work. He could have just fired me."

The next Saturday Emmy and Kristen were in downtown South Hampshire shopping and talking about Kenny and John when they walked past the old Lincoln Hotel.

"How about this place?" Kristen paused and pointed to the building. "Have you ever thought about it?"

"Thought about it for what?" Emmy stopped and ran her hands over the red bricks.

"As a place to have your reception. You will be getting married one of these days. You should start thinking about things now while you have the time."

Emmy grinned and said, "I guess I have dreamed about having a reception in this place. It's really beautiful, but it's kinda expensive. I could never afford to have my reception here."

"Emily Colasanti, how many times are you planning to get married?"

"Oh, I don't know. Maybe four or five times."

"I'm gonna smack you."

"Just once, why?"

"Then spend the money to have your reception in a fancy hall. You know Kenny will help you pay for it."

"Why should he? He hasn't proposed. I'm beginning to doubt he ever will."

"We're going to check it out and get some information about it. If you like it, and it's available for whenever you're getting married, you're going to book it. Do you understand?"

"Okay, Krissy. It will be fun to check it out even though I'm not engaged. I guess there's no harm in that."

Kristen grabbed Emmy's hand and pulled her toward the ornate front doors. Emmy rubbed a hand over the polished wood and gleaming bronze door handles as they walked inside the hotel, which had been renovated and restored to look as good as the day it opened in 1905.

"Come on, Em. Let's talk to the concierge. He can tell us who we need to ask about a reception."

Five minutes later, Kristen and Emmy were escorted around the different rooms which would serve their purpose.

"Kristen, why did you mention your grandpa? He didn't own this place, did he?"

"Not exactly."

"What does that mean?"

"He kinda contributed some money to help with the restoration. He was also on the board of directors of the company that actually owns the hotel." *I'm pretty sure that would give me, and you, an inside track when it comes to reserving a room. They might even cut you a deal.*

Emmy was awed by the splendor of the old hotel. *No wonder you wanted to check it out. I wonder how many hours it took the artists to create the plaster designs.*

"Isn't this just gorgeous, Em?" Kristen pointed to the grand staircase.

"Yeah, it's amazing." Emmy ran up one side of the marble staircase and then down the other.

Kristen shook her head. "You are a total goof, Emmy."

Kristen took over and discovered how far in advance the

hotel needed to be booked. She made sure Emmy was busy and spent a few minutes talking about a certain date.

As they were in the car heading home, Emmy looked at Kristen and said, "Thank you, Krissy. If you hadn't been there, I would never have been able to even look at such an expensive place. If I ever get married, I want to have the reception there."

"No problem, Em. I like to spend money—especially when it isn't mine."

Emmy bit her lip as she thought about the cost. *I might have to use some of the royalty money I get for the songs I helped Kenny write. I really hate to do that. I want to save that money for when I get old. I don't want to live paycheck to paycheck like Mom and Dad.*

Kristen smiled at Emmy. *You know Kenny Colwell, or his parents, would pay for the room without batting an eye at the cost.*

Kristen also checked about the price of rooms for guests who might want to stay overnight at the hotel. Even though Emmy was not officially engaged, Kristen had a feeling that might change in the near future.

Chapter Five

After the Saturday night concert in Cincinnati, Ohio, Kenny flew home. He wanted to surprise Emmy, but Kristen knew he was coming. He planned to go to the Crest Ridge church in the morning, but wouldn't let Emmy know he was there.

Emmy and Kristen woke up at seven on Sunday morning. They needed to be at the church by eight. As far as Emmy knew today was just like any other Sunday. The Bears were playing the Vikings in Minnesota, so Emmy planned to watch the game at home. Kristen excelled at keeping secrets and surprising people. She had done that when Tony and Mama threw a surprise party for Emmy's twentieth birthday. Emmy had no clue whatsoever Kenny was in town. Emmy waited for Kristen to finish getting ready. By a quarter to eight, they were on their way to the church.

"We might miss the start of the game, Em. Is that okay with you?" Kristen asked.

"We shouldn't miss too much if we don't hang around church too long."

"You do have to spend some time talking to people. That's part of your responsibility as a member of the worship team."

"I know. Maybe we should just start taping the games and watch them after they are over."

"That sucks, and you know you would turn on the game to see the end, anyway."

"Yeah, you're right. I guess church is probably more important than football."

"You're such a goof, Em." Kristen shook her head. *You are going to be so surprised today.*

They arrived at the church and rehearsed the songs for the morning service. At nine-thirty they joined their Sunday School class. After class, Emmy and Kristen hurried to the music room. Chase and the guys in the band were already there.

"Emmy, would it be all right with you if we make a last minute change?" Chase asked.

"Sure, what is it?"

"Pastor Herb has had a request from someone for the song

you sing for the teens sometimes."

Kristen grinned. *I know who made the request, but I can't tell you.*

"Which one? I hope it's not 'Yolanda's Song.' You know I still get emotional whenever I sing that one."

"No, it's 'I Will Be True To You.' We all know it so it shouldn't be too hard to add it."

"It's okay with me. Where will it fall in the service?"

"After the message. We will all come back to the platform and play it."

"Sure, we can handle that," Emmy said and didn't give the change to the order of service another thought.

The service proceeded as planned, and the worship team returned to the platform as Pastor Ausland prayed. Chase played his keyboard in the background.

Emmy glanced at the clock on the back wall and closed her eyes. *If we get out of here by noon, we won't miss too much of the game. I hope Kristen doesn't want to hang around too long*

When Pastor Herb finished, Chase and the band started to play. Only then did Emmy notice someone beside her playing the guitar. She turned to look and smiled.

She held the mic down at her side and whispered, "You are in deep trouble, Mr. Colwell. I suppose you requested this song?"

Kenny smiled and said, "You take the lead, and I'll join you on the chorus. We'll sing verses two and three together just like always."

"You better not make me cry, or else I will hate you forever."

Even though she tried very hard to not become emotional, tears flowed down her face by the time they sang verse three. They finished the song, and she put her mic back in the stand. Kenny set the guitar in a stand and turned to face her.

"Do you hate me, Em?"

"Yes, with all my heart," she answered as she embraced him. "When did you get home?"

"Late last night. We have two days off before the next show in St. Louis, so I thought I would pop in and see you."

Many of the people in the congregation knew Kenny Colwell, and that he and the guys in Fridays At Five originally wrote this song with some input from Emmy. She later changed some of the lyrics, so the song was now sung to God and not to another person. Some of the teens wanted to talk to Kenny, so he stayed around to talk and sign a few autographs.

Come on, Kenny. We need to get home. I want to watch the game. Emmy shifted her weight from one foot to the other.

By the time Kenny, Emmy and Kristen got home, the first quarter was over.

"Crap! They're getting their butts kicked," Emmy whined as she plopped down on the couch. "They're down by seventeen. This is worse than last week when they lost to the Lions."

They didn't bother to eat and watched the rest of the first half. Kenny got up and turned off the TV as the half ended.

"Hey! It's not over. They might come back in the second half," Emmy hollered. "Turn it back on."

Kristen knew what was going to happen, so she grabbed Emmy's arm to make sure she stayed on the couch. Then she smiled at Kenny.

"I know this may not be as romantic as taking you out for a fancy dinner at Ciao Bella, but," Kenny said as he got down on one knee and took a small box out of his pocket. Emmy saw what he was doing and started to cry immediately. "Will you marry me, Emmy? I love you, and I want you to be my wife and companion for as long as we live. Will you..."

"Yes! Yes! Yes!" Emmy shouted as she leaped off of the couch, hugged Kenny and knocked him over. "Yes! Yes! Yes!" She kissed him all over his face as they hugged and she lay on top of him.

Kristen reached for the ring. "Let me have this before you break it."

He handed her the ring and kept kissing Emmy. Kristen sat and watched with tears running down her face. She knew now that Kenny and Emmy belonged together. She felt a sense of relief in a way. Though she had always hoped Emmy and Tony would get married, she could sense the love that filled the small room as

Kenny and Emmy kissed and held each other.

"Do you even want to see the ring, Emmy?" Kristen asked after a couple of minutes.

Emmy was on the floor on her knees in front of Kristen with Kenny beside her. Kristen opened the box and for the first time Emmy really saw the ring.

"It's perfect! I love it." She stared closely at the ring and then looked at Kristen. "It looks familiar."

Kenny looked at Kristen and then at Emmy.

"There's something you need to know, Em," Kristen said.

"What's that?"

"Do you remember the day we stopped at Watson's just to kill some time?"

Emmy nodded. "Yeah, we looked at a bunch of jewelry. You bought a bracelet."

"And you found a ring you thought would be perfect."

"But it cost a fortune."

Kenny held her shoulders. "This is the ring, Em. Tony bought it. I don't know if that will bother you or not. If it does we can pick out another one and put this one away."

"Tony really picked out this ring? I don't understand."

Kristen explained, "I went with him and helped, but he spotted this ring by himself. For some reason he was drawn to the same ring you were."

"I really don't understand. If Tony bought it, how did you get it? Did you buy it from Tony?" Emmy asked Kenny.

"Yes. Like I said, we can buy a different one..."

Emmy interrupted, "No! I love this one. I loved it the first moment I saw it. It doesn't bother me that it's the one Tony picked out. Did he really pick it out, Krissy?"

"Yes, I pretended the ring was for me, and that I was Tony's fiancee. I even kissed him a couple times when he was about to say your name. I'm sure that salesman will be so confused if you take it back to be resized."

"Don't you want to try it on, Em?" Kenny asked.

"Of course. Do I have to take it off after I put it on?"

"No, baby, you can keep wearing it. Let's see how it fits."

Kenny took the ring out and slipped it on her finger.

"How does it feel? Is it too loose?" Kristen asked.

Emmy's eyes sparkled as she gazed at the ring. "I don't think so." She tried to move it. "I think it fits just right."

"I knew it would be close because it was just a little tight on me. My fingers are slightly bigger than yours."

"We have to call your parents and mine. Would it be wrong to call Mama and tell her?" Emmy asked.

"You should call your parents first, Em. But I want to hear the conversation. They are gonna be blown away."

"You got that right!" Emmy squealed. "First Tony proposes and now you do. They won't know what to think." Emmy hugged Kenny and tackled him to the floor again. "I want to kiss you all day," Emmy said as she leaned over and kissed his face and neck.

Kristen shook her head. "Come on, you guys. Emmy needs to make some calls."

Emmy called her parents and put the call on the speaker.

"Hello," Mom answered.

"Hi, Mom. It's me. I have some news for you."

"What is it, Emmy? Why do you sound so funny?"

"I've got the phone on the speaker because Kenny and Kristen are here and want to talk to you, too."

"You mean they can hear what I say to you?"

"Yes, Mom, so you have to be nice."

"Hello, Mrs. Colasanti, this is Kenny."

"I'm here, too, Mrs. Colasanti," Kristen added.

"Hello, guys. What's going on, Emily?"

"Kenny just asked me to marry him, and I said yes," Emmy shouted into the phone. "We're gonna get married!"

Mom didn't answer.

"Did you hear me, Mom? Kenny proposed, and I said yes."

"You aren't trying to pull a joke on me, are you?" Mom asked. "Raymond! Come here and listen. Emmy's on the phone, and she said Kenny just proposed to her. Is there a button on this phone to put it on speaker?" Mom and Dad looked at the phone and saw the small button that allowed them to both listen and talk to Emmy.

"We're not kidding, Mrs. Colasanti. I asked Emmy to marry me, and she agreed."

Dad answered, "I'm very happy for you, Kenny. I know you and Emmy have been friends for a long time." He shrugged his shoulders as he looked at his wife.

"I don't suppose you have talked about a date since this just happened. Please, just tell me that you will get married here in SoHam."

"I'm pretty sure we will get married here since both our families are here," Kenny assured Emmy's parents while he pulled Emmy close. "We should go. We have to call my parents, so we'll talk to you later."

Emmy looked at Kenny after they hung up and said, "Mom was so surprised she didn't even ask me if I was pregnant."

"Can we call my parents now?" Kenny asked after he kissed Emmy again.

Come on, you guys. Kristen shook her head. *Maybe you should just elope because you are going to be impossible to live with now that you're engaged.*

Emmy asked, "Are they going to be surprised?"

Kenny grinned. "Not really. They knew what I was going to do today."

They called Kenny's parents and Emmy talked to them.

"Emmy, we have thought of you as part of the family for so long," Mrs. Colwell said. "This will just make it official. I couldn't be happier for you."

"You know how much I appreciate all the things you've done for me over the years, but I want to tell you that I love you again just so you know."

"We love you, too, dear. Come and see us when you have time. I want to see the ring."

Emmy asked, "Do you know the story behind the ring?"

"Yes, we know all about it."

"I don't mind that Tony bought it first. I can think of it as he bought it for Kenny before someone else could. If Tony hadn't seen it, someone else would have bought it, and it wouldn't be mine. Does that make any sense?" Emmy asked and then giggled. "I can't

59

believe I'm really engaged!"

"That's a great way of looking at it."

After talking to Mr. and Mrs. Colwell, Emmy called Mama Bertucci. She knew Tony was in Minnesota, and Mama would be at home watching the game, or at least listening to it. The phone rang and Mama checked the caller ID.

"Emmy, what is the matter with these Bears? Did they forget how to play defense? I will have to get after Tony when he gets home. He missed an easy tackle, and he hasn't intercepted a pass all game." Mama paused and patted her chest. "Oh, my, I shouldn't get so excited. It's only one game after all. How are you, dear? Is there anything wrong?"

"Mama, I have some news for you, and I'm not sure how you will feel about it."

"It doesn't matter. You just go ahead and tell me." Emmy couldn't see Mama smiling.

"We turned off the game at halftime, and Kenny asked me to marry him and I said yes. I hope you won't be mad at me."

"I'm not mad at all. I'm very happy for you. I know you and Kenny will be very happy together."

Emmy looked at Kenny as she twisted her hair. "How silly of me. You already know. You know Kenny bought the ring from Tony, don't you?"

"Yes, dear."

"Knowing you, it was probably your idea."

"I might have suggested it..."

"Oh, Mama, I love you. You will always be Mama to me even if I'm not married to Tony."

"And you will always be so precious to me. I love you and Kristen like you are my daughters, too."

"I guess Tony must know that Kenny was going to propose since he sold him the ring."

"That's true, but he doesn't know Kenny was going to ask you today, sweetie," Mama said.

"Then I want to tell Tony the news myself. I don't want him to hear it from you or my parents or anyone."

"I think that would be the proper way for him to hear the

60

news. He won't be home until this evening. But if you and Kenny want to come over later, it's okay."

Emmy looked at Kenny, and he nodded.

"We'll come over later if you don't mind."

"I'll call you when he gets home."

Kenny, Emmy and Kristen made quick stops at both parents' home so Emmy could show off her ring.

"Are you sure you're not expecting, dear?"

"Would you be happier if I was, Mom?" Emmy did not want to discuss this today.

This question stunned her mother for a few seconds.

"I'm not. It may be a few years before we have any kids," Emmy said. *If I ever have a baby.*

"I guess I'm hoping for a grandchild who doesn't live so far away."

After spending some time at her parents' house, Emmy, Kristen and Kenny walked over to his parents' home. They walked in, and Emmy saw Mr. Colwell in his recliner. He jumped up and hugged Emmy.

"I am so happy for you both." He managed to say before his voice choked up and the tears cascaded down his cheeks.

Mrs. Colwell walked into the living room. Emmy held out her hand to show her the ring.

"I can see why you like it so much. It's absolutely beautiful." She hugged Emmy, too. "Were you there when he proposed?" Mrs. Colwell asked Kristen.

"Yes, and I started crying." Kristen smiled at Emmy and Kenny. "He got on his knee, and she tackled him. It was amazing."

After visiting with Kenny's parents, they decided to grab some food at the most logical place—Darby's Dogs. When they walked in, they were surprised to see Mr. Darby working by the booths. Emmy ran over to see him.

"Hi, Mr. Darby, how are you?"

"I'm doing fine, Emmy. How are you?"

Emmy held out her hand and showed him the ring, "Kenny asked me to marry him today, and I said yes."

Mr. Darby held out his arms and she hugged him as he held her. He tried not to let her see the tears forming in his eyes. No one had ever seen him cry since his son was born.

"It's about time he finally got smart enough to propose," Mr. Darby said as he reverted to his usual gruff self. "I suppose he wants to order something not on the menu to celebrate."

Kenny shook hands with Mr. Darby, "Do you have any chocolate cake in the back and maybe some ice cream?"

"You know I keep some around, but it's just for special occasions. What makes you think this qualifies?"

"Please, Mr. Darby. Can we have some cake and ice cream?" Emmy asked in her most childlike voice.

He smiled at her and pictured her as a little girl coming into the store holding the hand of her slightly older friend and asking the very same question. His voice cracked a bit as he answered the same way he did back then. "I have some in the back, but it's only for good little girls who obey their parents. Have you been good?"

"I've been very good. May I have some chocolate syrup on mine, too?" Emmy asked with a smile.

"I will expect an invitation to your wedding and a new picture to put on the wall," Mr. Darby said.

"Consider it done, Mr. Darby." Kenny shook his hand.

While they were eating their cake and ice cream, Emmy's phone rang.

"I just wanted to let you know Tony's home, and you can come over if you want."

"Thanks, Mama, we'll be there in a little while."

They said goodbye to Mr. Darby and headed to the Bertucci home. Emmy led the way and walked right in the back door.

"Mama! We're here. Where are you?"

"We're in the living room, dear. Come on in."

Emmy looked at Kenny and Kristen and asked, "Should I go in first?"

"Yes, go on in, and we'll be there in a minute," Kenny said.

Emmy walked into the living room and held out her hand as she walked over to Mama.

"It looks lovely, dear."

Tony stood up. He and Emmy looked at each other without saying a word for a few seconds.

Oh, Tony, please don't hate me. I love Kenny, and I have to be with him. She bit her lip to keep it from quivering.

Tony remembered the first time he ever kissed Emmy. *You may not remember it, Em, but I actually kissed you before you ever met Kenny. You were four. You thought it meant we were going to get married. It's funny how things work out.*

Then he opened his arms, and she moved closer so he could hug her. He held her in his arms, picked her up and squeezed her.

"I'm happy for you, Em. I really am. Do you still like the ring?" he asked as he set her down.

"I love it, Tony. It's absolutely beautiful," she answered as Kenny and Kristen walked into the room.

Tony held out his hand and Kenny shook it.

"Congratulations, Kenny. I know you guys will be very happy together, but if she ever gets out of line, just let me know."

"I'll do that. I'm sure she will be rather difficult and stubborn at times."

"That's for sure." Tony pulled on her ponytail to tease her.

Emmy stomped her foot and glared at both guys. "I am not stubborn."

Mama motioned for Kristen to sit beside her and said, "Now we just have to work on that other guy and get him to propose to you."

"What guy would that be, Mama?" Kristen teased. She knew very well Mama was taking about John Randolph.

As soon as Emmy, Kenny and Kristen returned home, Emmy ran upstairs to her room and called Lynette Jefferson from church and told her the good news. "Kenny asked me to marry him today, and I said I would."

"Oh, Emmy, I'm so happy for you."

For some reason Emmy thought Lynette wasn't very surprised, so she asked, "Did Kristen already tell you?"

"Yeah, sorry, Em. Kristen called a little while ago. Please don't be upset with her. She just had to tell me. Is it all right if I say something on Wednesday?"

"You can go ahead and tell people, I guess. Oh, you should pray for Kristen because I'm gonna murder her."

Emmy called Diane, who lived in Toledo, Ohio.

"Hi, Diane. Guess what? Kenny proposed to me tonight, and I said yes. Please give me a call when you have a chance and kiss Carson for me."

Emmy hung up and flew down the stairs as she shouted, "Kristen Lynn Keasling! You are gonna get it."

Kristen was in the living room with Kenny, and she started laughing as Emmy rushed into the room.

"I'm sorry, Em, but I had to tell someone."

"Oh, I guess it's all right. Did you call your parents?"

"I called them and Derrick, but that's all."

"I'm gonna murder you in your sleep tonight, Krissy, so be careful," Emmy said as she hugged Kristen.

Kenny kissed Emmy after she stopped hugging Kristen.

Emmy asked, "Are you gonna stay here tonight?"

"Emily Olivia." Kristen stood with her hands on her hips and did her impersonation of Mama Bertucci. "Just because you are engaged does not mean you can sleep with Kenny... again." Kristen paused for a reaction and then added, "You have to wait."

"I suppose so, but I don't have to like it, do I?"

Kenny smiled and kissed her again. "I should get home. I'll come over after work tomorrow. We have a few things to discuss."

"We have to set a date, don't we?" Emmy remembered.

Before Emmy went to bed that night, she got on her knees and said her prayers. After she finished, she ran back downstairs and sat down at the computer desk. She pulled a piece of purple stationery out of the drawer and wrote a note.

"Today, October 27th, 2002, Kenneth Travis Robert Colwell asked me to marry him and I accepted."

Emmy filled the single piece of paper with her thoughts and then folded it. She placed the sheet of stationery in a matching envelope and carried it reverently upstairs to her room. She pulled out her music box, opened the secret drawer and placed the envelope inside. She had a thought. *Maybe in fifty years someone will open this and read about the happiest day of my life, so far.*

Chapter Six

Kenny came over at six the next day with Chinese carryout. He and Emmy kissed once and then kissed again. They kept kissing until Kristen stopped them.

"Just cool it, you guys. We have to eat dinner and get busy. We have a lot of work to do in a short time."

"What do you mean by a short time, Krissy?" Emmy asked.

"Do you want to have a real long engagement, or do you want to get married before you turn twenty-five?"

"I want to get married tomorrow," Emmy said as she kissed Kenny again.

"Stop it right now, young lady, and help me bring the food into the dining room. Kenny, will you get some plates and stuff?"

"Yes, Mama," they both said to Kristen as Emmy giggled.

Kristen sighed and rolled her eyes.

They began discussing the wedding as they shared the different dishes.

"Can I have some more of that stuff, please?" Emmy asked.

"It's called General Tso's chicken. Do you like it, Em?"

"Yes, it's got a bit of a kick to it. What is this other stuff called?"

"Chicken chop suey," Kristen answered.

Emmy rolled her eyes. "Not the chop suey. I know what it is. The other stuff."

"It's called Happy Family," Kenny said as he scooped more of the spicy chicken onto her plate.

"Can we have Chinese at the reception?" Emmy asked with a mouthful of rice.

Kristen and Kenny looked at Emmy to see if she was joking. She appeared to be serious.

"Emmy, you can't have Chinese food for your reception," Kristen said.

Emmy stuck out her lip and pouted. "Then I want Darby's. We can have chili dogs and beef sandwiches and tons of fries."

Kenny started laughing because he knew Emmy was teasing Kristen. Finally, Kristen caught on.

"Very funny, Em. Can we get serious for a while?"

"Okay, should we set the date first?"

"That would be a good place to start," Kristen said. "May I have more Happy Family, please?"

Emmy passed the container to Kristen. "I don't like this one. You can have it all."

"I was looking at our schedule, and we are going to be in Australia and New Zealand the last couple weeks of March, but then we have the whole month of April free. Do you think we could have an early April wedding, or is that too soon?" Kenny asked while taking more of the chop suey. *I won't order the chop suey again since no one is eating it except me.*

"It's not too soon for me," Emmy said. Then she realized, "April fifth is Grandma Isabel's birthday. What day is that on next year? We are talking about 2003, right?"

"Yes, Em. I know you can't wait until 2004." Kristen rolled her eyes as she looked at the calendar. She didn't really have to because she already knew the fifth was on a Saturday. Kenny knew it, too. "The fifth is on a Saturday."

"Can we get married on Grandma's birthday?" Emmy asked as she smiled at Kenny. "She would like that, and she has always done so much for me and Diane."

"That sounds like a great idea, Emmy. I'm glad you thought of it," Kristen said.

"We can get married at the church, and we have to find a place for the reception," Kenny said with a forkful of chop suey dangling above his plate.

"What about the Lincoln Hotel, Em?" Kristen asked. "You said you like that place. How about it for your reception?"

"It might not be available, but we can check."

Kristen smiled and Emmy looked at her and then at Kenny.

"All right. I can tell something's up. Spill it."

Kenny looked at Kristen before they both looked at Emmy.

"We were kinda hoping you would suggest April fifth, because..."

"Please tell me you didn't do what I think you did." Emmy shook her head.

"What might that be?" Kristen asked.

"Did you guys book it already? Did you guys plot together and set up the date, and now you're just trying to make me think it was my idea?"

"Sorta," Kenny said.

"I don't care if you did. I love it!" She paused for a moment before continuing, "You are a real stinker, Kristen Lynn Keasling. You knew Kenny was going to propose when we stopped at the hotel that day, didn't you?"

"Yeah, I did. Are you mad?"

"No, I'm glad you suggested that place because I never would have thought of it because it's too expensive. I would have wanted to find a cheaper place I could afford on my own."

"Wait a second, Em. You still have to pay for it on your own, I sure can't afford it on the measly allowance Andy gives me," Kenny teased.

"Just wait. I'll have a talk with him."

They finished eating and sat on the couch to make a list.

"I'll write this stuff down since you can't read your own writing, Em," Kristen volunteered.

"Okay, we've got the date and place set."

"We need to make sure we can use the church that day," Kenny said. "Who do we need to ask?"

"I suppose we need to ask Pastor Ausland." Emmy watched as Kristen wrote furiously. "What are you doing, Kristen?"

"Making a list. I've got invitations, flowers, photographer, music..." Kristen read her long list. "You have to decide how many bridesmaids, and who. You need to buy a dress." Kristen glared at Emmy. "Don't you dare say you're going to get married in jeans and a t-shirt, or I will smack you."

Kenny left two hours later. Emmy sat slumped on the couch with Kristen. "I'm exhausted. Maybe I should just elope and get it over with. By the time the wedding arrives I will be down to fifty pounds."

"You are not going to elope. I will help you, and we will get through all this. Besides, I already have my dress, and I can't wear it anywhere else."

67

For the first time ever, Emmy dropped a college class. She was just too busy and didn't have the time to devote to it.

Kristen teased, "You are just afraid you won't get an A."

"Well, I've never gotten anything less in any of my college classes. I don't want to take a chance."

"Did you ever get a B at Roosevelt?"

"Mrs. Vidales gave me a C in Spanish my freshman year," Emmy admitted sheepishly.

"Oh my God! You got a C on your report card. Did you get grounded?"

"Daddy spanked me," Emmy answered as she turned red.

Kristen hugged her and said, "I'm sorry. Sometimes I forget how you were treated."

"It's all right. I'm over it."

The rest of October and the beginning of November passed like a blur. Before they realized, it was almost Thanksgiving.

Mama called. "Emmy, what are your plans? I'm assuming you will be having dinner with Kenny and his parents."

"Actually, Mama, Kenny won't be home and his parents are going to be in Texas for a week. Mrs. Colwell asked me to go, but I have to work. What's up?"

"Would you do me a favor?"

"Of course."

"Will you help me cook Thanksgiving dinner? I've been feeling a little tired lately, and I could use some help."

"Are you sure you want me to help, Mama? I've never cooked a Thanksgiving meal before."

"You don't have to do the whole meal, Emmy, just help me out Thursday morning."

"You know I will help any way I can, Mama."

Mama and Emmy talked during the week about what Mama needed Emmy to do and what she could bring.

Emmy arrived at Mama's early Thursday morning and walked in through the back door.

Mama turned around and saw her. "I didn't expect you this

early, but I'm glad you're here. Tony's still sleeping."

"He sure wouldn't be able to sleep this late if we were married. I'm gonna wake him up, okay?"

"Be careful. He can be really cranky in the morning."

"Mama, you know he's a teddy bear. I'll be right back."

Emmy ran upstairs and into Tony's room. She jumped on the bed and kissed his forehead. "Wake up, sleepyhead. Time to rise and shine."

He opened one eye and looked at Emmy. "Go away, brat. I want to sleep."

"You can't. You have to get out of bed because I'm here."

"Says who?"

"Says me."

He groaned as he stretched his arms over his head. "What time is it? I want to sleep late today."

"It's time to get up. I'm here, and I want to see you. Isn't that a good enough reason?"

"I think it's a good reason to stay in bed."

Tony reached his arm around Emmy and pulled her close to him and wouldn't let go.

"Tony, what are you doing?"

"I'm holding you. What does it look like?"

"It looks like you are trying to pull the cover over me and take advantage of me before I'm married. You are, aren't you?" Emmy teased.

"Not at all. Why would I want to do that? It would be like kissing my sister."

Emmy slid under the covers and moved on top of Tony.

"What are you doing, Em? You know what happened the last time..."

"Shut up! I remember, and that's not gonna happen again." She giggled and said, "And don't you dare tickle me."

He knew she wanted him to tickle her. He pulled the blanket over the top of their heads. Emmy laughed as Tony tickled her sides. Mama walked in and could hear them laughing.

"What are you two doing under there? No wait! I don't want to know."

Emmy poked her head out from under the blanket to look at Mama. "Make him stop tickling me, Mama. He won't stop."

"Tony, you need to stop tickling her. She's engaged, remember?"

"She started it." Tony moved his hands over his head and grabbed the headboard.

"I did not!" Emmy giggled as she told a little lie.

"Yes, you did! I was sleeping, and you woke me up by jumping on the bed."

"I need you to do something for me, son."

"Tony, stop tickling me."

"I'm not touching you anywhere, Emmy."

"Tony, let her go so she can help me in the kitchen and get yourself up. I need you to run to the store and get me some more sweet potatoes and a few other things."

"I'm not tickling her or holding her. See! My hands are here." He waved his hands. "She's just trying to get me in trouble."

Emmy threw back the cover and started to get off the bed. Tony swatted her as she did.

"It was all her fault. She's the one who started it," Tony said.

Emmy stood in front of Mama and stuck her tongue out.

You are acting like a little sister, Emmy. A very young little sister. Mama put her hands on Emmy's shoulders and said, "It's a good thing you aren't marrying this one. He still acts like an overgrown child at times."

"That's for sure. He's so immature," Emmy said and then ducked behind Mama.

Tony grabbed a pillow and threatened to throw it at Emmy. "You're lucky Mama is protecting you, brat."

Mama pointed a finger at Tony. "Get up now." Then she turned to Emmy. "How are things going with the planning? It's just a little over four months away, dear."

"I know. Time is going by so fast. Kristen is helping, and we hired Paula Kratzsky to be the coordinator. She's already been a big help."

"Are you getting excited, Emmy?"

70

Emmy grinned at Mama and then Tony.

"Mama's not talking about that. She knows you're ready for sex."

Emmy rushed over to the bed and smacked Tony with a pillow. "I wish we were getting married tomorrow. I love him more everyday."

Emmy blushed because she didn't want to tell Mama how much she missed Kenny. Tony put his thumb to his nose and wiggled his fingers at Emmy, so she smacked him with the pillow again. Mama and Emmy went back downstairs to the kitchen. Tony got ready and came downstairs a few minutes later.

"Here's a list of what I need. Make sure the sweet potatoes look nice."

"Emmy, are you coming with me?" Tony asked.

"I can't. I need to stay and help Mama with the pies and the turkey."

"Can I have a kiss before I go?" Tony teased.

"No way! I'm never kissing you again. You're a dork." She smiled and then kissed him quickly on the cheek. She backed away when Tony tried to grab her around the waist. "There, now hurry back. We have work for you. You have to put the leaves in the table so everyone will have room."

"Yes, sir, General Colasanti." Tony snapped to attention and saluted Emmy.

A few hours later, everyone sat down to eat. Emmy said grace and everybody started digging in and passing the food around the table. Tony's sister Heather and her husband, Alex Khryzman, were home along with Kristen, her parents and John Randolph. Derrick Keasling was away at law school in Arizona and couldn't get back home for the holiday. Emmy's mom and dad were there, also.

Mama told Emmy's parents, "Emmy did a lot of the cooking by herself. She has been a big help to me today. You should be very proud of her."

"Really?" Mom turned and smiled at her daughter. "Emmy, I'm surprised. You never showed any interest in cooking before."

"Mama has been giving me lessons since I moved out and

71

started living on my own. I had a lot of practice cooking for him." She pointed at Tony who had a mouth full of mashed potatoes, a roll in one hand and a forkful of turkey in the other.

Eventually, everyone was stuffed, and they made their way to the living room. Kristen helped Emmy clean up, and they filled the dishwasher before they joined everyone. All the places to sit were taken so Emmy looked at Tony.

"Can I sit on your lap, dork?"

"You can, but I might pop. I ate so much."

Emmy sat on the arm of the recliner.

"Everything tasted so good, Emmy," Tony said. "Did she really help much, Mama?"

"She most certainly did. You better be nice to her if you expect her to ever invite you over for dinner after she's married."

Tony whispered in her ear, "Oh, I will be nice to you all right. Especially when I have you in bed like this morning."

Emmy blushed because she knew Kristen, standing next to her, could hear what Tony said.

"Emmy, will you help me in the kitchen for a minute. We left some Jell-O out of the fridge."

"No we didn't, Kristen. I'm sure we put everything away."

Kristen took Emmy by the hand and dragged her to the kitchen.

Emmy scanned the kitchen. "What, Kristen? There's no Jell-O anywhere."

"I know there's not, but I heard Mama say something about you and Tony in bed earlier, and now I hear this from Tony. What have you been doing? Did you forget who you are engaged to? And why on earth were you sitting so close? You were almost on his lap."

"There was no where else to sit. Kenny would understand."

"You could stand up like me." Kristen frowned. "What about this morning?"

"Kristen, I just went upstairs to wake him up. I got under the blanket and he started tickling me."

"Under the blanket? Sometimes I don't understand you at all. Why would you do that?"

72

"I don't know. I guess I wasn't thinking straight, but nothing happened."

"Are you sure?"

"Well, maybe, he was touching me a little, but it doesn't mean anything."

"I know it must be difficult to wait, but you only have a few months to go before the wedding."

"I know. I'm counting the days."

"Just make sure you don't get carried away with Tony."

"I won't. He treats me the same way he treats you."

"*I* don't get in bed with him and let him *tickle* me. You shouldn't either, young lady."

Later, Emmy said goodbye to her parents, and the Keaslings also headed home. After falling asleep while watching some football, the guys woke up ready to eat again.

"Mama, I'm hungry. Is there anything left to eat?"

"Not much, you and John ate most everything before. Kristen, will you help Emmy see if there's anything left for these gigantic stomachs on legs?"

Emmy joined Kristen in the kitchen, and they got out the food again. They warmed the turkey, potatoes and dressing in the oven. They used the microwave to warm some gravy and vegetables. Tony, John and Alex sat at the dining room table and filled up again. By the time everyone left later that night, there wasn't enough food left to save for leftovers.

Mama sighed. "I will just have to make more food for next Thanksgiving."

Chapter Seven

The days after Thanksgiving and before Christmas flew by for Emmy. She and Kristen stayed busier than normal at Robertson Industries. Emmy was relieved when the semester ended at North Park College. She decided to take the spring semester off since she would be busy with work, the worship band tour and the wedding.

The countdown to Christmas continued. After work on Wednesday, just one week before Christmas, Emmy and Kristen stopped at the mall, determined to find gifts for the guys.

"Kristen, I'm getting desperate. We need to get our Christmas shopping done before it's too late. Do you know what you're getting John?" Emmy asked as she threaded her way through the crowded mall.

"He mentioned he needs a few things for his apartment."

"You can't just buy things for his apartment. You need to buy something personal for him," Emmy said as a shopper walked right in front of her and hit her with a shopping bag. *Well, excuse me for being invisible.*

"What are you getting Kenny?" Kristen asked as the crowd magically parted for her.

How do you do that? Emmy shrugged and said, "I don't have a clue. Mrs. Colwell said he needs some new clothes, but I'm not sure exactly what. I want to find something for Tony, too. What are we gonna do?"

"Gift cards. Then they can buy whatever they want."

"We can't do that. We need to come up with something special to get them."

"What about power tools? All men need power tools to do their man stuff," Kristen suggested.

"Has John ever asked for a power tool?"

"Well, no, but he might want one," Kristen said.

"Let's go to Best Buy. There's got to be something there they would like," Emmy said.

They left the mall and stopped at the Best Buy across the road.

"Kristen, come look at this. We can get each of them a

74

PlayStation2 and some games. They would love it. They're just overgrown kids, anyway."

"Are you sure you don't want to buy it for yourself, Em? You're just as much a kid as Kenny or Tony."

"I admit it, it would be fun to have one. But we don't have to tell the guys, do we?" Emmy asked as she grinned.

They ended up buying three PS2s and a bunch of games. Later, Emmy also bought some dress shirts after Mrs. Colwell told her what size to buy. Kristen bought John a drill set just in case.

Kenny and the band had been touring throughout the South and Southwest. They played a show in Dallas on the twentieth, and Kenny called Emmy as soon as he arrived home.

"Em, how are you? I just got back and had to call you."

"What time is it?"

"It's just after three."

"I was sleeping."

"Should I call you in the morning?"

"No, you should come over here and sleep with me. I have missed you so much."

"Em, we have to wait until the wedding."

"Why? Oh yeah, I forgot."

"I'll call you in the morning. I love you!"

"I love you, too."

She fell right back to sleep and dreamed about Kenny.

He called again at seven.

"How are the wedding plans going? I know I haven't been much help lately, but I'm home now until the end of January, and I can help with whatever you need."

"Oh, Kenny, Kristen and I have both been super busy. Between work, school and the wedding, I never have a moment to sit down and chill. I had to drop my Business 373 class, and I've never done that before. I've decided not to take any classes next semester. I'm going to be too busy with other things."

"There must be something I can do to help you."

"Sure. I need a back rub, and I need ideas about what to get my parents for Christmas. You have to help me pick out the invitations." She hopped up and sat on the kitchen counter. "Mom gave me a list of people to invite, and I have no clue who some of them are. I think she wants to invite everyone she has ever met."

"Have you talked to Mom about our side of the family?"

"Yes, I had dinner with your parents last week, and she has a list of people to invite. We will have to spend a lot of time together while you're home. Can you come over now and spend this weekend with me?"

"Are you sure that's a good idea? We might be tempted to... you know."

"Kristen will be here. She will do her best to make sure nothing happens." Emmy grinned at Kristen, who was sitting at the kitchen table. "Tony and John have a game in Carolina, and they're leaving today. Wanna watch the game with us?"

"Sure, do they still have a shot at making the playoffs?"

"Not really, but they can still finish with a winning record."

"I have to finish my Christmas shopping. Want to help me, or are you too busy?" Kenny asked.

"I could go with you this afternoon. I need to do some work around here this morning." Emmy jumped down because Kristen was frowning at her.

"How about I pick you up at one, and we can grab lunch and go shopping?"

"Okay, I'll see if Kristen wants to go, too. Is that all right?"

Kristen shook her head. "I'm not fighting the crowds."

"Of course. See you later."

Tony and John left for Halas Hall on Saturday morning. They flew into Charlotte, North Carolina, and prepared for the game against the Panthers in Ericsson Stadium on Sunday.

Kenny stopped by to pick up Emmy and Kristen. He walked in the back door and saw Kristen in the kitchen putting glasses in the cupboard.

"Hi, Kristen. How have you been?"

"Busy!" Kristen dropped a glass but Kenny caught it before it fell to the floor. "Even with Paula helping, the wedding planning is keeping us very busy. Nice catch, by the way."

"I'm sorry I haven't been much help lately."

"That's all right. We're doing stuff you wouldn't be much help with anyway. Do I get a hug?"

"Of course. It's good to see you."

Kenny hugged Kristen, and they were hugging when Emmy walked into the kitchen.

"Hey!" Emmy frowned and put her hands on her hips. "Have you been gone so long you forgot which one of us you are marrying?"

Kenny played along. "I know it is one of you girls, but I can't remember for sure. Maybe I should kiss you both and that will jog my memory."

Emmy waved a fist at him. "I'll jog your memory with a smack to the head unless you let go of Kristen and kiss me."

"You're the one I'm marrying, huh? I think I need more than a kiss. I want..."

Emmy squealed and took off running. Kenny chased her and cornered her in the living room. She let him catch her and they started kissing. Kristen followed Kenny and watched.

"Ahem. I think that's enough kissing for now."

"You're a spoil sport, Kristen."

"And don't you forget it, young lady," Kristen said as she headed back to the kitchen.

"Now let me see the ring," Kenny commanded. "I want to make sure you are still wearing it."

"What ring?"

"You know which ring."

"No, seriously. What ring are you talking about?" Emmy shrugged. "I never wear jewelry."

"The engagement ring."

"Oh! That old thing." Emmy stuck out her hand and proudly showed Kenny her engagement ring. "Do you still like it?"

"It's beautiful, just like you. I'm so happy you like it, Em."

Emmy brought Kenny over to the couch, and they talked as they sat close together. After a couple of minutes, Emmy told him, "Kristen doesn't want to go shopping, so it's just the two of us. She doesn't want to fight the crowds."

"There won't be any crowds where I'm going. She can go

with if she wants."

"Where are we going?" Emmy asked. "Every place is crowded at this time of year."

"We are going to Darby's for lunch, and then I need to stop at Paul's Bookstore on Polk St."

"Are you buying everyone a book for Christmas?"

"No, I did all my shopping online. I want to pick up a couple books I ordered. You remember the book I got you for your birthday?"

"I remember it."

"Well, Mr. Tockstein is the man who helped me find it. He knows more about old books than anyone in the country. He located the copy you have in New York City. I try to buy a few books from him every year."

"Kristen, did you hear that?" Emmy hollered. "We aren't going to have to fight crowds."

Kristen ran into the living room. "I'll go since we aren't going to the mall or anything. John likes books. Maybe I can find one for him."

"Were you eavesdropping on us?" Emmy frowned.

"I wanted to make sure you guys didn't start making out."

They headed to Darby's and ate lunch. Kenny was recognized by some tourists, signed a few autographs and had his picture taken. Kenny knew they were tourists because the local people from SoHam didn't treat him like a celebrity. To them he was just a local kid who happened to play music for a living.

After lunch they drove to Polk St. where Paul's Bookstore occupied the first three floors of a five-story building. Many of the businesses had moved out of downtown South Hampshire, but Paul had kept his bookstore in the same location for over twenty years. Kenny parked the car in the parking deck a block away, and they walked to the store. Kenny listened as Emmy sang "Best I Could Do," a Fridays At Five song.

"I like that scarf, Kristen," Kenny said. "Where did you get it?"

"I can't remember for sure. Probably in the mall."

Emmy stopped singing. "Does that mean you don't like my

stocking cap? I've been wearing it since high school."

"I know, Em. Maybe it's time to retire it and buy something nicer."

"He does have a point, Em." Kristen adjusted her scarf.

"Yeah, on top of his head from the lump I'm gonna give him." Emmy jumped and pretended to give Kenny a smack on his head. "I suppose I can afford something a bit more fashionable."

"How about retiring your old army coat, too?" Kenny suggested.

"I have a nice coat, but this is so comfortable. How about I just wear it around the house, or in the neighborhood?"

"I can live with that, Em."

Kenny held the door open for Emmy and Kristen.

"Thank you, Kenny," Kristen said.

Emmy bumped into Kristen, who had stopped just inside the door.

"Em, can you watch where you're going, please?"

"Sorry."

Kenny walked toward the checkout registers as Emmy and Kristen checked out the books on the front display. He smiled at the clerk. "You must really like candy canes."

She giggled and then said, "Yes, would you like one?" She ripped one off of her festive holiday vest.

"Thank you." He slipped it into a pocket. "Is Mr. Tockstein around today?"

"Yes, he's here somewhere. He might be on the second floor. He just got a bunch of books about the Civil War and was sorting through them. Should I page him for you?"

"No, we'll see if we can find him."

"Okay." The girl behind the counter giggled again. "I know who you are. Can I have an autograph?"

"If you promise not to call your friends and tell them I'm in the store, I will sign something for you on our way out. We can even take a picture together if you want."

"I won't tell anyone, I promise."

Kenny waved at the girls, and they headed upstairs. Kenny spotted Mr. Tockstein sorting books in the third aisle.

79

"Hello, Mr. Tockstein, how are you?"

He looked up and recognized Kenny. "Well, look who's here. How are you? It's been a while since you were in the store."

"Yes, it has. This is my friend, Kristen Keasling, and this is my fiancee, Emmy Colasanti. Ladies, this is Mr. Tockstein."

"It's a pleasure to meet you, but I hope you will call me Paul." He held a large book in his hand as he stood up. "I can never convince Kenny to call me that. He makes me feel old sometimes. Congratulations on your engagement, Emmy."

"Thank you, Mr. Tockstein."

"Emmy is the great-great...I can't remember how many greats it is. But do you remember the book you found?"

"Sure. The book by Pietro Jacovelli. 'Una Storia Dell'arte Di Fare Carillon' if I remember correctly."

"Yes! That book was for Emmy."

"That was a rather rare book. I'm happy I was able to find a copy for you."

"Thank you very much, Paul." Emmy said slowly emphasizing Paul as she looked at Kenny. "It means a lot to me."

"Kenny told me you have one of his music boxes."

"Yes, Grandma Colasanti gave it to me."

"Does it still play music?" Mr. Tockstein looked at the photo of Confederate cavalry on the cover and then set the book on a shelf.

"Yes, but I don't often play it."

"You should play it a few times a year just to make sure it still works properly. It's better for the box than just letting it sit."

"I'll remember that. Thank you."

"Those music boxes are a real hot item now. Collector's are paying over ten thousand dollars for ones in fair shape. If you have one that's in mint condition, it could be worth over fifty thousand dollars."

Emmy looked at him wondering if he was pulling her leg.

"I can see you are shocked, but I am being honest with you. Try to keep yours in the best condition possible, but don't ever replace any parts. That lessens the value considerably."

"I won't. I could never sell my music box no matter how

80

much it's worth. It was the last present Grandma ever gave me."

"I totally understand that." He paused and then added, "Kenny, I have the books you wanted in my office."

"Were they hard to find?"

"The first one was more difficult to locate, but the second book is more common. I actually located five of them."

"What books did you buy, Kenny?" Emmy asked.

"One is *Life On The Farm* by Elsie Blanche, and the second is *One Room Is Enough* by the same author. The first is about growing up on a small farm, and the other is about teaching in a one-room schoolhouse. They are out-of-print and have been for a long time."

"Who are they for?" Kristen asked as she browsed.

"They're for Jeff. He was born in southern Illinois, and his grandfather was actually a student of the author."

Paul added, "I read the book about the schoolhouse. It's only fifty pages long, and the schoolhouse was called Green Ridge School. I remember because there used to be a school here in town by that name."

Mr. Tockstein took them to his office and showed Kenny the books. They looked very old and fragile. Mr. Tockstein handled them carefully and wrapped them up for Kenny.

"Was what I gave you enough to cover everything?" Kenny asked.

"Yes, I should give you some money back."

"That's not necessary. I'm just happy you were able to find them."

"You know how much I love hunting down old books. I love the challenge and the thrill when I am successful. Have a happy holiday, and it was a pleasure to meet you young ladies."

"Merry Christmas, Paul, and thanks again for finding that book for Kenny and me." Emmy shook his hand.

"You're welcome. Maybe one day you will let me see your music box. I would love to see one that's in good shape."

"I'll do that sometime," Emmy promised.

"We're gonna look around the store for awhile," Kenny said.

"You know where the music section is, right?"

"Yes, I'll take a good look there. Thanks again."

They wandered around the store for an hour. Kenny found two books for himself, and Emmy found a book to give to Lynette at church. Kristen selected two Chip Hilton books for John.

Emmy opened one of the Clair Bee authored books. "Why are you buying these, Krissy? They look so old." She read a few paragraphs. "They must have been written for junior high kids. What goofy names. Speed Morris. Biggie Cohen. Who is Chip Hilton?"

"Give that back, Em." Kristen grabbed the book from Emmy. "He told me his father collected these when he was a kid."

"John or his father?"

"When his father was a kid. Look! This one was published in 1948."

"How much are they?" Emmy asked.

"Two hundred dollars each," Kristen admitted.

"You're nuts!" Emmy shook her head.

They headed to the checkout counter, and Kenny kept his promise to the cashier. He gave her an autograph, and Emmy took a picture of her standing with Kenny using the checkout girl's phone.

As they were walking back to the parking deck, Emmy tugged on Kenny's arm and asked, "How much did you pay for those books?"

"I gave Mr. Tockstein two thousand dollars if you must know. He probably had to pay close to a thousand dollars for each book, but if he didn't, it's okay with me. I'm just glad he still keeps the store open."

Emmy stopped walking and looked at Kristen. *He must be nuts to pay that much for an old book.* Emmy made a circle around her ear.

Kristen frowned and grabbed Emmy's stocking cap. She stretched her arm and held it up as high as she could.

"Hey! Give that back," Emmy shouted as she jumped and tried to grab it. "I need it."

Kristen turned her back to Emmy. "What use could you

possibly have for this ratty old thing? It's starting to fall apart."

Emmy wrapped her arms around Kristen and almost tackled her. "I need it because I wore it to a show once."

"What are you talking about?" Kristen reluctantly handed the stocking cap back to Emmy. "A movie?"

"No." Emmy put the cap back on.

Kenny shook his head, but then he smiled at Emmy. "She wore that cap to our first gig, and I don't think she's washed it since."

"I have so." Emmy stuck out her tongue.

Kenny took the girls home and later helped Emmy make dinner. Kristen stayed out of the kitchen after she caught them kissing and getting playful with each other. After dinner, they gathered in the TV room to talk about the wedding.

"Kenny, do you know who you want to be in the wedding party?" Emmy asked.

"I want all the guys in the band, of course. Do you know how many bridesmaids you are going to have?"

"Well, I want Kristen, Diane, Lynette from church, maybe Heather if she's available, and I was thinking about Linda Newton, too, but I don't see or hear from her much anymore."

"So I need five guys." Kenny thought about who else he might ask. He grinned. "I'm not sure he would, but I'll ask Andy..."

"He better say yes, or else I'll disown him as a cousin." Emmy frowned at Kenny.

Kenny laughed and said, "I've already asked him to be my best man, and he agreed as long as you promise to dance with him."

"I suppose I could dance with him one time. Who else are you gonna ask? What about Frankie? He's been with the band from the beginning."

"I asked him, but he refused. He said he would die if he had to wear a tuxedo and stand up in front of people." Kenny looked at Emmy. "Since neither one of us has a brother, I was thinking. Would it be too weird if I ask Tony?"

Emmy looked at Kristen and then back at Kenny. "Let me think about that. What do you think, Krissy?"

"I think some people might find it weird, but you and Tony are still close friends." Kristen thought about it. "Actually, very few people know Tony proposed, so it should be all right."

"It's just a thought, Em." Kenny rubbed his jaw. "I could ask one of the other guys from the organization."

"But if you do, then the others might be upset. I can see asking Andy and the guys since they are your partners. I don't think I would have a problem with you asking Tony. Of course he might say no because he might feel too weird about it."

"If Heather is going to be in the wedding party, he might not feel as weird. Is there anyone else you might want to ask?"

"I was thinking about Sloane Beckett from church. We're pretty close now."

Kristen added, "I was thinking she might be a better fit than Linda. Linda's expecting a baby sometime next year."

"That's right. You did hear that. I'll ask Sloane tomorrow, and I'll call Heather to ask her. If Heather agrees then you can ask Tony."

"Em, you do know Heather is expecting, right?" Kristen asked.

"I didn't know that!" Emmy exclaimed. "You never told me she was pregnant."

"I didn't know until this week. You know how Heather never tells anyone, except Mama, anything about her private life. Mama mentioned it to me, and I guess I forgot to tell you."

Emmy slumped her shoulders. *Who can I ask that isn't pregnant? Oh! I know someone.* She straightened up and smiled. "I guess I could ask Lindsey Cameron from church. She's a good friend of Sloane's, and I like her a lot, too."

"What about Tony?" Kenny asked.

"Go ahead and ask him. Lindsey and Sloane are both single so maybe we can set him up with one of them."

"You're becoming as devious as me, Emmy," Kristen said as she grinned.

Chapter Eight

Emmy and Kristen went to the Crest Ridge church in the morning while Kenny attended Faith Bible with his parents. He came over afterward, and they watched the Bear's game at Emmy's house.

"Isn't this exciting?" Emmy sat on the edge of the couch as the final seconds of the game ticked away. "There's only time for two plays at the most."

"What play would you call, Em?" Kenny asked.

"Well, the Panthers are going to be covering the sidelines," she said. "I would run a play where John blocks, then goes up the middle of the field. They might lose track of him in all the confusion."

The Bears attempted a quick pass to the sideline, but it sailed out of bounds.

"Well, at least they stopped the clock. They've got eight seconds left."

Kristen pointed out. "They have to score a touchdown. A field goal won't matter since they're down by four."

"You've learned a lot about football since you met John," Emmy teased.

"I followed football before that. I always went to Tony's games if I could."

"Will you girls be quiet?" Kenny hushed them. "This is the final play."

Bobby McMullen took the snap in shotgun formation. He looked to his left, but the receiver was double covered. He scooted to his left to avoid a sack, stepped up in the pocket and then spotted John Randolph breaking open.

"Throw it to John!" Emmy screamed as she jumped up and waved her arms. "Look out!"

McMullen got the pass away, but then got leveled by two Panthers. John Randolph caught it, broke one tackle and dove into the end zone.

Emmy jumped up and down. "All right! The Bears still have a chance to make the playoffs. They just have to hope the

Giants lose their last two games."

The Bears were eliminated from the playoffs later that day when the Giants won. Even if the Bears won their final game and the Giants lost, New York had the edge in the tiebreaker.

After practice on Monday, Tony and John stopped at O'Hare Airport. Without telling anyone, Tony had been talking to his brother Marco. They had worked through most of the differences that kept them apart in the past, and Marco was flying home for Christmas. John dropped Tony off at terminal one, and he headed inside to wait for Marco. John parked the truck and joined Tony about ten minutes later. Tony kept looking around and finally spotted Marco.

"There he is, John." Tony pointed to his brother.

John looked at Marco. "He doesn't look anything like you or Heather, and that full beard makes him look sinister or something."

"Yeah, he looks like my father, and Heather and I look like Mama and the Lombardi side of the family.

Tony waved to get Marco's attention, and they walked toward each other. Tony offered his hand and Marco shook it. Then Tony surprised Marco with a hug. Marco shied away at first, but then hugged Tony back.

"It's good to see you, Marco. How was the flight?"

"Bearable. The plane was packed, and we departed late, but I made it. Does Mama know I'm coming?"

"No, I haven't told her or Heather. I haven't told anyone except John. Oh, this is John Randolph."

"Hello, John. I'm Marco Bertucci. Tony's older, but much smaller brother."

"Is this all your luggage?" Tony asked.

"I like to travel light."

Tony took Marco's two carry-on bags. "The truck is in the parking deck. John was my roommate at Notre Dame, and now we're teammates on the Bears."

"Yes, I know. I do follow your football career, even though I'm not a rabid sports fan."

Tony and Marco talked as John drove them to Mama's house. After a few minutes of talk about Marco's continuing education at Johns Hopkins University, Tony mentioned Emmy.

"Do you remember Emmy Colasanti? You met her at Heather's wedding, and you might have met her at Roosevelt. Anyway, she and Kenny Colwell from Fridays At Five are engaged. Have you heard about that?"

"Yes, Heather told me." Marco looked at Tony. "I don't know a lot about your relationship with Emmy, but I do remember you were dating in high school. From what I saw at Heather's wedding, the two of you could still be dating."

"I guess I should have filled you in more about stuff."

"I don't blame you for that." Marco glanced up at John. *I suppose it's all right to talk about this in front of you.* "We've never really been close, and I take all the blame for that. I never even told you I was getting married, or even told you after Nancy and I were married. It's something Heather and I share in common. We are both very close-mouthed about our personal life."

"You do share stuff with her."

"And she reciprocates, but we keep the information private."

"I don't want to dwell on the past." Tony waved a hand dismissively. "You are my only brother, and I would like to think we can put our past differences behind us. Maybe you could come to one of my games sometime. I don't know when we might play in Baltimore, but maybe you could come to a game in Chicago."

"Will you give me some time to think about it? I don't remember the last time I saw you play in person. I did see a few games in high school. I've watched parts of games on TV, but you know I've never shared your interest in sports."

"Sure. I understand."

John parked in the driveway, and Tony led the way to the house. "Marco, you should walk in first. Mama will probably be in the kitchen."

He tugged on his beard. "I hope she doesn't suffer a heart attack when she sees me."

They walked quietly through the back door and into the

kitchen. Marco led the way. He stopped as he saw his mother. Mama was busy at the stove when she heard the door open.

"Dinner will be ready in a few minutes, Tony," she said. Then she turned around and dropped her stirring spoon. "Marco, oh, Marco," she whispered.

"Hello, Mama, Merry Christmas. It's good to see you."

Mama opened her arms, and Marco walked over and received a hug. "I'm so happy to see you, son. This is a very pleasant surprise. I didn't have any idea you were coming. I always hope you will come home for Christmas, and I always buy you some gifts."

"I know you do, Mama, and I appreciate that. Heather always makes sure I get them. Is she here?"

"They are coming tomorrow evening. They have to work until four, but they should be here by seven or eight. Does Heather know you're coming?"

"No one knows. I wanted to surprise everyone," Tony said.

"I will set an extra place at the table. Tony, why don't you take Marco's bags up to his room?"

"It's okay. I can get them." Marco grabbed his bags and headed upstairs to his old room. He turned on the light and looked around. It didn't look much different than when he left for college. He sat on the edge of the bed for a moment to gather his thoughts. He wondered how soon he would see Emily Colasanti. Tony told him that she usually came to the house at Christmastime. He needed to talk to her about something that had bothered him since Heather's wedding.

Tony picked up John early Christmas Eve morning. They would have a shorter practice today. Marco was alone with Mama, and they had a chance to sit down and talk.

"How are Nancy and the kids?" Mama asked as she straightened the cushions on the living room couch.

"Nancy is doing well. She and the boys are in Florida with her parents."

Mama sat down on the couch and patted a spot next to her. "I bet they have grown so much. Nancy does send me pictures once in a while."

"Mama, is it true Tony asked Emmy to marry him, and she said no?" Marco sat down.

"Yes, it was a sad situation." Mama paused and reflected for a moment. "At one time they were in love with each other, but that changed. They were too young at the time."

"How well do you know Emmy? What is she really like?"

"She's the sweetest girl in the world, and Tony adores her—the same way he adores Kristen. She's just a tiny little thing. I keep trying to fatten her up, but she's just tiny. It's rather humorous to see them dancing together."

"Will you listen to something I need to tell you without interrupting me?"

"Certainly, son."

Marco stood up and began pacing back and forth as he collected his thoughts.

"Tony might despise me again after he learns about this, but I will have to take that chance. When I was a senior at Roosevelt, I hung out with this kid named Todd Delaney. I didn't have many friends, and I never should have hung around with this guy, but it took me a while to realize that. He was a troublemaker, and he had a grudge against Emily Colasanti for some reason. I was jealous of Tony, as you know, but I didn't know he knew Emmy or anything. I didn't really know her. I never met her and never really saw her except from a distance. I don't think I ever even knew her last name." Marco paused to catch his breath.

"Is your asthma bothering you again?" Mama asked.

"Not very often." He waved a hand. "Anyway, Todd convinced me and one other guy to help him spread the truth about her, as he called it. He convinced us she was, to put it bluntly, rather promiscuous. He wrote notes about her, and we would stuff them in her locker. We told some of the other guys what Todd told us about her. He somehow convinced us he had proof that she was different from what the other students believed."

He stood in front of the fireplace and looked at the family photos for a moment.

"One day after school I was with Todd, and he was going to

89

make a big scene to try to really embarrass Emmy. He yelled at her and tried to grab her, but Tony was there, and he stopped Todd in his tracks. I saw Tony and, like a coward, I ran away. I was really confused and scared. If Tony knew this girl, and she wasn't what Todd accused her of being, then I was helping to ruin an innocent girl's reputation. I knew Tony well enough to know he would never be talking to a slut, pardon my French, Mama."

He sat back down on the couch.

"Well, later, I learned why Todd had a grudge against Emmy, and I learned she was not the way he portrayed her to be. By then the damage had been done." Marco looked at Mama, "I totally lost my temper and beat the crap out of that kid and never talked to him again. I didn't know how to make it up to Emmy or Tony." Marco stopped.

Mama put a hand on his shoulder and asked, "Is that why you left home and stayed with Grandma Dorothea?"

"Yes, I was afraid to face Tony. Later, I learned he and Emmy were dating. That's why I took all the pictures of me out of the living room. I didn't want her to see them."

"Do you think Emmy knows it was you?"

"I can't be sure, but when I see her, I'm going to confess. Then I will tell Tony about my part in the matter."

Later that evening, after dinner, Heather and Alex arrived. They were both very pleasantly surprised to see Marco. Emmy and Kristen stopped by for a quick visit. After Emmy had a chance to talk to Heather, Mama pulled her to the side.

"Sweetheart, Marco is upstairs, and he needs to talk to you in private. Would you feel comfortable talking to him?"

"All right," Emmy answered nervously thinking she knew why. "I'll talk to him."

Mama took Emmy into her bedroom where Marco was waiting. She left the door open as she walked out into the hall. Marco was standing beside Mama's bed and Emmy sat in Mama's chair.

"Emmy, I need to tell you something. After I met you at Heather's wedding, I went home thinking I knew you somehow. One day I heard some news from another old classmate about Todd

90

Delaney. He was a kid I ran around with for a time in high school. Oh, you probably remember that, unfortunately for you... Anyway, it dawned on me. You were the pretty young girl Todd treated so poorly." Marco covered his eyes with a hand as he started crying. "Emmy, I am so, so sorry for what I did. Can you ever forgive me? I don't deserve your forgiveness, I suppose, but I am so sorry."

Emmy jumped up, took Marco's hand and said, "I forgive you, Marco. I forgave you the moment I gave my life to Jesus, and He asked me to forgive the people who had wronged me." Emmy gave Marco a hug and held him tight. "Marco, I love you, and more importantly Jesus loves you, too."

Marco was too stunned to say anything for a moment. He expected to be slapped or something worse. Finally, he replied, "I was a fool for ever believing Delaney. When I realized the truth, I beat the crap out of him, and I moved out of the house. I acted like a coward. I was afraid to face Tony, or you, and admit what I had done. I took all the pictures of me so you wouldn't recognize me. I knew you and Tony were dating by this time. I'm going to tell Tony what I did even though he'll probably hate me."

"He already knows, Marco. You don't have to tell him, and you don't need to worry. He won't hate you. He gave his heart and life to Jesus, too. He's not the same person he was before."

"You knew it was me then, huh?"

"I thought I recognized you at Heather's rehearsal, and I told Tony."

"How did he react? Did he punch a wall?"

"No, he didn't get all mad. He didn't lose his temper. I think it made him sad."

I wish I could change the past..."

Emmy waved a hand. "No need. I've moved past it, but if I ever see Todd Delaney again, I will punch him where it will hurt the most, if you get my drift." Emmy smiled at Marco and he grinned back at her.

Chapter Nine

Emmy poked Kristen's shoulder. "Kristen, wake up. I have to leave now."

Kristen rolled over and opened her eyes. "You stinker! Did you just wake me up to tell me you're leaving?"

"Yeah, I have to be at Kenny's house by eight."

"I hope you enjoy your last day on earth because I'm gonna strangle you when I see you again." Kristen closed her eyes, but reached out for a hug.

"We're coming over to Mama's later," Emmy said. "I'm taking an overnight bag because I might not stay here tonight."

"Why?"

"I'm not sure how late I'll be at Kenny's tonight."

"Will you stay in the house, or out in the apartment?"

Emmy bit her lip. "Not sure, yet."

"I love you whatever you decide."

"You're the best friend in the world, Krissy."

"I know, but you're still gonna get it later," Kristen said as she snuggled deeper into her bed.

"Don't stay in bed too long. You're supposed to help Mama make breakfast," Emmy reminded her.

"I'm gonna stay in bed all day. It's too cold to leave the comfort of this comforter."

Emmy laughed as she tucked the blanket around Kristen. "You're so goofy when you're sleepy."

Emmy arrived in time to help Mrs. Colwell in the kitchen. Tom and Sherry Hanna arrived a few minutes later.

"Emmy, let me see your ring. I am so thrilled you and Kenny are engaged," Sherry said.

Emmy held out her hand to show Sherry and then saw Tom.

"Merry Christmas, Mr. Hanna. Do you want to see my ring?"

"Nope," he said as he leaned against the countertop. "I'm not interested in looking at your ring... unless you stop calling me Mr. Hanna. I haven't been your teacher for a long time and since you're going to be part of the family, I insist you call me Tom."

"Okay, I guess it's all right now. Tom, would you like to see my engagement ring?" Emmy held out her hand.

"Nope. Not interested," Tom said without glancing at her.

"But I called you Tom."

Tom held out his hands and smiled at her. "I'm teasing. Let me see that ring, and I want a hug."

Emmy let him see the ring and then gave him a big hug. He lifted her off her feet as he held her close.

"Kenny was right. You don't weigh fifty pounds."

"I weigh more than fifty pounds," Emmy said just as Kenny walked into the kitchen. She saw him and asked, "Did you tell Tom that I weigh fifty pounds?"

"I might have," Kenny said.

"I weigh more than that, and you know it," Emmy said just before she kissed him.

Kristen eventually got out of bed and headed over to Mama's house to help with breakfast. Mama let Kristen help make the scrambled eggs, but kept a close eye on her.

"Do they look all right, Mama?"

"Yes, dear, you are getting better in the kitchen."

Kristen smiled because Emmy still teased her about not knowing how to boil water.

"Sometimes I make breakfast at home now."

"What do you make?" Tony asked as he walked into the kitchen. "Cold cereal? Or maybe instant oatmeal?"

"FYI, I can make pancakes and eggs, and I can fry bacon."

"Can you make pancakes from scratch?" Tony opened the fridge and grabbed the gallon of milk. He sniffed it to make sure it was all right. Then he poured himself a glass.

"No, I use the mix where you just add water." She blew a stray hair off of her face.

"What are you gonna do after Em and Kenny are married?" Tony asked as he sniffed the scrambled eggs.

"What do you mean?" Kristen tried to shove Tony away from the stove but couldn't budge him.

"You're going to move out, right?" Tony grabbed a slice of bacon. "Get your own place and all."

"Why would I do that? I'm planning to stay in the house with Emmy. Kenny can stay at the carriage house apartment, and they can see each other on weekends, or once a month or something. Just because they're married doesn't mean he will be around all the time," Kristen said with a straight face.

Mama laughed as she saw Tony's reaction. "I think she just got you big-time, son."

"I knew you were kidding," Tony told Kristen as he grabbed her around the waist from behind and picked her up.

"Put me down! You thought I was serious. Admit it."

"So what. It's too early to be thinking straight, and I'm gonna send back any present I might have got you." Tony looked out the window. "John's almost here."

"How can you tell?" Kristen asked.

"His old truck needs a new exhaust system. I can hear him from a mile away."

John Randolph walked in the back door a minute later and saw Tony holding Kristen. Kristen saw John and yelled, "Make him put me down."

"Why? You probably deserve whatever it is you're getting," John said as he walked over to Mama.

"Merry Christmas, John," Mama said.

"Merry Christmas to you, too, Mama," John replied as he gave her a hug. "Have these two been causing trouble already?"

Mama rolled her eyes. "They are teasing each other like they always have."

After breakfast at the Colwell home, it was time to open gifts. The first Christmas present Emmy opened was from Kenny. She kissed him before she ripped the wrapping paper.

She looked at the box. "Is this really from Victoria's Secret?"

"What? No, you aren't supposed to open that one in the house," Kenny said. "I must have mixed it up with another one."

"Should I go ahead and open it?" Emmy asked.

"Maybe you shouldn't," Kenny said.

"Why not?" Dad Colwell asked.

"Because it's something to wear to bed," Kenny said.

"Like a nightgown?" his father asked.

"Sorta."

Emmy opened the box, squealed and closed the lid. "It's a negligee. A sexy one."

Sherry said, "Pull it out, Emmy. We want to see."

"I can't in front of everyone." Emmy bit her lip as she looked at Mr. Colwell and Tom Hanna.

"Don't be a baby. You're getting married in a few months. Show us what Kenny got for you." Sherry tried to grab the box, but Emmy moved it out of reach.

"Let us see," Sherry insisted.

Emmy reluctantly took the negligee out of the box and stood up. She held it up in front of her. The top part was totally sheer and the bottom part only marginally more modest.

Mrs. Colwell looked at Kenny. "Kenneth Travis Robert Colwell! Why did you buy this for Emmy now? You know she can't wear it until April."

"Did you get it for half price because there's not much to that nightgown?" Dad Colwell asked.

"Carter, it's not a nightgown," Mom Colwell said. "It's different."

"What's the difference?" Dad Colwell shrugged.

"The flannel things I wear to bed are nightgowns. This is lingerie. There's a big difference," Mrs. Colwell said as she smiled.

Sherry grinned and smirked, "Emmy, why don't you try it on to make sure it fits?"

"Sherry, don't encourage her. She's not going to try that on with us here," Tom told his wife as he smiled at Emmy.

Emmy looked at Tom and Mr. Colwell as she held the negligee up in front of her. "I don't know what all the fuss is about." She stood up and slipped the negligee over her jeans and top. "No one can see anything."

Everyone laughed and then Sherry said, "I think you're supposed to wear the negligee without anything underneath it."

Emmy replied in her girlish voice, "But if I do that, Kenny will see me naked. I can't let him see me like that!"

"Not even after we're married?" Kenny asked.

"No way! If I let you see me without my clothes on, you might want to have sex. I'm too young and innocent to do that."

Emmy passed around the gifts she had for Mr. and Mrs. Colwell and everyone watched as they opened their gifts—Emmy found sweatshirts with a picture of a large boulder on the front. On the back was the phrase "My son is a rock star." She also bought them each a book from their wishlist at Amazon.com. Then Emmy pulled another gift out of the bag and handed it to Kenny.

"I guess this might be for you, but you probably don't deserve it." Emmy was excited because she thought Kenny would really enjoy her gift.

He tore off the wrapping paper and saw that the box had no identifying label. It was taped shut so Mr. Colwell handed Kenny his pocketknife. Kenny opened the box and removed the packing material. Inside were four new CDs. Two were by The Lyricon—*Let It Fly* and *Free Flying Soul*. One was by Jesus People—*Innocent Blood* and the fourth one Kenny really freaked out over—*Horrendous Disc* by David Solomon.

"Oh, my God! Emmy, where did you find this? This is one of my favorite albums of all time. I have an old vinyl LP of this, but it's so scratched up. This is, as Andy would say, awesome!" Kenny put his arm around Emmy and pulled her close. He kissed her cheek and whispered, "Thank you so much. I hope we can play this later."

"I might stick around," Emmy teased. "I want to hear how the CD sounds."

Kenny grabbed her, pulled her onto his lap and kissed her.

"Stop It! We have more presents to open." Emmy kissed him once more, but then squirmed off of his lap.

They kept opening presents for another thirty minutes. Finally, there were just two gifts left under the tree.

Emmy handed them to Kenny and said, "These two are for you. You have to open the... I guess it really doesn't matter. You can open either one first."

Kenny looked at the gifts. "I'll open the bigger one first."

He did, and it was the PlayStation2. Now he knew what was probably in the other present. He opened the smaller gift and looked at the games Emmy bought.

"Thank you, Emmy."

"Can we set it up out in the carriage house?"

"I suppose. Did you buy this for me, or for you?"

Emmy grinned and said, "A little of both."

Kenny hugged, kissed her and said, "Thank you, Em."

"I have some coffee in the kitchen if anyone would like a cup," Mrs. Colwell mentioned.

"I would love a cup of coffee, Aunt Elly. Come on, Tom. Let's have some coffee." Sherry glared at him because he was staring at Kenny and Emmy.

"I'm not thirsty right now."

"Yes, you are, dear." Sherry took his elbow and yanked.

"Oh, right. I need some coffee. Thanks, Aunt Elly."

Mr. Colwell smiled at his wife. "I could really use a good cup of coffee about now." He kissed his wife, put his arm around her waist, and they headed to the kitchen.

Kenny and Emmy didn't notice everyone had left the room. When they finished kissing, Emmy whispered to Kenny, "Maybe we can go out to the carriage house later, and I could try on my negligee for real. What if it doesn't fit? We should find out now so you can take it back and get one that fits better." She bit her lip and looked coquettishly at him.

"That sounds mighty tempting, but Mom was right." He pulled her onto his lap again, put a hand on her stomach and rubbed it. "You have to save it for after April fifth."

"April fifth? That date jogs my memory for some reason. Is there something I need to do that day? Hmmm." Emmy put a finger to her chin. "Oh, I remember now. That's the day I have to re-fold all the towels in my bathroom."

"You are such a comedian." Kenny looked around. "Where did everyone go?"

"They must be in the kitchen because I can smell fresh coffee." Emmy yawned and said, "I need a nap. Are you sleepy?"

Kenny smiled at her and replied, "Come to think of it, I am a little sleepy myself."

"Maybe we can take a short nap later, huh?"

"Did you forget? We have to go see your parents, and you promised Mama we would come over today," Kenny said.

"I didn't forget, but maybe we'll feel better and be able to stay up later if we take a quick nap." She touched his cheek.

"What time did Mama say they were eating?"

"I think she said four. Heather and Alex are home and so is Marco. Have you ever met Marco?" Emmy asked.

"I think I remember him a little from Roosevelt High. He's a couple years younger than me, right?"

"Yeah, he actually graduated with my class because he missed part of a year because of a serious accident. Heather told me once that he almost died. Tony kept him alive until the paramedics arrived."

"I think I remember hearing about that."

"Derrick will be there, and Mr. and Mrs. Keasling are coming over."

"Aren't we supposed to bring gifts for a grab bag thing?"

"Yes, and I have two for us."

Tom and Sherry needed to leave to visit her parents. They still had to make a stop at Tom's parents' house, also.

"It was nice to see you again, Emmy. If you need any help with the wedding, just let me know. I would be glad to help," Sherry said.

Emmy jumped up from Kenny's lap. "Thanks, Sherry. I might just take you up on that."

It took several minutes for everyone to say goodbye, and, as soon as Tom and Sherry left, Emmy took Kenny's hand.

"We should go see my parents now."

"Are you ready?"

"Yes, I just said a prayer, and I'm ready to go."

They walked over to her parents' house. Kenny carried a bag with the gifts they bought. She hung onto Kenny's arm as they walked up the sidewalk and climbed the steps to the front door. Emmy rang the bell and waited. Mom opened the door and smiled.

"Merry Christmas, Mom."

"Merry Christmas, Emmy. How are you?"

"We're fine. How's Daddy doing? Is he here?"

"He's doing better, but I can't get him to give up his beer. He's outside in the garage. He's looking for his drill or something. He still can't find it."

Emmy and Kenny smiled at each other. Emmy asked, "Kenny, would you go outside and bring him in the house?"

"Sure, be right back." Kenny walked through the house and out the back door.

Emmy told her mother, "We bought Daddy a new cordless drill because he threw his old one away. Doesn't he remember?"

"I don't know. You'll have to ask him."

Kenny noticed the overhead garage was open, so he walked right in and saw his soon-to-be father-in-law talking to a neighbor. They both had a bottle of beer in their hand.

"Hello, Mr. Colasanti. Merry Christmas."

"Hello, Kenny. Merry Christmas to you, too. Want a beer?"

"No, thanks."

"You can have one. I've got plenty. Oh, this is Nick Francona. He lives across the alley. This is Kenny Colwell from down the street. He's in the band Fridays At Five, and he's engaged to Emmy, my youngest daughter."

"Good to meet you, Kenny."

The two men finished their beer, and Mr. Colasanti opened the fridge to grab another one for Nick and himself. Kenny noticed the fridge was full of beer. After the guys finished their second beer, Mr. Colasanti came back in the house with Kenny.

Emmy was in the kitchen with her mother when the guys entered.

"Hi, Daddy. Merry Christmas." Emmy hugged her father and kissed his cheek. "I can smell the beer. Are you being careful? You know what the doctor said."

"I just have two a day."

Everyone made their way into the living room, and Emmy passed out the gifts to her parents. Her father opened his first gift. Emmy always bought a shirt for her father for Christmas. Mom opened her two gifts—A wool sweater and a new cookbook containing recipes from many of the ladies from church. Her father opened his second gift and was surprised.

"Thanks, I need a new drill. My other one was crap, so I tossed it out."

"Kenny's father helped us pick it out. It's cordless and heavy duty. It's eighteen volts—Mr. Keasling recommended it."

"Thank you, sweetheart, and you, too, Kenny."

Mom handed Emmy a card and inside the Christmas card was a gift card from Kerry's Pizza and Pasta.

"Thank you, we love the pizza there. That's where we're going to have the rehearsal dinner, in fact."

Everyone sat, and they talked for a half hour.

Mom asked, "Are you staying for lunch? I can make something if you are."

"We are going to see Kristen and Tony later. Mama Bertucci is making a big dinner for everyone."

Mom raised her eyebrows. *Why are you going over there, Emmy? You turned down his marriage proposal.* She didn't understand why they were still friends. "That's all right. We are going to see Betty and Cliff later."

"We should be going. Have a good time with Aunt Betty. I'll call you later this week."

Emmy hugged her parents, and she and Kenny walked back to his house. They grabbed the PS2 and the games and hurried upstairs to the apartment, but instead of a nap, they set up the PS2 and played the games Emmy bought.

"Kenny, it's three thirty. We should get going. Mama wants to eat at four."

"I'm ready if you are, Em." Kenny shut down the PS2.

A little while later, they pulled into the driveway and walked in the front door of the Bertucci house. The first person Emmy saw was Derrick.

"Well, if it isn't the princess. Merry Christmas! About time you guys got here. Everyone else is waiting. Let me see that ring, and I need a hug."

Emmy held out her hand to show Derrick the ring. He examined it, approved it, and then gave her a hug. He hadn't seen her since Kristen and Tony's graduation party in June.

"I'm very happy for you guys," he said as he shook hands

100

with Kenny. "I might try to make it to the wedding."

Kristen walked into the entryway and saw Emmy and Kenny.

"Did you remember to bring the grab bag gifts and the other ones?"

"Yes, they're in the car. Should we bring them in now?"

"You can wait until after we eat. We are going to do the grab bag right after dinner."

"Where's Mama?"

"In the kitchen with Mom. We're about ready to eat."

Emmy took Kenny to the kitchen, and they wished everyone a merry Christmas. Emmy held out her hand so everyone could admire the ring.

"Emmy, that's a gorgeous ring," Heather held up Emmy's hand. "Aunt Karla, don't you think this is fabulous?"

Kristen's mother admired the ring. "It has been cut so perfectly. It must be about a carat."

"It's not as big as yours, Mother, but it is beautiful." Kristen knew her mother would compare Emmy's ring to her own.

Soon everything was ready, and Mama called everyone into the dining room.

"Derrick, would you run downstairs and let Tony and John know dinner is ready?"

"I'll do it, Mama." Emmy ran downstairs to get the guys. They were on the couch and Emmy walked up behind them. "You guys are watching the Bulls and Lakers, huh? What's the score?"

"Lakers are up ten," Tony said without taking his eyes off of the TV.

"In your face!" John yelled as Jalen Webber hammered home a monster dunk.

"Mama said you have to come upstairs now to eat."

"Be there in a second."

"Mama said now!"

Tony stood up, grabbed Emmy and held her on his shoulder.

"Okay, we're coming."

John turned off the TV and followed as Tony carried Emmy

upstairs and into the dining room. Mama looked at him and shook her head. Emmy looked at Kenny, and he was grinning. He loved the fact Tony and Emmy were still such good friends.

Mama explained, "There are twelve of us here and only room for ten at this table so I thought you younger people could eat in here and I'll eat in the kitchen with Karla and Daniel."

Kenny suggested, "Maybe it would be better if Emmy and I eat in the kitchen. Maybe Kristen and John can join us and you can eat in here, Mama."

"Yes, I like that better," Karla said emphatically. "You're not going to eat in the kitchen, Maria."

Everyone liked this idea because it allowed Mama to eat with her kids and her sister. Tony moved the extra chairs to the kitchen, said a prayer and soon everyone was busy eating.

After the food was put away and the kitchen cleaned, everyone gathered in the living room to open the grab bag gifts.

Kristen explained the rules. "Everyone has a number and whoever has the number one goes first. You can open the gift so everyone can see. Then whoever is number two can either steal the opened gift or take a new one. A gift can only be stolen three times. Got it?"

"It sounds easy enough," Derrick teased his sister.

Emmy looked at her number. She had number two. John had number one. He picked a gift and opened it. It was a cookbook, so Emmy stole it. The game continued, and Emmy hung onto the cookbook until Kristen stole it. Finally, it got down to Kenny who had number twelve. By now all the gifts had been opened except one. He looked at the unopened gift and then turned to Kristen.

"I think I'll steal the cookbook from you."

Kristen reluctantly surrendered the cookbook, "You just want this so you can give it to Emmy. That's all right. We can both use it since we live together."

Kristen opened the last gift, which was a DVD, and the game was over.

"We're going to see Carmen and Sharon," Karla said. "Bobby and Brian are home. I don't often see my nephews."

"They are grown men with busy lives," Mama said.

Derrick hugged Emmy and left with his parents.

Kenny ran out to the car and brought in the presents Emmy and Kristen bought for Tony and John along with his own purchases. They went into the living room so the guys could open the gifts. Kenny knew the girls bought Play Stations for Tony and John.

"Merry Christmas, guys. Kristen and I bought these. We thought you might like them. Kristen, will you take a picture, please?"

Kristen took pictures as Tony and John opened the boxes containing the PS2s. They were as excited as little kids as soon as they realized what was in the boxes. They opened up the games, also.

"Can we set one up now?" Tony asked.

"That's why we bought them," Kristen teased.

"This is for you, too, Tony. I hope you don't already have them." Kenny told Tony as he handed him a gift.

Tony opened the gift and inside were two books—*The Frank Leahy Legend* and *Rockne of Notre Dame: The Making of a Football Legend*.

"All right! Thanks, Kenny. I don't have either of these books." Tony showed them to Emmy and asked, "Do you know who these guys are?"

"Duh! They are econ professors at North Park," Emmy said.

Tony told Kenny, "Grab her so I can tickle her to death."

Kenny held onto Emmy while Tony tickled her behind her knees. She started laughing so hard and tried to get away but couldn't.

"I give! Stop! I know they are famous football coaches."

By now Emmy was in tears as she was lying across Tony and Kenny on her stomach. Tony let go of her legs, so she turned over.

"You will both get it later. You're so mean to me." Emmy sat up and looked Tony and Kenny and then at John and Kristen, who were sitting in the recliners and laughing. "I still think those guys are econ professors."

She tried to get up and get away from the guys, but Kenny managed to grab a belt loop of her jeans and hung on. He pulled her onto his lap, kissed her then said, "If you behave yourself, maybe later I will check to see if Santa brought you something even though you don't deserve it."

Emmy relaxed and slid off Kenny's lap and and sat in the middle of the couch. "I've been good most of the time," she said quietly as she glanced at Kristen.

They headed down to the basement, and Tony hooked up his PS2. He and John began playing Madden 2002 football. Kenny and Emmy challenged Derrick and Kristen to a game of pool. Derrick was the best player and he made more shots than the rest of them combined.

After a couple of hours, they headed back upstairs to the living room.

"Can we have the cookies now, Mama?" Tony patted his stomach. "I'm hungry."

"Okay, but don't eat all of them. You'll make yourself sick. Go get them." Mama waved. "They're in the garage."

Tony hurried to the garage and returned with several containers of many different kinds of holiday cookies. Tony opened one of the containers and showed Emmy.

"These are my favorite. I think they're called macaroons and the lemon bars are good, too."

Emmy tried a couple of different kinds. "I bet they are all good, Tony. I like the peanut butter with the chocolate kiss."

They tried several different kinds before Mama reminded them, "Those are for Marco, Heather and Alex, too. You might want to let them have some before you eat all your favorites."

Tony passed one container to Alex. "Mama always makes these cookies for Christmas. It's the only time of year she makes all these different kinds."

"They are really good, Mama. Will you show me how you make them someday, please?" Emmy asked.

"Of course I will, dear. You will need to know so you can carry on the tradition. Some of these cookies I learned how to make from my mother, and she probably watched her mother make them. Heather doesn't enjoy baking, so I'll be happy to show you. We'll have to wait until next Christmas though."

"I'll look forward to it, Mama."

Shortly after that Kristen needed to talk to Emmy alone.

"What is it, Krissy?" Emmy asked as Kristen pulled her into Mama's sewing room and closed the door.

"John asked me to come to Defiance for a few days after the last game, and he wants me to come over to his apartment now. He wants us to have our own Christmas."

Emmy grinned and asked, "Are you gonna spend the night?"

"He mentioned that. What are you gonna do?"

"Chances are, I'll spend the night at Kenny's house." Emmy put a finger to her mouth. "That means neither of us will be home tonight. Who's gonna let the dog out for a walk?"

"What dog? We don't have a dog, Em."

"I know, but what if we did? One of us would have to be there to let him out."

"You're a goof." Kristen sat in Mama's rocking chair. "I'm a little nervous about going to Ohio to see his family," Kristen confessed as she began rocking back and forth.

Emmy put her hands on the arms of the rocker. "You know his family loves you. They would have to be insane otherwise."

"When they met me before, they were busy with graduation. This time they will have more of a chance to get to know me."

"That's a good thing. They will appreciate you even more." Emmy pulled Kristen out of the rocker and hugged her.

"I have to say good night to everyone. I hope Mama doesn't get mad at me for leaving with John."

"Krissy, we are both adults now. We can do what we please without having to ask Mama for permission," Emmy said.

"Does that mean you will tell her you're spending the night with Kenny?"

Emmy grinned and then shook her head. "Not a chance! She would ground me if she knew."

John gathered up his and Kristen's gifts as she told everyone good night.

"Drive safely, John. I hope nothing happens to your transmission," Tony said as he shook John's hand.

"I'm not taking a chance. We're going to drive Kristen's car," John said. "Unless I decide to get a new truck."

Tony, Emmy and Kenny watched as John and Kristen left. They went back inside and Emmy told Mama, "Thank you for everything. We are gonna take off, too."

"Merry Christmas, dear. I expect you to stop and see me once in a while."

"We will."

Tony walked out to the car with them.

"Merry Christmas, guys. Thanks for the PS2, Em."

"You're welcome. Maybe the next time I'm over I'll challenge you to a game of football. You won't have much of a chance to beat me, but I'll take it easy on you."

Emmy hugged Tony and Kenny shook his hand.

Emmy and Kenny headed back to the Colwell home and sat on the couch across from his parents, who sat in their recliners.

Kenny whispered to Emmy, "Have you really been good this year?"

"I've been good most of the time," she said quietly.

"Let me check in the den to see if there's anything else for you." Kenny smiled and Emmy bit her lip. He went into the den and came back a minute later with a gift. "This doesn't have a name on it. Do you know who it's for, Mom?"

"I didn't buy it, and I know Carter didn't, either," Mom said as she looked at Kenny's father. "You didn't buy it, did you, dear?"

"Can't say that I did."

Kenny handed it to Emmy and said, "I suppose we might as well give it to you then."

Emmy grinned and eagerly took the rather heavy package from Kenny. She quickly ripped off the paper and realized it was a laptop computer just like Kenny's.

"Oh, Kenny, thank you so much. This is just like yours, right?"

"It's an upgraded version of mine. Yours is an IBM ThinkPad 380Z. It's better than mine, but I'm going to get a new one soon."

"Thank you, Kenny. You are so generous to me."

"Now you don't have any excuse for not keeping in touch."

She stuck a finger in his ribs. "I always keep in touch. You're the one who forgets to check his email."

Kenny and Emmy headed out to the carriage house to listen to his new CDs. She pulled him over to the old couch and she sat at one end. She had him sit in the middle, then pulled his head onto her lap as he lay on his back.

"Thank you for the laptop, but you can't keep buying me expensive presents. I need to live on what I make."

"It wasn't that expensive, Em. Besides, after we get married you are going to have more money than you could ever spend."

"I want to save most of our money. I don't want to blow it all on fancy cars. Buying a brand new Civic. How extravagant was that?" Emmy teased.

"I should have bought a Corvette like you suggested," Kenny teased back. "Have you thought about where we're going to live after the wedding?"

"At my house, why?"

"Maybe we should buy a house instead of renting one."

"I can't afford to buy a house."

"*We* can! Are you forgetting that my money will be yours and vice versa. It won't be yours and mine anymore. We will be a team."

"I guess I'm just so used to doing everything on my own."

"We will save money on taxes if we buy a house, let alone being able to file as married."

"I don't want to think about all that stuff yet."

"I know you just want to be married so you can have sex without feeling guilty about it."

Emmy was about to answer back when she stopped. She leaned forward and whispered into Kenny's ear.

"Do you feel guilty?"

"No," he whispered back as he kissed her quickly.

107

"When are you leaving again?" Emmy asked.

"We leave January thirteenth to continue the tour in the States. Then in March we head overseas. I'll be home at the end of February for a few days. I'll have a lot of things to get done then, but I'm going to Florida with my parents Sunday afternoon."

"I didn't know that. Where are you going?"

"We're staying on Sanibel Island..."

"Can I go with you?" Emmy asked excitedly.

"I thought you had to work? If you don't, you can come with us."

"I forgot about work. How long are you gonna be gone?"

"We'll be gone a week."

"If you get a chance, you should go see Grandma. She would love to see you."

"I'll make sure we go see her."

"I just thought of something," she said.

"What?"

"I'll have to add you to my health insurance after we get married."

"No, you don't. I have health insurance already. Everyone in the band does and all of the full-time employees."

"I didn't know that. Good. I won't make you get a real job then," Emmy said and then giggled.

After listening to music and having fun for two more hours, they were ready to fall asleep.

"I want to stay out here with you, but I know I shouldn't."

"I know. I want you to stay, too."

"I should go back in the house. My overnight bag is in your room. I have to work in the morning, but just a half day. I'll be home around one. Should I come straight here, or will you come to my house?"

"I'll meet you at your house. We can make an early dinner and listen to CDs and maybe watch a movie."

"I might need another nap, too," Emmy mentioned as she bit her lip.

Chapter Ten

When Emmy woke up, she could smell breakfast being prepared. She made a pit stop and headed downstairs. She saw Kenny working at the stove so she quietly snuck up behind him.

"I love the smell of bacon in the morning. What time did you get up?" she asked as she wrapped her arms around his waist.

"Morning, Em. I got up at six. Took my shower and got dressed. How did you sleep?"

"Okay, but it was kinda lonely..."

He chuckled and asked, "You always sleep alone, so why was last night any different?"

"Because I kept thinking about you in the carriage house."

"What time do you have to pick up Kristen?"

"By seven-thirty. We're just working till noon. Are you still coming over so we can work on the guest list?"

"I'll be there when you get home. Should I make lunch, or will you stop and pick up something?"

"Why don't you make lunch for us? There's some stuff in the fridge that needs to get used."

"I'll see what I can do. How many strips of bacon do you want?"

"Three is enough for me."

"I've got some scrambled eggs and some potatoes ready."

Because his parents were still in bed, Kenny and Emmy ate breakfast in the kitchen by themselves.

"Remind me to give you a fresh overnight bag to bring back here. I will have to wear jeans to the office today unless I change at home."

"Will Mr. Oliver mind if you wear jeans since it's the day after Christmas?"

"No, he's kinda relaxed the office dress code. I don't think any of the other guys will be there today except Mr. Oliver. Did I tell you he's going to retire in June?"

"I don't remember you saying anything about that." Kenny looked at Emmy and asked, "What are you going to do after we get married? Are you gonna keep working, or should I find you a spot in the band? There are always openings."

"We need to talk about that. We have to make some important decisions about our future."

Emmy drove back to the house, ran in the back door and yelled, "Kristen! Are you here?"

Emmy heard footsteps coming down the stairs.

"I'm here and ready to go."

"Did you sleep here last night, or did you stay at John's?"

"He brought me home around one, so I didn't get a lot of sleep."

Emmy was about to ask Kristen about her time at John's apartment, but from the look on Kristen's face, Emmy knew she shouldn't.

They spent a half day at the office. Emmy and Mr. Oliver were the only ones working from their team. Kristen's team was working a full day, but she got off at noon. Emmy met Kristen at her office and they had a chance to talk as they walked out of the fifteen-story building together.

"Are you hungry, Em? Should we stop and grab something for lunch?"

"I got a text from Kenny. He's making taco salad. Will that be all right?"

"Sure, I love taco salad. Is he coming over, or are we going over there?"

"We're going home. We have to work on the guest list. Can you help us for a little while?"

"Yeah, but I'm supposed to meet John after they get home from practice."

"What are you guys doing tonight? There's no practice at church this week."

"Not sure. John mentioned going out to eat, but we'll just play it by ear," Kristen said and then asked, "Where did you sleep last night?"

Emmy grinned and Kristen gave her a hard stare.

"Don't tell me you both slept in the carriage house."

"No, I slept in the house, and he stayed in the apartment. I just wanted to see how you would react."

110

"You have to behave until you're married. The time will go by faster than you realize," Kristen said. *I don't care what you've done in the past, Emmy.*

"I know, but sometimes..." Emmy nudged Kristen's side. "How did you guys celebrate your *own* Christmas?"

"He set up the PS2, and we played with that."

"And..." Emmy said slowly. "What else?"

"We stayed out of his bedroom." Kristen changed the subject. "How does Kenny make taco salad?"

"Fine! Be that way."

"Does Kenny have a key to the house?"

"He has a full set of keys. Both doors, the garage and the spare key for the car. You know I'm paranoid about losing my keys. You're not upset that he has a house key, are you?"

"No, I guess not. John has a key, too."

Emmy had a little trouble starting Kenny's old Civic. It finally started and warmed up after a time.

"Em, do you think maybe it's time for a new car? After you get married at least."

"I might not need a new car then, Krissy. I might not be working for Robertson Industries."

"Oh, no! You can't quit! I will miss you if we aren't working together."

"I've been thinking about whether I will stay, or start working with Kenny in some capacity."

"Have you mentioned anything to Mr. Oliver?"

"Not yet. He's retiring in June, so it might be a good time to leave."

Kristen tried to talk Emmy out of leaving during the ride home.

"I'm not going to make a decision today. We have to pray about it, and God will provide the answer."

"I said a prayer and asked Him already. He told me that He needs you to stay and work with me," Kristen teased.

"You're so funny," Emmy said. "I'm serious about this. I'm not working in April, and Kenny is leaving in June. I want to go with him, so I'm pretty sure I will quit by then."

111

"I know you guys don't need the money, but what will you do if you leave?"

"Duh!"

"Besides that," Kristen said as she rolled her eyes.

"This isn't an easy choice, Krissy. Mr. Robertson is a great boss. I don't want to come across as being ungrateful."

"You could stick it our for two more months."

"I'll see," Emmy said.

Kenny had the taco salad made and the kitchen table set by the time Emmy and Kristen arrived home. Kristen walked in the back door first and saw Kenny.

"How was work today?"

"Not too busy. The taco salad smells good. Thanks for making lunch. I gotta run upstairs to change, but I'll be right back."

Kenny wondered why she made it so clear she would be right back. "Okay, should I fill a bowl of taco salad for you?" he asked slowly.

Kristen realized how she sounded. "Sorry, I guess I just wanted to make sure you guys didn't start kissing or anything."

Emmy walked into the kitchen after having checked the mailbox on the front of the house.

"What's this about kissing? Who's been kissing?"

"Nothing, Em. I'll be right back."

Emmy wondered what Kristen was thinking about, and then she kissed Kenny. "The taco salad looks good. Is it ready?"

"It's good to go. Kristen was reminding me she will be right back so we didn't start kissing or anything."

"She asked me where I slept last night."

"What did you tell her? Did you tease her and tell her we slept together?"

"Not really. I just grinned at first, but then I told her the truth. Let's eat, then get started on the wedding plans."

They each ate second helpings of taco salad before moving into the dining room to take a look at the guest list. Emmy looked at the list her mother gave her.

"I don't even know half these people."

Kenny was looking at the list his mother gave him. "Same

112

thing here. Maybe we should come up with a number of guests we want to invite first. Then we can start eliminating people until we get down to the magic number."

"I think that's a good idea, you guys," Kristen said. "I read somewhere that the first thing you need to decide is how many guests you are going to invite. There is an equation that takes in the size of the reception hall and everything. The room at the hotel can accommodate over five hundred guests easily."

Emmy looked at Kenny and asked, "Are we gonna have to invite some of your celebrity friends?"

"Do you mean like Bono Evans or Michael Buck? People like that, or are you talking about people like Mr. Kesson?"

Emmy laughed. "I guess I was thinking about people like Mr. Kesson. He does own the record company. I wasn't thinking about rock stars."

"That's good because I don't want this to turn into a circus. I want it to be a normal wedding for people from the church. I don't think we can invite everyone from both churches though. That could get kinda crazy."

"I agree. Are we gonna invite children to the reception, or just adults?"

"If you make it strictly for adults, you won't be able to go, Em," Kristen said with a straight face. "You're just a kid, too."

"Very funny. Oh, Kenny, before I forget, did you ask Tony about standing up for you?"

"Yes, and he said there was no way he would ever do that. He said he doesn't even want to go to the wedding or reception."

Emmy looked stunned and her lip quivered.

Kenny and Kristen began to laugh. "I'm teasing, Em," Kenny said. "I'm sorry. I didn't think it would make you cry. Tony said he would be honored and would do it on one condition."

"What is that?"

"Two things really. First he wants to be able to kiss the bride and give her a hug. And he wants you to promise you will dance with him at least once."

Emmy smiled. "He drives a hard bargain, but I accept his conditions."

Kristen looked at her and asked, "Did you really think he wouldn't go to your wedding?"

"I guess I was thinking he was mad at me since he asked me first."

"You are a goof sometimes."

Kenny got them back on track. "Okay, we need to come up with a number of guests we can invite."

"How much did Paula say it would cost us per guest?" Emmy asked.

"I wrote it down," Kristen said. She looked at her notes. "Here it is. She said we should figure a hundred dollars a guest."

Kenny used the calculator. "Five hundred times one hundred is fifty thousand."

"Dollars? Fifty thousand dollars?" Emmy asked. "There's no way I can afford to pay that much."

Kenny chuckled and said, "Emmy, you don't have to pay for everything yourself. I think I might be able to help a little."

"Oh, I guess I wasn't thinking about that, but we still have to come up with a lower number."

"Why?" Kristen asked.

"Because that's way too much money. Maybe we can cut down on some of the expenses."

Kenny looked at Kristen and offered a suggestion, "Yeah, we could eliminate flowers and the photographer and not have any food at the reception."

"That sounds like a good idea, Kenny," Kristen said as she nodded. "You could not hire a band and just play music on the band's PA. What about eliminating the open bar? You could just serve water. Maybe pop, too."

Emmy crossed her arms across her chest and listened to Kristen and Kenny. "Are you through?"

"You said we need to lower the cost. Do you have a better idea?"

"You guys are teasing me."

Kenny kissed her and said, "Em, do you remember that I have a few dollars stashed away?"

Kristen looked at Kenny and, though she had never asked

114

him about money before, she asked, "How much did you make last year? Was it over a million dollars?"

Kenny smiled, but didn't say anything.

"Higher? Over ten million dollars?"

He answered, "A bit higher than that."

"Oh my God!" Kristen's eyes opened wide. "Does everyone in the band make that much money?"

"I probably make a bit more because I write more songs than the other guys. Dave doesn't write many songs, but he does other things for the band." Kenny paused and looked at Emmy. "What do you do with your royalty checks? Have you spent all that money?"

"What royalty checks?" Kristen asked.

Emmy didn't say anything as she pulled her knees to her chest.

"Emmy!" Kristen said slowly. "Answer me."

Emmy bit her lip and twisted her hair into a braid, but she still didn't say anything.

"Emmy gets royalties on the songs she helped write," Kenny answered for her.

"I haven't spent any of that money. I gave the church ten percent and repaid Grandma the money she paid on rent for me and Diane. I gave some to Mom, but the rest was invested. Mr. Robertson's financial guy took care of it for me."

"How much money are we talking about?" Kristen asked.

"The last check I saw was for over a hundred thousand dollars," Kenny said.

"Are you kidding me?" Kristen stood up rather quickly and knocked over her glass of water as she put her hands on the table. "For crying out loud, Emmy, if you have that much money in the bank, then why on earth do you cut out all those coupons, and you never buy anything unless it's on sale. You won't buy a new dress unless it's reduced to half price or less."

"I don't want to use that money. It's for a rainy day. I might lose my job or something might happen to Daddy or..."

Kristen ran into the kitchen, grabbed some paper towels and wiped up the water. "Oh my God! You are unbelievable. You

115

guys are unreal. We go grocery shopping, and I worry about every cent. We buy the house brand to save a few pennies." Kristen started to laugh. "Emmy Colasanti, you are going to have the best wedding we can put together, and if I hear one more word about how much something costs, I am gonna swat your butt."

Emmy looked at Kristen and said, "I saw a wedding dress that was fifty percent off that I like."

Kristen threw her arms in the air and cried out, "Lord, help me. She's worse than my grandmother who was raised during the depression and has a reason to be the way she is."

"I can't help it if I try to be careful with the money I make from my job. We never had much growing up, so that's how I learned to live."

"Oh, sweetie!" Kristen moved over behind her and hugged Emmy. "I'm not trying to change you, or make fun of you. I guess I assumed you were as broke as you act. I'm glad that you have some money invested for the future."

"Can we agree that we can afford to spend whatever it takes to make this a nice wedding?" Kenny asked. "I'm not saying we go nuts, but we can afford to invite as many people as the reception hall can hold."

Emmy looked at Kenny, then Kristen. "All right, but I'm not letting you pay for the whole thing."

"I will if I need to, but you can pay for part of it, too."

They agreed to spend the money and then started looking at the guest list. Emmy was looking at the list her mother provided.

"I have no idea who George and Bessie Williams are. I can't believe my mother expects me to invite the Sanders family." Emmy kept looking at the list. "There's no way I'm inviting the Fronczeks."

"Who are they?"

"They're the people who used to live next door to us. They're probably a hundred years old, and they moved away ten years ago."

"I think it's safe to cross them off the list, Em."

After working on the list for three hours, they had cut it down to 550 people not counting kids.

"I think we have to eliminate kids from the reception. They can come to the wedding, but how about we say no kids at the reception?"

"Can I make a suggestion?" Kristen asked.

"What?"

Kristen explained, "You could look into setting up a day care room for the parents with small kids who might otherwise not be able to come."

"I bet we could use the church's facility for that," Emmy said. "We could hire some of the teens and a few adults who wouldn't be coming."

"That sounds like a plan."

"Okay, then let's say no kids, but offer the babysitting option."

Kenny looked at the clock and was surprised at the time. "I gotta run. I'll see you later."

Kristen said to Emmy, "We should take my car to work tomorrow. I'm afraid yours is gonna quit on us because of the cold weather."

Kenny looked at Emmy and asked, "Are you having trouble with the Civic?"

"I think it needs a tune-up or something. Maybe a new battery. It's getting harder to start in the morning and after sitting outside at work all day."

"We can trade it in, Em. You don't have to keep it just because I gave it to you. You won't hurt my feelings if you want a new car."

Emmy looked at him for a moment and then grinned.

Kenny saw the grin and told her, "You're not getting a Corvette or a Ferrari or some fancy sports car. It has to be something sensible and practical."

"Some rock star you are. I suppose it has to be a Honda."

"It doesn't have to be, but they are very reliable."

Emmy kissed him. "I love you even if you are the dorkiest rock star in the world."

Chapter Eleven

Three days later, on the twenty-ninth, Tony, John and the Bears prepared to play their final game of the season at home against Tampa Bay. Before she and Kristen left for the game, Emmy was able to see Kenny for a few minutes. He would be flying to Florida that afternoon. He stopped over at their house and brought health food, as he called them—chocolate muffins with chocolate chips.

"You brought my favorites. Thank you, sweetie." Emmy kissed Kenny as Kristen watched from the kitchen doorway.

"I know you like blueberry muffins, so I brought two of them for you, Kristen."

"That was thoughtful of you. What time do you have to leave for the airport?" Kristen asked.

"I guess we need to be there by one."

"How are you getting there?" Emmy asked as she took a large bite of a muffin.

"Andy is going to drive us."

"Tell him I said hi when you see him," Emmy said.

Kenny stuck around for a few minutes, but then had to leave so he could make it to church on time.

"I'll miss you, but at least you'll only be gone for a week," Emmy told him as she kissed him again.

"I will miss you, too. I'm sorry I'm gonna miss the New Year's Eve party, Kristen."

"That's all right. To tell you the truth I'd rather be in Florida myself," Kristen said. "I don't like cold weather anymore."

Emmy kissed Kenny one more time. "Have a good time and don't get sunburned."

"I won't, and I'll try to go see Grandma Isabel. You know you could always quit your job, and we could just live on my earnings. Then you could go on vacation all the time."

"Like you do," Emmy teased.

"If you call being on tour a vacation, you are sorely mistaken, young lady. You should come with me sometime for a few months, and you'll realize it's work."

118

"I offered to go with you before," Emmy said.

"I know, but it wasn't the right time. After April it might just be the right time."

"I'll see you when you get back. I need to let you get to church."

"Stay warm at the game today, Em. It's going to be cold."

"I'll have Kristen with me. We'll keep each other warm."

After a hug and another kiss, Kenny was out the door.

Later, Emmy and Kristen huddled together at Soldier Field to keep warm. The temperature was in the twenties with a slight breeze.

"My feet are freezing," Kristen complained.

"Don't be a wimp. Just keep moving them."

"If they win today, they will finish with a winning record, right?"

"Yeah, they would be nine and seven. Tampa Bay has a tough defense, though. It won't be easy to score against them."

"Do they sell hot chocolate here, Em? I need something to warm up my insides."

The fan next to Kristen overheard her. "I have some hot apple cider in this thermos. I snuck it in. I'll share with you ladies."

Since he sat next to them all season, Emmy and Kristen knew him.

"Thanks. How did you sneak it in?"

"Our son actually works for the Bears. My name's Fred Baxter and this is my wife Marilyn. Do you girls have season tickets?"

"Actually, our boyfriends are on the team."

"I thought so. Didn't I tell you that, Marilyn? I've listened to you, but I didn't want to pry. Who is your boyfriend?"

"Number eighty-four, John Randolph, the tight end. My name's Kristen Keasling and this is Emmy Colasanti."

"I know her boyfriend is Tony Bertucci because she yells his name all the time."

"Well, technically, he's not her boyfriend. He's my cousin, and he and Emmy are good friends."

Fred handed Kristen a paper cup of hot apple cider.

119

"Thanks, Mr. Baxter."

"You're welcome. Maybe we will see you next year. We've had the same seats for a long time."

"Next year the Bears are gonna win the Super Bowl," Emmy predicted.

The offense sputtered and the Bears lost to finish the year 8-8. Injuries had taken a toll on the team this year though Tony and John managed to make it through unscathed. However, they were worn down after the long season.

Tuesday night was the New Year's Eve party at the Keasling home.

"I'm glad your parents are letting you have the party here even though you don't live here anymore," Emmy said as she and Kristen arrived at the house.

"They're at the cabin in Wisconsin, so they don't care."

"There's so much more room here than at our house," Emmy said as she helped Kristen with some holiday decorations a little later. "Are we still planning to crash here tonight?"

"I guess it depends on how late we stay up. I don't want to drive home in the middle of the night. There will be too many drunks on the road."

"It's not that far, Krissy."

"That's not the point. We could get hit by a drunk driver just down the street. I'd rather stay here. You did bring an overnight bag, right?"

"I've been keeping one in the car." Emmy positioned a centerpiece just right. "Are you still going to Ohio tomorrow?"

"Yes, John wants to leave right after breakfast."

"Then we should go home after the party. Derrick will be here. He can clean up the house," Emmy said.

"Good idea. I still need to finish packing."

"I assume Tony's coming alone. Maybe he will keep me company since Kenny's in Florida."

But Tony surprised Emmy, and Kristen, too, when he arrived shortly after nine with Sloane Beckett from church. Emmy and Kristen saw them as they walked into the family room.

120

"Hey guys, happy new year," Kristen told Tony and Sloane. "I'm glad you could make it."

Sloane turned 360 degrees as she looked at the house. "I'm happy to be here. This is a fantastic house, Kristen. Tony told me a little about it on the way over here."

"Thanks, Sloane. Mom and Dad talk about selling it and getting a smaller place since Derrick and I are gone, but I hope they don't. This is still home to me."

"Hi, Sloane."

"Hi, Emmy, is Kenny here?"

"No, he had a trip planned with his parents. They're in Florida right now."

"Do you have to work? Is that why you didn't go with him?" Sloane asked.

"Unfortunately, I have to work the rest of the week," Emmy said. She looked up at Tony and asked, "Do I get a hug tonight?"

"I suppose I can spare one hug. It's good to see you, Em. You look nice tonight. Is that a new dress?"

"You know it's not new. I wore it when we went to dinner at Ciao Bella," Emmy said, but then she realized that might not sound right to Sloane. Emmy looked up at Sloane.

Sloane smiled at Emmy and put her at ease. "It's okay. I know you guys are friends and used to date. You don't have to try to hide that."

In some ways the party was a reunion of Roosevelt High grads. Most of them had graduated from college already. Some of them from North Park College, but not all. Emmy saw Barry and Linda Newton for the first time in quite a while.

"Hi, guys. I didn't know if you would make it." Emmy stood in front of them as they sat on the couch in the family room.

"Hi, Emmy. Just a few more months and you and Kenny will be married."

"And it won't be too long before you are a daddy. I still can't picture you with a baby, Barry. No offense meant."

"None taken. Sometimes I wonder about that myself."

"How are you doing, Linda?"

"Okay. I feel as big as a house, though." Linda rubbed her

121

belly. "I make Barry rub my feet for me because I can't."

Later, as she wandered through the house, Emmy heard the latest news about Damon Barclay and Diana Ahronson Barclay. They had only been married since June and Diana was expecting already. Emmy spotted Adrien and Elaine Coyle talking to Cindy Mackens in the living room. She overheard the news that Cindy broke off her engagement with Bryce Harper after she learned he was seeing another woman. Mace Franklin and his wife Erin were talking with Elaine and Cindy. Mace was coaching basketball at Roosevelt High and teaching physical education. As Emmy was leaning against the large arched entrance to the living room, she felt a tap on her shoulder and turned around.

"Annie O'Dell! How are you?"

"Hi, Emmy. I'm doing all right. Let me see that ring. I heard you were engaged. Congratulations. Have you guys set a date yet?"

Emmy held out her hand. "It's April fifth. Oh, Annie, I need your address. Where are you living these days?"

"I'm living in Daddy's old house. He built a new one on the farm. He and Elisabeth and Keyshon are living there."

"How is your grandfather doing?" *I should send him a thank you note for helping out with Daddy.*

"He's doing great. He loves being retired."

Emmy glanced around. "Are you here by yourself? Where's Matt?"

"At work. When his father died, he inherited The Hungry Lion. He's been working seventy hours a week. Sometimes more."

Emmy made sure she had Annie's current information so she could invite her to the wedding.

"Emmy! Where have you been? I've been looking all over for you."

"Hi, Kristen. I've been talking to friends from high school."

Kristen pulled Emmy into the dining room where they could talk more privately.

"Did you hear that Maris Harris is expecting again?"

"No, I hadn't heard that. I still can't get used to her name. Maris Harris. Grady should have changed his name. He could be Grady Miller." Emmy grinned.

"They could have changed their names to Harris-Miller."

"Where's Derrick?" Emmy looked around. "I haven't seen him anywhere."

"He and Amber are upstairs. Amber wanted to change her dress or something."

"Do you think they will ever get married?"

"Who knows?" Kristen shrugged. "I don't think Derrick wants to get married until he's finished with school and has a practice somewhere."

"I got an email from Kenny yesterday. He said he would text me when it was midnight down there."

Kristen asked, "Did you know Tony was bringing Sloane Beckett to the party?"

"I didn't know, but I'm glad he did. This will give him a chance to get to know her better. I'm not sure if I should pair him up with Sloane or Lindsey Cameron."

"Maybe you should let Tony choose who he wants to date."

Emmy poked Kristen in the ribs. "No, not that kind of pairing up. I meant for the wedding. Both Sloane and Lindsey have agreed to be bridesmaids."

"That great. I like both of them. They're such sweet girls. Sloane might make a better partner for Tony since she is taller than Lindsey," Kristen said. Then she turned Emmy around and pulled on Emmy's braid. "What do you think of Sloane's hairstyle? We could get ours cut that short."

"I would look like a boy if my hair was that short," Emmy said. "Where did Tony go?"

"I think he's watching TV with Sloane and a bunch of guys," Kristen answered. "Did you know Sloane played basketball in college?"

"No, but she is as tall as Heather. Where did she go?"

"Olivet Nazarene University. She must have been pretty good to get a scholarship to play ball."

Just then Emmy's cell phone buzzed.

"It's probably Kenny," she told Kristen.

"You should go in there." Kristen pointed. "Even if you're just texting."

123

Emmy walked into the butler's pantry for some privacy.

"Happy New Year!" Kenny texted.

"What are you doing?"

"Listening to some band. Are you having fun?"

"It would be more fun if you were here. Gotta go. Talk to you later. Love you!"

"Love you, too. Bye."

Kristen waited until Emmy was finished and asked, "Do you remember hearing me talk about Solomon Berkshire and Ashley Zeigler?"

"Weren't they the computer geeks from North Park?"

"Yeah, that's them. They both have doctorates already. I heard they were living in California and working for some computer company," Kristen said.

Emmy and Kristen mingled with the guests and kept hearing all the latest news about people from high school and college. It surprised them to hear that so many of them had moved away from the area. Adrien and Elaine Coyle were living in Colorado Springs where he served on the staff of a large church.

"Hi, Emmy."

Emmy heard Derrick's voice and turned around to face him. "There you are. I was looking for you. What have you guys been doing all night?"

Derrick moved close and hugged Emmy. "Are you sure you want to know?"

"Not if it's what I think it was."

"We were studying. You were probably thinking about something else."

Emmy grinned at Derrick.

"You look fantastic, Emmy. I guess you are enjoying being engaged."

Kristen put her arm around Emmy's waist. "She wishes she was married already. All she can talk about is having sex."

"Kristen! I do not." She pushed Kristen's arm away.

Kristen gave Emmy a dirty look. "Don't lie."

"Not all the time, anyway. Where's Amber?" Emmy asked.

"She's in the kitchen. She needed some water."

"How are things between you guys?"

"We're not getting married anytime soon if that's what you're asking. We're both too busy with school."

"Maybe someday, though?"

"Probably. I hear you're a recording star now, Emmy."

"I'm not a recording star, Derrick." She poked him in the chest. "Kenny produced a CD for the worship band from church."

"What's the name of the band? Kristen told me, but I forgot."

"Crest Ridge Worship Band."

"Isn't it actually Crest Ridge Worship Band featuring Emmy Colasanti?"

"I suppose if you want to get technical, but that was not my decision. Mr. Kesson at Steward Music wanted it that way. He thought he might want me to make another CD someday."

"You mean he saw the potential in you, Emmy. You could have a career as a singer if you want it."

"I'm not sure that's what God has planned for me, Derrick."

"You never know, Em. It might be."

When the countdown arrived, most of the guests had a glass of champagne for the toast. Emmy, Kristen, Tony and Sloane drank sparkling grape juice.

A few minutes later, Emmy saw Tony and Sloane in the living room and asked, "Did you know Sloane played basketball for Olivet?"

"Yeah, she told me the first time we went out..."

"The first time? I didn't know you guys went on a date before tonight."

Tony held Emmy's shoulders and smiled at her, "I don't tell you everything, Em."

"How many times have you gone out?"

Sloane looked at Tony and then at Emmy. "I guess tonight is the fourth time we've been out together."

"Good for you guys. Maybe we can go out for dinner after Kenny gets back from Florida."

"When is he getting back?" Tony asked and then added, "I bet you get tired of hearing that question."

"Yeah, I hear that a lot. They're coming back on Sunday. The tour starts on January thirteenth. He will be home at the end of February for a couple days. They will be gone during March, but home for the whole month of April."

"Oooh! A whole month. Where are you going on your honeymoon, Em?" Tony asked.

"We haven't decided yet, but I know where we're spending our first night."

"Will you tell me where you're gonna go on your honeymoon, or is that too personal?"

"Tony! You shouldn't pry." Sloane grabbed his arm.

"It doesn't matter if you know. I'm sure we will tell our friends."

"What about your wedding night?" Tony asked with a grin because he was sure that would embarrass Emmy.

"We gonna stay in the apartment above the carriage house," Emmy answered without a hint of embarrassment.

"Tony, you shouldn't try to embarrass Emmy like that," Sloane said.

"It's okay. I think Tony would be more embarrassed if I told him the details afterward." She grinned and she and Sloane both giggled as Tony turned red and fidgeted with his collar and tie.

"Sloane, have I ever told you how I hang Emmy from the ceiling at home?" Tony asked.

"No, what do you mean?"

"I used to grab her ankles and lift her up. I won't do it now, but I could if she wasn't wearing a dress."

Sloane looked at Tony and said, "You better not try that with me. I don't care how strong you are."

"I won't try it here, but I bet I could do it at home. I have been doing that to Emmy almost since we first met."

"Yeah, Sloane, he has always treated me like a little sister. Don't let him get away with treating you like that."

"Believe me. He won't." Sloane smiled at Tony and then kissed him.

Chapter Twelve

"Did you finish packing?" Emmy asked Kristen the next morning while making breakfast.

"All done. John should be here in an hour. Pancakes, huh?"

"You can have some. I made enough." Emmy flipped some of the pancakes over. "Are you nervous about seeing his family?"

"I've got butterflies."

"You'll be all right. They will love you."

Kristen set the table and pulled the maple syrup and butter from the fridge. "Do you think there's a chance they won't?"

"Certainly!" Emmy turned to face Kristen. "His family could be certifiably insane."

"You're a big help," Kristen said.

"Don't worry. They will love you as much as you love John."

"Easy for you to say. Kenny's parents have always loved you like a daughter."

Emmy frowned. "How do you mean?"

"Not like that, you goof."

"I know what you mean." Emmy stacked the pancakes on a plate. "I want to hear all the details when you get home." Emmy smiled. "And I mean all the details."

Kristen shook her head. "Not a chance. I'm glad we came home after the party. I'm more used to living here."

Forty-five minutes later, Emmy hollered from the kitchen. "Kristen, John just pulled in the driveway. Is this the only suitcase you're taking?"

"That large blue one, and I have my small travel case," Kristen responded from the bathroom.

Emmy tried to lift the blue suitcase. "You do realize you're only going to be gone for three days, right? This thing weighs a ton."

John knocked on the back door.

"Come on in, John," Emmy yelled.

Kristen walked out of the bathroom and into the kitchen from one doorway as John entered from the pantry area.

127

"Morning, John," Kristen said.

"She packed enough for a month," Emmy said.

John lifted the suitcase as though it weighed less than a pillow. "Here are my keys, Emmy. You can use the truck if you want while we're gone."

Emmy laughed. "I would be afraid to drive it. It might fall apart and leave me stranded."

"My car is getting old. I might need to buy a new Acura soon," Kristen said as she grabbed her purse.

John loaded the luggage into Kristen's 1996 Acura CL and moved his truck out of the way.

Emmy walked outside and hugged Kristen. "Have fun and call me when you get there."

"Yes, Mom."

Four hours later, John pulled onto the concrete driveway of his parents 60s-era ranch home and they got out of the car. "Well, this is it. We made it."

Kristen spotted Mr. Randolph just inside the front door. "I'm a bit nervous, John."

"Relax! Mom and Dad are fond of you for some reason."

"Evalyn!" Jerry Randolph hollered as he stepped outside. "They're here." He walked over to the car and waited.

"Hi, Dad. We made it." John hefted Kristen's suitcase out of the trunk.

"How was the traffic?" Mr. Randolph smiled at Kristen. "Let me look at you." He shook his head and then laughed. "I still can't believe Johnny has such a beautiful girlfriend."

"Did you say that to all his girlfriends?" Kristen held her travel case in one hand and her purse over her shoulder as she waved to Mrs. Randolph.

John said, "I don't think he's ever called any of my old girlfriends beautiful. He must really meant it, Krissy."

Mrs. Randolph scurried over to Kristen. "Please forgive my appearance." She patted her hair. "I've been baking pies and haven't had a chance to clean up.

Kristen noticed what appeared to be a cherry or possibly strawberry stain on Mrs. Randolph's white apron. "You look fabulous, Mrs. Randolph," Kristen said as they hugged.

"Thank you and please call me Evie."

Kristen's nervousness vanished.

"Come on in. We're watching football. You do like football, right?" Mr. Randolph asked.

"I'm not a maniac like Emmy, but I do like to watch," Kristen said.

Mr. Randolph put an arm around her shoulder. "We're flipping back and forth between games now, but the Rose Bowl will be on later. We always watch that together."

"Are Kirk and Keith coming over?" John asked.

"Of course. Everyone will be here for dinner," Mom said. "You will have to miss part of a game in order to eat."

"Do you need any help in the kitchen?" Kristen asked.

"I've got it under control, dear. Roslyn and Pam are bringing some food. I'm making pies and a pot of sloppy joe mix. We keep it simple on New Year's. The guys watch football all day."

Kristen smiled. *Did Tony tell John to tell you I don't know how to cook? I do know how to do some things.* Kristen noticed the brick planter next to the sidewalk under the overhang as she walked into the house. *I bet you plant lots of flowers.*

John held the door open for Kristen, and she grinned at him. "Are you being gallant today?"

"I open doors for you." He put a hand on the small of her back.

She stepped into the living room and immediately noticed the walnut-colored paneling along the far wall. *That reminds me of the paneling in Grandpa Keasling's house.*

"John, would you put Kristen's luggage in the spare bedroom, please? You can use your old room," Mom said.

John had described the house on the drive. There were three bedrooms and one bath upstairs. In the early 70s, Mr. Randolph had finished the basement and added two bedrooms and a second full bath. The rest of the basement was divided between a large family room and the unfinished laundry and furnace area.

"I need to check my pies," Mom said. "I don't want them to burn."

Kristen followed Mrs. Randolph into the farm-style kitchen and noticed the cabinets matched the paneling. "How many will there be for dinner? I could set the table," Kristen said as she gazed at the long table at the other end of the room.

"Technically, only eight," Evalyn said as she grinned.

Kristen tilted her head.

"Roslyn and Pam are both expecting. We will have two grandchildren in three months."

John's brothers and their wives arrived at halftime of the Rose Bowl. John reintroduced Kristen to his brothers and their wives. She shook hands with the guys. *All of you are taller than Tony, but I think John is the tallest.*

"When are you due?" Kristen asked as she helped set the table for dinner.

"April fifteenth. Both of us," Roslyn answered as she patted her baby bump. "We didn't plan it that way."

Later that night, Kristen sat beside John until the end of the Orange Bowl. "I need to go to bed. It's been a long day," she said.

John walked up the stairs with her. "Would you mind if I show you around town tomorrow? I'd like to show you the high school where we went. Dad teaches science there. And the hospital where Mom works. She's a nurse."

"I'd love to see some of the places where you grew up."

After breakfast, John took Kristen on a tour of the city.

"What's the population of Defiance?" Kristen asked.

"Fifteen, sixteen thousand, I guess. Give or take. That's the courthouse." John pointed.

"That's a unique building. I like the reddish brick, and the windows are different on each of the three floors."

John drove past the single-story high school and pointed out the football stadium. "It's called the Fred Brown Stadium."

"Who was he?"

"As far as I know, he was a local baker who donated a lot of dough to build it. Never met him myself."

"Real funny," Kristen said. "You probably told me before, but where do your brothers live?"

130

"Kirk and Roslyn live in Lima. They're both teachers. Keith and Pam live in Findlay."

"What do they do?"

"Keith sells insurance and Pam works in a doctor's office part-time. I'm not sure if they'll keep working after the babies are born. Roslyn will go back to teaching, I suppose."

By the time Kristen got ready to leave Defiance on Friday, she felt completely at ease with his family.

"You make sure to come back and see us soon, okay?" Mrs. Randolph baked two apple pies for John to take home. "Don't let him eat these all at once."

Mr. Randolph walked her out to the car and opened the door for her. "Hurry back, Kristen. You can bring him if you want."

"I might have to do that."

A few minutes later, John stopped at a red light and laughed for no apparent reason.

"What's so funny?"

"You have really charmed Dad. He never made such a fuss over Roslyn or Pam. He must really think you're special."

"Maybe I am, John Randolph," she said. "By the way, you have a green light."

John pulled into Emmy and Kristen's driveway just after five on Friday.

"See! I told you we would get home in plenty of time for the game," Kristen said. "But I don't know why you want to watch. Miami is going to kick Ohio State's butt."

"We'll see. They might surprise you."

Emmy heard them arrive and ran outside without a coat. "You're early. I didn't expect you back until later."

"Where's your coat? It's snowing. You'll freeze," Kristen said.

"How was the trip? Did his family love you? Did you sleep in his bedroom?"

"Get your butt inside before I smack you!" Kristen pointed toward the door as she frowned.

131

"I want to know," Emmy hollered over her shoulder while dashing back inside.

John brought Kristen's suitcase inside and kissed her. "I promised Tony I would watch the game with him. I had a lovely time, Krissy." John kissed her, grabbed his keys and then left.

"Did you guys have a fight?" Emmy asked from her spot on the kitchen countertop.

"No, we didn't have a fight. Why would you think that?"

Emmy mimicked John. "Thank you for the lovely time, Krissy."

"We had a good time, you stinker. And, FYI, we didn't share a bedroom."

"Too bad!" Emmy jumped down. "My money's on Ohio State tonight."

Kenny and his parents were returning from Florida on Saturday the fourth. Andy Walker had agreed to pick them up. Emmy called him that morning.

"Hi, cuz, would you mind if I run up to the airport to get Kenny and his parents? I want to surprise him."

"No! Absolutely not," Andy told her sternly.

"Oh, please! I haven't seen him for a week, and I miss him. Please, can I go?" Andy started laughing and Emmy realized he was teasing her. "You stinker! You don't care if I get him, do you?"

"You are more than welcome to run to the airport. I've got enough work here to keep me busy all weekend. Do you know how to get there?"

"I know how to get to Midway. I'm not geographically challenged—just height challenged."

"They're supposed to get in at two. Oh, he was going to call my cell phone when he was ready to be picked up. I was going to wait at a restaurant on Cicero Ave."

"I'll park and go in to wait for them. It can't cost much to park for thirty minutes or so."

"They should make a parking lot close to the airport where people with cell phones could wait in their cars. That way the people arriving could just call and be picked up. The drivers

132

wouldn't have to keep circling around."

"You're always coming up with brilliant ideas, Andy."

Emmy got to Midway before two, parked the car in the deck and hurried inside. Fifteen minutes later she saw Mr. Colwell coming down the escalator, but not Kenny or his mother.

"Hi, Mr. Colwell!" She waved as she dodged through the crowd. "I'm here to pick you up instead of Andy. Where's Kenny?"

Mr. Colwell grinned and answered, "Oh, sorry, Emmy, but he decided to stay in Florida until they leave on tour."

Emmy's jaw dropped, and she looked so sad that Mr. Colwell felt bad.

"I'm sorry, sweetie. I'm just kidding. He stopped to wait for his mother. They'll be here in a minute."

"You really had me going."

"I'm sorry I teased you like that. Let's move out of the way. I think our luggage will be coming out on carousel six."

A couple of minutes later, Mr. Colwell looked back and saw Kenny walking toward him. "Here they come. Why don't you hide so he doesn't see you, and you can surprise him?"

Emmy moved out of sight. Kenny and his mother approached, and he was looking around for someone.

"I should call Andy. He was going to park somewhere and wait." Kenny took out his phone and was about to call when Emmy stepped out.

"Would it be all right if I take you home with me, Mister?" Emmy asked seductively. She tried to be seductive, but she looked like an innocent high school kid.

Kenny smiled and put his phone away. "I'm not sure. I'm supposed to be engaged, but as long as my fiancee doesn't find out I went home with a beautiful girl who picked me up at the airport, I guess it's okay."

"Is your fiancee as pretty as me?"

Kenny wasn't sure how he should answer this. "She's almost as pretty as you, but I haven't seen her for such a long tome, it's difficult to remember. I miss her so much..."

"I guess that's a good enough answer." Emmy stepped forward and kissed him. "Come on, let's get the luggage, and you

133

can tell me all about Florida."

Emmy stayed with Kenny until ten that night, but then went home. She needed to be at church by nine to go over some songs. When she pulled in the driveway, she saw John's old truck. She walked in the back door, and the house was dark. She listened, but didn't hear anything.

"Kristen, are you home?"

She didn't hear an answer, so she crept quietly up the stairs. She paused as the third step from the top squeaked. She didn't hear anything, so she kept going. The door to Kristen's room was closed. Emmy wasn't sure if she should, but she knocked on the door.

"Krissy, are you guys in there?" Still there was no answer.

Emmy went to her room and changed into pajamas. She walked back downstairs and made some Celestial Seasoning Country Peach Passion tea. She got comfortable in the TV room with a book and ten minutes later she heard Kristen and John talking as they walked in the back door.

"Kristen, I'm in here. Where have you guys been?"

"Just a sec, Em, I'll be right there." Kristen and John hung up their coats, removed their caps and gloves then walked into the TV room. "It was such a nice night that we decided to go for a walk. How long have you been home?"

"It was after ten when I got back."

"How is Kenny? Did he get a good tan?"

"He's okay, and he did look more tanned than before he left." Emmy paused, "When I got home the house was all dark, so I thought you guys were upstairs."

"You thought we were fooling around, huh?"

"The thought crossed my mind. I was almost afraid to knock on your door."

"I didn't put the *Do Not Disturb* sign on the doorknob, so you should have known it was safe to enter." Kristen was teasing, but John looked at her like she was being serious.

Kristen saw the expression on his face and grinned. "I'm not serious. You should see the look on your face."

John felt a little guilty because he and Tony did have a way

134

to notify each other the dorm room was occupied and not to *disturb* the occupant. John stuck around for an hour before heading home.

After church, Emmy drove over to Kenny's. They worked on the wedding plans and took an afternoon nap in the carriage house. Before she fell asleep, Emmy whispered to Kenny, "I hope we can still take naps together after we are married. It feels good to just cuddle and let you hold me."

"We can still cuddle after we're married, Em."

Kenny woke up before Emmy and looked around the carriage house. He had a tape measure and began checking the end of the apartment closest to the house. He had decided to go ahead and have that end of the apartment remodeled into a master bedroom. Emmy woke up and watched as he measured the space.

"What are you doing?"

"I think it's time to have a real bedroom up here. If we are going to spend our wedding night here, I want it to be on a real bed."

"I like that idea." Emmy jumped off the futon and helped Kenny measure the space. "We can put new windows in this wall and a closet over here."

"Em, are you sure you want to spend our wedding night here?"

"Absolutely!" she answered, as she looked at the old couch.

Emmy kept busy at work on Monday and Tuesday. Kenny used that time to take care of band business and met with the contractor who would do the bedroom remodel. On Tuesday night, Kenny and Emmy went shopping at Turk Brothers Furniture and picked out a bedroom set. They picked out paint colors and even purchased curtains for the new bedroom. The work would be done while Kenny and the band was away on tour. Mr. Colwell would oversee the work.

Kenny called Emmy at work on Wednesday.

"Would you be interested in coming to my church tonight?

I'm gonna sing for the teens."

"Sure, I'd love to hear you sing," she teased.

"You have to sing with me, Em."

"Oh, all right. I suppose I could do that."

Emmy dropped Kristen off at the house and rushed over to Kenny's.

"Do I have time to eat before we have to go?"

"We need to leave in fifteen minutes. Mom made taco crusties for dinner."

Emmy sat with Kenny in the breakfast nook and inhaled her food.

"I'm ready to go," she said as she placed her plate in the sink.

They didn't have time to practice before the service, so they stuck to familiar songs. At the end of the service, Pastor Ronnie Rojas made an announcement.

"I'm sure this is old news to you, but I just want to congratulate Kenny and Emmy on their engagement. I hope that after you guys are married, you will still come and sing for us occasionally."

"I'm sure we will make time in our schedule, but Emmy and I will be attending her church after the wedding."

The girls wanted to see Emmy's ring after the service, and the guys shook hands with Kenny.

Thursday night Emmy and Kristen practiced with the Crest Ridge worship band.

On the way home Kristen asked, "Do you guys wanna join us tomorrow night?"

"What are you guys doing?"

"John and I are having dinner with Tony and Sloane. I think we're going to Kerry Lynn's for pizza. It will be fun. You should come with us."

"Maybe, but I think we're gonna..." Emmy paused because she had planned to spend the night at the carriage house apartment. She was going to make Kenny sleep on the couch, but even that didn't feel like the proper thing to do. She felt a bit guilty because she would be disappointed if Kristen spent the night at John's apartment, even if they didn't sleep together. "I'll think about it and let you know on the way home from work."

As they waited at a red light on the way home from work the next day, Emmy bit her lip as she looked at Kristen.

"What's that look for, Em? Have you decided whether you're going with us tonight?"

"I have a confession to make," Emmy said as she moved ahead with the traffic.

"What is it?"

"I had originally planned to stay with Kenny tonight. Just the two of us... in the carriage house."

"Okay," Kristen said slowly.

"I thought about it after lunch, and God just kinda let me know that I needed to set a good example for the teens at church."

"And the teens who aren't in church, too."

"You're right. Anyway, I called Kenny, and he agreed with me. So I guess we're going to Kerry Lynn's with you guys."

"Rats! We made reservations for four. I don't know if we can change them."

"They don't take reservations there." Emmy pulled around a car going twenty-five miles an hour. "You're teasing me."

"I can't fool you, huh?"

Later, Tony arrived with John and Sloane. "Should we try to squeeze everyone into the Envoy?" Tony asked. "Emmy is so small she could fit in between you guys."

Emmy stuck out her tongue at Tony. "Kenny and I will drive separately. We might want to go somewhere after we eat. We might go to the Riverwalk or Swallow Cliff."

They took two vehicles for the ride to Kerry Lynn's Pizza and Pasta. They found a table for six, ordered pop to drink and decided to order two large pizzas. They still loved eating there though the guys were asked to sign autographs.

Later, a preteen girl walked over to their table and asked timidly. "Are you Emmy Colasanti?"

Surprised that anyone would recognize her, Emmy

137

answered, "Yes, I am. What is your name?"

"I'm Lacey and my big brother Adreian has your CD. He lets me play it, and I really love it."

"Thank you so much, Lacey."

"My favorite song is the last one."

Emmy's hand went to her heart.

"Adreian comes to visit me in the hospital."

All conversation stopped as everyone looked at Lacey.

"I'm gonna be a singer just like you when I grow up." Lacey smiled and then ran back to her booth.

Emmy watched as Lacey climbed into the booth next to her mother. Lacey's mom put an arm around her as Lacey hugged her. Then Emmy noticed Lacey's mom straighten up her daughter's blonde wig as she mouthed a silent "thank you" to Emmy. Emmy bit her lip... hard... as she realized the truth.

Everyone looked at Kenny.

"What?"

"Just waiting to see if you're gonna write another song like at Darby's that night," Tony said.

"I think "Yolanda's Song" was a once in a lifetime thing," Kenny said.

As Tony explained to Sloane what had happened, Emmy closed her eyes and remembered the evening Juanita Rosa Garcia approached her in Darby's and told Emmy about the death of her sister Yolanda. Kenny had been inspired by God and wrote the lyrics to what became "Yolanda's Song" on a couple of napkins. Emmy recorded the song for the first Crest Ridge Worship Band CD. It was the last track.

An hour later as they were getting ready to leave the restaurant and head home, Emmy began to weep. Kenny knew why.

"Em, what's the matter?" Kristen asked.

Emmy wiped her nose with Kenny's handkerchief. "If I hadn't followed God's direction and done what I wanted to do, I wouldn't have met Lacey."

"She was a cute kid," Tony said as he helped Sloane with her coat.

138

"Yes, she was," Kenny answered for Emmy. He had noticed Lacey's wig immediately. Silently, he sang the lines of the chorus for a new song.

The rest of the weekend passed quickly, and Kenny and the band left early on Monday morning. They wouldn't be home until the end of February. Emmy and Kenny hugged and kissed as he left, but she didn't cry. She knew he would return to her in a few weeks.

When she got to the office that morning, Mr. Oliver needed to talk to her.

"Yes, Mr. Oliver, what is it?"

"Have a seat, Emily." He pointed to a chair. "I'm sorry. I know I should call you Emmy, but sometimes I forget and I'm too formal. Let me start again. Good morning, Emmy. How was your weekend?"

"It was busy. Kenny and the guys left this morning. How was your weekend?"

"Not as busy as yours which is just the way I like them. I have an opportunity for you and also Kristen Keasling if you are interested."

"An opportunity, huh? Did I screw something up?"

"No, no. Nothing like that. There is a team going to San Diego next week. They will fly out on Wednesday and return on Friday night. They need two assistants. Stephen Butler is in charge of everything and he asked if you would be interested and available. You remember him, correct?"

"Yes, he was always pleasant to work with."

"Well, he wanted you, and I told him I would ask. You would be staying at a hotel in the Pacific Beach area. Real close to the ocean and the beach if that makes your decision any easier."

"How soon do you need an answer?"

"By the end of tomorrow if possible. If you aren't interested Stephen needs to find other assistants."

"I'll call Kristen, and let you know by noon. I'm interested, and I think Kristen will be, but I don't want to say for sure until I talk to her."

Emmy talked to Kristen as soon as she got back to her desk.

"Hey, Kristen, I was just talking to my boss about this..."

"The trip to San Diego?"

"Yes, how do you know about it?"

"My boss knows Stephen Butler, and one of the guys from our team is going."

"Are you interested?" Emmy asked.

"Interested? Is the sky blue?"

"Sometimes."

"You goof! Yeah, I wanna go. It will be so much fun. Yeah, I know we will be working all day, so we can't work on our tans, but we will be free at night."

"I'll tell Mr. Oliver that I talked you into going, but it wasn't easy."

"We might need to go shopping this week. I need to pick up a new..."

"Now who's being a goof?"

Later, Emmy called Kenny and mentioned the trip.

"You will love San Diego and especially the Pacific Beach area."

"Too bad you guys will be on the other side of the country," Emmy said. "We could have seen each other."

"Have fun and let me know how it goes."

The week flew by for Emmy and Kristen. They went shopping on Saturday morning, and Emmy even bought some new clothes to wear on the trip.

"Hey, Em, do you wanna go out with us tonight?" Kristen asked as they ate lunch.

"Who's going? Is it just you and John?"

"No, Tony and Sloane are coming. I think maybe Lindsey Cameron, too. You should come with us. You and Lindsey could keep each other company."

"Yeah, sure. It would be better than sitting at home and moping for Kenny."

"Good. Tony made reservations at The Hungry Lion for

eight o'clock. Tony's going to pick up Sloane and Lindsey. You can ride with John and me."

In the afternoon, Emmy and Kristen worked on wedding plans. John picked them up at seven thirty. They drove to the restaurant and arrived just after Tony.

"Hey, Em, I'm glad you decided to grace us with your presence tonight," Tony said as they were escorted to their table. "Kristen said you've been in a funk all week."

"I just miss Kenny."

Tony put an arm around her shoulders and squeezed tenderly. "I can understand that."

They sat at a table in the back corner. Although Emmy had met Lindsey and Sloane several months ago and had become good friends with both of them, she didn't know a lot about their background. While the two couples chatted, Emmy and Lindsey got to know more about each other.

"So, you and Sloane grew up together, huh?" Emmy said after Lindsey talked about going to school with Sloane in Troy, Ohio.

Lindsey's glasses slipped down her nose as she nodded. "We've been best friends forever."

"Kenny's been my best friend since I was seven."

"That's so sweet. Now you're engaged. I've always dreamed about marrying my high school sweetheart."

"What's his name?" Emmy asked.

Lindsey laughed. "Oh, I haven't met him, yet. I didn't date much in high school and only a few times in college. But I'll meet him someday. I just know it."

After church the next day, Emmy ate lunch with the Colwells and even stopped to visit with her parents.

Her mother let her in and immediately asked, "Are you still planning to get married in that church you go to?"

"Yes, Mom, why?"

They walked into the living room and Mom sat in her recliner. Emmy looked at her father's recliner, but couldn't bring herself to sit there. She sat in her customary place on the couch.

"I was talking to Father Thomas, and told him I thought you need to get married at St. John's. We are Catholic, you know."

"Did you explain that we go to a different church now, Mom?"

"You're not going to change your mind, are you?"

"No, Mom, I'm not."

"Are you...?"

"I'm not pregnant as far as I know," Emmy said intending it as a joke.

"I was going to ask if you were going somewhere exciting on a honeymoon."

"It might not be real exciting, but right now we are planning to go to Ireland and England. That might change, but that's the plan as of now."

Emmy stayed for a while but needed to get home.

"Where is Daddy? You haven't said anything about him. He's not down at Miller's Bar is he?"

"No, he went with Nick Francona to buy some lumber. He's working on his basement and your father is helping him. He hasn't been to Miller's for a while."

Emmy closed her eyes. *Thank you, Lord, for that good news.*

Chapter Thirteen

Emmy and Kristen spent Tuesday evening packing and talking about the trip. They used the Internet to research San Diego. They got to bed early, but Emmy had trouble falling asleep. After tossing and turning for over an hour, she slipped quietly into Kristen's room and got in bed with her. Kristen was sound asleep and didn't even know Emmy was there until the morning when she woke up and could feel Emmy in the bed.

"Emmy, are you all right?"

Emmy opened her eyes and yawned as she stretched her arms. "I couldn't sleep so I came in here with you. Sometimes I miss having Diane around. I remember we always would complain about sharing our small bed, but sometimes now I miss it."

"We need to get ready. Are you getting as excited as I am?"

"I'll be more excited once we are in San Diego."

They got ready and were picked up for the early morning trip to O'Hare Airport. They made it through security and proceeded to gate twenty-eight. There they were introduced to the rest of the team. In addition to Stephen Butler, who was in charge, there was Harold Bernanke from Kristen's office. He was over six feet six, slender with thinning gray hair and wire-rimmed glasses. Nolan Kelley was from Stephen Butler's team. He was under six feet tall and nearly as wide as he was tall. Just then the final member of the team came around the corner carrying coffee for the guys. Emmy and Kristen looked at each other as they saw him. He needed no introduction—unfortunately.

"Hello, Emmy, I didn't realize until a few minutes ago that you and Kristen were our assistants for this trip. It's good to see you again."

"Hello, Richard, how have you been?" Emmy asked Richard Demarco without smiling.

Stephen Butler said, "We need to talk about the project for a few minutes. Then we won't have to waste time on the plane."

The team spent the next forty-five minutes going over details before they boarded the plane. Emmy and Kristen were sitting together and could talk without being heard by the team.

"Are you going to be okay, Em?"

"I'll be fine. What happened between us was such a long time ago. Maybe he has changed."

Emmy thought about her relationship with Richard that ended when he made unwelcome sexual advances toward her.

"Leopards don't get rid of their spots, Em."

"What does that mean?" Emmy asked as laughed.

"I don't know, but I've heard Daddy use that phrase."

"Well, I'm not gonna let Richard Demarco ruin my week. We have to see him during the day, but we don't necessarily have to see him at night," Emmy said.

Later, as they were close to landing, Emmy nudged Kristen and asked, "Is that the ocean?"

"I don't know, Em. It might be. It's water at least."

The gentleman sitting on the aisle spoke up. "That's actually North San Diego Bay. You really can't see the Pacific yet."

The team landed at San Diego International and rode a shuttle to the Pacific Beach neighborhood. They checked in at the Ocean Park Inn.

Stephen Butler informed the team, "We need to meet downstairs at noon. We are starting right away. We will work at the naval station until six today. For the rest of the week we will meet in the lobby at six thirty and be driven to the base. We should be finished by four at the latest every day so you will have some time to enjoy the sun and water. If there are any questions, just ask."

Emmy and Kristen went up to their room on the top floor.

Emmy opened the drapes. "Kristen! This has to be the ocean."

"I think you're right, Em."

"Which bed do you want, Krissy?'

"Doesn't matter. Go ahead and take the one closest to the window. I know you want it," Kristen said.

Emmy called Kenny before she unpacked. "We're at the hotel. It's right on the ocean on Grand Avenue. We've got a great view of the Pacific."

"I hope you have time to spend at the beach, Em."

"Mr. Butler assured us we would. I'll keep my phone with

me after we finish working, so you can call me when you can."

After they finished for the day, Emmy and Kristen hurried back to their room before any of the guys could talk to them. Not that the guys were interested—except maybe Richard and Stephen. They changed clothes, headed downstairs and walked to the beach. They gobbled down some food and drank bottled water at an outdoor restaurant. They were having a good time until they spotted Richard walking toward them.

"I just wanted to stop by and say I'm pleased you are part of the team, Emmy. It's nice to finally meet you, Kristen. Mr. Butler has had nothing but high praise for your work. If there's anything I can help you with during our stay, please ask. I'm talking about during the day while we are working. I won't bother you after hours, as it were."

"Thank you, Richard. We'll see you in the morning," Kristen said. *You stay away from Emmy.*

"Have a fun evening, ladies."

Kristen stared at him until he disappeared from view. "Don't let him talk to you, Emmy."

"I have to be civil," Emmy replied.

The next two days were filled with hard work, but they did finish by four and were back at the hotel by four-thirty. That allowed Emmy and Kristen to spend some time at the beach. Mr. Butler saw them after dinner on Friday and walked over.

"This place is perfect," Emmy said.

"It is," he said as he glanced at the ocean. "I have bad news, or maybe you will see it as good news. I'm not sure."

"What is it?" Emmy asked.

"We were planning to fly home in the morning, but we are going to be here longer. It's possible we could be here until next Wednesday. Sometimes these government projects are more difficult than originally planned. Would you be willing to stay until then? I know you will miss church and I apologize for that."

"How did you know that, Mr. Butler?" Kristen asked.

"Richard told me you were both very active in your church and might not want to be away for the weekend."

Emmy looked at Kristen, and they both grinned.

"We are both off this Sunday. We would still go to church, but we weren't going to sing. We can stay until the job is finished," Emmy said.

"Thank you. I appreciate the cooperation. We will be working tomorrow, but not Sunday. You will be free to do as you please all day long."

Later, Kristen headed back to the room to call John. Emmy saw Richard on the beach and walked over to talk to him.

"Hi," she said while listening to the waves breaking.

He turned and smiled. "Hi, Emmy. Are you enjoying the weather? Isn't it gorgeous here?"

"Yes, and I wanted to thank you for telling Mr. Butler about church."

"I thought he should know."

He turned back and watched the people walking along the beach. Emmy watched with him and then asked, "Would you like to go for a walk, Richard?"

"Sure, should we wait for Kristen?"

"She was going back to the room to call her boyfriend. I'm afraid you will have to put up with me alone." *Shoot! Shoot! I hope that didn't sound like I was flirting. Kristen is always getting after me for that.*

"I heard you are engaged."

She smiled as she held out her hand to show off her ring. "Yes, I'm getting married in April to Kenny Colwell from my old neighborhood. We've been friends since we were kids."

"I'm happy for you, Emmy."

"What about you? Are you seeing anyone?" Emmy listened to the waves and the squawking of the seagulls. *I love the salty smell of the ocean.*

"No, I've been concentrating on work. I've been on a couple dates, but nothing serious. I even gave up drinking beer."

"You did? That's great!" Emmy was sincerely pleased by the news. "I know how much you enjoyed your beer."

"Yeah, but I didn't want to end up a drunk like my father."

"I know what it's like to have a father with an alcohol

146

problem," Emmy admitted. "Daddy has a problem, but he's been getting treatment. How is your father?"

"He died two months ago. His liver was shot."

"I'm sorry to hear that."

"I got to see him before he died. It made me realize I needed to make an adjustment in my life. If I remember correctly, you don't drink at all."

"Not very often. I grew up drinking wine with dinner and I would sneak one of Daddy's beers once in a while, but now I don't normally have anything stronger than pop or coffee."

Richard looked at her and remembered how he treated her one night. "I'm sorry about that night. I won't blame it on the beer, but that was part of the problem."

"I think I realized that afterward, and I don't hold it against you. You can be very charming and I still think you are very attractive for an..."

"For an older man. It's okay. I realize most people would think I am your father."

"I know I teased you about that, but I never thought of you as old enough to be my father. Daddy is sixty-six, so he's a lot older than you. I'm twenty-two now and you must be..."

"I'm twenty-nine and holding. I tell people I'm prematurely gray."

Emmy laughed and realized Richard still retained his charm and sense of humor.

After their walk, they sat at the outdoor bar and drank bottled water. This time Richard didn't crave the beer like he did before. They talked until after ten and then Emmy went back to her room. Richard walked along with her and Emmy noticed that he behaved like a changed man.

"Good night, Emmy. I'll see you in the morning."

"Good night. Thanks for the walk."

The team stayed busy until five on Saturday. Then Mr. Butler took the team out for dinner at Scenes, a fancy Italian restaurant. Emmy ended up sitting across the table from Richard, and she smiled at him several times throughout the dinner. Three of

147

the guys ordered wine and cocktails, but Emmy, Kristen and Richard stuck to bottled water. Afterward, the whole team spent an hour at the outdoor bar. All of the guys were drinking to help unwind from the busy week, except for Richard. When Kristen was busy talking to Mr. Butler and Harold Bernanke, from her office, Emmy had an opportunity to talk to Richard.

"Do you ever have a beer anymore?" Emmy asked.

"No, I'm afraid if I have one I won't want to stop. I do have a glass of wine once in a while, but no beer."

"I'll have a glass of wine with you, if you want one."

He stared at her for a moment. "All right. I suppose one glass of wine would help me relax and chill out."

"I'll let you order because you probably can pick out a better one than me."

Richard ordered a California wine he enjoyed. Emmy liked it so much she had a second glass.

"That's enough for me," she told Richard. "Are we going for another walk?"

"I will if Kristen comes along." *I'm not going anywhere with you after you've had some wine.*

"I'll make her come with us."

Kristen joined them, and they enjoyed the walk along the ocean. Kristen had gotten to know Richard a little better this week. She realized he didn't act like the same man Emmy knew before. *I still don't completely trust you. You are still a leopard as far as I'm concerned.*

As they were walking back toward the hotel, Emmy asked, "Have you been to church lately, Richard?"

"No, the last time I was in church was that day I took you."

"You know you would always be welcome to visit us some Sunday. I'm not going to preach at you or anything like that, but I will pray for you whether you want me to or not," Emmy said.

"I bet you will." Richard chuckled. "I'm not sure I would be comfortable going back to your church because of how I treated you that night, but if you could recommend another one, I will give it a try."

Emmy mentioned several other churches, but then added,

148

"Just as Jesus forgives us of our sins, the church, I mean the people in the church, also forgive. I don't harbor any ill feelings toward you and there are only a few people who know about our... relationship."

"That might be true, but I know you and Kristen and probably Tony and certainly Kenny know, and I don't think I will ever be able to forgive myself. I tried to take advantage of your youth and innocence just for my physical pleasure. I never gave a thought to your feelings."

Kristen stared at him. *Holy moly! Either you are the slickest liar I have ever met, or else you've really done a one eighty.*

"As much as I would love for you to come to our church, I can understand your feelings. I would certainly rather see you in another church where you feel comfortable than feel ill at ease in ours," Emmy said.

"Of course, the other churches don't have Emmy singing on the platform," Kristen pointed out. *I'll cut you some slack for now, but I'm watching you.*

"That's a good point," Richard responded with a laugh.

"There are plenty of other churches that have singers a lot better than me."

"Oh, Em, stop being so modest," Kristen said.

Richard looked at the two girls, as he thought of them, and admitted, "I've never really been interested in church. I went when my parents made me, but once I was old enough to make my own decisions, I stayed away. I was more interested in living my life as I wanted to and that was chasing women and having a good time."

That's for damn sure. Kristen thought.

"I never told you much about my marriage, Emmy. It was a disaster from the start. Two weeks after I was married, I cheated with a woman from work. Anyway, after I stopped drinking I realized there had to be more to life than what I was experiencing. This trip with the two of you has made me realize I have overlooked something. I mentioned my parents basically dragged me to church once in a while, but I didn't tell you the whole story. The place they dragged me to was my grandfather's church. He was the preacher there. My father grew up in the church and he rebelled against his father, and I guess I rebelled against both of them. My grandfather never stopped believing in his way of life and he always... prayed... I guess for his son and grandson. He died about ten years ago."

Richard paused and Emmy looked up at his face. She could see a tear on his cheek. She whispered to him, "It's never too late to change. Jesus is waiting with open arms."

They walked and Richard said, "I can't go to church. If the people there find out about my past, there will toss me in the street."

"If you confess your sins, He forgives you and doesn't even remember them anymore. You will remember, but God won't."

"You really believe God will forget what I've done?"

Emmy looked him right in the eye and said, "In Jeremiah it says, 'For I will forgive their wickedness and remember their sins no more.' I believe that applies to everyone who confesses their sins. I was raised in a Catholic home, but we stopped going to mass when I was a young girl. When I was a teenager I started going to church with Kenny, but I didn't really accept Christ into my life until I was older. I wish I had done it sooner, but my point is that it's always the right time to accept Him into your life."

"But I'm such a mess. My life is still screwed up."

"So is mine! I'm far from perfect. I lose my temper."

"That's a fact." Kristen laughed.

"I sometimes swear like a sailor, and I get really horny."

Kristen poked her in the side.

"Ooops!" Emmy turned red. "Maybe I shouldn't have mentioned that."

Richard doesn't need to hear about your love life. Kristen tried to communicate with her frown.

"I'm sure you've heard this before, but you don't wait till you get well to see a doctor."

"Emmy and I are going to church in the morning. You're welcome to join us if you would like," Kristen offered.

"I'll think about it, okay?" Richard said.

In the morning Emmy called Richard's room, but he didn't answer. She left a message for him, and they waited as long as they could before they needed to leave for the church they found close by.

"Some people take longer to realize they need to trust in Jesus," Emmy said.

After church and lunch, Emmy talked Kristen into coming with her to Belmont Park.

"You'll love it. There's an old wooden roller coaster called The Great Dipper and lots of other stuff to do. Admission is free!"

"Free? Let me see that brochure." Kristen read it. "You have to pay to go on the rides, Em, but it's not much. I'll go with you."

They took their time walking down Ocean Front Walk. They stopped occasionally to watch the crowd.

Kristen turned Emmy away from the water. "Look at that juggler. He's on a skateboard."

"Cool!"

Kristen pulled Emmy aside as two rollerbladers roared past.

"They were flying," Emmy said as she watched them disappear in the crowd.

"Maybe they were trying to escape those cops on the bicycles."

They spent the rest of the afternoon at Belmont Park. Emmy convinced Kristen to ride The Great Dipper four times.

"That's all for me, Em. I'm gonna puke if I don't take a break. If you want to keep riding it, I'm sure those guys would be willing to join you." Kristen pointed to three guys who were watching them.

"They look like they're in high school."

"Right. They're just the right age for you," Kristen teased.

Emmy stuck out her tongue.

"Proves my point."

They stayed at the park until seven. On the way back to the hotel, Kenny called.

"Hey, Kenny, you'll never guess what I've been doing this afternoon."

151

"I suppose you aren't at the beach. That would be too easy to guess."

"We're walking along the beach right now, but Kristen and I spent the afternoon at Belmont Park. I made Krissy ride the roller coaster with me four times."

"Are you talking about The Great Dipper?"

"Yeah. Do you know about it?"

"I've been on it. Andy brought us there, and we rode it together. He grew up in San Diego, remember?"

"Oh, that's right. I should have talked to him about things to do. We really haven't left the beach area."

"He probably would have told you to stay at the beach."

They talked as the girls walked back to the hotel.

"There's a chance we might get done on Monday. As much as I love the ocean and beach, I'll be glad to get home."

"I should let you go, Em. Say hi to Kristen for me."

As soon as Mr. Butler realized the team would finish the project early Monday afternoon, he called the main office. He talked to Mrs. Walters, who handled travel arrangements for the company, and they were booked on a flight later that evening. On the flight back to Chicago, Emmy had another chance to talk to Richard. He agreed to try a couple of the churches Emmy suggested.

"Please stay in touch and let me know how you're doing," Emmy said because she was genuinely concerned about him.

"I will, Emmy. I'll make an honest effort to be in church on Sunday morning. I know we don't see each other at the office very often, but I'll try to let you know how it goes."

"Good. I'm still in the same office. You can look up my number in the directory if you ever want to call."

Chapter Fourteen

Kenny and the band arrived home on the twenty-third of February. Kenny planned to use the coming week to finalize details about the wedding. He had promised Emmy he would take care of hiring a band for the reception. He convinced Paul Joseph and the rest of The Notable Exceptions to play at the reception.

"I might sit in with you guys, but I will be kinda busy that night," Kenny explained to P.J.

"That sounds like a plan. Will we have a chance to rehearse with you?"

"I don't think we'll need to rehearse."

Kenny filled P.J. in on the details and then swore him to secrecy. Kenny also figured Fridays at Five would play a few songs, too. He told P.J. they could play music over the PA, like a DJ would, at times when the band needed a break.

Kenny called Emmy at work on Tuesday and said, "The bedroom is ready. Can you stop over here after work?"

"Sure, I can't wait to see it. I haven't been in the carriage house for a month. Does it look as good as we hoped?"

"Even better. I really like the summer blue color on the walls and the carpet feels good on bare feet."

"How about the bathroom?" Emmy asked.

"It's really bright in there. I'm glad we put in a walk-in shower and a skylight."

Emmy bit her lip for a second. "Do you think you spent too much money on it? We probably won't ever live there all the time?"

"No, I'm glad we did it like this this, Em. Who knows what might happen down the road? We might be living somewhere other than SoHam, and this will be the place we stay when we come back to visit."

Emmy and Kristen stopped at the carriage house after work. Kenny showed them the new bedroom and bathroom.

"What do you think, Kristen?" Emmy asked.

"This is adorable, Em. It reminds me of a room in an old

153

English house. I love that you left this brick wall exposed. The red in the brick goes well with the gray carpet, and the blue paint really pulls out the different colors of this old brick. I like the skylights and the way the ceiling is open to the roof. There's just one thing."

"What?"

"I'm not sure I like the closet doors. I don't think I would have chosen mirrored doors."

"We can always change them," Emmy said. "The bathroom isn't super huge like yours, but it's big enough for us."

Kristen walked into the bathroom and saw the shower. "This is perfect. I wish I had one like this at home. Is that countertop granite?"

"Yeah, Kenny found it. It really blends in well."

Kristen ran her hand over the countertop. "I love the blue specks, and I like how you painted the bathroom the same blue."

"We had to cover up the brick in here. I think it had something to do with the high moisture content."

Kristen looked at Emmy and asked, "Are you going to live here after you're married? Am I gonna have to move out of the house, or stay there by myself?"

"I don't think we will live here full-time," Kenny answered. He knew Emmy did not want to live this close to her parents. "I'm sure there might be times when we crash here, though."

Emmy looked at the king-size bed and pulled Kenny over to it. She grinned at Kristen.

"It feels so comfortable."

"Get up! Please tell me you aren't going to stay here tonight to try it out," Kristen said very seriously.

"Oh, all right. I'll come home. Party pooper. Are you going to sleep here tonight?" Emmy asked Kenny.

"Would you rather I didn't?"

"I was thinking maybe we could not use the new bed until..." She paused and looked at Kristen. "Maybe we won't sleep in the new bedroom until our wedding night."

"You better not, Emmy!" Kristen exclaimed.

"We should try out the shower before then," Kenny said innocently.

154

Kristen looked at them.

"I didn't mean together, Kristen," Kenny explained.

"Yeah, sure," Kristen replied as she frowned at Emmy, who was grinning and nodding her head.

On Saturday morning, the first of March, with the wedding just over a month away, Kenny and Emmy met at the church with senior pastor Dr. Ausland.

"Come on in and have a seat." He pointed to the oversize leather chairs in front of his large wooden desk. "I always meet with a couple before I marry them to offer counseling and to pray with them."

Kenny looked at the floor-to-ceiling bookcase which covered an entire wall. Emmy grinned at the family photos on the wall behind Pastor Herb.

"Is that a photo of your grandkids?" She pointed to one on the end.

Pastor Herb knew which one she meant. He turned a photo around on his desk. "We have five grandkids now. These three live in the states. Colorado Springs to be exact, and the youngest two live in the Philippines."

"Oh, that's so far away."

"We usually see them three times a year."

"They are adorable, Pastor Herb," Kenny said.

Pastor Herb smiled as he gazed at the photo. "Well, I should get down to business. Sometimes I have to caution couples about the decision they are making if I feel they are making an unwise choice, for any number of reasons. I am so overjoyed to tell you I have no such concerns about you, Emmy, or you, Kenny. I have known you for only a short time, but I have observed your growth as a couple and Emmy's growth as a new believer. I realize you are both fairly young to be taking this important step, but I have found you both to be very intelligent, dedicated and mature young adults. Excepting the times, Emmy, when I have noticed you acting like a young teenager. I remember watching you play basketball with some of the teens one night."

"I remember that night," Emmy said.

155

Dr. Ausland chuckled as he recalled. "I remember when one of the taller boys held Emmy up to the rim so she could slam dunk the ball. She threw the ball through the rim with ferocity, then he set her down and they gave each other high-fives. Emmy had such a look of joy on her face. But that look pales in comparison to the way she looks at you. When you are together, she lights up from the inside. Emmy, I know you have gone through some struggles over the last several years, and I know you and Kenny have been friends for most of your life. I'm so pleased that those doubts and concerns are behind you now." Pastor Herb paused and then chuckled before he continued, "My biggest concern is rather selfish in a way. I hope I can make it through the ceremony without breaking down and shedding a few tears. I have done countless weddings over the past forty years, and I don't remember the last time I so looked forward to a wedding as I am for yours."

"That's so sweet," Emmy said as she squeezed Kenny's hand.

Dr. Ausland paused as he wiped a tear away. "Do you have any questions for me? Anything about the ceremony or anything else?"

"Pastor Herb, would it be all right if Kenny and I write our own vows?"

"Certainly, Emmy. Many couples are doing that these days. It's not very often anymore that I have to use the old-fashioned vows that were so prevalent years ago. I remember just a few months ago I was conducting a ceremony and the couple had written their own vows. I was listening and got so caught up in what they were saying to each other that I nearly lost my concentration, and forgot what I was supposed to say next."

As the session neared it's end, Dr. Ausland tenderly placed an arm around their shoulders and prayed for Kenny and Emmy. He remarked afterward, "Kenny, I know you have been attending the church where you grew up, but have you decided what you will do after the wedding? I don't mean to take you away from your own church, but I strongly feel a couple should worship together. We would love to have you as a member of our congregation, but I will not try to persuade you one way or the other. I will leave that

156

to the Holy Spirit to guide your decision. Emmy, I will see you in the morning, correct? We are having the Copelands, a missionary couple from the Philippines visiting us if you remember."

"We will both be here, Pastor Herb."

Kristen and her mom had organized a bridal shower for Emmy and Kenny at the Keasling home for later that afternoon. Diane offered to help, but was too busy with her son Carson to be of much assistance, even if she wasn't in Toledo, Ohio. Diane made it to the shower and brought Carson, who just recently turned one. Emmy didn't get too many opportunities to see her nephew, but she took advantage of this visit. Carson was shy and usually didn't like to be held by anyone other than his mommy, but he willingly let Aunt Emmy hold him. Emmy held onto Carson's hands as he walked around.

"It won't be long before you're walking on your own. You're getting so big."

Carson grinned at her and babbled, "Em-Em."

"Aw! That is so adorable," Emmy said.

Diane laughed. "Don't read too much into it. He calls everything and everyone Em-Em."

The shower started at two and guests began arriving immediately. Kenny hesitated to come to the shower with Emmy, since he would likely be the only guy there. Emmy glanced around the family room at the guests and saw her three moms. Her mother was talking to Mrs. Colwell and Mama Bertucci. Emmy felt so blessed to have three people who loved her the way these ladies did. Emmy and her mother had grown closer in the short time since she had been engaged. She hoped it would last.

Emmy saw Linda Newton, who was due in two weeks, sitting in a chair and walked over to talk to her.

"Linda, it is so good to see you. How much longer?"

"Another week or so. I can't wait to see my feet again."

"How is Barry holding up?"

"He's been working a lot of hours, but he did get the nursery ready."

"Do you guys have a name picked out yet?"

Linda shook her head. "We still haven't made up our minds. We keep changing from one name to another."

"Maybe you should give him several names," Emmy suggested.

"Yeah, we could please everyone that way."

Emmy was delighted to see many of her friends from church. Emmy's closest church friend Lynette Jefferson gave her a beautiful fine bone china tea set.

"This is absolutely gorgeous. Thank you, Lynette."

"I know it's not the most practical gift, but you might use it when you get older."

"True," Emmy said and then giggled. "I can't believe Barry bought me a PS2 game. Did you see the look on Linda's face when I opened it and thanked her?"

"I noticed you liked the game, though."

"It's one I can play with Kenny and probably beat him."

As Emmy and Kristen were getting ready for bed later that night, Emmy walked across the hall to Kristen's bedroom and asked, "Kristen, you will be my maid of honor, right? I guess I have been assuming you would be, but I should formally ask you. Will you?"

"I'd love to be your maid of honor."

They hugged, but then Kristen realized something.

"Emmy, don't you think maybe you should ask Diane?"

"Why?"

"She is your sister, and I'm just a friend."

"Just a friend! Kristen, you are way more than *just a friend*. You're the best friend in the whole world." Emmy spread her arms out as wide as she could.

"Oh, Emmy, you're so sweet, but I still think you should ask Diane."

"If we were closer maybe I would, but we hardly ever talk to each other and we almost never see each other."

"Still, she is your sister."

"I don't know. Wouldn't you be insulted if I didn't ask you?" Emmy asked.

"Diane might take it as an insult if you don't ask her."

158

Emmy couldn't make up her mind. She had a tough decision to make because Kristen was her best friend and constant companion. Emmy and Diane had not seen each other since Diane's wedding until today, and they had never been as close as Emmy was with Kristen.

"We'll ask Mama in the morning. She will know what I should do."

"I'll go along with whatever Mama decides, Emmy."

When Emmy woke up, she opened the window to smell the fresh air and listened as the birds sang their morning songs. She knew Mama would be up so she called her.

"Hi, Mama, I need some advice about the wedding."

"What is it, dear? Nothing serious, I hope."

"It's this. I want to ask Kristen to be my maid of honor, but she thinks I should ask Diane since she is my sister. Kristen is worried Diane might be offended if I don't ask her. I'm so much closer to Kristen than Diane. What should I do?"

Mama laughed for a moment. "That's easy, Emmy. You ask Diane to be your matron of honor, and you ask Kristen to be your maid of honor. There's no law that says you can't have both."

"Are you sure I can do that?"

"Of course you can. That way both of them will be a special part of your wedding."

"I knew you would have the answer, Mama!"

As usual, Mama helped Emmy make the right choice.

Later that morning, Kenny stopped by to take Emmy and Kristen to church. The ladies needed to be there early for practice. Emmy dragged Kenny along to the music suite where the worship band was warming up.

"Morning, guys." Emmy walked over to the table with the coffee pots and donuts. "Who bought the donuts today?" she asked as she bit into a chocolate glazed one.

"I bought an extra dozen because I know how many you eat," Hank Lysenko said.

"Thank you, Hank. You know it's Kristen who loves donuts, right? She sometimes eats a whole dozen by herself."

Kristen shook her head. "How can you lie like that in church, Em?"

"It's not a real lie. I'm just teasing you."

Emmy turned around and saw Chase enter the room. "Hey, Chase, I brought this guy with me this morning who claims he can play guitar and sing. I don't know if he can or not, but I promised to let him audition."

"An audition, huh?"

Emmy nodded. "I told him the guys in the band are real professionals, but he still wants to try out. Do you have a couple of minutes to listen to him? I'm sure it won't take long for him to realize he's just an amateur compared to our guys."

Chase laughed as Emmy teased Kenny. "Good morning, Kenny. I know you can play and sing, so that's not an issue. What we really need is someone to take over as lead singer. We've been using this young girl, and while she is maybe kinda pretty and she certainly tries hard, but... we really need someone who can sing on key."

Emmy stuck out her tongue at Chase and Kenny. "Fine! If that's what you want then you should ask Mrs. Ceranzo to start singing again."

Chase laughed at Emmy and asked Kenny, "Is she serious? Are you willing to play guitar and sing with us?"

"I certainly don't want to take anyone's spot, but I'd be willing to play guitar and sing harmony if you're willing to have me. You know I'm gone a lot, but when I'm home I think we will be worshiping here."

"That would be great." Chase handed Kenny the list of the songs they were doing that morning. "Do you know these songs?"

Kenny glanced at the list. "I believe I am familiar with all of them except this one. I don't think I've ever heard 'Freedom Is Here' before."

"It's a brand new song for us. Today is the first time we are using it. Here's the chord sheet. Key of F."

Kenny looked over the music and it looked easy enough. "Do you have an extra guitar handy, by chance?"

"I think we might be able to rustle up something for you to

160

play." Steve Van Zant opened a case and pulled out a Fender Stratocaster. "Will this work?"

"I'm kinda familiar with this one."

Kenny practiced with the worship band and fit right in—after all he had played with them before. The new song was not a problem. During the service Kenny's appearance on the platform did not create a distraction—not even with the teens. Most of them had met him before and were not as in awe of him as previously.

After the service, Kenny and Emmy rushed home to have a quick lunch before he had to leave. Kristen went home with Tony because she was meeting John for lunch. John had been taking Mama to mass on Sunday mornings. Kenny picked up some Chinese carryout, and he and Emmy had an hour to be together.

They sat at the kitchen table to eat. "Is everything set for your tour, Em? Do you have any questions? I might be able to help answer them if they're easy."

Emmy giggled and then said, "This is nothing compared to what you guys do. I'm getting excited, but a little nervous."

"You'll do fine. Chase will take care of you." Kenny jumped up, left the room, and then returned holding a small notepad and a large journal. "I bought this stuff for you to use on your tour."

"You didn't have to. I could have picked one up."

"I thought you might forget with everything on your mind." He opened the journal and laid it on the table. "You can write down all the stuff that happens during your tour. You can keep the small notebook with you and write it in during the day, then transfer it to... You get the picture."

"Then maybe someday when I'm old and gray I can read through it."

"You could write a book about the first tour of the world famous Emmy Colasanti. It'll sell millions," Kenny said.

"Thank you, Kenny." She kissed him and smeared sweet and sour sauce on his lips. "I'll try to take care of wedding stuff when I have some time."

"If there's anything we need to take care of while I'm gone, just call me. I don't care about the time difference. Just call."

"If it's something minor, should I just take care of it?"

"If you want. I trust your judgment. Just don't be afraid to spend the money if it's something that will cost more than we planned."

"Okay, I'll spend your money."

They finished lunch and soon Emmy needed to run Kenny over to his house.

"Promise me you will use my car while I'm gone. We really need to replace the older Civic. I won't worry as much if I know you're using the newer car."

"Yes, I will use your fancy new car." Emmy rolled her eyes. "Maybe we should look at getting something like Tony has. It wouldn't be as good on gas mileage, but he won't ever get stuck in the snow."

"Have you ever driven his Envoy?"

"Just when he bought it. I took it for a test drive. I like the way it sits up higher."

"Maybe we can look for something when we get back from our honeymoon. You can check with the dealer if you want."

"We could get by with one car. At least while you're gone," Emmy said.

"True, but I think we'll need a second car for when I'm home," Kenny said.

"Is it okay if I tell people where we're going?"

Kenny tilted his head.

"On our honeymoon, goofy."

"It won't bother me if you tell your friends. Just don't invite them along," Kenny teased.

"Why not? If I ask Kristen to come along, she can keep me company, so I don't get bored."

"I might be able to keep you busy somehow." Kenny smiled and kissed her cheek.

"You better!" Emmy teased back as she bit her lip.

Chapter Fifteen

"Are you sure you have enough clothes?" Kristen asked as she dropped Emmy off at the church Tuesday morning.

"We're only gonna be gone for five days. I don't need more than a pair of jeans and a t-shirt."

"You're gross." Kristen made a face.

"I'll carry your suitcases, Miss Emmy. I'll put them in the bedroom for you." Joe Zawaski easily lifted the heavy suitcases.

"Thank you, Joe."

Joe and his brother Jess would travel with the band and do all the heavy lifting.

"I've gotta run, Em. Have a good trip."

"I wish you were coming with us, Krissy. I'll get lonely."

"No, you won't! You've got a bus full of men who will treat you like a princess. You better not turn into a diva. I'll tell Kenny if you do. Make sure you keep your phone charged and turned on. Sometimes you forget."

"I will, promise." Emmy embraced Kristen and then hopped onto the tour bus the church had leased.

Two hours later, Chase sat beside Emmy on the leather couch in the lounge area of the bus. "What are you writing, Emmy? A book?"

"Maybe. Kenny bought me this journal. I'm supposed to keep a record of the tour." Emmy held the journal against her chest, so Chase couldn't see what she had written.

"So, we have to behave, or else you'll write it down and get us in trouble, huh?" Hank opened his eyes. He had been napping on the opposite couch.

"It's not like that, Hank, but I want to write down my thoughts and some of the information about our concerts."

"Oh, an info dump about how many tickets we sold and how many CDs and t-shirts the kids buy," Alan Vicini, the drummer, said.

"You know that's not why we're doing this, Alan."

"He's teasing you, Em." Chase patted her knee. "We know the reason for this tour is to spread the gospel through song."

"And dance!" Steve Van Zant said as he leaned against the counter by the microwave. "We all know how much Emmy likes to dance when she sings."

"I'm going to my room if you guys are gonna tease me." Emmy grinned, but didn't make a move to leave.

"We love you like a little..." Emmy expected Chase to say sister, instead he said, "brat."

The guys laughed as she stuck out her tongue.

Kristen, Lynette, Paula, Sloane and Lindsey met at Emmy's house one evening to work on the invitations. They sat at the dining room table and chatted as they worked.

"Where is the worship team tonight?" Paula asked.

"Louisville, Kentucky," Kristen answered.

The ladies kept at it for nearly two hours.

Kristen sighed as she placed a stamp on one final envelope. "There! That's the last one."

"Do you want me to take them to the post office?" Paula asked.

"I would really appreciate it if you could," Kristen said.

"No problem. I'll make sure they are there tomorrow. That way people should have them by the weekend."

"I'm gonna strangle Emmy when she gets home. Why did we let her go on tour and stick this job with us, huh?" Kristen stood up and stretched out her back. "She will be home Sunday and Monday."

"Oh, Kristen, you know you love her. She'd do the same for you," Lynette said.

"You better believe it. I'm gonna make her do all the invitations for my wedding."

"How was Emmy able to book the Lincoln Hotel for her reception?" Lindsey asked. "Sloane and I stopped in there one day. That place is fabulous."

Kristen grinned and said, "Actually, I kinda booked it for her."

Kristen explained about her grandfather Lombardi's connection and the day she and Emmy visited the hotel. "I've even

164

reserved a block of rooms for that night."

"It must cost a fortune to stay there," Sloane said.

"Just part of a leg," Kristen said, "and an entire arm."

For three weeks Emmy and the worship band traveled throughout the Midwest. They returned home each Sunday and left again on Tuesday. Emmy wrote in her journal about each day.

After arriving back at the church in the early morning hours of the twenty-third, the worship team caught a few hours of sleep before the morning service. Emmy came home after church to catch up on her sleep.

"Kristen, don't let Kenny know I said this, but touring is hard work. I'm gonna crash in bed for a week."

"You have to work in the morning, Em."

"Can't I call in sleepy?"

"No," Kristen said. "I'll drag you out of bed."

Kenny took care of the music before he resumed his tour. Emmy picked out a few songs she definitely wanted P.J. and his band to play. Paula made sure Emmy had enough people to handle the day-of-the-wedding jobs. Emmy lined up John Randolph, Derrick Keasling, Reggie Lennon, Tom Hanna and some men from church to act as ushers. Sherry Hanna, Amber Quinlan and Linda Newton were going to be in charge of the guest book. Paula even made last minute decisions with the photographer, caterer and the florist without bothering Emmy. She had enough to worry about.

After Emmy finished the tour, she and Kristen worked during the day and met with Paula in the evenings. They worked hard to pull together all the details of the wedding.

Kenny and the guys returned home from Australia on the thirty-first of March. They landed at O'Hare at seven PM. A limo dropped Kenny off at his parents' house and after talking to Mom and Dad for a few minutes, he called Emmy.

"Hi, sweetheart, you made it back," Emmy said.

"Just got here a few minutes ago. I'm so glad to be home, but I think everyone will need a couple of days to recover from jet lag. It was fun to be down under. We saw some fantastic scenery.

New Zealand is like paradise."

"Are you coming over to see me, or should I come over there?"

"Would you mind if we wait until tomorrow to get together? I'm so wasted from the flight. I need to sleep."

"Okay, I understand. I've got to work tomorrow and Wednesday, but then I'm off for three and a half weeks. Maybe we could do something together. Maybe take a trip somewhere." Emmy was teasing because they would be on their honeymoon.

"I'll come over to your house and be there when you guys get home from work."

"I love you, and I'm glad you're home."

"I love you, too, Emmy."

Emmy had a difficult time concentrating on her job while at work on Tuesday. Mr. Oliver knew why. He called her into his office at two o'clock.

"Yes, Mr. Oliver, how can I help you?"

"I know Kenny got home last night and you haven't seen him yet. Do you want to leave early? I know your mind is not on your work, and I can understand why."

"That's very nice of you to offer to let me go, but Kristen has to work until five and we rode in together."

"I'm sure we could find someone to take Kristen home," Mr. Oliver said.

"I've only got three hours left. I'll be okay. Besides, Kenny is probably sleeping."

Emmy made it through the rest of the day and met Kristen in the lobby at five.

"Should I drive, or will you be able to drive without getting a speeding ticket?"

"I'm not in that big a hurry to see Kenny."

Kristen rolled her eyes. "Yeah, right. Just get us home in one piece."

"Are you and John going to dinner with us tonight?"

"Are you sure you want us along?"

"I'm not going to attack him in the restaurant, Kristen!"

166

"Yeah, you'll wait till you get home."

"You got that right," Emmy said with a gleam in her eyes.

Emmy got them home safely and saw Kenny's father's car in the driveway. She had been using his new Civic while Kenny was gone. She slammed on the brakes and jumped out of the car and ran in the front door. Kristen was sitting in the car and saw Kenny run out the back door. She started to laugh as Kenny ran up to the car and asked, "Where's Em?"

"She went in the front door."

Kristen could hear Emmy hollering for Kenny inside the house. Kenny ran in the front door just as Emmy emerged from the back door. Emmy ran up to the car and asked, "He must be here, but I can't find him."

Kristen couldn't resist and told Emmy, "He just ran in the front door." So, the cycle started again. When Kenny emerged from the back door again, Kristen got out of the car. Even though she was almost in tears because she was laughing so hard, she managed to tell him, "Just wait here. She will be back in a second."

Sure enough Emmy came flying out the back door and Kenny saw her. Now he realized why Kristen was laughing so hard. He smiled at her, and waited for Emmy to get to him. By the time Kristen was finished explaining what happened Emmy wasn't listening. She was too busy kissing Kenny.

That evening Kenny, Emmy, Kristen, John, Tony and Sloane headed over to Larry's Uptown Grill for dinner. Larry's place was one of Kenny's favorite local venues. The band played there often in the early days. After they finished eating, everyone, except Sloane, started teasing Emmy about the upcoming wedding. Sloane listened as Emmy took the kidding without complaining. It became obvious to Sloane that Emmy enjoyed the good-natured ribbing and thrived on it. Sloane listened as Tony and John teased her as though she was their little sister.

Sloane thought as she watched Tony. *I hope we still see each other after the wedding because I think I'm in love with you. In fact, I'm sure of it.*

Tony stopped teasing Emmy long enough to smile at Sloane. He held her hand as he thought. *I sure hope you understand my feelings for Emmy are not the same as how I feel about you.*

Tony and John took Kristen and Sloane home while Kenny and Emmy stayed at the restaurant. Kristen waited up until one in the morning before she went to bed. She resisted calling Emmy's cell phone and assumed Emmy was spending the night at the carriage house. Kristen had just fallen asleep when Emmy got home. Kristen woke up and listened as Emmy was talking to Kenny. She heard them kiss good night, and Emmy ran up the stairs and into her room.

"Krissy, are you asleep?" Emmy asked as she sat on the edge of the bed.

"Not anymore. Where have you guys been? Do you know how late it is? We do have to go to work in the morning."

"I know. I'm sorry."

"I stayed up until one. I thought maybe you were going to stay at the apartment. What have you been doing? Wait! Do I want to know? Don't tell me if you were... you know."

"We weren't doing anything like that. We were talking about the future. We made some decisions about where we want to be in ten years and stuff like that."

"That's great, Em, but I'm so tired. Can you tell me in the morning?"

"Okay, I'm sorry I woke you up. I love you."

"Love you, too, Em. See you in the morning."

As Kristen expected, Emmy overslept in the morning. Kristen had to wake her up, and they rushed to get to work. Kristen drove and wanted to hear about Emmy's news, but Emmy fell asleep with her head against the window. They both got off early and headed home. Emmy wouldn't have to return to work for almost a month. Kenny was there when they arrived. Emmy kissed him and then ran upstairs to change clothes. Kristen talked to Kenny for a moment before heading upstairs. A few minutes later they were all sitting on the couch in the TV room.

"Now will you tell me what you guys were talking about last night?" Kristen pleaded.

"Okay, this is what we think we want to do. I'm going to keep working part-time until June, and when Mr. Oliver retires, I'm gonna leave, too. When the guys go on tour this summer, I'm going to go along and work on the support team. That way I will see how I like the travel. When school starts in the fall, I'm going to go to North Park full-time. I should be able to finish in three semesters. Once that's done, I can either work in the Fridays office or travel with the band or a combination of both."

"If you're going to leave Robertson Industries, then I might quit, too. I know Daddy needs help running the company, and I can work for him. At least until I get married. Of course, I could go back to school and get a masters degree and we could share a dorm room. How would that be?"

"I'm not going to live in the dorms. I will commute."

Kristen kept a straight face as she asked, "Don't you want to live in a dorm so you can go to wild parties and have guys spend the night in your room? Aren't you afraid of missing out on all that fun?"

Kenny didn't crack a smile as he added, "She's right, Em. You should probably live in the dorm. It will be a great way to explore your sexuality."

Emmy looked back and forth at them. Neither Kristen nor Kenny smiled. After fifteen seconds, Kristen started laughing.

"I wish I had a photo of how you looked. Did you really think we were serious?"

Emmy poked Kristen in the arm. "I knew you were kidding all along. You never did that stuff when you were at North Park."

"Are you going to live in this house after you're back from your honeymoon, or are you gonna move to the carriage house?"

"Here, for the time being." Emmy leaned against Kenny, and he put an arm around her shoulders. "We might buy some property somewhere and build a house one of these days."

Kenny added, "Who knows? In twenty years you could have a business together."

"That might be cool," Emmy said.

"Maybe we will be neighbors, too. Wouldn't it be nice if we lived next to each other somewhere?"

On Thursday morning Kenny, his father, Mr. Colasanti and all the guys who were wearing tuxedos met at Capista Formal Wear. The guys in the band gave Kenny a hard time about his tux even though it looked just like theirs. After the guys were finished, Kenny took them all over to Darby's to eat. Kenny had called Mr. Darby the day before to let him know they were coming.

"I hope it's okay. We should be there around noon."

"I don't take reservations," Mr. Darby said in his usual gruff manor, though Kenny knew he was joking.

There were not too many places in the world now where Fridays At Five could walk into a restaurant and not be hounded by fans, but Darby's was one. Since Kenny, Jeff and Jeremy grew up in SoHam—Dave came to SoHam to go to college—the sight of them in the city was not treated as a special event by the media. They were usually able to go about their business and daily life without the distractions they normally encountered on the road. Kenny's wedding was mentioned in the media around the globe, but in SoHam no one paid any extra attention. There were always a few teenage girls who got excited if they saw the band, but most adults didn't bother them. They walked into Darby's and Mr. Darby took their order. He surprised Kenny because he didn't complain when Kenny ordered red sauce on his beef.

When he didn't hassle Andy about his order Kenny asked, "Are you okay, Mr. Darby? You didn't give us any grief about our order."

"I guess I'm feeling a little nostalgic seeing you guys again. I remember when you first started coming in here, as a band, I mean. I know you and Emmy have been coming in here together from the time she was allowed to cross the street." He looked at Mr. Colasanti. He hadn't always thought much of Raymond Colasanti, but he knew Emmy loved her father deeply.

"We keep coming back, Mr. Darby," Jeremy said.

"That you do. Just like a bad penny," Mr. Darby joked and returned to normal. Only Kenny caught the small hint of irony.

The women met at Emmy's house to try on their dresses one last time. Diane was the only one not present. She would be

170

arriving on Friday because Craig had to work. Kristen took some pictures of Emmy in her beautiful wedding dress. After they were satisfied the dresses still fit, they talked about where to have lunch. They ended up at La Cantina. Emmy wanted to have a margarita, but Kristen objected.

"Emmy, have you forgotten what happened the last time you had a margarita? You got sick to your stomach." Kristen didn't mention that Emmy had more than one drink and was pretty buzzed as they were walking home.

"Please, can I just have one?" Emmy asked Kristen.

"Okay, but you have to wait until your food is here," Kristen said. "I don't want you to have any alcohol on an empty stomach."

Emmy and Kristen had a margarita, but the other girls, Lynette, Sloane and Lindsey, stuck to water or pop. The talk soon turned to sex and Kristen and Lynette teased Emmy.

"What will you do if you get your period on your honeymoon?"

"That's not going to happen," Emmy assured them.

"Are you going to break in the new bed at the carriage house?" Lynette asked.

"She might break the bed, the way she bounces around," Kristen teased.

"I do not bounce around in bed." Emmy poked Kristen in the ribs as she blushed.

Sloane and Lindsey smiled as they listened.

Lynette grinned as she said, "I remember our honeymoon. We didn't get out of bed until noon every day."

"I want to do more than just... you know."

"Get out! All you talk about at home is how much sex you're going to have."

Emmy blushed and would not answer any of their questions even though she talked about sex at home with Kristen all the time.

The week had passed quickly and April fourth, the day of the rehearsal and dinner arrived.

"Emmy, are you gonna stay in bed all day? It's after ten."

171

Emmy groaned. "I'm sick. I feel like I'm gonna puke."

Kristen sat on the edge of the bed. "Is it because of that margarita, or is it just nerves?"

"Just nerves." Emmy sat up. "I should have eloped."

"Well, it's too late now. The whole wedding party is here."

Emmy's eyes opened wide as she pulled the sheet up over her chest. "Why are they here now?"

Kristen laughed. "I didn't mean they're in the house. I meant they're all in SoHam."

"They all live here. Why wouldn't they be in town?"

"Diane and Andy don't live here."

"Andy might as well. He's here more than Albuquerque or San Diego."

"Do you feel better now?"

"Yeah, I'll get up now. I want to make sure the house is clean before Diane gets here. I can't wait to see Carson again."

"You saw him a month ago at the shower."

"Infants can change a lot in a month."

"Well, the house is a mess so you better get crackin'."

Kristen knew Emmy would keep herself occupied and not think about the wedding if she thought the house needed cleaning.

Diane, Craig and Carson arrived around noon. They would be staying the next two nights at Emmy's house—along with Kristen, of course.

"Diane, when did he start walking on his own?" Emmy asked as she watched Carson.

"A couple of weeks ago. He still falls down a lot, but he gets right back up. You better be quick, Em. He moves pretty fast."

Emmy spent a couple of hours playing with Carson. He loved his Aunt Emmy and could even say her name. At least he could make the *m* sound.

The Colwell house was full of people as friends stopped by to see Kenny all day long. Almost all of the people who worked full-time for the Fridays At Five organization were coming to the wedding and reception. There were even a few of the part-timers, the ones who lived in SoHam mainly, who were planning to attend the wedding ceremony at least.

Later that afternoon, Carson took a nap giving Emmy a chance to talk to Diane.

"Are you going to try to get along with Mom?" Emmy asked.

"Yes. I promised that I would bite my tongue. How have you guys been doing? Is she still trying to control everything about the wedding?"

"She tried at first, but once we hired Paula Kratzsky, Mom kinda shut up. Paula is an expert at handling mothers."

"Get out! How did you do that?"

"I threatened to elope," Emmy said and then giggled. "No, Paula has dealt with overbearing mothers before. She allowed Mom to have some input on certain matters."

"Where did you find Paula? I might want to hire her every time I have to visit Mom and Dad," Diane said. *The only reason I ever bother to see them is because they want to see Carson.*

"I met her at church," Emmy replied. "She makes a decent living coordinating weddings and large parties and stuff. I don't know what I would have done without her. She gets everything done in a timely manner and saves me from the stress."

"You sound like an advertising campaign."

"Maybe, but I really mean it," Emmy said.

The rehearsal was supposed to start at six and Emmy rushed out the door at ten till, leaving Kristen behind. Emmy was six blocks away when her cell phone rang.

"Emmy, did you forget to take something to the rehearsal with you?"

"No, I don't think so.... Oh, shoot, Kristen. I'm sorry. I forgot your car is in the shop. I'll be right back."

Emmy and Kristen made it to the church only a few minutes late.

"Sorry, everybody. I forgot Kristen and had to go back and get her."

After fifteen minutes of socializing, Dr. Ausland asked, "Emmy, would you like to get started now?"

"Yes, Pastor Herb, everybody is here and ready."

Paula helped situate everybody on the steps of the platform

and used blue tape to mark everybody's spot.

"Paula, what would I do without you? You are so organized and think of everything. I never would have thought to mark the spot with tape."

"I've learned from experience, Emmy," Paula said.

Emmy was using Chase Hillman and some of the other musicians and singers from church, and they rehearsed their part. Pastor Paul Jefferson was helping Dr. Ausland with the ceremony. Everything went well, except for a broken guitar string, and everyone headed out for dinner afterward.

Kenny chose his favorite pizza parlor for the rehearsal dinner, Kerry Lynn's Pizza and Pasta, and made sure there was a ton of food available—not just pizza, either.

After the entire wedding party had arrived and the pizzas were on the buffet table, Dr. Ausland offered grace. Emmy and Kristen were the first in line to eat.

Tony turned to John and nudged him in the ribs. "Look who's first in line to grab some food."

John chuckled and said, "Yeah, I noticed. I hope they save some for the rest of us."

"I'm starving. What kind of pizza is this one?" Emmy asked Kristen.

"It looks like their Super Seven special, Emmy," Kristen answered.

"Which one is the Veggie Supreme? I am giving up eating meat. I read this book last week about how animals are treated, and it broke my heart. I'm giving up all kinds of meat and becoming a veterinarian."

"Do you mean vegetarian?" Kristen corrected her.

"No, I mean veterinarian. You know, a doctor who works on animals instead of humans."

Kristen shook her head. "Sometimes I think you are totally goofy, Emmy. What are you going to eat when we go to Darby's? They don't have veggie dogs you know."

"Well, I guess I'll have to make an exception when we go there. I can't give up my chili dogs."

Emmy and Kristen loaded up their plates with pizza and

headed back to the table where all the women were going to be sitting. In a few minutes Emmy finished her pizza and was heading back up to the table for more.

"Emmy, don't eat too much and make yourself sick. You might miss your own wedding, then you won't be able to have sex tomorrow night," Diane teased.

Emmy was embarrassed because Dr. Ausland heard what Diane said. "I just had three small pieces, Diane. I'm not going to make myself sick."

Kenny and the guys were demolishing the pizzas as fast as the servers could bring them out. After everyone had eaten their fill, Kenny and Emmy passed out gifts to the wedding party and to everyone who was helping in some way at the ceremony and reception. Emmy found necklaces that she loved and gave one to each of her bridesmaids. Kenny bought PS2 games for his groomsmen.

Kristen groaned and rolled her eyes. "Typical! I hope they don't stay up all night playing games."

"It wouldn't surprise me if they do, Krissy," Emmy said.

Two hours later it was time to go home. Emmy kissed Kenny good night. They hugged each other until Kristen pulled Emmy off of him.

"Come on, Emmy. We've got to go home. Say good night to him already."

"Okay! I just want one more kiss." Emmy turned back to Kenny. "After tomorrow, you will never have to leave me at night to go home ever again. I love you, Kenny."

"I love you, too, Emmy. Get some sleep. Tomorrow will be a busy day. Me and the guys are going to catch a baseball game in the afternoon and..."

"Mr. Colwell!" Emmy stomped her foot and put her hands on her hips. "I think you will be too busy tomorrow to go to a ball game. Have you forgotten already? We are getting married."

"Oh my God! Is that tomorrow? I forgot. I promised the guys..."

Kenny smiled and Emmy said, "You are such a funny guy, aren't you? Just wait, we'll see who's doing the teasing tomorrow night. I might just decide to spend the night with Kristen and watch romantic movies in my ratty old bathrobe instead of wearing a certain negligee that someone gave me for Christmas."

"I think I might be able to make the wedding," Kenny said as he kissed the tip of her nose. "What time is it again?"

Emmy pushed him away and told him, "Get out of here. Kristen and I have to go home. Don't stay up all night playing games, either." *You just might need to pull an allnighter tomorrow.*

Emmy had trouble sleeping that night and went downstairs and poured herself a glass of white wine. Kristen came downstairs when she heard her. Kristen got a wine glass from the cupboard.

"I'll have some, too."

"I thought a small glass of wine would help me fall asleep. It usually makes me sleepy."

"Only after you drink the whole bottle, Em," Kristen teased.

Emmy stuck out her tongue.

"Are you nervous, Em?"

"Just a little. Not because I'm afraid of marrying Kenny, but because I am afraid I will wake up in the morning to find it's all been a dream, and I'll be all alone for the rest of my life."

"It's not a dream. You don't need to worry."

"I suppose I'm being silly."

"Yes, you are, but we all love you, anyway."

Kristen hugged her and talked to her until they went back upstairs to bed. Kristen stayed with Emmy until she fell asleep.

"Sweet dreams, my angel," Kristen said as she kissed Emmy on the forehead.

Chapter Sixteen

Emmy Colasanti woke up early, surprisingly calm on the morning of the biggest day of her life. She said her morning prayers and read her devotional book. There were many things to get done this morning, so she and Kristen started right away. Paula was already working hard at the church. The wedding started at one, and Emmy needed to be at the church by eleven.

"I don't want to spend a lot of time fixing my hair today," Emmy told Diane and Kristen with a straight face. "I'll just put it in a ponytail because that's easier."

Kristen smacked her butt. "Not a chance in hell. Now, get dressed because we have to be at the hairdresser's at eight thirty, and we have to do your makeup."

They laughed as Emmy pretended to be in her wedding dress with a ponytail and a ribbon in her hair.

Later, the hairdresser actually used a piece of purple ribbon in Emmy's hair.

"Why are you wearing that, Emmy?" Diane asked as she touched the ribbon.

"Have you ever heard that old saying about wearing something old, something borrowed and something blue?"

Kristen and Diane shook their heads.

"Well, Grandma told it to me. This ribbon sorta fits. It's kinda old because I've had it in my music box. Tony used it to tie my hair in a ponytail on our second date."

"Oh, that's so sweet," Kristen cooed.

"So it's borrowed because I got it from him and it sorta looks blue because it has faded a bit."

"Does Kenny know that Tony gave it to you?" Diane asked.

"I'm not sure if I ever showed it to him. I doubt if Tony even remembers it."

"Don't tell anyone. It's kinda weird," Diane said.

Kristen drove Emmy to the church. The other girls were already there. They started talking and didn't pay any attention to the time.

"We do have a wedding this afternoon." Paula tapped a pencil on the table. "I would suggest everyone start getting dressed, and no, Emmy, you can't wear jeans and a t-shirt."

"What? Why not? My jeans are perfectly comfortable," Emmy whined.

"Get dressed," Paula ordered.

Although the bridesmaid dresses were the same shade of lavender, each lady had a different design. Sloan, Lindsey and Lynette wore more modest dresses. Kristen's showed more skin and Diane's revealed more cleavage than the the rest of them combined.

Kenny and the guys met at the Colwell home and decided to play catch with a football before going to the church. Kenny didn't show any outward signs of nervousness, but inside he was anxious for the wedding to start. Thankfully, the guys didn't hurt each other and made their way to the church to get ready.

Paula Kratzsky had instructed the ushers to be at the church ready to work at noon. She was experienced enough with large weddings to know there would be people arriving early to get a good seat. She had also coordinated with the SoHam Police. There were six squad cars directing traffic in the area and three plainclothes officers acting as security inside. Guests started arriving at Crest Ridge United Nazarene shortly after twelve. Mr. Oliver and his wife, as well as all the guys from her office, were among the first guests to arrive. Fernando Ramos and Ethan Hanks were invited and showed up with dates. Ethan was still dating Camille Dempsey. Barry and Linda Newton arrived with baby Fender Isaac Gerald Newton. He was born on March first—just over a month old. This was his first public appearance.

"Linda, will you please help me? He needs a new diaper, and I've already changed three in the last two hours. Being a daddy is hard work." Barry took a deep breath and then sighed.

Linda scowled at Barry. "Give him to me."

"I can't help it, Linda. I'm trying."

Linda told the group of women gawking at her son, "It takes Barry two hours to change Fen's diaper sometimes."

Emmy, Kristen and the rest of the ladies were waiting in a

178

room off the main sanctuary normally used by mothers of small children during Sunday services. They could see out into the sanctuary, but the guests could not see into the fifteen by fifteen foot room.

"Krissy, can you believe how full the church is?" Emmy asked.

Diane walked over and stood behind Emmy with her hands on her shoulders. "Why are there so many people here? Are you sure they're at the right wedding?"

"I hope so. Should we ask the ushers to double check?"

"Very funny, Emmy."

Sloane and Lindsey sat on padded chairs and discussed their chances of getting hired at Jamie McGee Junior High for the next school year. Lynette read a book about a fairy princess to her twin girls to keep them from becoming bored.

"Look! The ushers are sure keeping busy. Did we really invite all these people, Kristen?" Emmy asked.

"Remember you wanted to invite everyone you ever met, Em, and besides, you don't need an invitation for the wedding. Some of these people might be Fridays At Five fans."

"Or Worship Band fans," Lynette said as she grinned.

"I wanted to elope," Emmy said to no one in particular as she plopped down onto a chair and blew her veil out of her face.

"Aren't you pleased now that you didn't?" Kristen checked her hair in a mirror and then turned to face Emmy. "Get up! You'll ruin your dress."

Emmy jumped up. "Yes, this is the happiest day of my life." *I'm so nervous. I think I'm going to puke.* Emmy closed her eyes and said a quick prayer. *Please, Lord, help me get through this day. I'm afraid I'm gonna make a fool of myself by crying and not being able to say my vows.*

Although Emmy's wedding dress was white, it looked very modern. It was full length but not tight. She wanted it that way so she could be more comfortable and able to dance easier.

Paula checked her watch. "Ladies, we need to do a final check. Flowers, hair, whatever else you want to check. Time for a quick trip to the bathroom."

Emmy turned toward the door.

"Not you, Emmy. You can't leave this room," Paula said.

A few minutes later, the bridesmaids were assembled and ready. Emmy's father knocked on the door, and Paula let him in.

"Is this flower on right?" he asked Paula.

"You look absolutely perfect, Mr. Colasanti." Paula adjusted his tie and the boutonniere. "There you go."

He closed his eyes. *I could use a beer about now.*

Emmy and her father moved to a corner of the room and had a moment to themselves just before the ceremony started. He looked at her and his eyes filled with tears. "Emmy, you look so beautiful today. I am so proud of you." He started to break down, and she hugged him. "I'm sorry I was not a better father to you. I should have done better."

"Daddy, you have been the best father I could have asked for. I love you very much. I am so glad you are even here. We almost lost you, you know. I prayed so hard for you to get better and you have. I thank God everyday for you and Mom."

Diane overheard the conversation and rolled her eyes. *Get real, Em. Dad and Mom have treated us like crap.*

"Okay, ushers. It's time to escort some ladies to their seats," Paula said.

Emmy watched as Kenny's grandmother Beatrice and her grandma Isabel were escorted to their seats. Then Tom Hanna escorted Mrs. Colwell and finally Derrick Keasling escorted Emmy's mother.

Emmy bit her lip as she watched her mother walk down the aisle. *I'm so proud of how you and Daddy have made an effort to not fight and argue as much.*

Her father had been sober for over two months now.

Just after the mothers were seated, but before the bridesmaids started down the aisle, Diane closed her eyes and let her mind wander. A thin, frail-looking man using a cane and a rather plump, but very short, lady walked in and took a seat at the back unseen by everyone but Diane. Diane opened her eyes as she heard the sound of a music box.

The men walked out onto the platform and took their places

180

at the front of the church. Kenny, Andy, Jeff, Jeremy, Dave and Tony lined up and waited. Emmy laughed as the guys kept looking down to make sure they were standing exactly on Paula's blue tape. Dr. Ausland stepped into position. The music started.

Paula said, "It's time, ladies. Remember to walk slowly and maintain exactly twenty-three feet between you and the person in front of you."

"What? You never said anything about that last night," Diane said.

"I'm kidding." Paula laughed. *I use that line at every wedding and it always gets the same response.*

Emmy watched as all the bridesmaids walked down the aisle. Sloane Beckett went first followed by Lindsey Cameron. Lynette Jefferson was next. Diane headed down the aisle with a smile on her face. Before Kristen started down the aisle, Emmy held her hand for just a moment.

"I love you, Krissy."

"I love you more, Em."

Paula whispered, "It's time, Kristen."

After Kristen was nearly to the front, Lynette's twin two-year-old girls, Ruth and Esther, scattered white rose petals as they slowly made their way to the front. They stopped when they saw their grandmother and grandfather sitting in the third row.

"Pa! Ta!"

They squealed and forgot about their mother who was trying to get them to come up to her. The crowd got a big kick out of the adorable little girls.

When the time came for Emmy to start down the aisle, she helped her father compose himself. Paula took a final look at Emmy and adjusted her veil.

"Thank you so much for everything, Paula. I don't know what I would have done without your help."

"It's been my pleasure, Emmy. You look so beautiful."

Emmy listened to the music for their cue. Her father looked at her. "Is it time, Emmy?"

"Not yet, Dad. Wait... Okay now."

Emmy's mother and Mrs. Colwell stood up, and then the

whole room stood as one body. Emmy began the journey. Memories of her childhood flowed through her mind. Images flashed before her eyes by the thousands. Time stood absolutely still for her. Her father walked Emmy down the aisle and stood beside her. She held his thin arm and supported him. Dr. Ausland started the ceremony with a prayer.

Soon Emmy heard the words, "Who gives this woman to be married here today?"

"Her mother and I," Raymond Colasanti announced proudly with a stronger voice than Emmy had heard from him in months.

Emmy turned to her daddy; he kissed her on the cheek and sat beside her mother. Emmy joined Kenny before Dr. Ausland.

"Emily Olivia Colasanti, do you take this man to be your lawful wedded husband? To have and to hold from this day forward until death do you part?"

"I do."

"Kenneth Travis Robert Colwell..." as Dr. Ausland said his name, Emmy got goosebumps all over her arms and a chill ran up her back and her heart fluttered... "do you take this woman to be your lawful wedded wife? To have and to hold from this day forward till death do you part?"

"I do," Kenny said with a smile as Emmy bit her lip. *I love the way your eyes sparkle, Em. Always have.*

Pastor Paul Jefferson read the scripture they had chosen, and the musicians and singers did their part. Emmy almost got through the ceremony without crying until she looked at Andy Walker. He was crying like a baby. She looked at Tony, and he was crying, too. Emmy looked at Mrs. Colwell and she was beaming with pride. Her mom and dad both had tears flowing down their faces. Emmy saw Mama Bertucci in the fourth row and she smiled at her. Mama smiled back and winked.

Dr. Ausland whispered softly, "It is now time for you to say your vows."

They exchanged rings...

"Emmy, today I become your husband and you become my wife. I promise to love you with all my heart. I promise to respect

182

you as a very unique and special person with your own interests, desires and needs, that sometimes I wonder about, but that I realize are every bit as important as my own and most likely smarter than my own. I promise to share my innermost thoughts, my fears and feelings, my secrets and my dreams. I promise I will strive to change and grow with you and to keep our relationship alive, exciting and never boring, which knowing you, Emmy, will not be a problem. I promise to love you in good times, bad times and all the times in between with my undivided heart, with all that I have to give and all that I am, in the only way I know how, completely and forever."

Dr. Ausland turned his attention to Emmy and nodded.

"Kenny, today I become your wife and you become my husband. I read a poem once that said 'This is the miracle that happens every time to those who really love. The more they give, the more they possess.' Kenny, you are the most generous, loving, unselfish person I know. I fell in love with you the moment you held my hand to help me cross the street on my first day of high school. After I first kissed you, I knew I wanted to spend my whole life with you. I want to grow old with you by my side as my best friend and lover. I promise to love you without reservation, comfort you in times of need, encourage you to achieve all your goals and aspirations, laugh with you and cry with you. I promise to always be open and honest with you even if it hurts. I promise to be true and loyal, but not like a puppy dog. You inspire me to be the best person I can be and lastly, I promise to cherish you forever."

After their vows were spoken, Emmy and Kenny walked to the wooden memorial table, took the two burning candles and lit a larger one in the middle to signify their two lives had become one.

Dr. Ausland announced, "By the power vested in me by the state of Illinois and the authority of God Almighty, I now pronounce you husband and wife. Kenny, you may now kiss your bride."

Emmy had goosebumps all over her body as Kenny took her in his arms.

"Don't you dare use your tongue," Emmy whispered.

He crushed her to his chest and locked his lips on hers.

Dr. Ausland held out his arms and smiled. "It is now my great pleasure to introduce Mr. and Mrs. Kenny and Emmy Colwell."

The music played and Kenny and Emmy held hands as they very quickly walked back out the aisle she had recently walked so slowly down. They were soon joined by the rest of the wedding party. Kristen kissed her and hugged her tightly.

"Don't cry, Em. It will ruin your makeup."

"And I spent five minutes getting it just right," Emmy said and then giggled.

Andy shook Kenny's hand. "Congratulations, you made it through the day."

"There's still a lot to do, Andy. It's early in the game, if you know what I mean."

Andy hugged Emmy and whispered, "Congratulations, cousin. Now I won't have to worry about you guys misbehaving."

Emmy whispered back, "I plan to 'misbehave' as often as I can now."

Emmy and Kenny stood together as the crowd passed them. The greeting line was like a blur to Emmy, and she couldn't even see the end. She held Kenny's hand as much as she could.

Diane stood by herself, closed her eyes and saw the frail looking man with the cane and the short, but rather plump, lady again. They appeared to be smiling. Another form materialized beside them carrying a small wooden box. He opened the box.

Suddenly, Emmy grabbed hold of Kenny's arm and squeezed it.

"What is it, Em?"

"Can you hear that?" she asked.

"Hear what? All I can hear are the people in line."

Emmy closed her eyes and turned her head slightly toward the side of the foyer.

Diane kept her eyes closed as the figures walked toward a side door of a large cathedral. She heard the music box again. They paused at the door, turned to look at Emmy, smiled and then disappeared. Diane opened her eyes, and the music stopped.

184

Emmy opened her eyes and tilted her head. "It's nothing. For a moment I thought I could hear 'Clair de Lune' just as clear as day."

"You mean the tune from your music box?" Kenny asked.

"Yeah. I thought I could hear it playing. Must have been my imagination."

They greeted the next people in line.

Diane looked at the side wall and walked over to it. She put her hand on the solid masonry wall as a single tear escaped.

It took ninety minutes for all the guests to get through the line, but there were still three hours to go before the reception. The time went by quickly as Paula made sure the photographers took all the shots Kenny and Emmy requested.

When they finally had a few minutes to themselves, Kenny told her, "I love you, and you are the most beautiful bride ever in the history of the world."

"Knock it off and quit exaggerating." Emmy poked his arm. "You're just saying that so I will sleep with you tonight."

"I'm not exaggerating. I asked all the guys and they told me the same thing. Anyway, that's what they said after I handed them a fifty dollar bill."

"You're gonna get it, Kenny Colwell."

Kenny smiled and kissed her. "I hope so! I've been waiting for a long time."

"Do you think you can wait a few more hours?" Emmy asked with a devilish grin on her face and a sparkle in her eyes.

"Only if I have to, Mrs. Colwell."

Limousines that Mrs. Moneywell arranged, and charged to Mr. Robertson, drove the wedding party from the church to the Lincoln Hotel. He gladly paid for them. When Emmy looked into the room, she was shocked.

"Oh, my God, Kenny! The place is packed."

"Did we really invite all these people?" Kenny stepped aside as two kids scampered past. "So much for our no kids policy."

Paula still coordinated everything. She appeared totally unruffled in the loose-fitting dress that hid her extra pounds. She

185

cued Chase Hillman, and he introduced the wedding party as they entered the large hall. Two large video screens on the wall displayed pictures of Emmy and Kenny from throughout their lives. The two photographers roamed the room and took pictures of everyone. Paula had also hired two men to film the reception.

Before the dinner was served, Kenny and Emmy walked around to talk to as many people as they could. Emmy saw Chase and Yvonne Hillman and they hugged each other. So many of her friends from church were here including all the guys in the worship band and the entire pastoral staff. It meant so much to Emmy to have her church family here tonight. Many of the people from Faith Bible Church were there also. Later, as the waiters served dinner, the sound of silverware clinking on the glasses remained nearly constant. She and Kenny spent so much time kissing for the crowd, they barely had time to eat.

Later, Paula informed Will Consoli, the sound engineer for Fridays At Five, "It's time for the best man speech. Do you have the mic?"

Will handed Paula a wireless mic, and she took it to Andy.

"It's time, Mr. Walker. After you finish, would you give the mic to Diane, please?"

"I'm ready. I have my notes in my pocket." Andy stood, coughed, cleared his throat and looked at Kenny and Emmy. "I remember the day I met Kenny and the guys. A friend had told me about this new band, and suggested I might be interested in talking to them about becoming their manager." He looked at Kenny again. "I met them in this room above a garage. I had actually met Jeff, Jeremy and Dave before. So, I looked around and saw this kid with funny looking ears tuning a guitar. My first thought was that Jeff was playing a practical joke on me." Andy paused while the audience laughed. "Then I thought maybe he was the guitar tech and Frankie was the other member of the band." Andy looked around the room and spotted Frankie in the back trying to be inconspicuous. "Then Kenny started playing his guitar. He sang the first verse of one of their songs, and I was blown away by this awesome kid. I decided right there that I wanted to work with them. I guess I made a good decision." Andy had to wait again

186

while the crowd roared. He talked about the early days with the band and how the guys worked so hard to become successful. "Let me conclude by saying that since Kenny is now a married man like the other guys, I will have to raise his allowance." All of the people from the Fridays At Five organization knew how tight Andy was with the band's money and they laughed. "From now on, Kenny, you can have three hundred dollars a week. Don't spend it all in one place."

Andy handed the mic to Diane as the crowd roared again.

Diane rose to her feet and cleared her throat. "I want to say a few words about growing up with Emmy. First of all, Kenny, I hope you have a large bed because she will take up every inch of it." Diane followed with another comical speech. Emmy covered her face with her hand as Diane told some stories to entertain the crowd.

"Diane! I did not drink a beer when I was six."

"Sorry, Em. I got that wrong. You were nine."

Emmy gave Diane a big hug and kiss after she finished.

Kristen took the mic from Diane. "I'll do my best to keep this short. Here goes. I was minding my own business in the bathroom at Roosevelt High when all of a sudden this little bundle of energy in a maroon dress burst in and smacked into me. I could tell something, or someone, had upset her because of the words coming out of her mouth." Kristen glanced over her shoulder at Emmy. "Sorry, Em, but you were swearing. Anyway, I asked her if she was okay, and she told me what had happened. That was my formal introduction to Emmy Colasanti. I think within two hours we became best friends and have been ever since. I think there are two different Emmys. One is quiet, shy and as innocent as a newborn lamb—then there is the real Emmy!"

The crowd erupted with laughter.

"She can be funny, and she's definitely intelligent, if a little naïve about some things—like boys. She can be just a wee tiny bit stubborn." Kristen held her fingers very close together.

Again Kristen had wait until the laughter subsided.

"Okay, she can be very stubborn, and I would give you a few examples, but I have to go to work on Monday. I don't need to tell anyone here how her life changed back in June of 2001 when she accepted Jesus into her life. She was always such a sweet and caring person before, but after that she became even more amazing. She's not perfect..."

The wedding party roared in agreement. Emmy frowned at them.

"But she strives to be. I know from living with her that she influenced me to become a better person. Especially in the kitchen. I know there were times when she managed to choke down my awful food without too much complaining. She learned pretty quickly not to let me near the stove. See! I told you she was intelligent. Emmy, I pray God grants you and Kenny a long and happy life together. A toast to the bride and groom!"

Before she sat down Kristen added, "There I went through my whole speech and didn't even mention sex and how unbearable you have become because you are so horny."

The guests howled with laughter. Emmy hugged Kristen and whispered in her ear, "You are so gonna get it."

A few minutes later, Emmy and Kenny cut the cake so the caterers could take it away to be prepared for later.

Diane needed to get Emmy out of the room for a few minutes so she improvised. "Emmy, come with me to the bathroom so you can help me fix my hair."

"What's wrong with your hair? It looks fine to me."

"Please, Emmy, just come with me. I need to ask you something." Diane dragged Emmy away and they found a restroom.

"Your hair is fine. What did you want to ask me?"

Diane wanted to ask about the music box, but instead she said, "I just want to know if there are any last minute questions you want to ask."

"What do you mean *last minute questions*? Questions about what?"

"You know, questions about sex. Tonight will be your first time, won't it?"

"Diane! I'm not gonna answer that and, no, I don't have any questions about sex. I think we will be able to manage just fine."

At this moment Emmy truly was a blushing bride.

"Sorry, Em, I shouldn't pry."

Emmy whispered, "I thought you were going to ask me about something else."

"What?"

"It's just something silly." Emmy put a finger to her mouth.

"Tell me, or else." Diane squeezed Emmy's arm.

"When Kenny and I were greeting all those people..."

Diane froze.

"... for a moment, I thought I heard my music box tune. I closed my eyes, but when I opened them again, it disappeared. Never mind, it was just my imagination."

"Did you see anything?"

"Sure! Lots of people and a lot of them were strangers. Why?"

"No reason." Diane smiled. *Maybe one of these days I will tell you everything.*

Emmy and Diane returned to the ballroom and Emmy waved at P.J. and the band.

Kenny looked at Emmy and said, "Well, don't just stand there, Emmy. This new band wants to play for you."

"Kenny, how did you ever get The Notable Exceptions back together? Did you offer them a ton of money?"

"You do realize that all The Notable Exceptions made a special effort to be here today."

"I wish they hadn't broken up," Emmy said as she waved to some other friends.

"Actually, Em, I didn't have to pay the guys anything. They're doing it for free."

"You better pay them something. It must have cost them a small fortune to fly here."

"I will take care of them," Kenny said. "Especially P.J."

The time for dancing had arrived. Emmy and Kenny had the first dance all to themselves. Emmy chose most of the songs for the early part of the reception. Kenny laughed when he first read the list—they were all Fridays At Five songs. Emmy had chosen "Hero For Hire" for her dance with Kenny. Kenny wowed

189

the crowd with his Fred Astaire moves and the crowd went wild when he dipped Emmy and kissed her at the end of the song. The photographers and the video men captured the moment. They had been practicing to get it just right and gave a performance worthy of *Dirty Dancing*. For her dance with her father, P.J. and the band slowed down the tempo of "Sweet Girl" to enable Emmy's father to dance with her for the first time in her life. She danced with her father and nearly ruined her makeup. Kenny danced with his mother. He even danced with Emmy's mom.

Later, she talked with P.J. and the band. "I am so shocked you got the band back together for this. How can I ever repay you?"

"You could save a dance for me later," P.J. said with a grin.

When Emmy got a chance to dance with Andy Walker, she asked, "Why were you crying during the ceremony?"

"My contacts were bothering me. That's all."

"When did you start wearing contacts, Andy? I didn't know you even wore them or glasses."

"I don't."

"You're a teddy bear!" she said and gave him a big hug in front of everyone. Including one of the photographers.

Emmy saw Annie O'Dell sitting with her longtime boyfriend, Matt Sullivan.

"Hi, guys. I'm so glad you were able to come."

"It was a beautiful ceremony, Emmy, and you look absolutely ravishing."

"Thank you, Annie. You look fantastic yourself. Have you guys been dancing?"

"Just a couple of times. Matty twisted his ankle at work a few days ago." Annie pointed to his shoe.

Matt shrugged. "I wasn't watching were I was walking and landed on the edge of a step. Just foolish of me."

"I hope it gets better quick. If you want to dance with us girls, Annie, you're more than welcome. We're having fun."

"Thanks, Emmy, maybe I will."

Emmy even danced with Tony who whispered, "Kenny loves you very much, and now you can misbehave all you want."

190

"Believe me, I plan to be very naughty from now on."

Later, Emmy let Kenny remove her garter. Kenny tossed the garter to the guys and Tony grabbed it away from John Randolph. When Emmy threw her bouquet, Kristen caught it. She showed John the bouquet and he smiled at her.

"You know what this means, don't you, Johnny boy? It's a tradition."

"Does it mean that you and Tony are going to get married?" John asked.

"No! I can't marry my cousin. Maybe you can think of someone else who might want to marry me."

"I think you and Tony would make a good pair."

Kristen smacked John's arm. "If that's what you want, then I guess I'll spend the rest of the night with him." She turned to walk away.

He grabbed her around her waist. "I might be able to think of someone else who might be persuaded to marry you."

A few minutes later, Kenny announced, "There has been a special request, uh, by me, for the song 'I Will Be True To You.' I don't remember all the words, but there is someone here who does, I hope. Emmy, would you please come here?"

Emmy looked at him as he handed her a microphone. "Kenny Colwell, you are in big trouble. Are you making me sing at my own wedding?"

"Please! I think everyone wants to hear you sing," he whispered. Then he asked the crowd if they wanted to hear Emmy sing, and they started clapping and hollering. "I guess they want to hear you, Em."

"Fine! But you will pay later."

He smiled, and the band played as Emmy sang her song to Kenny. After she finished Kenny gave her a big kiss and hug as the crowd applauded. Emmy kissed him back and whispered, "Thanks for being such a great friend and never giving up on me."

"As if I could ever forget the first love of my life."

"Oh, Kenny! I love you so much."

Later, Kenny and the other members of Fridays At Five played a few tunes. They finished and Kenny told the crowd, "I

191

have a 'new' song for you if you would allow me to indulge myself. I actually wrote this song years ago for Emmy when she was just a wee little lass." He held his hand waist high to show how tall Emmy was then. "I guess she's still a wee lass even now."

The crowd laughed as Emmy looked at Kenny and stuck out her tongue at him. *You are such a dork.*

"Anyway, I wrote this for Emmy, but I never told her. I never even sang it for her, or anybody, for that matter. This will be the first time anyone has ever heard the song, except me, of course."

He grabbed an acoustic guitar and plugged in. He made sure it was in tune and then motioned to Will Consoli, the sound guy. Will started recording. Kenny faced the band. "I'll do this one by myself." He turned back to the crowd and said, "I guess this one is called 'You Have My Heart' and it goes like this." Kenny proceeded to sing the song he wrote for Emmy.

Emmy listened to the words and tried in vain to fight back her tears. Kenny finished and set the guitar down as she walked over to hug him tightly.

He whispered in her ear, "Emmy, I love you very much, and I always will. You are the dearest friend I have in the whole world."

"I love you, too, Kenny. That was the most beautiful song I ever heard. Are you going to record it sometime?"

"I just did, Emmy. It's my present to you. I wrote it just for you and nobody else."

Emmy's parents needed to leave so Emmy and Kenny spent a few moments with them.

"Thanks for everything, Mom. I'll talk to you when we get back."

"You look so beautiful, Emmy. I guess you're all grown up now for real."

Emmy hugged her mother and then turned to her father. "Oh, Daddy," were the only words she got out before she couldn't say anything more. Her father hugged her and kissed her cheek without saying a word.

Kenny hugged his mother-in-law and shook hands with his

new father-in-law. "We will talk to you in a couple weeks. Thanks for everything."

Emmy saw Mr. Robertson sitting with Mrs. Moneywell. She went over to talk to them.

"Thank you for being here. I know you guys were in France and had to fly back. I really appreciate it."

"We wouldn't have missed this for anything, Emmy," Mrs. Moneywell told her because Mr. Robertson lost his voice for a moment. "You look absolutely gorgeous, Emmy. I love that purple ribbon in your hair."

Emmy shrugged. "It's something I've had for a long time."

Mr. Robertson regained the use of his voice and asked Emmy for a dance. She danced with him, and he thought of her grandfather Joseph Colasanti and how proud he would be of her.

Emmy and Kristen spent much of the rest of the time dancing together. Annie O'Dell joined them, and Emmy thought about how she always got along great with Annie, but their paths didn't cross often. Kenny grabbed a guitar and joined the band. He and P.J. took turns playing solos to entertain the crowd.

Just before the party ended, Emmy danced one more time with Kenny. He told her, "Emmy, you are the most beautiful girl in the world, ever."

She kissed him and asked, "Who is the second most beautiful?"

He teased her and said, "Mom, is the second most beautiful woman ever."

"Who is third?"

He answered, "My grandmothers would tie for third."

"You're still my dorky rock star," Emmy said as she laughed. "I am so in love with you."

He pulled her close and kissed her. "How was that?"

"I love it when you use your tongue."

The ever-present photographers captured the moment.

Before Emmy and Kenny left they had to say good night to Mama Bertucci. She was ready to leave with Heather and Alex.

Mama put her hands on Emmy's shoulders and squeezed. "Emmy, you are the most radiant bride I have ever seen."

"Thank you, Mama. I don't know what I would have done without you these last few years. You have been my anchor in a stormy sea."

"Oh, sweetie. You are the light of my life. I love you so much. You make sure you come and see me when you get home. I'll have some food ready for you."

"I know you will."

Mama hugged Emmy as they both had tears flowing down their cheeks. Tony hugged Emmy and kissed her cheek.

As Tony and Emmy were talking, Mama told Kenny, "You take good care of your little one now."

"I will, Mama. I will."

Tony shook Kenny's hand and told him, "It was a totally awesome day. I'm happy you let me be a part of it."

"Thank you for sharing this day with us and for still being a good friend to Emmy... and me, too."

There were only a handful of people left—the hardcore party-people. The guys in the band were hanging around and Emmy thanked each one and gave them a hug. She pulled Andy aside to talk to him privately.

"Have I ever told you how much I love you?"

Andy rubbed his jaw and tilted his head. "No, I don't think you ever have, cuz." *What are you thinking, Emmy?*

"Well, I do and I appreciate how hard you've worked for the band all these years."

"If you are angling for a bigger raise in his allowance, forget it. You will have to make due with what I give him." Andy pulled Emmy out of the way of a busboy pushing a cart.

She stuck out her bottom lip. "How am I supposed to live like a rock star's wife unless you give me more money?"

"I'm sure you will find a way. Now give me a hug so I can get home. I've got to start planning the next tour."

It was after midnight when Emmy and Kenny finally left the reception in their limo. They arrived at the carriage house mentally and physically exhausted from the long day. They staggered to the top of the stairs. Emmy rested her head on Kenny's back as she waited for him to open the door.

"Are you gonna carry me inside?"

Kenny struggled for a moment before getting the door unlocked and opened. He turned and picked her up. "I will since we're an old married couple now."

"I love you, Kenny," Emmy said as she lay her head on his chest. "I've said that a lot today, but I really mean it." She yawned and closed her eyes. "I am so wiped out."

"It's been a long week and several hard days nights."

"Are you going to sing old songs to me now?"

"Not unless you have a special request," he said as he smiled.

"Maybe later," she answered while yawning.

He wondered how long she could stay awake. He carried her into the bedroom and set her down gently on the bed. "I'll help you get undressed as soon as I get out of this tux."

"Don't take too long," she said as she stretched her arms and snuggled into the pillows.

He shook his head as Emmy closed her eyes and didn't move. He quickly shed his tux and everything except his boxers.

"Em, if you sit up, I'll help you out of this dress."

Moments later he hung her dress on a hanger in the closet.

"That's a nice dress, Em. Too bad you only get to wear it once," Kenny said as he walked up to the bed and smiled at her. "Do you want to wear your negligee? It's right here."

She sat on the edge of the bed and shook her head. "I don't need it."

He scratched his ear as his eyes moved from her knees upward along her body. He paused and licked his lips as he stared at her breasts.

She giggled as she noticed some movement in his white boxers with red hearts. "I'm getting in bed now."

He watched as she stood up, threw back the sheet and blanket and lay down. He turned off the light and joined her under the covers. He scooted close to her and put an arm over her as she lay on her side. "Emmy, are you still awake enough? Should we wait until the morning?"

"No, I don't want to wait," she said softly as she moved

195

onto her back and tried to pull him on top. She yawned again. "Why are you still wearing your boxers?" she asked as she reached down and slipped a hand under them.

"I wasn't sure if I should remove them yet. Should I?"

"It might make it easier," she said as she smiled but then yawned again. "I'm sorry for yawning so much."

"It's all right," he said as he yawned. "It's contagious, Em."

He leaned closer, kissed her and raised up. "Are you nervous? You are kinda trembling. You're not too cold are you? I could turn up the heat."

"It is a little chilly in here, but that might be because of what I'm wearing," she whispered as she grabbed his hand and placed it on her hip.

"You aren't wearing... Oh, I get it," he said as he touched her stomach and then higher. "I'll turn up the heat. Would you like a bottle of water or anything while I'm up? Are you hungry? We didn't have much to eat, and it was hours ago," he asked as he slipped out from under the covers.

"Maybe some water, please," she answered.

"Right. Be right back," he said. "Don't go away."

"I'll be right here, silly," she said as she pulled the sheet up over her chest, giggled and yawned again.

He backed up and bumped against the doorframe. "I won't be long."

He adjusted the thermostat and heard the furnace kick on as he opened the fridge. He grabbed a bottle of water, opened it, took a sip and spotted a piece of fried chicken left over from earlier in the week. "I love cold chicken. Especially the crispy kind." He picked it up and felt the texture of the chicken breast. "Should I bring this with me?" He hesitated as he saw some leftover homemade potato salad. "We could have a snack before we... Uh... go to sleep." He looked back and forth between the chicken and the potato salad. "Maybe for breakfast." He put the chicken back and headed to the bedroom.

"Ow!" he hollered as he banged his knee against the desk. He hopped on one leg as he rubbed his knee. "I should remember to turn on a light."

He waited until his knee felt better and then slipped quietly into the bedroom. "I've got some water, m'lady," he whispered as he moved under the covers. "Em," he said softly when she didn't respond. The skylight allowed enough moonlight into the room for him to see Emmy. He listened to her breathing and stared at her for a moment before he smiled. "We can wait a little longer," he said as he placed the water on the nightstand.

Two hours later Kenny heard a soft voice and felt a warm body snuggling close to him.

"Are you awake, Em? Can't you sleep?"

"I'm awake now. Are you awake?" she asked.

"I am now," he answered. "Are you thirsty? I have some water for you."

She turned on her side and raised up. He could feel her soft, luxurious hair on his chest as she rubbed his chest and pressed into him.

"I'm not thirsty at the moment," she said as she leaned closer and ran her fingers through his hair. She giggled as she felt his ears.

"I'm not thirsty either," he said. He touched her bare back and then explored some more.

His heart raced as he felt her soft lips on his. They kissed for an eternity which lasted only a moment before she moved onto her back and urged him on top of her.

"Should I take off my boxers now, Em?"

"Yes, m'lord. Please do."

He smiled and whispered, "I'm a dork, huh?"

"Yes, but you're mine." Her eyes sparkled as she helped him tug his boxers down.

They held each other afterward. She fell asleep in his arms. He moved her hair away from her eyes and kissed her tenderly. She fell asleep too soon for him to make love to her again. In the early morning though, it was a different story.

Chapter Seventeen

Kenny leaned on his elbow and watched Emmy sleeping peacefully on the bed in the carriage house. She finally began to stir and opened her eyes. She saw Kenny and smiled as she stretched.

"Good morning, Mrs. Colwell. Did you sleep well?"

"Mmmmm, I slept very well. What time is it?"

He looked at the clock on the nightstand on Emmy's side of the bed.

"It's eight o'clock."

"What time do we have to meet Kristen and John?"

"We're meeting for lunch at noon."

"I guess we have some time to kill, huh? Is there anything you want to do?" Emmy asked as she smiled shyly and bit her bottom lip.

Three hours later they got out of bed. Emmy put on the negligee Kenny had given her for Christmas. She didn't have a chance to wear it last night.

"I finally get to wear this. Do you like it?"

He pretended to study the negligee as he looked at it from all sides.

"I like what I see. It really is your color."

"Stop it."

Emmy grinned as she spun around dancing to the beat of the song she sang to Kenny at the reception. Kenny sat on the edge of the bed as he watched and listened to his new bride. He stood up, grabbed her and held her in his arms as they kissed again and again.

"We have to get dressed. We can't meet Kristen and John looking like this."

"You can go first, Emmy. It won't take me long to get ready. Now I really appreciate everything Paula did for us. I didn't see the reason to pack a suitcase just for one night but now I understand. Everything is already packed for our honeymoon."

Emmy looked at Kenny and he asked, "What? Why are you looking at me like that?"

"I was just remembering how quiet you were and now..."

"If you want me to stop talking, just kiss me."

Emmy kissed him quickly. Then she needed to get ready.

John and Kristen were waiting as Kenny and Emmy entered La Cantina. Kristen spotted Emmy and waved. Kenny and Emmy held hands as they walked over to the table.

"Good morning, guys."

"Good afternoon, Mrs. Colwell. You look adorable in that dress, Emmy."

"Thank you, Krissy. We picked it out together remember."

"I remember. Sit next to me. I want to hear everything."

Kristen pulled Emmy onto the bench next to her, and they quietly whispered to each other. Emmy looked over at the guys sitting across from them. She smiled at Kenny and then at John. She turned back to Kristen, and they continued to whisper to each other.

"Are you telling Kristen everything about last night, Em?"

"Everything I can remember about last night and this morning," Emmy said with a grin.

"At least you didn't take out your journal to make notes," Kenny said.

Eventually they needed to get going. They had a five o'clock flight to catch at O'Hare. John and Kristen drove them to the airport. Emmy and Kristen hugged one last time.

"Remember to go outside once in a while, Em," Kristen said.

"Why? It rains all the time."

"Is that why you picked Ireland?"

"Only partially," Emmy said and then giggled.

Kenny and Emmy had discussed many different places to go for their honeymoon, but settled on Ireland and England. They flew into Dublin, then on to County Kerry. They stayed for a week in Killarney at a bed and breakfast called Ashville House. They had beautiful views of the mountains and took long walks together. That is when they got out of bed. From there they flew into Heathrow and took the train to Thorpe. Kenny had leased Sheila Cottage for two weeks. Kenny had met some great people on his previous visits to Thorpe, and he loved the area. They went sightseeing with Kenny's friends the Kennedys. They even went into London to see Derek Clayton at The Royal Albert Hall.

After the honeymoon, Kenny moved into the house with Emmy. They adjusted to married life very quickly. One thing Kenny learned was that Emmy still moved all over the bed in her sleep. He often woke up to find Emmy in different positions. Many times she slept with her head on his chest or her legs on top of his. Kristen moved out and stayed with her parents even though Emmy wanted Kristen to stay.

Emmy learned to cook Kenny's favorite foods, and he learned how to do housework and her laundry without ruining her unmentionables. Emmy went back to work and told Mr. Oliver about her plans to leave when he retired in June. She made an appointment to see Mr. Robertson. She wanted to tell him in person about her decision. She was a little nervous as she entered his office.

"Good morning, Emmy. You look very pretty today."

"Thank you, Mrs. Moneywell."

"Did you and Kenny enjoy your trip to Ireland?"

Emmy blushed a bit, grinned and said, "We had a great time."

"He's ready for you, so you can go on in."

"Emmy, how are you? How is Kenny?"

"We're doing great." Emmy looked up at Mr. Robertson and bit her lip. "I have to tell you something."

"Have a seat next to me on the couch and tell me." He already had a good idea what she was going to say.

She sat next to him and paused. She took a deep breath and began, "I want you to know how much I appreciate everything you've done for me, and Diane, too, but... I'm going to leave when Mr. Oliver retires. I feel as though I'm being ungrateful because I have this perfect job and two great bosses. Kenny and I both prayed a lot about this, so it's not just a decision we made lightly or without a lot of thought. He is going to be on tour a lot the next couple years, and I want to be with him." She paused again and then asked, "Are you mad at me?"

Mr. Robertson put his arm tenderly around her shoulder and hugged her. "I'm not upset you're leaving. Quite the contrary, I'm very happy for you. Actually, I didn't think you would return after your wedding. I will miss you, and it will be difficult to find someone as capable to replace you, but you are making the right choice. You need to be able to spend time with your husband, and he needs to have you with him. May I ask if Kenny's band has a healthcare plan for their employees?"

"Yes, they have healthcare for all the full-time employees and some of the seasonal personnel also have coverage."

"You may not think it's important now because you are young, but it will become more important as you get older."

"If you are talking about babies, I might not be able to have any. At least that's what my doctor thought."

"Doctors aren't always right, Emmy. God may have a say in the matter," he said and then chuckled. "Just so you know, if you ever decide you want to stop traveling, or working for the band, you will always be welcome here. We are also beginning to allow some employees to work from home. I will always be able to use someone as capable and intelligent as you, even if it's just on a part-time basis."

"Thank you, Mr. Robertson. I'm gonna be with Kenny all summer. Then I'm going to be a full-time student at North Park. It will take me three semesters to get my degree."

"I know that means a lot to you, Emmy."

"It's been my dream to get a college degree."

They stood up, and Emmy gave him a big hug.

"You should tell Mrs. Moneywell about your decision as you leave. I'll walk you out. I'm afraid she will start crying when you tell her."

Mr. Robertson and Emmy walked out to see Mrs. Moneywell. She did start to cry as Emmy shared her decision.

"I will miss our little visits, and you had better come and see me once in a while."

"I will, Mrs. Moneywell."

One day as Kenny was cleaning up their bedroom, he found a box of old photos. Emmy came into the bedroom as he was looking at them. She sat on the bed beside him, and they looked at the photos together.

He found many pictures of Emmy and him together and held one up. "Do you remember anything about this one, Em?"

Emmy looked at the photo. "I was ten, I think, so you were thirteen. This was taken in your backyard. Probably by your mom. Most of these were taken by your mom. I don't remember my mother ever taking many pictures of us when we were kids. Grandma Isabel took pictures though."

"You were very pretty even then."

"That's sweet of you to say, but I was a total tomboy and my hair was always a mess."

Kenny kissed her and told her, "I'm still think you look like a tomboy most of the time."

Kenny kept looking through the photos and found one of Emmy with Barry Newton.

"Is this Barry?"

"Yeah, he was really skinny back then."

He looked at the photos Brady Robertson had taken of her and Diane. She blushed and thought he was going to be upset with her, but he smiled at her and told her. "You look so innocent in all of these pictures, but yet so sexy, too. Look at this one. Where was it taken?"

"Brady took it at the park down the street. I was thinking about you when he took it."

"I want to get a larger copy of that picture and keep it on my nightstand."

Kenny kissed her and pulled her onto the bed.

"I want to make love to you right now."

"It's noon. Aren't you hungry?"

"I'm ravenous, and you are what I need."

Chapter Eighteen

The grass turned green, and the flowers popped up as spring arrived. The days grew warmer, and Emmy enjoyed being outdoors in the sun. She and Kenny ran almost every morning before she left for work. They also took walks around the neighborhood in the evenings. They occasionally ran into Fernando and Ethan who hadn't gone anywhere—Ethan still lived right across the street, and Fernando's place was down at the other end. The guys still teased Emmy and accused Kenny of robbing the cradle. Emmy invited them over to dinner one night, and Kenny got to know them better. He met them the day of the wedding, but didn't have much of a chance to talk to them.

As they were sitting at the dining room table, Fernando asked Emmy, "Tell me again how you managed to get a marriage license at the age of thirteen."

Emmy smiled and explained, "I just smiled sweetly at the clerk and told him I was really sixteen and needed to get married in a hurry."

Ethan added, "I was talking to Mr. Robertson and Mr. Oliver at the reception, and I heard them say something about a promotion and a raise. Did you get moved to a new team?"

"Not a new team, but I have a new title. I am now Mrs.-executive-administrative-aide Colwell, and I got a hundred dollar a month raise."

"Congratulations, Emmy, I'm sure you deserve it," Fernando said without teasing her.

"Thanks, but I feel guilty since I've hardly been there the last couple months. Plus, I'm leaving the company in June when Mr. Oliver retires. I need to be able to travel with Kenny."

Emmy thought about asking Annie O'Dell and Matt Sullivan over sometime soon. She kept thinking about it and decided she wanted to have a lot of people over.

"Kenny, since the weather is getting nicer, I would like to have a big cookout and invite all our friends over before we leave on tour."

203

"When? It's still a roll of the dice with the weather at this time of year."

"Later, when it's warmer. Maybe early June."

Emmy talked Kenny into throwing a big outdoor party at their house and inviting everybody they had ever known, at least it felt that way to him.

Kenny checked the list of people Emmy wanted to invite. "You can't invite the whole world, you know. Do you think you could cut it down a little? We don't have room for this many people."

"I'll try. I guess we could have another party someday and invite different people."

Kenny chuckled as she spotted a familiar name. "Emmy, I don't think you need to invite Mrs. Hogan from church."

"Why not? She's always been so nice to everybody."

"Emmy, she passed away last March, remember?"

"Oh, that's right, I forgot. I really do need to pay more attention to the older people at church. I'm sorry."

Kenny convinced her to trim down the guest list to a more manageable number, and she tried. They decided on the last Saturday in May because they would be on the road after that. She invited all of her and Kenny's close friends and family. They asked some of their friends from church and ended up inviting over seventy people.

Emmy again had trouble with Kenny's old Civic, so they made a trip to see the same salesman at the dealership where Tony bought his GMC Envoy. They got the same great deal Tony did and Emmy drove away with a brand new 2003 gray GMC Envoy.

"Are you sad to see your old car go?" Emmy asked as they waited at a red light.

"No, it was time. It didn't make any sense to keep pouring money into it."

"We could get by without a second car," Emmy said. "My parents never had two cars until Diane bought one."

"I thought about that, but we can afford a new car. Now I won't have to worry about you being stranded on the side of the

204

road in a broken-down car."

"Thank you, Kenny. I love you."

"I love you more, Mrs. Colwell."

Emmy looked over her shoulder. "There's lots of room in the back seat. Should we break it in?" she asked as she grinned.

"Are you forgetting that we have to be at the church so we can get up to Elgin?"

"I wasn't forgetting. What time do we need to be at the church?"

"Chase wants to leave around noon. You should be there before that."

"I suppose. I really like how much higher this is than the Civic. I feel like I can see everything so much better."

"Just be careful, Em. This has more horsepower than the Civic. You don't realize how fast you're going."

Kenny leaned toward Emmy and checked the speedometer. "This is a forty-five mile-an-hour zone, and you're clipping along at fifty-five. Slow down or else you'll get a ticket, and I'll have to take your new car away."

"You're right. I didn't realize I was going that fast."

Emmy slowed down just as they passed a SoHam patrol car.

"Ooops! Is he gonna stop me?"

Kenny looked out the rear window. "Looks like you're safe, Em. He's turning onto Springfield."

Emmy pressed on the accelerator and giggled.

"You're paying for all your traffic tickets," Kenny warned.

They pulled into their driveway without being stopped for speeding.

"So are you going up to Elgin with me, or riding with your parents?" Emmy asked later as she finished getting ready. "Chase said we're taking three vans, so there should be room for you."

"Dad said he knows how to get there, so I guess I can ride up there with you. Do you think Chase will mind?" Kenny asked as he lay on the bed watching Emmy.

"I don't think he will mind." She flipped her hair out of her face. "Besides, I'm a diva. I can throw a fit to get my way."

Kenny reacted and sat on the edge of the bed and pulled Emmy onto his lap. "You are the exact opposite of a diva."

"And you're the exact opposite of a rock star. You're a dork!" she squealed as he tried to kiss her. "We can't do that now. You have to wait until tonight."

"I want a kiss before I let you go."

One kiss led to one more and then another.

Kenny rode up to Elgin in a van with Emmy, and they arrived at Hemmens Auditorium in plenty of time. The three vans pulled up in the back of the auditorium, and everyone entered through the backstage doors.

"Chase, do you think we should let Kenny hang out with us backstage?" Emmy asked.

Chase laughed as he said, "I thought he was here to keep you in line."

"I've been behaving," Emmy said with a grin. "Haven't I been good, Kenny?"

Chase and Kenny laughed.

"Yes, dear, you've been very, very good," Kenny said and then kissed her cheek. "I promised Dixie and Alan I would talk to them about the new band they want to start. I'll be back in a few minutes." Kenny kissed Emmy again and walked over toward the guys.

"Hi, Kenny," Dixie said as he and Alan shook his hand.

Kenny led the guys to a corner of the backstage area where they could talk without having to shout. "So, Em told me you guys are starting a band."

Martin "Dixie" Case had played guitar and sang for a number of bands before landing the gig as the rhythm guitar player for the Crest Ridge Worship Band. Born in a small town in Alabama, Dixie's good looks and southern drawl captivated young women wherever he went.

Alan Vicini played drums for the band and also owned a music store in SoHam.

"Yeah, I've always wanted to have my own band," Dixie said.

Alan added, "It's really going to be Dixie's band. I don't

want to be more than just a drummer. I have my business to consider, but I want to help Dixie get his band up and running. He can always find a better drummer down the road."

Kenny talked to the guys for close to thirty minutes about life on the road and other things Dixie would face as a bandleader.

"Will you be home on Wednesday?" Dixie asked Kenny.

"We should be. Why do you ask?"

"We're doing a showcase at Larry's Uptown Grill that night. I almost hate to ask, but..."

"I'd love to hear you guys. I'll put it on our calendar."

"That would be great," Dixie said. "We're going on at nine, so you guys can still make it to church."

Kenny rejoined Emmy and hung around with her before the show. He signed a few autographs and posed for some photos before sitting with his parents during the concert. They left immediately afterward because he knew Emmy would be busy, and he didn't want to be a distraction.

After the show, Dixie found Emmy and said, "I told Kenny about the gig at Larry's."

"Did he agree to listen to you guys?" Emmy asked.

"He did."

"I knew he would. He likes to check out new bands. I can't wait to hear you guys."

On Wednesday night, Kenny and Emmy drove to Larry's Uptown Grill after church to hear Dixie and Alan's new band.

"Dixie brought a couple of guys he knows up from Alabama after we got back from our tour. Wells Callaghan and Stuart Dengel. One of them plays lead and the other switches back and forth between guitar and keys. I can't remember who does what though. Dixie told me they have been practicing for six hours a day since then," Emmy informed Kenny as they pulled into the parking lot.

Kenny nodded. "They should be pretty tight. I know Larry wouldn't let them have a showcase if he didn't think they were talented and ready."

Mr. Kesson, the owner of the Steward Music Group, met

207

them there with his wife, but he didn't want Dixie or the band to be aware of his presence. He wanted to hear the band without the pressure of them knowing they were auditioning for his label.

"Hello, guys, it's good to see you. How was your trip to Ireland?" Mr. Kesson asked. "Did you have a chance to see the country?" He grinned at Emmy.

"Not really," Kenny answered. "Emmy kept me pretty busy."

"You are going to get it, Kenny." Emmy blushed.

"Have they come up with a name for the band yet?" Mr. Kesson asked.

"Not as far as I know," Kenny answered.

"I suggested they use 'The Dixie Case Band,'" Emmy said. "I didn't say it was original, but it fits."

"We tried to convince Dixie to use that but he won't," Kenny said.

"How about 'Dixie Case and The Plaintiffs' then?" Emmy offered.

"That's kinda catchy, Emmy. I like it," Mr. Kesson said. "I'll talk to you guys later. We're going to find a table in the back."

Mr. Kesson would have the final say about signing the band since it was his company and his money.

Emmy sat with Kenny near the front for the first set. The addition of Dixie's friends from Alabama made quite a favorable impression on Kenny—especially the lead guitar player.

"What did you think?" Emmy asked between sets.

"I think they have some talent. Dixie is good and Alan is a good fit. Steve Van Zant was not, though. He's all right as a player, but he is not creative enough to go in the studio. I'm glad Dixie and Jimmy Cronin are getting along so well. I thought Jimmy would be a good fit for Dixie."

"Steve doesn't want to quit his job. He told Chase he might do a tour in the fall but that would be it for him. I don't blame him at all. He has a family to support."

"Don't get me wrong. I love Steve. He's a great guy. I can understand his decision, though. He's still going to play at church."

Emmy excused herself to use the restroom. Dixie saw her

leave the table and knew where she was going. He waited in the narrow, dark-wood-paneled hallway.

"Hi, Dixie. Are you waiting for me?"

"Yes. Did Kenny say anything about us?"

"He really likes your new lead guitar player."

"All right!" Dixie pumped his fist. "Did he say anything else?"

"I'll tell you, but you can't tell anyone, okay?"

"Okay Emmy. I won't. What did he say?"

"He told me that... I have pretty eyes!"

Dixie shook his head as Emmy giggled and ran away. Then he laughed because she was so good at teasing him.

Kenny and Emmy stayed for all three sets. It was nearly one o'clock before they left. Kenny had a chance to talk to Dixie backstage as Emmy held onto his arm.

"I like the changes you have made. Nothing against Steve Van Zant, but the other guys are a better fit."

"Yeah. I agree. I like Steve, but he doesn't have the same goals. Do you want to meet my friends?"

"I do, but maybe another time. I need to get Emmy home before she falls asleep. She has to work in the morning. She only has seven more days at Robertson Industries. Mr. Robertson has been so good to her. He has allowed her to work part-time and even gave her extra vacation time to go on tour."

"All right. Thanks for coming out to see us." Dixie turned to face Emmy. "Thanks for bringing Kenny."

"It was my pleasure. We both had a good time."

"You're leaving soon, right?" Dixie asked.

"Yes, a week from this Sunday. I get to be on the road with Kenny and the guys for the whole summer. I'm looking forward to it."

Emmy waved goodbye as she and Kenny left. In the car she asked, "Are they really good?"

"Yes, Emmy, they really are. Mr. Kesson thinks so, too."

"I thought they were, but I wanted your opinion."

They arrived home and Emmy asked, "Do you want some ice cream or something? I'm still too keyed up to go to bed."

"I guess that means the honeymoon's over, huh?"

"I didn't mean it like that. I meant I wasn't ready to go to sleep. We can still make love."

"Okay. I'm sure we have some ice cream in the fridge."

Emmy dished out some ice cream and warmed up some hot fudge. "We don't have any whipping cream. Sorry."

"That's all right. I like it better without."

They sat close together on the couch and talked quietly.

"Mr. Kesson talked to me about Dixie's band. He wants to sign them, and he wants me to produce the CD."

"That would be so cool, Kenny." Emmy wiped some hot fudge from Kenny's chin.

"I listened to the teen worship band, Em. Those guys have a lot of talent. I could see them making a career of music."

"They are really good, and they're good kids. I shouldn't call them kids because other than Bobby, none of them are teenagers anymore."

"I know this might sound strange, but just hear me out."

"Okay. I'm listening." Emmy ate another spoonful of ice cream.

"Since most of the other guys in your worship band have jobs, or families and commitments with the church, you should think about using the teen band as your touring band. They are all single."

"I should hope so!"

Emmy cuddled close to Kenny as she ate her ice cream and hot fudge. He had finished his.

"They are very talented. I know you like having Dixie along to keep you company, but he wants his own band. Chase doesn't like to leave his family any more than the other guys do. It's just something to think about. Steve and Hank are not really interested in traveling much."

"I never thought about using the younger guys. Are they really that good?" She pictured Adam Vicini, Boyd Goldman, Perry Johnstone, Ryan Lederer, Skip Mason and Bobby O'Connor on stage together.

"Given enough time to play together, they will be better

than the older guys. Adam may not be as experienced on keys as Chase, and his voice isn't as strong as Chase's, but he is talented. He will get better as he gains experience. Boyd and Perry are already good on guitar and they will even get better. Ryan is rock solid on bass. I'm not sure who would be a better fit on drums."

"Bobby and Skip have both taken lessons from the same guy. I don't think there's much of a difference in their styles."

"Skip has a stronger left hand and his timing is better, but Bobby is a lot easier to get along with. That makes a difference, you know."

"I'll think about it, Kenny. You're probably right. Is it difficult to keep your ego in check knowing that you are always right about everything?"

"It's a burden I have to bear, Em!"

She poked him in his ribs as they both laughed.

"Mr. Kesson wants you to travel a little more and this might be just the way to accomplish that. He is looking at you as a long term investment. He knows you place God and our marriage ahead of any career as a singer, but he still thinks you could travel a bit and maybe release a CD every couple of years."

"I suppose I can see myself doing that."

"We should get to bed. It's getting late, and you have to get up in the morning."

"I still have some time before I need to fall asleep," she whispered. He kissed her and carried her upstairs to their bedroom.

Chapter Nineteen

"Kenny! Wake up! Your parents will be here any moment." Emmy jumped out of bed and threw on some shorts and a t-shirt.

Kenny opened his eyes and groggily looked at the clock. "Wow! It's almost nine. I never usually sleep this late."

"It's because we were up so late."

"We went to bed at ten," Kenny reminded her.

"True, but..." Emmy grinned. "I'm going to check the forecast. I hope we have a sunny day."

When Kenny made it downstairs ten minutes later, Emmy was sitting at her computer.

"We might get lucky. The forecast is for sunny skies, temps in the upper eighties and no chance of precipitation."

Kenny walked up behind her and kissed the top of her head. "That's great, Em. Looks like the last Saturday of the month was a wise choice. Have you been praying for good weather?"

She spun around in her chair. "Of course. Why wouldn't I? Is that being selfish?"

"I guess not."

Mr. and Mrs. Colwell had planned on being there around nine, but were running late. They arrived at ten-thirty.

"I'm sorry we're late, dear. Carter's brother called. They had to take care of some family business."

"It's all right. I doubt if any of the guests will be here before noon."

"What can I do to help?"

Emmy and Mrs. Colwell worked on the potato salad while Kenny and his father ran to the store. Kristen arrived and pitched in wherever Emmy asked.

Emmy heard a knock on the back door, heard the door open, and then heard footsteps.

"Hey, Emmy, are you dressed, or are you running around naked?" Tony hollered.

Mama smacked his arm as she followed him. "Stop that. I'm sure she doesn't run around the house naked."

"I'm not so sure about that," Tony said as he grinned.

"I'm in the kitchen with Kenny's mother," Emmy answered as she held a large spoon in her hand. "Thanks for trying to embarrass me." She shook the spoon at Tony and then tried to swat him. "I don't always run around like that, you know."

Tony dodged and then grabbed the spoon out of her hand. "Kristen told me you did. She wouldn't lie."

Emmy glared at Kristen.

Kristen frowned at Tony. "I might have mentioned it, but he was supposed to keep his big mouth shut."

Tony and Mama Bertucci arrived early because Mama wanted to help in the kitchen. Sloane Beckett and Lindsey Cameron arrived together, but it soon became apparent Sloane was there to see Tony.

Kristen checked her phone. "Em, I need to pick up John."

"What time does his flight arrive?"

"Eleven-thirty, so I need to run. We'll be back as soon as we can. I'm sorry I can't stay and help with the cooking."

"That's okay," Emmy and Mama said simultaneously.

"I'm getting better in the kitchen." Kristen made a face to express her displeasure.

"Yes, you are, dear. Now go pick up John and hurry back," Mama said. Then she inspected the potatoes Kristen had been peeling. "Emmy, I do hope and pray that whoever Kristen marries makes enough money for them to hire a cook. She missed a bunch of spots on the potatoes."

Jeff and his wife, Frances, arrived right at noon since they only lived a few blocks away. Frances was expecting their first child in a month after having a miscarriage once before.

"Thank you, guys, for coming over early," Emmy said. "Frances, I don't want you to do anything too strenuous, okay?"

"I'll be careful, Emmy, but I'm still able to do some work."

"Don't you be lifting anything. You might have the baby right here."

Kenny and his father returned from the store with enough plastic plates, cups and utensils for an army.

A moment later, Andy Walker arrived with a box full of fresh steaks, hamburger patties and chicken breasts. "I am claiming the grills as my domain."

"Do you want any help?" Jeff asked.

"Sure. You can assist me, but you can't lift anything heavy," Andy teased as he put an arm around Jeff's shoulder. "Oh, I forgot. Frances can't lift anything. You can do all the heavy lifting."

Emmy's parents arrived. She helped her father up the steps. His hip had been bothering him, so he was using a cane.

"Daddy, why don't you sit on the couch?" Emmy held his arm as they walked into the living room.

Mr. Colwell sat in the recliner and they talked about the neighborhood while they waited.

Mom Colasanti walked into the kitchen and asked, "Do you need my help?"

"We've got it under control, Mom," Emmy said.

"In that case, I will have a seat at the table. This kitchen isn't big enough four four women." She had become better friends with Mrs. Colwell and Mama Bertucci since the wedding.

They worked at getting all the food ready—everything that didn't have to be cooked on the grill, that is. The guys were in charge of the grills. Kenny had rented tables and chairs to handle the large group of people who were expected. He and Tony used John's old pick-up truck to bring the tables and chairs to the house.

After getting everything ready for the cookout, Emmy wanted to shower and change into clean clothes. Ten minutes later, she headed back downstairs, and Mama put her to work again.

"More guests will start arriving anytime now. Emmy, I want you to clear off the dining room table."

"Mama, we're going to eat outside."

Mama turned Emmy around and pointed her in the direction of the dining room. "I know, Emmy, but some of the guests might come in the house, and I want it to look its best."

"All right. I know if I don't take care of it that you will." Emmy quickly cleared off the table.

Kristen and John walked in the back door, "We're back."

"That was quick," Emmy said while sampling the potato salad.

Mama swatted Emmy's hand. "It's good to see you, John.

214

Kenny and Tony are outside in the back setting up tables if you want to help."

John gave Mama a kiss on the cheek and a hug. "It's good to see you, too, Mrs. Bertucci."

"John Randolph! You know better than to be so formal."

"Sorry, Mama. I was just trying to be polite."

John and Kristen met when Tony was hurt in a car accident back at Notre Dame fourteen months ago.

Emmy took John's arm and said, "You better propose to her soon if you know what's good for you. You guys are perfect for each other."

Kenny came back inside. "Hey, John, I didn't know you were here."

"We just got here. Need any help outside?"

"Nope, got it all set. I'm gonna run upstairs and shower and change. I need a kiss and a hug, Em."

"Yuck, you're all sweaty, and I just showered. Go upstairs and clean up. Then you can kiss me."

Kenny chased Emmy around the house trying to kiss her and hold her against his sweaty body. She squealed childishly as he captured her.

"Just one kiss, and don't touch me except with your lips."

Kenny kissed her tenderly, but then licked her face.

"Yuck, go away and don't come back until you are clean and don't smell so sweaty."

Kenny showered and changed into shorts and a t-shirt and came back downstairs. "Emmy, where are you? I want my kiss and hug now."

His mother told him, "They are out in the backyard getting everything ready. Go help them and don't be messing around. You have guests coming."

"Yes, Mom." Kenny kissed his mother on the cheek.

"Go! Help your little one with the tables and such."

Kenny came out to help them and gave his wife a big kiss and a hug as he picked her up. He whispered in her ear, "You look very nice today. I think I will have to take you behind the garage and kiss you some more."

215

"Normally, that would be all right, but we have guests coming, and they might wonder where we are and come looking for us. You wouldn't want them to catch us kissing. Would you?" She put a finger to her mouth. "Hold that thought for later tonight."

"No, of course not. Now give me another kiss, and I'll put you down."

She asked, "Do I really look all right in this or should I put something else on?"

"You look perfect just the way you are."

"Did you turn into Billy Joel or something? Go on with you," Emmy teased in her best imitation of an Irish accent.

The guests started arriving a few at a time. Jeremy, his wife Amanda, and their son Joshua arrived followed a few minutes later by Dave and his wife Macy. Soon the long driveway and the street were filled with cars. Many of the guests wanted to see the house so they came inside. Mama looked at Emmy with a smile as if to say, "I told you so."

"You were right, Mama," Emmy said.

Emmy spotted Annie O'Dell and Matt Sullivan as they arrived. "Hey, guys! I'm glad you could make it. Is your ankle all right?" She hadn't seen Annie or Matt since the wedding.

"It's as good as new, Emmy. Thanks for asking." He hopped up and down to show her. "Do you need help with anything?"

"No, everything is about ready. You look lovely, Annie."

"So do you, Emmy. Married life must be agreeing with you," Annie said. "Matty, would you see if you can find Kenny and the guys? I need to talk to Emmy for a moment."

Matt understood why. He kissed Annie before he headed out to the backyard.

Annie turned to Emmy, and they smiled at each other. Emmy whispered softly, "The sex is great. We waited for so long, but we're making up for it now."

Emmy and Annie spent several minutes catching up on important news.

After all the guests arrived and all the food was ready, Mrs. Colwell and Mama chased everyone out of the house and into the backyard. Kenny offered thanks and told them to dig in. There

216

were so many guests that Andy and Jeff spent all their time at the grills. Andy thoroughly enjoyed being the grillmaster. Tony and John helped out and eventually they had a chance to eat, also. Emmy and Kenny decided to stick with bottled water and pop for the cookout even though some of the guests might have preferred beer or wine.

Barry and Linda Newton were running late as usual. Linda held her son as they walked up the long driveway. She sniffed his bottom and wrinkled her face. "Barry, Fen needs a fresh one. Did you remember to bring the diaper bag?"

"Yes, Linda I brought the diaper bag and most everything else that was in the apartment, too." Barry struggled to carry it all. "Shoot! I dropped something."

Emmy and Kristen saw Barry and Linda and ran to greet them.

"Did you drop this, Barry?" Emmy asked and then giggled.

Barry snatched the box of Pampers from Emmy and dropped a bag of dirty diapers.

Emmy picked it up and held it away from her. "And you brought these because?"

"We had to change him on the way here," Barry answered.

"How is little Fig doing, Barry?" Kristen asked as she and Emmy made faces and funny noises at him until he smiled.

"You guys are never going to quit calling him that are you?" Barry asked.

"Nope. Maybe you should change his name," Emmy suggested.

"Oh, yeah. What should we change his name to? I suppose you have some suggestions."

"How about Van? As in van-illa wafer or maybe Chip, you know Chocolate Chip. If you have a girl are you gonna name her Lorna Doone?"

"Are you girls finished?" Barry sighed.

"Barry, you know we love ya, and we love Fen, too."

Thirty minutes later, after he had filled a plate for Linda, made sure Fen was dry and happy, Barry sat down to eat. He put his hamburger up to his mouth. *This is gonna taste so good. I haven't had a decent hamburger in years it seems.* After he finished his second burger, Barry asked, "Emmy, we need some music. Got any CDs by The Notable Exceptions handy?"

Emmy brought out an old boombox to play some music. Emmy put on her CD of the band and she and Kristen sang along. Soon she and Kristen were dancing, then Annie, Sloane, and Lindsey joined them. Tony and the guys were sitting around talking about sports and not paying much attention to the girls.

The backyard was big enough so some of the guys wanted to play football. Kenny grabbed a football from the garage and the guys started tossing it around. Emmy decided she wanted to play.

"Tony, can I play? I want to show you how fast I can run."

"Okay you can play but if I catch you..."

"Don't worry you won't," Emmy said as she tried to take the football away.

Tony tried to tackle Emmy and she ran away. Tony and John boxed her in, and Tony finally caught her and tackled her to the ground. He sat on top of her and wouldn't let her up as he tickled her behind her knees.

"Stop it! You're gonna make me wet my pants. Let me up!"

"I told you I could catch you."

"You only caught me because I let you. Just because you can do a forty-four-second-forty in a straight line doesn't mean you can catch someone with the moves I have," Emmy teased.

"Okay, Barry Sanders. And that's a four-point-four second forty not forty-four seconds."

Emmy finally made him stop, and he let her up.

"You can try to tackle me if you think you can," Tony said.

Emmy got Kristen and Annie to help her try to tackle Tony. Sloane watched as the girls ganged up on Tony. He saw her watching and smiled. Tony walked along as the girls jumped on him and tried to stop him. He finally stopped and let them tackle him. Emmy started to tickle him but it didn't bother him.

"You know I'm not ticklish, Emmy," Tony said.

"You could at least pretend so I could have some fun."

"Is Kenny ticklish?"

"Hmmm, wouldn't you like to know?" Emmy giggled.

218

Not really. Tony thought. *But I'm sure he likes to tickle you.*

"There's more burgers and chicken breasts left," Kenny hollered. "I know you can eat more. Tony, John, another burger?"

"I'll take one," Tony answered. "I haven't eaten for a couple of hours."

"I knew you'd be hungry again. You only had four of them earlier," Emmy teased.

"You're going to get it, brat," Tony said.

Emmy's parents offered to stay and help with the cleanup, but Emmy wouldn't allow it. "You should take Daddy home. He looks tired, and we can clean up all right. There are enough friends here to help."

"Okay, your father is tired. It was a very nice party, Emmy. You did a good job!"

"Thanks, Mom!" Emmy beamed with pride.

By nine most of the guests, including the guys in the band and their wives, were gone—Andy was still around.

"I'm going to clean this grill and then head home."

"Thanks, Andy. You did a great job with the meat."

"It was my pleasure, cuz," he said as he grinned at Emmy.

"Emmy, will you help me out back?" Kenny hollered.

"Sure, Kenny. What do you want me to do?" She left Andy's side and ran to the backyard.

Kenny pointed. "We need to clean up the mess."

"Oh, I thought you were thinking of something else."

Tony and John heard Emmy.

"Geez, Emmy, can't you wait until we're gone?" Tony teased.

John laughed and said, "I'll pull my truck into the driveway so we can start loading up these tables and chairs."

Annie O'Dell and Matt Sullivan pitched in to help without even being asked. Annie helped Emmy while Matt helped Kenny. Mama and Mrs. Colwell cleaned up inside. Emmy wanted to enjoy the warm night air so she stayed outside to work.

"Can I have one kiss?" Emmy pleaded.

"Fine. One kiss, but then we have to take this garbage to the garage and get the recycling bins."

She kissed Kenny and unbuttoned her top as he watched with a smile. She teased him by showing him the camisole she was wearing.

"Stop that, Em. You have to wait until everyone's gone."

"I know, but I like teasing you."

"You better behave until everyone is gone," Kenny warned her with a grin as he tried to button her top without success.

"I'll fix it in a minute."

They continued to clean up the backyard. Matt Sullivan helped Tony and John load the tables and chairs onto John's old pickup truck so he could take them back to Grand Rental Station in the morning. Andy scrubbed the grill until it looked brand new.

"Em, do you know your top is unbuttoned?" Kristen pointed out.

Emmy looked down at her top. "I was starting to sweat, so I unbuttoned it partway."

Tony grinned at her. "You mean you and Kenny were starting to fool around. You better not let Mama see you like that. She'll get after you."

"It doesn't matter because you're like my brother now, and, besides, I'm covered up."

Just then Mama walked out the back door and heard her name. "Who will be in trouble?"

"Nobody, Mama."

Mama looked at Emmy. "Emmy, fix your top this instant! There are men here."

"Mama!" Emmy exclaimed.

"Just because you are married does not mean you don't have to listen to me." Mama pointed a finger, but then she laughed.

Emmy bit her lip. "I'm sorry. I was hot and didn't want to get too sweaty."

Kristen was standing beside Annie and told Emmy, "Honey, we girls don't sweat, we just glisten."

Annie high-fived Kristen as they laughed.

Mr. and Mrs. Colwell walked outside. "What's going on? Who was Maria yelling at?" Mrs. Colwell asked.

Kenny pointed at his wife.

Emmy smacked Kenny on the arm and told her in-laws, "I unbuttoned my top partway because I was too hot."

Mrs. Colwell got after Kenny, "Stop embarrassing your wife like that."

"She started it."

Andy said, "I'm finished with the grill and was going to head home, but I think I had better stick around." He put his hands on Emmy's shoulders and spun her around. "You better do what Mama said."

Emmy looked up at him as she fixed her top. "Nobody could see anything. What's the big deal?"

"It's not, so just drop it," Andy said.

Emmy bit her lip because Andy was disappointed with her.

"Don't worry. I still love you, cuz," Andy said as he hugged her.

John came back after moving his truck out of the driveway and stood next to Kristen.

Kristen told Emmy, "John is spending the night with me."

"Kristen Lynn Keasling! What did you say?" Mama asked.

"Mama, I didn't mean he's staying in my room. He's just spending the night at the house."

Mama threw her hands up in exasperation. "I'm getting too old to deal with you kids. John, will you hurry up and marry her so I can quit worrying."

Emmy kissed them both good night and whispered to John, "Don't forget what I told you."

John smiled at Emmy and said, "I won't forget."

Annie and Matt were ready to leave.

"Thanks so much for coming and helping with the clean-up. You didn't have to do that, you know," Emmy told them.

"We know, but we're used to hard work. We help on the farm a lot. We had a good time, Emmy. Thanks for inviting us. Maybe we can invite you guys out to the farm sometime. There's a lake where we like to go swimming."

"I'd like that, Annie. We really should get together more often. Thanks again for helping." Emmy hugged Annie and then looked at Matt. She gave him a hug as well.

221

Kenny's parents were spending the night because they were all going to church together in the morning. Later that night after his parents were asleep, Emmy and Kenny went out to the backyard. Kenny brought a large piece of foam from the garage and Emmy carried the double wide sleeping bag and they lay under the stars.

"Isn't the sky so full of stars tonight, honey?"

"Emmy, there aren't any more stars out tonight than any other night. It's just that you can see more of them."

"Sweetheart, are you trying to spoil this romantic night, or are you just dense? I know how many stars there are."

"You do, huh? Tell me, Mrs. Einstein, how many stars are there."

"You know what I mean."

It was a beautiful night, and they were enjoying it. Kenny kissed her, but then stopped.

"Are you going to make love to me or not?" Emmy asked.

"You better believe I am."

"Well, then get in the bag with me. I'm not going to do it on top. What if somebody saw us? Your father could wander out here in his sleep."

"Do you think Dad walks in his sleep?" Kenny asked.

"No, but he and your mom might get the same idea we had."

He laughed as he shook his head. "I don't think Mom and Dad are going to be sleeping on the hard ground at their age."

"Yeah, I guess not. Now get in here with me."

"If you insist."

"I do."

"You said that once before. Where was it? Oh, yeah, at the church when we got married. Have I told you lately that I love you, Mrs. Colwell?"

"Not in the last ten minutes. Tell me again, and I thought my name was Mrs. Einstein." Emmy giggled as Kenny climbed in the sleeping bag with her.

Chapter Twenty

"Emmy, Emmy, wake up. It's light. We should go inside."

"No, I don't want to. I'm still sleepy. What time is it?" Emmy complained.

"You can go back to bed inside. It's still early. We don't have to be at church until nine. Where are your pajamas?"

"They're in here somewhere. If you get out, I will have more room, and I can put them on easier."

"Okay, don't go back to sleep. Have I told you that I love you yet today?"

"No, you haven't. You've been awake for a whole minute, and you haven't told me yet. I guess the honeymoon's over."

Emmy found her pajamas and put them on. She crawled out of the sleeping bag and helped Kenny roll it up. She carried the sleeping bag, and he carried the foam padding. They stored them in the garage.

"We are going to need a bigger garage someday to keep kids' bikes and all their stuff... Oh, baby, I'm sorry. I wasn't thinking. I forget sometimes."

"It's all right, Kenny. If we keep praying about it, maybe God will find a way."

"Come on. We better get in the house before anyone wakes up."

"Did you have fun yesterday and last night?" she asked.

"I think everyone had a good time at the cookout." Kenny grinned. *I know you are asking about sleeping outside.*

"What about camping out?" She twisted her hair into a braid. *We've never had that much fun camping out before.*

"Oh, that. Yeah, that was all right." He kissed her. *It was better than all right. Maybe next time we can set up the tent.*

"You are so sweet. I think I should marry you someday. Oh wait. I already did that."

"Yes, you did."

They walked up the steps to the back door hand in hand not paying any attention to anything but each other.

In the kitchen Mrs. Colwell scooped some scrambled eggs

onto a plate for Mr. Colwell, who sat at the kitchen table drinking coffee and reading yesterday's newspaper. Emmy walked in first.

"Mom, what are you doing up so early?"

Mrs. Colwell turned to see Emmy and Kenny behind her. "Good morning, dear. It looks like it's going to be another beautiful day."

As Emmy passed the open pantry area, she saw Mr. Colwell sitting at the table.

"What are you guys doing up so early?" Kenny asked.

"I couldn't sleep, so I woke your father up and we came downstairs to have breakfast. It was more difficult to sleep in a different bed than I realized. We should have gone home last night after all. What were you guys doing outside? Never mind! I can guess."

"We camped out last night because it was such a beautiful night."

"Breakfast will be ready in a few minutes. You kids should scoot upstairs and get dressed."

"Thanks for making breakfast, Mom," Emmy said as she checked the stove. "Everything smells so good."

Mom Colwell glanced at Emmy's pajamas and sighed.

"I'll be right back to help." Emmy ran past Dad Colwell and up the stairs to her bedroom.

"You get yourself upstairs, too," Mrs. Colwell scolded. "Don't be walking around in front of your mother in just your boxers and a t-shirt."

"Yes, Mom."

"Just git and don't sass me young man, or I will use this spatula on you."

Kenny hugged his mother. "I love you." He kissed her on the cheek and asked, "You're still going to church with us, right? Tony will be there with Sloane, and Kristen is bringing John."

"Yes, we still plan on going so we can check out a service. It's so much bigger than Faith Bible, though. I'm afraid we will get lost."

"You won't get lost, Mom. You have to come back here for lunch because we have a ton of leftovers to eat. I don't want that food to be wasted."

"We will," she said and then pointed upstairs.

Kenny got the hint.

Mrs. Colwell leaned back against the counter. After a minute or two, Mr. Colwell set down the paper and looked at her. "What are you thinking about, Elly?"

"Do you remember when they would camp out in the backyard?"

He thought about it for a moment and then laughed. "Yeah, that was a long time ago. They were just kids."

It wasn't that long ago, Mrs. Colwell thought. "Did you ever dream that they would still be camping out after all these years?"

"Is that what they did last night?" he asked as he sipped his coffee.

"I heard them get up. They were trying to be real quiet, but I heard Emmy giggle. It reminded me of how she used to giggle when she was a little girl."

"Oh! You mean they were 'camping out', huh?"

Mrs. Colwell smiled. "Carter, you pretend not to have a clue, but I know you do."

He stood up and hugged his wife. "Do you want to go camping again sometime?"

"Only if we use a motorhome," she said and then laughed.

A few minutes later Emmy dashed into the kitchen after galloping down the stairs. "I'm dressed now."

"Emmy, do you have to run down the stairs like that? You could fall and hurt yourself. You're not a tomboy anymore, young lady!"

"I'm ready for breakfast, Mrs. Colwell? I could eat a horse."

"It's ready, dear."

"Did you have fun camping out?" Mr. Colwell asked.

"Carter!" Mrs. Colwell frowned at him.

Emmy grinned, but she also blushed.

"What? I used to ask Emmy the same thing when they used to camp out in the backyard at home."

"Times have changed." Mrs. Colwell rolled her eyes.

Emmy got a plate out of the cupboard. "We did have fun, but we didn't talk all night like we used to." Emmy giggled as she filled her plate with scrambled eggs and a slice of ham.

Just then, Kenny came down the stairs. "What's going on? Breakfast smells good."

"It is good. I was telling your father how much fun it was to camp out last night," Emmy said as she grinned.

Kenny didn't say another word.

Mr. Colwell nearly dropped his cup of coffee.

Mrs. Colwell sighed and turned away. "Dear Lord! What am I supposed to do with these two?"

After she ate breakfast, Emmy hurried to get ready for church. Her in-laws had decided to check out Crest Ridge United Nazarene even though they had been members of the smaller Faith Bible Church, which was much closer to where they lived, for over thirty years.

Kenny drove and escorted his parents to one of the adult Sunday School classes.

"Mr. Cartwright, I would like to introduce you to my parents. Mom, Dad, this is Mr. Cartwright."

"It's a pleasure to meet you. My name is Bob Cartwright, and this is my wife Rosa."

"Hello, I'm Carter Colwell and this is my wife Elly."

They shook hands and found seats together.

Elly said, "No one calls him Carter. He goes by Bob."

Kenny met his parents after the class ended.

"Did you guys do all right? I feel bad that I had to leave you, but we're doing a couple of new songs today, and I needed to be at practice."

"That's okay. We did fine. The Cartwrights are very nice."

"I'll take you to the sanctuary and help you find a seat."

"Kenny, we can manage just fine on our own. We were here for the wedding remember. I'd rather we go by ourselves so we get a better feel of the place."

"Okay, if you can, save us two seats."

"We'll try."

Kenny rejoined Emmy in the music suite.

"Did you show your parents around?" she asked.

"No, they want to get a feel for the church on their own."

"That's probably a good idea."

Kenny's parents found a place to sit, but weren't able to save two seats for Kenny and Emmy because they were joined by the Cartwrights and other members of the Sunday School class. The service finished just before noon, and Kenny and Emmy met his parents in the foyer. They socialized with some of the people for a time and then headed home.

"Well, what did you think?" Kenny asked in the car.

"I admit it was much friendlier than I imagined it would be. I always assumed because it was so large the people would not be as sociable, but everyone I talked to made us feel welcome."

"But you aren't going to switch churches, are you?"

"Did you really expect us to, son?"

"No, not really, but I'm glad you came today. How did you like the music?"

"It was louder than at our church, but I guess it needs to be because it's so big."

"I liked that solo you did on that one song," Dad told Kenny. "And of course, Emmy sounded like an angel."

"Didn't you hear her go flat for a couple notes?"

"You shouldn't be so critical."

"Thank you, Mr. Colwell." Emmy grinned and stuck out her tongue. "I did not go flat. I have perfect pitch, remember?"

When they got home, Kenny chased Emmy up the stairs to the bedroom. He tackled her onto the bed and she started to giggle.

"You need to behave because your parents are here."

"No, I don't," Kenny said as he kissed her and moved his hand to an intimate area.

"If you don't behave, I will scream!"

"Go ahead. They will think you are having... fun"

"They will not. You can kiss me, but then we need to change and get lunch ready."

Kenny kissed her a few times and she responded.

"Can we finish this after your parents leave?" Emmy

227

whispered as she looked at Kenny with adoration.

"Just try and stop me."

They changed clothes and went downstairs. Mom Colwell was already getting leftovers out of the fridge. Dad Colwell was relaxing in a recliner in the living room.

"You don't need to do that, Mom. I can do it. You can relax if you want."

"I don't mind helping, dear." Mrs. Colwell smiled and hugged Emmy. "It makes me feel so good that you are calling me Mom."

"I was hoping you wouldn't mind."

"Oh, Emmy, I've known you for so many years, and I've always loved you like a daughter. I'm so pleased that now you really are my daughter."

They ate lunch together, but by two o'clock Mrs. Colwell was ready to go home.

"I hate to eat and run, but I need to take my Sunday afternoon nap, and I want to take it in my own recliner. Thanks for lunch. Let's go, Carter."

"All right. You don't have to push me out the door."

Emmy hugged them as they left.

"Why were you in such a big hurry to leave?" Mr. Colwell asked as they drove home. "You could have taken a nap in the recliner in the living room. It's just like the one you have at home."

"We needed to leave so they could be alone. Have you forgotten how we were when we were first married?"

He looked at his wife and grinned. "Oh, right, I forgot how anxious we would be when your parents would come to visit."

Emmy and Kenny were able to finish what they started earlier, but it took them the rest of the afternoon.

In the evening, Kenny and Emmy talked about the tour.

"You might be excited for the first week, but it will get old soon enough."

"It might to you, but I think I will be excited because I will be able to see new cities."

"You won't be able to see much of the cities we visit, Em. Not if you stay with me. Our days will be filled with requests from radio stations, magazine writers looking for a story, meet and greet events for fan club members."

"Will we have any time to ourselves?" Emmy asked.

Kenny grinned and answered, "We will have time for that, Em. We will be in our bedroom on the bus overnight as we travel."

"Will we be alone on the bus?"

"We will be sharing our bus with Jeff and Jeremy. Frances and Amanda are not going. Frances because of the baby, and Amanda has to manage the office here in SoHam. Andy will be along for a couple of weeks. He will keep you busy."

"How?"

"He will put you to work in the production office."

"What do you mean?"

"In all the large venues we play we always have a production office set up to handle stuff. You'll see."

"I'm already beginning to see that you guys work harder than I imagined."

Emmy returned to work Monday morning. It was her final week, at least for now, at Robertson Industries. The week flew fly by, and on Friday Mr. Robertson took the whole team out to lunch. They were celebrating Mr. Oliver's retirement, but later in the office they also had a cake with Emmy's name on it.

"We will miss you so much, Emmy."

"You were the best assistant we've ever had."

All the guys had a chance to say goodbye to her. Ethan Hanks even stopped by to wish her well. He didn't say goodbye since they were still neighbors and would see each other again.

As soon as she walked in the back door after work, she could smell lasagna, garlic bread and a fresh cut green pepper. She saw Kenny chopping vegetables for one of his scrumptious salads. She walked up behind him and put her arms around his waist.

"Is that really lasagna I smell in the oven? I can see you are making a salad, and I know there's garlic bread in the oven, but did you put the lasagna together?"

"I would like to take all the credit, but I can't. Mama Bertucci put it together for me. I just had to pop it in the oven, but the salad is all mine."

"It smells delicious. Can I have a kiss before I run upstairs to change?"

"I have one or two kisses left, but maybe you can wait to change until after dinner. I invited Mama and Tony over since she was kind enough to put it together for us. I think Tony is bringing Sloane, too."

"Okay, do you need help setting the table or anything?"

"It's all done," Kenny said as he kissed her.

She peeked into the dining room and saw the table was already set and there was a bouquet of flowers in the center of the table.

"I see that you've been busy."

"I did as much laundry as I could, too. The only things I didn't do are your delicates. I thought you could do them later."

"Do we have enough time to... you know?"

"Not now because Tony just pulled in the driveway." Kenny grinned as he kissed her nose and then licked it.

"Stop that!"

"Stop kissing you?"

"No, stop licking my nose."

They heard a knock at the back door and then heard it open.

"We're here! Is it safe to come in?"

"No!" Emmy hollered. "We're in the dining room and I'm naked. Kenny attacked me as soon as I got home."

"She's lying," Kenny said as he walked into the kitchen. "Come on in. Dinner should be ready in a few minutes."

Mama could smell the lasagna and garlic bread. "It smells very good, Kenny."

"Thank you, Mama. I already told Emmy you put it together so she knows."

Emmy walked into the kitchen and turned her back to Kenny, "Will you zip up my dress for me? I can't reach it and since you were the one who unzipped it..." Emmy began to laugh and couldn't keep a straight face. "He didn't unzip it. I did it just to tease him."

Tony grinned and said, "Sure, Em. Kristen told me how bad

you guys are."

"We're not that bad," Emmy said with a grin. "Hi, Sloane, don't believe anything Tony tells you about me."

"I know you well enough by now to know how you act." Sloane smiled and Emmy grinned back.

"Are we going to eat, or are you guys going to talk about Kenny and Emmy all night?" Mama asked as she pulled the lasagna out of the oven.

"Let's eat. I'm hungry and everything smells so good," Emmy answered.

They sat at the dining room table and talked as they ate. Emmy mentioned, "Hey, did I tell you we saw Dixie Case's new band at Larry's Uptown Grill last week?"

"You told me you were going. How was it?" Tony asked.

"They were really good. Even Kenny thought so."

Mama asked, "Who are you talking about, Emmy?"

"Dixie Case is one of the guitar players in the worship band. The touring band, actually, but he plays on Sundays once in a while, too. He and some of the other guys have started a new rock band."

Tony looked at Kenny. "Were they really any good?"

"Yes, and I think Mr. Kesson might offer them a recording deal."

After they finished dinner, Kenny loaded up the dishwasher while everyone else sat in the living room to relax.

"Are you sad to be leaving your job, Emmy?" Sloane asked.

"In a way. It certainly wasn't an easy decision. I really enjoyed working there, and Mr. Robertson is the best boss in the world."

"Are you going to travel with the band all the time?" Tony asked.

"Just until the fall semester at North Park. Then I'm going to take a full load. Actually, more than a full load. I'm going to take eighteen hours. I want to finish my degree in a year and a half."

"So, when Kenny is on tour you will be here in SoHam by yourself, is that right?" Tony asked.

231

"Yes," Emmy answered slowly as she grabbed a small pillow from the end of the couch. "What's your point?"

Tony smiled and Emmy threw the pillow at him.

"You are so mean to me."

"I'm just wondering how you will survive without being able to... with having to..."

"Get by without sex. You can say *sex* in front of Mama."

Sloane got after Tony, "You shouldn't tease her about sex. After all she's still a newlywed. She wouldn't tease you if you were in her shoes."

"She likes to tease me just as much as I tease her," Tony said in his defense.

Kenny was finished in the kitchen and had heard most of the conversation. He walked into the living room and sat next to Emmy.

"Tony's teasing me about sex."

"He is! Now why would he do that? Doesn't he know that we never have sex anymore?"

"Or any less," Tony teased.

"Okay, that's enough talk about sex. Why don't you talk about church or something?" Mama suggested.

"You're right, Mama," Emmy said and then remembered. "Did you hear who is getting married?"

"No, who?" Sloane asked.

"Reggie Lennon and Maria Juneau. I heard it from Lynette. He asked her to marry him last week, and she said yes."

"Have they been dating very long?" Sloane asked.

"A little over a year. I'm not sure if they've set a date or anything, but they are both really nice. I actually went out a couple times with Reggie. They were kinda more like going out as friends rather than romantic dates. I can't remember for sure if he ever kissed me. Probably not."

"I can understand why he wouldn't want to kiss you," Tony said.

"You're a creep!" Emmy stuck out her tongue at Tony.

"Wasn't Maria married once before?" Sloane asked.

"I don't know. I've never heard that," Emmy answered.

232

"Lynette would know."

Tony looked at Kenny and asked, "How do you feel about taking Emmy with you on tour? It's kinda like taking your wife to work with you. I could never imagine taking my wife to football practice."

"It's going to be a challenge," Kenny said and Emmy stuck her tongue out at him.

Mama rolled her eyes.

"Do the other wives ever go?" Sloane asked.

"They have at times, but not as much anymore. If we're going to be gone for a long time, like a couple of months without being home, they might fly to wherever we are for a night or two."

Tony looked at Emmy and grinned. "Well, Em, I guess you will have to take advantage of your time together this summer. Once school starts you will be too busy to see each other."

"Don't remind me. I do want to get my degree though, and the time will pass quickly. I feel like you just started at Notre Dame. Then before we knew it, you were finished."

Mama stood up and told Emmy and Kenny, "Thank you for a lovely dinner. It was very good, Kenny."

"Of course it was. You made the lasagna. All I did was heat it up," Kenny said.

"Are you leaving?" Emmy asked.

"Thank you for inviting us," Sloane told Emmy as she hugged her.

"Thank you for coming. I'm sorry you had to share dinner with him." Emmy pointed to Tony.

Tony moved over behind Emmy and asked Sloane, "Did you have a good time tonight?"

"It was a thoroughly enjoyable evening," she answered.

"Even though the brat was here?" Tony asked.

"You guys are goofy at times." Sloane laughed.

Emmy glared at Tony for a moment before giggling.

"Come on. Let's say good night and let the two newlyweds have some time alone," Mama said.

They took advantage of Mama's suggestion.

Chapter Twenty-One

While Kenny and the guys in the band met at the Steward Music Group office, the road crew employees loaded up the semitrailers at the band's warehouse. For the summer portion of the 'Johnny March Tour' the band would be performing outdoors at large stadiums. Two road crews, two stages and two sets of gear would leapfrog the country. While one crew set up in one city, the other crew would race to the next venue. They would also use up to two hundred local workers at each stop of the tour. Twelve of the sixteen total buses would depart today for the west coast.

In the office, Andy Walker, Ralph Glissman, Tim Perino, Randy Lemmert and Phil Barnes met to go over details of the tour. Emmy joined them and listened as the details were discussed.

"Is it always like this?" Emmy asked Kenny. "Forty trucks of gear?"

"Yeah, this is the biggest tour we've ever done. Not the longest though."

"Thank God for that," Emmy said. She read through the 'travel bible' as Andy called it. "I have one question."

"What's that, Em?" Andy asked.

She blushed as everyone stared at her. "Uh, I see how each day is planned out, but aren't you leaving out one major detail?"

Andy tilted his head. "Would you care to elaborate, Ms. Colasanti?"

"When do we get to use the bathroom?"

"If you would read section seven, paragraph fifteen, it clearly states that all calls of nature will be handled between noon and 12:05."

Emmy frowned at Andy and then stuck out her tongue. "I'll keep my mouth shut from now on. Sorry."

"The planning and attention to detail have always been a part of our mission, but we didn't have as much gear in the beginning. You know how it was," Kenny said as he rubbed her back.

"I remember the early days, I guess I was wondering when it all got so big."

234

"After *Transitions* came out and we started headlining, it just kinda grew into what we have today. In some ways it would be nice to scale it back, but while we can, we need to play the big stadiums. One of these days that will change."

"I know the lights have changed from when you started," Emmy said.

"Yeah, we use LEDs for the most part now. They are lighter, don't produce as much heat and we don't need as many of them because they change color."

"And we're using digital mixing boards, too. They're lighter and we can do more processing with them," Phil mentioned. "The speakers are more efficient and smaller."

"Does that mean the guitars and drums will start getting smaller, too?" Emmy joked.

The meeting ended and everyone headed home. They would return at one tomorrow to leave for Seattle.

"I'm glad we brought most of our luggage today," Kenny said as they loaded it into the bus.

"We just have a couple of suitcases to bring tomorrow."

"Smart thinking, huh?" Kenny said as he smiled.

"What are we gonna do with the rest of the day?" Emmy asked as they headed back to the house. "I know we have to finish packing, and I have a little bit of laundry to do. I want to clean the house so it looks nice for Kristen."

"I promised Mom we would have dinner with them, and we should stop and see your parents, too."

"We can check out the carriage house," Emmy said with a gleam in her eye.

"I know why you want to do that."

"I just want to make sure it's okay. We haven't been there since..."

"You just want to be naughty again," Kenny teased.

"Don't you want to be naughty?" Emmy asked with a grin.

"Let's get everything done and see how much time we have left."

By the time they got all the laundry done, the house cleaned and most everything packed, it was time to go see the parents.

They parked in front of the carriage house and decided to go to her parents' house first. They walked over, and Emmy rang the front doorbell. Her mother opened the door and was surprised to see them.

"I didn't know you were coming, Emmy. I don't have anything for dinner."

"It's okay, Mom. We're going to have dinner with the Colwells, but I did call you earlier this week, remember?"

"I guess it just slipped my mind."

"We're leaving after church tomorrow, so this is the last time we can see you, unless you come to church with us in the morning." Emmy always hoped her parents would someday accept Christ and prayed for them daily.

"I don't think so. Come and sit down. Your father is in back working on the yard."

"Why don't we go outside and sit at the picnic table? It's a beautiful day," Emmy suggested.

"Okay, would you like something to drink?"

"Do you have any bottled water?"

"There's some in the fridge. Help yourself, dear."

Emmy grabbed two bottles, and they headed outside. Her father didn't hear them at first because of his electric trimmer. He finished trimming an overgrown bush and turned around. He saw the kids and turned off his trimmer.

"Hi, Daddy, we came to see you because we're leaving tomorrow, and I won't be back until the end of August." She walked over and kissed her father's sweaty cheek. "How have you been feeling?"

"I'm doing better. My hip doesn't hurt as much, and I haven't had to use that darn cane lately."

"That's good to hear. Why don't you take a break? I brought out some water for you."

"Thanks, sweetie. How are you guys doing? Everything all right?"

They sat down at the wooden picnic table and listened to two blue jays screeching at each other.

"Married life is wonderful!" Emmy answered gleefully.

236

"How have you and Mom been getting along?"

"She still drives me nuts at times, but we don't argue as much anymore. I haven't been drinking at all."

"That's good news." She wondered if it was really true.

Emmy and Kenny spent an hour with her parents before they said goodbye and walked over to see the Colwells. They walked in the front door, and Emmy could smell fried chicken. She saw Mr. Colwell in his recliner, with a book on his lap, sound asleep. She walked up behind him, kissed the top of his head, and he looked up.

"Hello, sweetheart, is it that late already? I must have been asleep longer than I planned. How are you? Where's Kenny?"

"I'm here, Dad."

"I'm gonna see if Mom needs any help in the kitchen."

Emmy headed to the kitchen, and Kenny sat on the couch to talk to his father.

"Are you ready to hit the road?" Dad asked as he closed the book.

"Just a little packing to finish tomorrow."

"Are you excited to have Emmy going with you? Silly question, I know."

"I just hope she doesn't get discouraged by the travel. It can really wear a person down after a while."

"She will have adrenaline keeping her going for a couple of weeks since this is her first trip. The first trip with you guys, I mean. It's a lot different than touring with her worship band. After that she might start to wear down a little."

"The tour with the worship band was like a trial run. This summer will be a true test of whether she can handle the stress." Kenny could hear his mother and Emmy laughing in the kitchen.

"Do you know who's going to be on your bus?"

"My assistant, Brent Luckey, will be on our bus the whole tour. Andy, Ralph and Tim will be riding with us at the start. You know Andy will only be with us for a couple of weeks at most. After that, I'm not sure who will be riding with us. Maybe no one and we can have a little more privacy."

"Just make sure you pay her a lot of attention. I know how

237

busy you can get on these tours," Dad said.

"I will."

Later that night after they checked out the carriage house, they finished packing.

"I don't think there's anything left in the dresser. I'm taking just about everything I own," Emmy told Kenny.

"You will learn to pack lighter with more experience. It's a science."

"You mean you wear the same underwear for a week at a time," she said and then giggled.

They woke up at seven and, after cuddling in bed for a time, got up to get ready for church. They ate breakfast, arrived at the church shortly after eight and saw Chase and Yvonne Hillman in the music room.

"Morning, guys, are you ready for your trip, Emmy?" Chase asked.

"I'm all packed and excited. I know it's not a big deal to Kenny, but I'm looking forward to the tour."

"Where is the first show?" Yvonne asked as she printed out several copies of the order of service.

"Seattle, Washington. It will take us over thirty hours to get there. It's over two thousand miles. If we were in a hurry, we would fly, but Andy insisted we take the bus."

"Surely you mean buses?"

"Oh, right. There are several buses. It's a huge trip to coordinate. All of the crew has already left."

Emmy explained as much as she could to Chase and Yvonne. They offered a prayer for the safe travel of the band and their organization., Emmy and Kenny hurried home after the service, and Kristen followed them.

"Thank you so much for agreeing to house-sit for us."

"It's not a problem, Em. At least you guys don't have any pets."

"You still have a bunch of your clothes in your old room."

After a very quick lunch, Kristen drove them over to the Steward Music Group site.

"Have a safe trip and call me when you arrive," Kristen said as she put her hands on Emmy's shoulders.

"I will. Thanks for taking care of the house."

"Are you going to take pictures?" Kristen asked.

"Yes, and I'm going to write in my journal."

"We need to go, Em. It's time," Kenny said.

Emmy hugged Kristen and then she and Kenny boarded the bus.

Shortly after one, the remaining four buses rolled out and were on the way. Kenny and Emmy were using the bedroom at the rear of the large blue Prevost XL2 bus. Each of the guys in the band would travel in their own bus along with members of the production team.

The buses pulled into the Four Seasons Hotel after over thirty hours on the road. Everyone would spend the night here and head over to Seahawk Stadium tomorrow.

After Kenny and Emmy were settled in their hotel room for the night, she asked, "Why haven't I met Brent before? How long has he been traveling with you?"

"He started at the beginning of the 'Johnny March Tour.'"

"So, why haven't you mentioned him before?"

"I guess I just never thought about it. He's just the guy who keeps track of my schedule while I'm on tour. He helps out with whatever the guys on this bus need. All the guys have someone like Brent. They come and go because it's a tough job and doesn't pay a whole lot. That's why we hire young college grads, like Brent. They usually only stick around for one tour, but then move on to a better job."

"Have you always hired guys for the job?"

"I did have a female for the Transition Tour."

"What was her name? Do you remember?"

"It was Nina something, but I can't remember her last name. She was only with us for a couple of months."

"I still can't believe how many buses and trucks it requires for your tour." Emmy lay on her stomach and flipped through the TV channels.

"Just wait until tomorrow, Em. You will be amazed at how many people are working at the stadium."

He lay next to her and rubbed her back. She turned off the TV as he pulled her t-shirt over her head.

In the morning Emmy and Kenny ate breakfast in the room and then his workday began. Between interviews, meeting fans, soundchecks and meeting more fans Kenny kept busy all day. They ate dinner and then it was showtime–the only time of the day Kenny really relaxed and enjoyed himself. He appreciated the fans, but it got more difficult every year to sit through the interviews and face the attention of the media.

A reporter for a local tabloid asked, "Where is your wife? We heard a rumor that she's here with you."

"She is traveling with me this summer, but she won't be available for interviews at the present time," Kenny answered.

"Are you gonna have her sing with the band? I read that she is a singer in her own right."

"Is it true your wife just turned eighteen?"

On and on the questions came. They became more absurd as the interview progressed. Kenny knew Emmy was listening and probably laughing at the ridiculous questions he, and the other guys, had to answer over and over.

Emmy soon adjusted her internal clock to going to bed at two in the morning and sleeping until ten. The time they spent secluded in their bedroom after the show, and traveling to the next city, was the only time she and Kenny had to themselves all day. The tour took the band south along the coast, with a side trip to Salt Lake City. They performed in San Francisco for two nights and after two days off, spend four nights in Los Angeles. While in LA, they arranged to join Becky Morrison for dinner. They met at Cafe Blue in Studio City, the neighborhood where Becky lived.

"Becky, it's good to see you. How have you been?" Emmy asked as she and Becky embraced.

"I've been doing great. This is Taylor Claussen. Taylor, this is Kenny Colwell and his wife Emmy Colasanti."

240

Kenny and Taylor shook hands, and he smiled at Emmy.

"It's a pleasure to meet you. I've been a fan of your music for several years, and I also enjoy listening to your CD, Emmy."

"Really? You have our CD?"

"He plays it all the time," Becky said. "Are you having fun traveling? I know from experience it can take a toll on a person."

"It's still exciting to me, but we haven't been gone that long."

The wannabe-actress-hostess seated them in a booth in the back corner of the trendy restaurant, and, after ordering drinks and appetizers, they had a chance to talk.

"Taylor is now on the staff of Living Water Church, Kenny," Becky explained. "He's the associate pastor in charge of the senior adult ministry."

Emmy giggled.

"That's great and what is so funny, Emmy?"

"Taylor is too young to deal with senior citizens."

"It's only temporary," Taylor said. "But I do enjoy it. They treat me like a son."

"Is Dr. Behren still there?"

"Yes, and he was asking about you the other day. He asked me to say hi and offered his congratulations on your marriage."

Later that night back in the hotel room, Emmy passed her thoughts along to Kenny. "You do know that Becky and Taylor are in love, right?"

"Why do you think that, Em?"

"Because of the way her eyes light up when she looks at him. I'm so happy for her. She's gonna make the perfect pastor's wife."

"Did she say anything about getting married?" Kenny thought about his relationship with Becky.

"Not in so many words. Are you still happy you married me instead of her?"

Kenny held Emmy in his arms and kissed her. "Do you really have to ask?"

Emmy giggled and then said, "I think you're gonna show me your answer."

Chapter Twenty-Two

"What would you like to do on your first birthday as a married woman, Emmy?" Kenny asked as he and Emmy squeezed into a booth with Andy Walker and Ralph Glissman, the tour manager, at Cisco Franklin's Bar-B-Que in Austin, Texas.

"Remember to be polite in front of us, Emmy. We know what you really want to do," Andy teased.

"Kenny gave me that present this morning," Emmy answered with a gleam in her eye that made Andy and Ralph blush. "The food smells delicious."

"It's awesome!" Andy proclaimed. "I recommend the brisket or the pulled pork. They're both great."

"I take it you've been here before then, cuz."

"Several times." Andy turned to Ralph. "Every time one of the guys got married and brought their wife along on tour, it was like a honeymoon. They lost their concentration on what's really important."

"What would that be, Andy?" Ralph knew where Andy was going and set him up like the perfect straight man.

"Making more money for me." Andy punched his fist into the air and then laughed as he delivered his line. "That's the most important, and really the only reason as far as I'm concerned, to be on the road like this. I'm getting too old to work this hard."

"I'm surprised you're still with us. You never stay on the road for this long. What gives?" Kenny asked.

"It's summer, the weather is nice and I wanted to spend time with my favorite cousin." Andy smiled at Emmy and squeezed her hand. "I need to show her the ropes so she can take over one of these days."

"If I ever take over, we are gonna fly everywhere," Emmy said. "Why aren't we flying anyway? You used to."

Andy looked at Kenny.

"She doesn't know," Kenny said.

Emmy looked at Kenny and then Andy. Ralph developed a sudden interest in the menu.

"What don't I know? You guys better tell me. Ralph, do you

242

know what they're talking about? Do I have to call Alice?"

"You should tell her, Kenny," Andy said.

"Okay." Kenny looked at Emmy and held her hand. "A couple of years ago we almost crashed. We had to make an emergency landing and the pilot managed to get us back down safely. After that, we decided to stay on the ground most of the time. It's not that we aren't ever going to fly again, but when it's feasible, we are going to travel by bus. That's why this tour was set up with so many days off."

"You never told me about that," Emmy said softly.

"I'm sorry. I didn't want you to worry. I told Tony because he heard about it, but I made him promise not to tell you."

"I don't know what I would do if I ever lost you." Emmy started to cry.

"Oh, Em, I'm not going anywhere." Kenny put his arm around her shoulders.

"Don't you guys know the safest way to travel is by air? It's been statistically proven."

"Don't you like the bus, Em?" Andy asked. "There aren't any bedrooms on a plane."

She blushed but managed to smile. "That's the best part of traveling on a bus."

"I know what I want for lunch," Ralph said as he set his menu down.

"What might that be?" Andy grinned.

"A pulled pork sandwich with coleslaw and mac and cheese as my sides."

"Really, Ralph? You are indeed quite the adventurous type," Andy said and then he and Kenny laughed.

"What's so funny?" Emmy didn't understand why the guys were laughing at Ralph.

"Ralph orders the same thing for lunch if at all possible. He's like you and your blueberry pancakes for breakfast."

Emmy crossed her arms over her chest and frowned. "I happen to like blueberry pancakes."

"Oh, don't be mad at me." Kenny tried to kiss her, but she turned her head.

"You shouldn't be so mean to Ralph."

"Okay. We'll try not to tease him anymore."

Since the band had a night off, Kenny took Emmy out for dinner that evening. After they ate, he asked, "Would you like to hear some live music, Em? I know a couple of places, or we could just go back to the hotel."

"I'd like to hear some good music for my birthday," she teased.

"Fine! Be that way."

"I'm teasing. We can go out. Maybe I can convince you to dance with me."

"I know where a bunch of guys from the crew are going. We could join them."

"Sounds like a plan to me."

They checked out the local music scene and saw two bands they both liked—The Motorcars and The Stragglers. Emmy did get Kenny to dance with her. She danced with some crew members and even dragged Frankie Hanna onto the dance floor.

"I don't know how to dance, Emmy," Frankie admitted.

"It doesn't matter. You just put this hand in mine and put your other one right here on my waist. Now you move your feet around. We'll take it nice and slow." Emmy guided him.

"Sorry," he apologized.

"That's okay. Kenny has stepped on my foot before."

By the end of the song, Frankie had relaxed enough to not totally hate having to dance.

Emmy smiled and said, "That wasn't too terrible, was it?"

"It was all right."

"If you want to try it again, just let me know. We can pick out a slow song."

Frankie smiled. "I'm glad you and Kenny got married. You guys were always best friends when you were kids."

"Thank you, Frankie. I sorta remember when you and Tom would come over to visit. You were always quiet." Emmy recalled, *You hardly talked at all. In fact, I didn't think you could talk.*

"Still am," Frankie said.

244

Emmy was eating breakfast at the hotel in Dallas early Thursday morning when her cell phone rang. Emmy thought she knew who might be calling—it was probably Mama Bertucci calling with important news. Emmy checked the caller ID and saw that she was correct and answered the phone, "Hello, Mama, did Heather have the baby?"

"Yes, she had a baby boy. His name is Peter Anthony, and he arrived this morning at four o'clock. You were very close to the right date, Emmy. You thought Heather would have the baby on the eleventh, and he came a day early. He weighed seven pounds and eight ounces and he's twenty inches long."

Emmy hollered to Kenny, "Heather had her baby. Come and talk to Mama."

Emmy handed Kenny her phone.

"Good morning, Kenny." Mama said.

"Good morning, Grandma," Kenny said as he emphasized "Grandma."

Kenny asked for the details, so Mama repeated everything for his benefit. Emmy couldn't wait to see the baby. Kenny knew Emmy was happy for Heather and Alex, but in her heart she had an ache and felt an emptiness. Emmy wished she could have a baby.

Heather and baby Peter were doing great and were able to go home late Friday afternoon. Mama and Tony arrived at Alex and Heather's apartment an hour later along with her sister Karla.

"Mama, he is so little," Tony said.

Mama told him, "He's not that small. Over seven pounds is pretty normal. You were just over seven pounds when you were born."

"Was I really that tiny?" Tony couldn't imagine he was ever this small.

"You were a little longer if I remember correctly."

Tony could see that Heather was thrilled to a mother, and Mama was as happy as she could possibly be in her new role as a grandmother. Mama and Karla made dinner while Heather took care of Peter. Alex and Tony sat in the living room.

"We've started looking for a house," Alex mentioned.

"So, you guys are gonna stay in South Bend?"

"Yeah, I think we'll be here for a few years, but eventually I'd like to move back to the Baltimore area."

Around ten o'clock, Tony, Mama and Karla headed to the hotel where they were spending the night. They spent most of Saturday in South Bend and Tony and Aunt Karla headed home in the evening. Mama was staying with Heather to help take care of the apartment and baby because Alex would be busy at the hospital.

On Sunday afternoon, the thirteenth, Emmy's cell phone rang. She didn't answer because she was "taking a nap" with Kenny. When the phone rang again, she sighed and looked to see who was calling.

"It's Kristen," she told Kenny. "Maybe I should take the call and then we can continue with our nap."

"Okay, but we only have an hour," Kenny said.

"Hi, Kristen. What's up?"

"I'm sorry to bother you because you are probably busy..."

"We were just taking a nap."

"Oh crap! I'm sorry, Em." Kristen knew what Emmy meant. "But I just have to tell you what happened at church this morning."

"What happened? Is everyone okay? Did something bad happen, or is it something good?"

"Bad! Very, very bad!" Kristen was near tears so Emmy knew it was something serious.

"Just calm down and tell me, Krissy." Emmy tried to console her friend with a soothing voice.

"Pastor Herb is leaving. He's retiring in October and moving to the Philippines. The Philippines! Can you believe it?"

"Oh, no! Are you sure?"

"Yes, he announced it at the end of the service today. He said something about teaching at a college, or a seminary or something like that, for six months before they return home. Everyone was shocked, and the place was totally quiet. He went on to say this was a decision he had been praying about for several months, and the church board knew about his decision two weeks

246

ago. Do you know who is on the church board? I don't have any idea who he meant."

"I know a few of them. They are the older men, and I think there are some women, too, but they are the people who make the decisions about running the church."

"Oh, I don't know about any of that stuff. I just know I started crying and so did a lot of other people."

"You know, in a way, I'm not surprised. He has told us before that he's getting older, and I think his wife was born in the Philippines. I know her parents served as missionaries there, and he has grandkids there."

"Who will they get to replace him? Will they just promote Paul Jefferson, or one of the other guys?"

"I'm not sure, Kristen. They might need to find an older pastor with more experience than Paul or the guys. Didn't you tell me there was a different preacher a few weeks ago?"

"Yeah, it was when Pastor Herb was on vacation. His name was Behren, I think."

When Emmy heard this name she looked at Kenny. He had heard most everything and looked at Emmy.

"I wasn't supposed to say anything until it was official, but Becky did email something about Dr. Behren possibly leaving California to be closer to his daughters and their families. Maybe he has made up his mind."

"You stinker! You should have told me."

Kenny shrugged. "Sorry, Em, but I couldn't."

"Did you hear that?" Emmy asked Kristen.

"Yeah, I can hear."

"Kenny knows Dr. Behren because he is the pastor at Becky's church where Kenny totally gave his life to Christ."

"What are we going to do, Em? What if we don't like the new pastor?"

"We just have to give him a chance. The church wouldn't hire him if they didn't believe it was God's will."

"I hope you're right. I'm sorry I bothered you. You guys can finish your 'nap' now."

"I don't think I can now," Emmy said.

Emmy and Kristen didn't realize the church board had been interviewing Dr. Behren and some of them had even flown out to California to meet him and visit his church.

Kristen rushed to Kenny and Emmy's house after work on Friday and changed clothes. John arrived five minutes later.

"Kristen, where are you?"

"I'm upstairs. I'll be right down. Are Tony and Sloane meeting us here?"

"Yeah, they should be here shortly." John wandered into the dining room and looked at the piles of mail. He picked up a *Billboard* and thumbed through it.

Kristen walked up next to him. "How was your day?"

John leaned down and kissed her. "Tony and I worked out for three hours. I think we're gonna be in better shape for training camp than last year. Did your team invent anything new today?"

"Maybe, but I can't tell you. It's super top secret."

John looked at the sorted stacks of mail. "How do you know what to do with all this?"

"The junk mail gets tossed. Anything that looks like a bill, I open and pass on to Kenny's parents if I need to. Some of it is stuff they might want to see, but not real important."

"When is Emmy coming home? You told me, but I forgot."

"August twentieth," Kristen said as she saw Tony pull into the driveway. "Let's go. They're here."

Sloane moved into the back seat to allow John to have more legroom.

"Is everyone ready for some pizza?" Tony asked as he backed out.

"You are so predictable." Kristen shook her head. "Don't you ever take Sloane out for a romantic evening at a fancy restaurant?"

"She likes the pizza at Kerry Lynn's."

Kristen looked at Sloane, who shrugged her shoulders.

"What can I say? He's not gonna change."

"Just don't let him treat you like he does Emmy and me."

"Hey! I heard that. I know better than to treat Sloane like a

248

cousin, or a little sister." Tony turned the corner a bit too fast.

"Hey! Hot rod, get us there in one piece," Kristen scolded.

"Are we going anywhere after we eat?" Sloane asked.

"I suppose we could go back to my house," Tony said as Kristen mouthed the words along with him.

"Why don't we do something different tonight? We always go to your house. John only likes to go because Mama always sends him home with a ton of food."

"What do you have in mind, Kristen?" John turned in his seat to look at her.

"Why don't we go back to my place?"

"You mean Kenny and Emmy's place, right?"

"Yes, if you want to get technical, although I have been house sitting for over a month."

"Doesn't make it your place," Tony reminded her.

"Fine. Let's go to Kenny and Emmy's house."

"Why?"

"God! You guys are imbeciles, I swear."

Tony and John looked at each other. Finally, it dawned on them.

"I get it. You want to go there because no one is there. You want to watch one of those romantic movies you and Emmy used to watch. Then you will want to make out."

"Aha! You're not totally brain dead." Kristen clapped her hands while Sloane laughed.

After spending an hour and a half at Kerry Lynn's, they headed out to Tony's Envoy. Tony whispered to Kristen, "I know you want to have some time alone with John, since we'll be leaving soon, but I'm gonna take Sloane to my house. I'll drop you guys off."

"Is it that obvious that I'm going to miss him?"

"You're not as bad as Emmy."

"John won't spend the night." Kristen twirled her hair with a finger.

"I'm not gonna judge you, Kristen."

Later that night, Kristen felt guilty and made John go home earlier than usual.

Fridays At Five continued to play stadiums across the country for the duration of the summer. Emmy stayed with Kenny until August twentieth. She needed to get home to prepare for classes which started on the twenty-fifth. The band was in Cincinnati, and Kenny and Andy took Emmy to the Cincinnati/Northern Kentucky International Airport. Kristen had agreed to pick her up at Midway Airport.

"Are you sure you've got enough clean clothes for the rest of the week?" Emmy asked Kenny.

"Yes, Em. I'll be all right. Brent will take care of things."

"I'm going to miss you so much," Emmy said as she kissed him again.

"Not as much as I will miss you."

Andy looked at them and sighed. "Are you guys gonna keep this up? You've been saying goodbye to each other for the last two days. I know you're still newlyweds, but come on. We'll be home for a month in just a few weeks. Surely you can go that long without seeing each other."

"It won't be easy, cousin, but I am anxious to start classes," Emmy said.

"I will have Brent send the rest of your clothes and stuff home. I know the airplane can't hold everything," Kenny teased.

"I don't have that much stuff left on the bus."

Andy hugged her and kissed her cheek. Kenny and Emmy kissed one more time, and she joined the line of people going through the security checkpoint. Kenny watched until she was out of sight.

Andy looked at Kenny and patted his back. "The time will go by faster than you know it and then you'll be back home."

"I suppose. It was so good to have her with me though. What will I do the next time we leave, and she has to stay behind?"

"She will be finished with school by the end of next year. We're only going to be gone for five months or so between now and the end of the tour in May." Andy counted up the months in his head. "So out of the next nine months, you will only be apart for five of them."

"Nine months, huh?"

Andy looked at Kenny, "Is that significant? Is she pregnant already? I thought you said..."

"She's not, but we aren't using anything to prevent it. Maybe her doctor was right."

"Doctors aren't always right. Just keep praying and God will answer your prayer—one way or another."

Emmy's flight landed at Midway Airport on time, and she called Kristen, who was waiting inside the terminal.

Kristen saw her and hollered, "Em! Em!"

Emmy saw Kristen and rushed over to hug her friend.

"How was the flight?"

"Uneventful. Just the way I like them. Did you know that Kenny almost crashed?" Emmy explained what almost happened to the band as they walked to the car.

"I never knew anything about that, Em. I swear."

They made it home, and Emmy immediately called Kenny.

"Did you have a good flight, Em?"

"Yes, and I told Kristen why you guys aren't flying. I miss you already."

"I miss you, too. We'll be home soon."

Before she went to bed, Emmy asked Kristen, "Why don't you stay at the house with me while Kenny is gone? It will be like old times."

"I'll stay as long as you promise not to complain about Kenny being gone every night."

"I won't. I can wait until he gets back to make love. I'm not in any hurry for him to get home." Emmy bit her lip. *No one would ever believe that lie.*

"I'll believe that as soon as soon as gas hits three dollars a gallon."

"That won't ever happen," Emmy said.

"And neither will you going without sex for a month."

"I will have to because he's still gone."

"I meant you won't ever go for a month...oh, never mind, Em. You know what I mean."

Chapter Twenty-Three

"Hey, Krissy, I've got dinner ready. We do have time to eat before we have to be at the church for practice, right?"

"Sure, we have time." Kristen stopped in front of the stove. "This smells good. What is it?"

"It's a special recipe for gumbo I got in New Orleans. I'll dish it out while you change." Emmy filled two bowls with the steaming soup. "How was work?"

"A typical day. I saw Stephen Butler. He said to say hi."

"Do you ever see Richard Demarco?" Emmy asked as she set the gumbo on the table.

"I haven't seen him since San Diego," Kristen hollered as she ran upstairs.

Later, on the way to church, Emmy apologized, "I'm sorry the gumbo sucked. I must have written the recipe down wrong."

"It's all right. You've had to eat plenty of my mistakes."

"I put in way too much salt. We can grab a burger or something on the way home," Emmy said as they passed Burger Bob's. "Do you think the guys missed me this summer?"

"No, I never heard them mention your name. I think they were glad you were gone," Kristen said with a straight face.

Emmy parked her GMC Envoy, and they hopped out. "Were you kidding about the guys not missing me?"

"You can be so gullible at times, Em."

Emmy grinned. "So they did miss me."

"Not really." Kristen held the door open. *Of course they missed you, you goof. You keep life from becoming dull and routine.*

As she and Kristen walked into the music suite, Emmy didn't know what to expect. *Maybe Kristen wasn't teasing. Maybe they just moved on and don't need me.*

"Emmy!" Skip Mason ran to her and almost knocked her over. "Boy, are we glad to see you. It's been a rough summer without you."

"Finally, we have a singer who sounds great." Steve Van Zant grinned as he looked at Chase Hillman.

Hank Lysenko didn't say anything, but walked over to Emmy and embraced her.

"I'm glad to be home. I missed you guys, too, but it was an interesting summer. I learned first-hand how difficult it is to be a rock star. It's not as easy as people might think."

"Are you gonna go on the road with the band again sometime?" Skip asked. "Are you gonna sing with them?"

"Probably yes to both questions, but I will be busy at North Park for the next year and a half." Emmy shook her head at Kristen. "So, they didn't miss me at all, huh?"

"I guess they missed you a teeny tiny bit." Kristen held her fingers very close together.

Emmy was happy to be back with her friends in the worship band. She couldn't wait until Sunday to see all her friends from church.

Sloane Beckett and Lindsey Cameron, both now teachers at Jamie McGee Junior High in SoHam, shared a two-bedroom apartment not too far from where John Randolph lived in the Reedswood neighborhood. On the Friday before school started, with only the teachers present, Lindsey met the teacher from the classroom across the hall.

"Hi, I'm Cam Frees, and my classroom is right there," he said as he pointed to his room.

"Hi, Cam, I'm Lindsey Cameron. You look familiar for some reason, but I can't quite place you."

"I think I've seen you before, too." Cam thought for a moment before asking, "Do you attend the United Nazarene church on Canton Lane in Crest Ridge?"

"Yes! That's it. That's where I've seen you."

"I just started attending there a few weeks ago. This is my second year at Jamie McGee—I teach seventh grade math, by the way. I went to Olivet Nazarene University my first year, but then I switched and finished at Ohio State. I wasn't real familiar with South Hampshire, but jobs back home were rather scarce."

"My roommate and best friend, Sloane Beckett, and I both graduated from Olivet just last year. In May of '02, I mean."

"I saw you with another teacher who looked familiar."

"That was Sloane. She is teaching here, too. Her room is on the second floor. She teaches eighth grade math. You mentioned Ohio State, why did you switch to that school?"

"I grew up in Sidney, Ohio, and my father went to Ohio State."

"Oh, my gosh!" Lindsey put a hand to her mouth. "I grew up in Troy."

"You're kidding. For real?"

"Yes, I've lived there all my life—until I went away to college. Sloane and I were roommates at Olivet. We've been friends since we were three years old. After we graduated, we were looking for teaching jobs, but all we could get was positions as subs here in South Hampshire. We moved here, found an apartment and worked part-time all last year. We were both hired this year, and we're working on master's degrees at North Park."

"I will have to make sure I look for you at church this Sunday," Cam said. *I like how you part your long hair on the side. It frames your face perfectly.*

"Yes, I would like that very much." Lindsey looked up at him. *You're pretty tall. You must be a few inches over six feet.* "Do you know Emmy Colasanti by any chance?"

"I don't really know her, but I've heard the name. Didn't she sing in the worship band?" Cam tried not to stare, but he was captivated by Lindsey's long, dark hair and her big brown eyes.

"Yes! She was gone for a couple of months, but she's back. Sloane and I were in her wedding. We were both bridesmaids."

"Her wedding? I've only seen pictures of her with the worship band, but I thought she was in high school. Is she really married, or are you joking?"

"She's really married."

"I never would have guessed she would be married."

"She got married in April. I'll introduce you to her this Sunday and her husband the next time he's in town. He travels a lot because of his job." Because Lindsey wanted to surprise Cam, she didn't mention Emmy's husband's name.

254

Emmy woke up early on Sunday morning and quickly got her clothes out for church. She went into Kristen's room, sat on the edge of the bed and touched her shoulder.

Kristen woke with a start. "Go away. I want to sleep."

"Krissy, it's time to get up. I want to get to church early."

"It can't be time to get up. I didn't hear the alarm go off."

"It hasn't gone off yet. It's only six forty-five."

"Can't I stay in bed until seven? We don't have to be there until eight."

"I want to get there early." Emmy pulled back the covers. "Please, will you indulge me this one time?"

"No!" Kristen pulled the sheet over her head. "Go away."

"Please?" Emmy asked sweetly.

Kristen lowered the sheet, turned onto her back and sighed. "All right, but you owe me."

"I'll shower first and that will give you five extra minutes."

"Take a longer shower. I need ten more minutes." Kristen rolled over and closed her eyes.

They arrived at church fifteen minutes early and headed to the music suite. Chase was already there.

"I didn't expect you this early," he said as he sorted the music charts.

"Emmy dragged me out of bed before the alarm went off." Kristen gravitated toward the table with the coffee pots. "Is there any coffee made?"

"It should be ready in a couple of minutes," Yvonne Hillman told Kristen as she hugged her and then Emmy. "I'm so happy you're home. Chase has been stressing out all summer because he had to lead the songs. He's spoiled having you here."

The rest of the worship team arrived one by one.

"All right, donuts!" Skip Mason grabbed his favorite. "Wow! You guys are here early." He was genuinely surprised to see Emmy and Kristen. He inhaled his first donut and then grabbed another.

They went over the songs for the service again. They were finished by nine-fifteen, and Emmy and Kristen headed to their young adult Sunday School class. They saw Lindsey and Sloane talking to a young man they didn't know.

Lindsey saw them, waved excitedly and brought the young man over to them, "Cam, this is Emmy and Kristen. They are both singers for the worship band. This is Cam Frees. He teaches across the hall from me."

Emmy didn't say much and tried to hide behind Kristen, but Kristen talked to Cam as if he were her oldest friend in the world.

"How are you, Cam? How do you like teaching at Jamie McGee?"

"I like it. It's my second year there."

"My cousin Tony Bertucci went there, but that was several years ago. I went to The Barclay Academy..." Kristen carried on.

Emmy glanced at Cam. *You remind me of Buddy Holly because of those glasses, and you're as tall as John Randolph.*

"I've seen you singing on the platform this summer," Cam told Kristen.

"I sing harmony and background parts. Have you been coming to our church very long?" Kristen asked. "I think I might have seen you, but I know we haven't been introduced."

"I started in July. Before that I was going to the Baptist church on Belmont Avenue down the street from my apartment. I like this church better. I already feel at home."

"I remember when I first started coming here. The people were so friendly. I had always thought people who went to church were dull and went around wearing frowns all the time. Now I know better." When Cam glanced away, Kristen nudged Emmy. "Say something."

"Like what?"

"You can be so frustrating." Kristen rolled her eyes.

Sloane quietly told Emmy, "I think Lindsey likes Cam. She's been talking to him on the phone a lot. Oh, he doesn't know who you're married to, and I think Lindsey wants to surprise him. She wants to introduce Cam to Kenny when he gets back."

Emmy smiled and said, "I won't say anything to spoil the surprise, but he might hear it from other people."

"You're probably right, but we'll see how it goes."

Emmy called Kenny later that Sunday as she lay in bed.

"My classes start tomorrow."

"I know, Em. I've got the twenty-fifth marked on my phone. Are you nervous? You won't get lost, will you?"

"No, I know my way around campus. I've taken classes there before," she said. "I am a little nervous, though."

"You'll do fine. The classes won't be any trouble for you. You're the smartest person I know."

"I think I'm more worried about the social aspect." She rolled over onto her back.

"Are you worried about the guys hitting on you? They will because you'll be the prettiest girl on campus."

"You're so sweet. I should let you take me on a date sometime."

"Would you let me take you to bed on our first date?" Kenny teased.

"That depends. Are you a handsome debonair heartbreaker, or are you a dorky rock star?"

"I'm definitely the former."

"Too bad! I only sleep with dorky rock stars," Emmy said and then giggled.

Emmy may have looked like a freshman to the other students, but few, if any, of them wore a wedding ring. She heard some of the guys in her classes talk about her.

"Do you think she wears that ring just so guys will think she's married?"

"She probably wears it so guys like us don't hit on her."

"She can't be married. She doesn't even look old enough to be going to college."

"She's here, dorkbrain, so she must be out of high school."

She remembered how guys gossiped about her in high school. *At least they're not assuming I'm like Diane. I doubt if anyone knows Diane. These guys are a little more mature.*

Although she still used her maiden name, word eventually got around campus that she was married to Kenny Colwell. She noticed some of the other students treated her differently. They didn't usually bother her, but did stare at her. She didn't realize it, but she was becoming a celebrity in her own right. The CD she and the worship team recorded was still on the *Billboard* charts, and many of the students had bought a copy. She began to notice more of the North Park students at Crest Ridge United Nazarene.

With Kenny still on tour, Kristen stayed at the house with Emmy. She still worked at Robertson Industries and kept Emmy up to date.

"Mr. Robertson is starting to turn more and more of the day-to-day operations over to Brady. He doesn't want to retire, but he is taking it easier," Kristen mentioned as they ate dinner in the TV room.

"I heard he does a lot of traveling now. I know he was in France just before the wedding. And I think he was with Mrs. Moneywell," Emmy said.

"I've met her a few times. She's so funny. She cracks me up at times." Kristen laughed.

"Do you think Mr. Robertson and Mrs. Moneywell will get married someday?"

"Who knows? They might, or they might just be friends."

"Oh, Kenny told me the live CD and DVD is going to be released on September second."

"Is that the stuff they recorded... like three years ago? I seem to recall you talking about it."

"Yeah. This will be the first official live recording released by Steward Music Group. Kenny said there have been bootlegs recordings, but they probably don't have the same production value."

"You're starting to sound like a veteran recording star yourself, Em," Kristen said as she grinned.

"Stop it!" Emmy kicked Kristen's foot. "I've never going to be a recording star like Kenny."

Chapter Twenty-Four

Though Tony and the Bears split their preseason games, he had high expectations for the season. His goal was to make it to the Super Bowl. The Bears opened the season on September seventh in San Francisco. The 49ers scored on their first three possessions, and the Bears got blown out by forty-two points. Tony sat in front of his locker after the game. He could not remember ever being involved in such a lopsided defeat.

The team traveled to Minnesota the following week and turned things around on offense though they still trailed by four points late in the fourth quarter. The defense stopped the Vikings and forced them to punt.

"Yes!" Emmy screamed. "Did you see the way Tony creamed that running back?" She bounced up and down on the couch next to Kristen.

"Settle down, Em. You are going to need a new couch if you break this one."

"I can't help it. I get more excited than the players." *And I wouldn't mind a new couch if I can find one on sale.*

The Bears had the ball on their own twenty-eight yard line with just under two minutes to play and one timeout left.

"Mama, you should watch. There's only two minutes left, and the Bears have the ball," Emmy hollered.

Mama stood in the kitchen doorway to answer. "I'll listen to you guys. I'll be able to tell if the Bears win by your reaction."

Quarterback Bobby McMullen led the offense down the field. They reached the nine yard line with thirteen seconds to go, but used their final timeout.

"Lymore, what are you doing? You've gotta get out of bounds." Emmy almost knocked Kristen off the couch as she yelled at the TV.

The Bears had time for maybe two plays. Bobby called the play in the huddle and added, "Make sure you listen for an audible. All right, break."

The team broke the huddle and took their positions. McMullen surveyed the defense and saw the two inside linebackers cheating up toward the line. He knew they were going to blitz, so he called an audible. Not everyone heard the audible and the result was a busted play. Bobby scrambled out of the pocket and threw the ball away to kill the clock. He kept his cool and got the team back in the huddle. It would come down to the last play of the game. McMullen called a pass with the primary target being the slot receiver on the left. The ball was snapped and Bobby looked right and then back to the left.

"No! Lookout!" Emmy screamed, as the right tackle lost contact with the defensive end.

His primary receiver was covered, but Bobby saw the tight end break open. He threw the ball up high just before he got smashed to the ground, hoping John Randolph could go up and get it. John made the catch and the Bears scored.

Emmy jumped off the couch. "He caught it! Did you see that, Krissy? John caught it with one hand." Emmy pulled Kristen off the couch, grabbed her hands and started dancing.

"I knew they would win," Kristen said calmly, though her heart was pounding. "That was cutting it close."

Emmy hollered so loud that Mama, who was still in the kitchen, ran into the TV room to see what happened.

"John caught a pass on the last play of the game and the Bears won! Isn't that great, Mama?" Emmy was so excited she high-fived Mama.

"Well, of course they won. They're the best team because they have Tony and John on their side," Mama said nonchalantly.

The Bears had a bye the third week of the NFL season. On Saturday Kristen found Emmy studying at the dining room table.

"It's the weekend. You need to take a break, Em. I invited the guys to come over."

"What are you guys gonna do, Krissy?"

"I'm not sure yet. I guess I'll play it by ear, and see what they want to do."

When John and Tony arrived, they didn't have any suggestions about what they wanted to do.

Kristen rolled her eyes and sighed. "You guys are no fun.

Come on. We have to do something. It's the weekend, and you guys don't have a game."

"Let's go rock climbing. There's a new thirty foot rock wall at the Sports Warehouse over by the mall. I would like to do that," Emmy suggested.

Kristen replied, "That sounds like fun. I wanna try it."

The guys looked at each other. They knew that even though they were professional athletes, climbing a thirty foot wall was beyond their talents.

Before they left the house, Kenny called Emmy. Although Kristen could only hear Emmy's side of the conversation, she knew they were talking about sex. Emmy looked at Kristen and smiled wickedly.

"Emmy Colasanti Colwell! You are so bad now. Is that all you can think about?" Kristen teased her as they both laughed.

"I can't help it if I miss Kenny. I haven't seen him for a month, and I'm getting rather... anxious... to see him."

Tony grabbed an apple from the fridge. "You're just horny."

Emmy smacked his arm and said, "You would be, too."

John shook his head. "It's a good thing Kenny is in as good as shape as a professional athlete, Emmy."

"If you would marry Kristen, then she could take advantage of her professional athlete, too," Emmy said. "That's my two cents worth of advice."

"Are you trying to tell me something, Emmy?" John asked.

Emmy smiled. "Let's just say I'm not the only one who feels horny."

"I'm going to smack you, Emmy." Kristen frowned as Emmy giggled.

They made their way to the Sports Warehouse. Emmy had been rock climbing before on a smaller wall.

"Come on, Kristen. Let's show these guys how easy it is."

"It's easy for you, Emmy, because you only weigh ninety pounds and have been a tomboy all your life," Tony said as John nodded in agreement.

"Well, hold the rope so we don't fall at least. Can you manage that, Mr. Professional Athlete?"

"What do you think, John? Should we let them get to the top and then let go?"

"Let's see if they make it that far." John kept a close eye on Kristen.

Emmy had no problem getting to the top. Kristen struggled, but eventually made it, too. They waved at the guys.

"We're coming down now."

Tony looked at John, "I suppose we should be on belay so they don't fall."

Emmy and Kristen made it down safely.

"Nice job, Kristen. I knew you could make it," Tony told Kristen and gave her a high-five.

"What about me?" Emmy asked.

"Oh, did you make it to the top, too, Emmy?"

She stuck her tongue out at Tony.

Tony responded, "You did a great job climbing, Emmy. I've never seen anyone climb so fast."

"Too late. If I was married to you, I think I might just give up sex for a few months."

Kristen snickered, "Fat chance of that happening, Em."

Emmy and Kristen spent more time climbing the wall. Then they ordered two pizzas and picked them up on the way home.

When they got back to Emmy's, Kristen told her, "Don't worry John and Tony won't stay too late. I know you really wish Kenny was home. You have to wait until Monday. What time do you think he will get here?"

"Can you blame me for missing him? He will be home in the morning, but I'll be at school."

"You could always skip classes for one day."

"I can't. It's difficult enough as it is. I can't afford to miss any classes and fall behind."

Kristen sighed as she looked at John. "I envy you, Emmy."

"I would still love you if you and John want to..."

"He sure wants to."

"What guy wouldn't? You are so beautiful."

Shortly after the pizzas were gone, John took Tony back to

262

his house. He stuck around for a while before going to his apartment. On the way to his empty apartment he thought about how enjoyable it would be to have Kristen with him.

Tony was able to be at church on Sunday morning for the first time in many weeks. Once football started in the summer, his Sundays were not free. He was running a few minutes late, but made it to the Sunday School class right at nine-thirty. He saw Sloane and smiled. He sat between Sloane and Lindsey. Cam sat to Lindsey's left. Directly across the round table were Emmy and Kristen.

Tony smiled at Kristen. "Morning, Kristen. It's good to see you here."

"I've been here every week unlike someone else."

When Tony looked at Emmy, she made a face and then giggled at him. Tony made a face back at her.

Kristen poked Emmy in the side and scolded her. "Will you ever grow up and learn to behave like an adult? We're in Sunday School now so act accordingly."

"All right, I was just saying hi to Tony," Emmy replied meekly.

After the class ended, Lindsey had a brief moment to talk to Emmy. "Cam still doesn't know Kenny is your husband."

"Really?"

"It helps that everyone still calls you Emmy Colasanti."

Emmy grinned and then said, "Kenny will be here next Sunday, so maybe we can actually pull this off. Gotta run. See you later." She and Kristen ran off to the music suite to get prepared for the worship service.

After the service, Tony invited his friends over to the house. "Mama is making fried chicken and tons of food. She told me to bring home as many friends as I wanted."

"Doesn't Mama realize you don't have any friends?" Emmy asked without cracking a smile.

"I consider Kristen and John to be my friends. Sloane, Lindsey and Cam are friends, too. I'm not sure about you, though."

"Can I please be your friend for just today? I'm hungry, and

263

I know Mama will want to see me." Emmy pretended to be pleading as she joked with Tony.

"Oh, I suppose you can be my friend, but just for today."

Emmy hugged Tony and whispered, "It was good to see you in church today even if I made a face at you. I know you can't be here during the season. Did you like the songs today?"

"Yes, I thought Kristen did a fantastic job," Tony said.

Kristen watched as Tony and Emmy teased each other. *I'm so thankful you guys are still good friends and that Tony and Sloane are getting along better and better.*

When they arrived at Tony's house, John was helping Mama in the kitchen by sampling the food. He had taken Mama to mass the night before.

"John, get away from the potatoes. If you keep tasting them, we won't have enough for lunch. Now scoot!" Mama waved him away.

John smiled and said, "Yes, Mama, I was just making sure everything was okay."

"You don't have to worry. I made extra for you and put it away already. You won't starve this week."

Tony offered grace, and the eight people at the table began eating. Emmy listened as everyone around the table talked as they ate. Mama noticed Emmy and Tony looking at each other and smiling instead of teasing each other the way they normally did. Afterward, Emmy helped Mama clear the table while the other kids headed downstairs.

"I can take care of this, dear. You can go downstairs and have fun."

"I will in a few minutes, Mama."

"Are you all right, sweetie? I noticed you were very quiet while we ate. I also saw you and Tony smiling at each other."

"I'm all right. I guess I was just thinking about how grateful I am that Tony doesn't hate me because I wouldn't marry him. If we weren't still friends, then I wouldn't be able to come over here and see you."

"Tony could never hate you. He loves you and now that you're married and he has found someone, you are able to love

264

each other as close friends."

"He treats me like his sister, and I realize that's the way God wanted our relationship to be. We tried to make it into something else, and it just didn't work. Now we get along so much better, and I think I love him more than I ever did before. It's just in a different way. Does that make any sense to you?"

"Yes, dear, it makes perfect sense. You run along and have some fun. I know you are excited that Kenny will be home tomorrow."

Emmy looked up at Mama and grinned. "I can't wait till classes are over tomorrow."

Emmy joined the others downstairs. She sat in a recliner and watched Tony and John play pool. Kristen kept close to John, and they talked between shots.

Emmy closed her eyes and let her imagination run free. *I think John will propose to Kristen soon, and I can even picture Tony and Sloane getting married.* She listened to Sloane, Lindsey and Cam talk about school as they at on the couch and watched the football game. *Cam and Lindsey act like they've been together forever. If Tony and John don't get their acts together, Cam and Lindsey might be engaged before anyone else.* Emmy's thoughts then turned to Kenny. *I can't wait to see you. We're going to make up for the last month.*

Somehow the subject of Kenny coming home didn't reach Cam's ears, so the secret was safe. Emmy looked around the room and realized that, except for Tony, she was the youngest one in the room, and the only one who was married. She closed her eyes and offered a quick prayer of thanks for her special friends.

Her reverie was interrupted by Tony. "Hey, Em, you wanna be on my team? Kristen wants to play."

Emmy shook her head. "You should have Sloane on your team. She's better than me."

Sloane stood up and said, "Yeah, I'll play," as she continued talking to Lindsey. "I have five kids in my second period I'd love to strangle."

"I know what you mean," Lindsey agreed. "I have a few students that need to be disciplined constantly."

Emmy glanced at Cam, bit her lip and turned her attention to the game.

Cam smiled. *You really are shy. Maybe it's because you're married.*

Emmy and Kristen were both up early Monday morning. Emmy had an eight o'clock class, and Kristen had to get to work.

"Oh, Krissy, I'm not sure how I will make it through the day," Emmy said as she ate a banana and drank a glass of apple juice.

"Just be patient." Kristen rolled her eyes while waiting on the toaster. "I won't be here after work, so you guys will have the house to yourselves."

Emmy took the time to write Kenny a note before she left and placed it on the kitchen table where he was certain to see it.

"Promise me you won't read it?" Emmy asked Kristen.

"I'm not going to read your love letter to Kenny. I'm sure it's all about how much you missed him and how you can't wait until you see him so you can have sex again."

Emmy bit her lip but then grinned. "I told him I have an hour between classes at noon, and if he wants to see me..."

"You are so bad, Em. Just where are you planning to meet him?"

"I thought we could go for a walk along the river or something," Emmy answered demurely.

"You do realize other people use the Riverwalk, too, right?"

"I know. I'm not going to attack him in public. I just want to kiss him and let him hold me in his arms. It will be so romantic."

"Oh, Em, you are so in love... and such a goof at times."

Kenny arrived home shortly after ten in the morning. He saw the note on the table and read it. He smiled as he looked at the clock. He had time to shower and make a quick stop at Darby's. He would surprise Emmy with lunch from her favorite restaurant.

"Hey, Mr. Darby, how's things goin'?"

"Hey, Kenny, when did you get back in town? How's married life treating you?"

266

"Great! Emmy was with me until she had to get back for school. She's going to North Park full-time so she can finish her degree."

"That's good. I want to thank you guys for inviting me to the wedding. Did I already tell you that?"

"We were honored you took the time to make it to the ceremony and the reception and thanks for the gift. I know we sent out thank you cards, but I just thought I would tell you in person."

"It was nothing. What can I get you today?"

"I'm going to meet Em for lunch, and I thought I would bring her something I know she loves."

"I know just what she likes. I'll wrap it in foil and put it in one of these new warming boxes."

"Could we have two pieces of chocolate cake, also?"

"Sure. You make sure you tell her to study hard, and I expect to see her sometime real soon."

"I'll pass that along."

Kenny took the food and managed to make it to the campus just as Emmy's class finished. He waited for her outside Lancashire Hall. She walked outside with some new friends, and they saw Kenny waiting with a bag from Darby's in his hand and a smile on his face. Emmy pretended to be shy as she walked over to him.

"Hello there, young lady, I was in the neighborhood, and I just happen to have an extra chili dog and fries with me. I was hoping to pick up a pretty college girl to share lunch with and maybe fool around a little. Would you be interested?"

"I love chili dogs from Darby's, but I can't fool around with you. I'm just an innocent girl, and I have a boyfriend in high school."

Kenny looked at the other girls, who recognized him right away, and teased them, "Would either of you pretty girls be interested in..."

Emmy dropped her backpack on the sidewalk and rushed to Kenny's arms.

"You better not try to pick up my friends."

Kenny held her in his arms as they kissed. They didn't pay any attention to the other students who were now watching them.

"Are you happy to see me, or is that..."

"Emmy! Behave. There are other people here," Kenny said.

She turned around and smiled at her friends. "I'm just happy to see my husband. He's been gone for a month."

"We understand, Emmy. See you tomorrow," one of her friends said and then they all giggled.

"I stopped at Darby's and picked up some lunch. We should eat it before it gets cold."

They walked to the Quad and found a spot to eat. Emmy was so excited to see Kenny that it took her thirty minutes to finish her chili dog and fries.

"You know if you eat first and then ask questions, your fries won't get cold."

"It's okay, What else do you have in the bag?"

"Two pieces of chocolate cake. Do you want to eat them now or save them for later? If we save them, we have time to go for a walk before your next class."

"Let's save them for later."

She and Kenny strolled arm in arm along the asphalt trail next to the river.

"Is there anything special you want for dinner tonight, Em?" he asked. "And don't say what I know you are thinking about."

"I'd like a salad, but that's all. I have two hours of reading to finish tonight, but then my night is free."

"I'll make sure you have a good nutritious salad for dinner, but I think I'll order a pizza for myself. I haven't had a pizza from Kerry Lynn's for so long."

"Will you share some of your pizza?" Emmy asked as she used her charming smile to persuade Kenny.

"I thought you just wanted to eat healthy food?"

"Pizza is good for you. It's got vegetables and a dairy product."

"I'll share the pizza, Em, if you promise not to read all night."

Emmy patted his hip. "Oooh! That sounds like you missed me as much as I missed you."

After classes were finished for the day, Emmy rushed home. She parked the Envoy in the driveway and sprinted up the steps to the back door. She ran into the kitchen and hollered, "I'm home! Where are you?" She scurried into the dining room as she yelled, "I want to rip off all our clothes and attack you." Emmy stopped in mid-sentence as she saw Pastor Ausland and Chase Hillman sitting on the couch and Kenny in his recliner. "Oh crap!" Emmy said slowly as she turned red.

"Em, we have company. Maybe you can rip my clothes off later."

"I'm sorry. I didn't know you were here, Pastor Herb."

"It's okay, Emmy. I understand your feelings, and we were just leaving. We stopped by to talk to Kenny about the possibility of doing a new recording at the church."

Everyone stood, and Kenny put his hands on Emmy's shoulders as she stood in front of him.

"I guess I was so excited to get home that I didn't pay any attention to the car parked out front. I was just kidding about what I said before."

Chase laughed. "I know you well enough to know you were deadly serious about that."

She looked at Pastor Ausland and then made a face at Chase. "Well, we haven't seen each other for over a month."

Even Pastor Ausland laughed as Emmy was obviously embarrassed.

"Please think about what we have discussed and spend time in prayer. If you feel it was something that God leads you to do, then let us know."

"I will, Pastor Herb."

"I apologize for staying so long. We will let you have your dinner now."

Pastor Ausland shook hands with Kenny and smiled at Emmy. Chase shook his hand and hugged Emmy.

Chase whispered in her ear, "We might have to come right back because Pastor Herb's Bible is on the couch. You might want to wait a few minutes before you... you know."

Emmy whispered back, "You are going to get it for

269

embarrassing me so much." She walked over to the couch and picked up the Bible. "Does this belong to you, Pastor Herb?"

"Oh, yes. Thank you, dear. I can't forget that."

Emmy handed the Bible to him and made a face at Chase. He smiled at her as he left.

"Will we see you on Wednesday?" Pastor Herb asked.

"We will try to be there," Kenny answered.

Pastor Herb walked down the steps and headed to the car. Kenny and Emmy were with Chase on the front porch.

Chase reminded Emmy, "Don't forget. We have practice Thursday evening, and we're learning three new songs. You need to be there."

"I'll be there if I'm not in bed," she teased as she grabbed Kenny's butt.

Chase laughed again and waved goodbye. Emmy and Kenny went back in the house.

"Why didn't you warn me? I couldn't have been more embarrassed."

"You would have been more embarrassed if you started taking off your clothes as soon as you walked in the house," Kenny said.

"I don't do that."

"I remember a couple times when you..."

"Hush! That was different. We've been married far too long for me to do that now."

"Should I wait to order the pizza, Em?" Kenny asked.

"That would be a good idea," Emmy answered as she began to unbutton his shirt.

With Kenny home from touring, he and Emmy began recording a new project. Originally planned to be the second Crest Ridge Worship Band CD, it soon became apparent to Kenny and Mr. Kesson that it would really be Emmy's first solo project. They would work on tracks as time allowed. Kenny was shooting for an early 2004 release.

Chapter Twenty-Five

Since meeting at the beginning of the school year, Lindsey Cameron and Cam Frees had started dating—exclusively. They looked for each other at church the Sunday after they met and had been inseparable ever since. After that first Sunday, Cam picked up Lindsey and Sloane for church since he lived close by.

In the Sunday School classroom Lindsey sat next to Emmy and quietly asked, "Is Kenny here today?"

"Yes, but he won't be in class. He's helping Chase and Bruce right now. They're having some technical issue in the sound booth." Emmy glanced at Cam as he talked to two of the other guys in the class.

"So, Cam won't see him until service starts, right?" Lindsey asked.

"Probably not unless you want to introduce them beforehand."

Lindsey made sure Cam couldn't hear. "I'll try to keep Cam away from the sanctuary until you guys start singing."

Emmy grinned as she asked, "Do you think Cam will recognize Kenny?"

"Definitely! He's a fan so he will know him."

"But he won't know we are married, unless you tell him. It's not like I'm gonna to announce it from the platform, or walk over and kiss him," Emmy said and then giggled.

"If he doesn't see you guys sitting together, then he won't see you together until after the service."

Emmy shook her head. "Kenny will probably run upstairs to the tech booth to see if he can help Bruce in case they have the same issue he had last Sunday."

"Good. Then we'll see you guys after the service," Lindsey said.

Cam did recognize Kenny as soon as he saw him on the platform.

"Lindsey, do you know who that is?" Cam asked excitedly.

"Yes, I know, so shush. We're in church now. Maybe you can meet him later."

"I didn't know he went to church here. I knew he was from..."

Lindsey poked him in the side to keep him quiet.

Kenny did go upstairs after the worship team finished. Emmy sat with Kristen. Tony and Sloane were right in front of them.

Emmy leaned forward and tapped Tony on his shoulder. "Could you move over, please? I can't see Pastor Herb through you."

"Maybe you should be in the kids' service until you grow up, little girl," Tony answered.

"Knock it off, Em. You and Tony can tease each other after the service. Right now you need to pay attention. Maybe you will learn something," Kristen scolded, but with a smile.

Emmy made a face at Kristen and whispered in Tony's ear, "It's so good to see you in church again today. I think all your games should be on Monday night." Emmy looked at Kristen, who was shaking her head. Emmy sat back in the chair and folded her arms across her chest as if she was upset with Kristen.

"Grow up," Kristen whispered. "Before I swat you."

After the service, Kenny spotted Emmy in the crowded foyer by the Coffee Club talking to Kristen, Sloane, Tony, Lindsey and Cam. Kenny walked up, stood behind Emmy and put his hands on her shoulders. He moved her hair and kissed her neck. When Cam saw this his eyes almost doubled in size.

Kenny knew they were trying to surprise Cam, so he played along. "Oh, I'm so sorry. I thought you were someone else. Please accept my apology, young lady."

Emmy turned to face him. "It's okay. I don't mind being kissed by a dorky rock star. If I wasn't married, I would go home with you."

Everyone laughed except Cam. He looked shocked.

After a few seconds, Lindsey spilled the secret. "Kenny, may I introduce Cam Frees. He's a teacher at Jamie McGee. Our classrooms are across the hall from each other. Cam, this is Kenny Colwell of Fridays At Five. He also happens to be Emmy's husband."

Kenny extended a hand and Cam shook it.

"It's a pleasure to meet you. I...I...I don't know what to say. I've been a fan for years."

Cam looked at Lindsey and then the other people. They were all grinning at him.

"What did you say about Emmy's husband?" Cam asked.

"Emmy is married to Kenny," Lindsey said.

"Get out! For real?"

Emmy pulled Kenny up close behind her and moved his arms around her waist. "So, it's really okay if I go home with him."

"You didn't have any idea, did you?" Lindsey asked as she took Cam's hand in hers.

"No, you just said Emmy's husband travels because of his job. You never mentioned his name or anything," he said. Then he looked at Emmy. "But your name is Colasanti. Not Colwell. Why?"

"Legally, I'm Emmy Colwell, but I use my maiden name for privacy."

Lindsey grinned at Cam. "We wanted to surprise you and somehow we managed to pull it off. Are you upset with me?"

"Not at all. I love you, and I would never be upset with you."

Both Cam and Lindsey realized he had said "I love you" for the first time. Lindsey responded, "I love you, too, Cam Frees." Cam took her in his arms, and, even though they were in church, he kissed her.

"Whoa! Did we just witness a first, Lins?" Sloane asked. "Was that the first time you have told each other that you love him, and her? You know what I mean."

"I guess it was," Cam answered.

"Wow! That was quick. You guys have only known each other for a month," Kristen said. *I knew you guys would fall in love. I should be a professional matchmaker.*

Lindsey and Cam looked at each other and then back at everyone else.

"It's like we've known each other forever."

"Then we need to go somewhere and celebrate," Sloane

273

said as she hugged her best friend.

Tony suggested, "Let's go to Darby's. I know there are other places closer, but I think it's worth the trip."

So, they ended up at Darby's. After they placed their order, which Kenny paid for in spite of their protests, Kenny showed Cam the photos on the wall.

"Is this Emmy? She looks like a child, almost. Please don't tell her I said that."

"Yes, that's Em. She was fourteen, but she looked even younger. She used to sing onstage with us back in the beginning."

"Have you known her a long time? Sorry for asking so many questions. I know you must get tired of fans bugging you."

"It usually doesn't bother me, and I don't get bothered that much here in SoHam. I've known Emmy since she was seven."

They heard laughter, and Kenny knew it was Emmy. He and Cam looked at Emmy and Tony. Emmy was laughing as Tony tickled her. Cam looked at Kenny.

"It's okay. They're close friends—almost like brother and sister. They treat each other like that a lot. I don't know if you are aware, but Tony and Kristen are cousins."

"I wasn't aware of that," Cam said.

Kenny tilted his head. "I hope it doesn't bother Sloane that Tony goofs around with Em so much."

"I don't think it does. She would have told Lindsey if it did." Cam chuckled as he watched Emmy and Tony. "Did you know Lindsey, Sloane and I grew up in Ohio just twenty miles from each other, but we never met until this year at Jamie McGee school?"

"I didn't know that. That's kinda funny." Kenny thought for a moment and then asked, "Have you ever heard of Defiance, Ohio? Tony's roommate, John Randolph, grew up there. I think it's in western Ohio somewhere."

"I have heard of it. It's farther north and maybe a hundred miles away. I think one of my father's friends is a teacher there. I'm pretty certain his name is Randolph."

Really?" Kenny looked at Cam and then hollered, "Em, will you bring Tony over here a second, please?"

274

Emmy pulled Tony by the hand over to where Kenny and Cam were standing.

"What is it? Am I in trouble for goofing around with my big teddy bear?" Emmy asked innocently.

"No, I need to ask Tony something. John is from Defiance, right?"

"Yeah."

"Isn't his father a teacher?"

"At the high school. Why?"

"Cam, Sloane and Lindsey are all from Ohio, and Cam thinks his father knew John's father."

"For real?"

"Maybe. Do you know John's father's name?"

"It's Jerry, and his mother's name is Evalyn, I think. Hey, Kristen, what's John's mom's name?"

"Come right over," Kristen said as she ended a call on her cell phone. She looked at Tony. "It's Evalyn, and his dad's name is Jerry. Why?"

"Come here, you guys." Tony waved at the girls.

"What's up? Oh, I like that picture. Is that you, Emmy?" Sloane asked.

"It's Emmy, but we need to figure something out. Cam's father might be friends with John's father."

Cam explained everything, and he decided to call his father to find out for sure. After a few minutes on the phone, it was confirmed. Cam's parents and John's parents knew each other and had for years. They went to school together, but hadn't been in close contact for a few years.

"What a small world!" Lindsey exclaimed. "Isn't it amazing how God has brought us all together in this place as good friends?"

It became even more amazing when John walked in a minute later.

"Kristen called me and said you were eating at Darby's, so I thought I would join you guys."

Kristen kissed John and told him, "You aren't going to believe this, but..."

275

Chapter Twenty-Six

Tony, John and the Bears played their home opener against the Green Bay Packers the next evening. Emmy and Kenny brought Diane and Craig to the game because they had never seen the Bears play before.

"How long are you going to be in town?" Emmy asked Diane.

"Craig's on vacation for a week. Why? Are you tired of us staying with you already?"

"Not yet," Emmy said. "I can't believe Mom and Dad volunteered to take care of Carson for the day."

"They don't get to see him that often. They want to spoil him while we're here."

Kristen used John's tickets and brought Sloane, Lindsey and Cam to the game. They had never been to a pro football game before, either.

"What do you guys think?" Emmy looked up at Cam.

"These are nice seats, and it's not as cold as I assumed it would be since we're right on the lake."

"You might have to cuddle with Lindsey," Emmy teased.

"I think I can handle that, Emmy." Cam smiled and put an arm around Lindsey's shoulders.

Emmy backed up against Kenny. "I'm gonna pretend to be freezing so Kenny will have to keep me warm."

Cam laughed. "That sounds like something you would do."

The Bears were leading in the third quarter by one point when Bobby McMullen, their starting quarterback, and Clinton Bishop, their top running back, suffered injuries on consecutive plays.

Emmy kicked the back of the empty seat in front of her. "This really sucks. It's gonna be up to the defense to win games now."

"They might not miss too many games," Kenny said as he tried to console her.

The Packers took advantage of the injuries, and the Bears subsequent inability to generate any offense. Back-up quarterback,

Dustin Terrell, was intercepted twice, and the Bears lost the game in the fourth quarter. Their record was now one win and two losses. Despite the loss, everyone enjoyed being at the game together.

Craig drove Diane and Carson back to Toledo on Wednesday afternoon after he argued with his father-in-law.

Emmy called Diane's cell phone and asked, "What happened?"

"Dad got after Carson for breaking a stupid old clock, and Craig yelled at Dad. Dad yelled back. Carson started crying. Mom yelled at them to stop yelling. I thought they were going to punch each other."

"I'll talk to Daddy."

"No need. It was Craig's fault. He used it as an excuse to leave. I'm so pissed at him. I'll talk to you later, Em."

"I'm glad I got to see you for a few days at least," Emmy said. *Craig can be such a jerk. Diane should leave him home the next time she visits.*

On Thursday evening the worship team met for practice. Chase had picked out several of Pastor Herb and Carolyn's favorite songs to do Sunday morning. He walked out of his office expecting to hear the usual chatter, but he entered a room filled with deafening silence. There was none of the normal banter. Chase looked at the sad faces. They ran through the first song, which they had sung several times before. At the end of the second verse, Chase waved his arms to stop everyone.

"This is a train wreck."

"Sorry, Chase, I thought we were going to the bridge," Steve Van Zant apologized.

"What key are we in? I thought it was supposed to be in A." John Patterson looked bewildered.

Emmy shuffled her music and half of it ended up on the floor. "Dammit!" she swore. "I mean shoot."

Everyone froze and didn't say a word for several seconds.

Chase finally spoke up. "Come on, everyone. I know this is a rather somber occasion. We are all going to miss Pastor Herb and

277

Carolyn. I've been working with him for ten years, and some of you have known them even longer."

"Chase is right," Hank said. "We want to be at our very best on Sunday. I would feel terrible if we didn't. Let's take a break and have a group prayer."

They held hands and prayed together for ten minutes. Then they went back to their instruments and mics.

Emmy spoke up, "Before we start I need to say something."

"Go ahead, Emmy." Chase suppressed a grin because he thought he knew what she wanted to say.

"I'm sorry I swore. I grew up in a family where swearing was just a part of our vocabulary. I know I shouldn't, but sometimes I use those words without even realizing it. If I get mad or upset, my mouth opens before my brain can filter it."

The guys chuckled. Most of them had heard her swear before.

"If you ever hear me swear, or use that one really bad word, please, just smack my butt."

"Emmy! No one is going to smack your butt." Kristen rolled her eyes. "Other than Kenny, I mean."

"Kristen! He doesn't do that." Emmy blushed as she looked at Kenny. "I guess I didn't mean that literally." Emmy looked around the room. "What I mean is you guys should call me out. Hold me accountable for what I say."

"I'm sure we have all slipped up and made mistakes. For some of us it might be something other than swearing." Chase grinned at Emmy. "None of us are perfect."

They started again and ran through the first song on the list.

"Yeah! This is more like it," Chase encouraged everyone.

This time everything fell into place.

After her last class on Friday, Emmy stopped at Best Buy and made an impulse purchase. She bought a digital camera, and gave it to Kenny when she got home.

"I bought this for your birthday. Do you like it?"

"I do. Was it like fifty percent off, and you couldn't pass it up?" he teased.

"No, it wasn't on sale at all."

"Really? That's not at all like you. You never buy anything unless it's on sale."

"I wanted to surprise you."

"I like it, but you do realize it's not even close to my birthday, right?"

"I know, but I didn't want you to have to wait until January," Emmy said.

He looked at her, and she started to grin. "You bought this because you wanted it, and now you're trying to pretend you bought it for me. I know how your devious mind operates, Em."

"You can use it, too. I want you to practice taking pictures and then take some of the house."

"Should I take pictures of you, Em?" Kenny asked.

"You can take a few pictures of me if you really want, but I'm not going to pose for them. I have housework to do."

Kenny spent the rest of the night learning how to use the camera by taking pictures of Emmy around the house.

"Will you stop it? You're starting to really bug me. I didn't buy you that camera to just take pictures of me."

"But I like taking pictures of you, sweetie. You are so pretty. I want to have lots of pictures to show everyone."

That night as they were getting into bed Kenny told her, "Thank you for the camera, Emmy. It's one of the nicest presents I ever got."

"I've got one more present for you, sweetie. I think you might like this one even more," Emmy said as she climbed on top of him.

On Saturday morning, Kenny used his new camera to take pictures of Emmy as she slept. He took pictures of her from many different angles, but when she woke up and realized what he was doing, she tried to hide. She turned over on her stomach and hid her face under a pillow.

"Stop it! My hair is a mess, and I look horrible."

"Emmy, I love the way you look in the morning. Turn over and let me see your pretty face."

279

"Pretty ugly face you mean. I don't have my makeup on."

"You don't wear makeup, Emmy." He poked her hip. "Turn over and let me take your picture, please."

After awhile she turned over and put a finger to her mouth. Kenny took some pictures of her as she started smiling at him.

"That didn't hurt now did it?"

Emmy stuck her tongue out at Kenny, but couldn't wait to see the pictures on the computer.

She showered and got dressed for the day. Kenny downloaded the images to the computer, and they looked at them together.

"I want to take more pictures."

"Go ahead, but I have work to do."

He spent a few more minutes taking pictures of her all over the house. He nearly ran her over as she picked up a laundry basket.

"Don't you have to listen to tracks at the studio or something today? You're really starting to get on my nerves."

"Not today. I don't have anything to do, or anywhere I have to be." He took another picture. "I can take pictures all day."

She dropped the plastic laundry basket and dirty towels tumbled out. "Just because you don't have to work this morning doesn't mean that I don't have things to do."

"Do you want me to help with anything?"

"Yes, could you take the laundry down to the basement, please? If we ever move, could we find a place where the washer and dryer aren't two floors below the bedrooms? That will really suck when I get older."

"I will build you a house with a washer and dryer on every floor if you want, Emmy." He grinned at her. *In fact I've been thinking about that very thing*

"I would settle for a house with the laundry facilities on the same floor as the bedrooms, but thanks, honey."

Chapter Twenty-Seven

Their alarm buzzed at six, and Kenny hit the snooze button for a few more minutes of sleep. He looked at Emmy and laughed. She was spread out over most of the large king-size bed leaving him only a foot or so on the very edge. She was almost sideways on the bed. Even after being married for six months, Emmy still amazed Kenny with her habit of wandering all over the bed as she slept. They both attributed it to her having to share a small bed with her sister during her entire childhood. He let her sleep a few more minutes as he got up and took his shower. He returned to the bed, sat on the edge and gently caressed her face.

"It's time to wake up, sleepyhead. We have to get ready for church. We need to be there early today."

Emmy stirred a bit but didn't wake up. Kenny finished getting dressed and tried again. This time he kissed her ear as he moved her hair away from her cheek.

"I will have to leave you at home if you don't wake up."

She swatted his hand away.

He kissed her once more and then used another trick to get her to wake up. He started rubbing her back and then slowly moved his hand lower. She began to stir. She opened her eyes and looked at him.

"What time is it? I didn't hear the alarm go off."

"It's six fifteen. You need to get out of bed. We have a big day ahead of us. Special music, the potluck dinner."

"I'm too tired to get up. I just want to stay in bed with you today." She closed her eyes again.

"Okay. I'll tell Pastor Herb you were too sleepy to come hear his last message. I'm sure he won't mind."

Emmy remembered today was Pastor Herb's final Sunday, and she got up on her hands and knees.

"Shoot! I almost forgot. You better get in the shower."

"I did already. The bathroom is all yours."

"I'm not looking forward to the service today. I think there are gonna be a lot of people who will be really sad."

"That's true. Even though I've only been going to the

church for a few months, I have learned to really appreciate Pastor Herb," Kenny said. "I heard someone say he's been the pastor for over twenty years."

She moved to the edge of the bed and dangled her feet over the side. "I would bet for a lot of the congregation he is the only pastor they have ever known."

"No doubt."

Emmy showered and dressed while Kenny made breakfast. He made blueberry muffins for Emmy because she liked them so much. When Emmy got out of the shower, she could smell the muffins and coffee. She got dressed quickly and headed downstairs.

"Good morning, sweetheart. What would you like for breakfast?"

"I can smell the muffins. Thank you for making them for me." She kissed his cheek and tried to grab one of the warm muffins.

He swatted her hand away. "The muffins are for you to take to church. I can make you eggs or pancakes. What would you like?"

"Bacon and eggs, I guess. I need more cholesterol in my system."

Kenny made breakfast for Emmy and even let her have one of the muffins.

"Do you think Tony is disappointed you guys aren't going to the game today?" Kenny asked as he added some hot sauce to his eggs.

"He understands. They're playing the Raiders, so they should win even with McMullen and Bishop hurt. Can I try some of that, please?"

"Don't pour too much on your eggs. It's pretty hot," Kenny said.

She tried a bite. "Ow!" She waved a hand in front of her face. "You're right. Why is it so hot? The stuff we usually buy isn't like that."

"This has habanero peppers in it."

"You should have warned me."

282

The children stayed in the sanctuary with their families today for this special service. The ushers added extra chairs to handle the expected crowd. Emmy was surprised when her in-laws arrived and even more surprised to see Mama Bertucci with them.

"I didn't know you would be here." She hugged them all, but then she and Kenny had to join the worship team in the music room. "I'll see you after the service. You are staying for the dinner, right?" Emmy asked Mrs. Colwell.

"Yes, dear, we are all staying."

"Thank you guys for coming today and bringing Mama. I know Tony was sorry he couldn't be here today, but he did have a chance to say goodbye on Wednesday."

"There are so many people here," Mama said. "It's not always this full, is it?"

"Close, but I see a lot of new faces," Emmy said as she glanced around the sanctuary.

The worship team began the service as though it was just a normal Sunday, but it soon became apparent it was not. Emmy looked out at the congregation and saw many sad faces. After the music, announcements and the offering, Dr. Ausland began his message with a prayer. Over the years, he developed a habit of walking around and mentioning people by name as he spoke. He amazed Mama with his ability to speak without any notes whatsoever. She wondered if he had memorized the entire Bible. Dr. Ausland had always been able to keep his emotions under control as he spoke—at least most of the time.

"Kenny, do you think Pastor Herb will make it through his message with getting emotional?"

"I would be shocked if he does, Em," Kenny answered.

They marveled at his ability to keep his emotions in check. He was nearly finished with his message when at last his composure broke. He stopped for a moment as the tears flowed down his face. The whole congregation shed tears as well. Grown men who would not normally show any signs of emotion wept openly. Pastor Herb finished his message with a prayer. Chase and the worship team returned to the platform to sing a special song for Pastor Herb and Carolyn.

After the song ended, George Whiteside walked slowly onto the platform using a cane as an aid. Mr. Whiteside was known for his jovial personality. He was an original member of the church, and he represented the church board this morning. Chase handed him a microphone.

"Pastor Herb, on behalf of the board and the entire congregation I would like to present you with this plaque." He stared at it for a moment. "I would read it, but my eyes are not working so good right now."

The congregation chuckled as many of them were aware of the cataracts which had rendered him almost blind. Chase came over and read the inscription which thanked the Auslands for their years of service and ended with one of Pastor Herb's favorite scriptures. Mr. Whiteside waited as Yvonne Hillman walked onto the platform with a bouquet of flowers.

"These are for you, Carolyn. We all know how much you love flowers."

"Thank you, Yvonne. They are lovely." Carolyn accepted the flowers from Yvonne and they hugged.

"You can continue now, Mr. Whiteside," Chase whispered.

"There is one more gift that we have for you but we couldn't bring it up here. I think if you look on the screens there might be a picture of it." Mr. Whiteside used the microphone to point to the screens.

The congregation watched as a picture of a brand new Honda Odyssey appeared on all the screens around the sanctuary. Pastor Herb put a hand to his mouth and his arm around his wife.

"I have some keys in my pocket somewhere. Oh, here they are." Mr. Whiteside pulled them out of his suit coat pocket. "We know your old car has over 200,000 miles on it, so we thought you might need a new vehicle. And this is a gas card for you to use. I've been told that it is for a thousand dollars. That should last a very long time. I don't know how much gas costs now because my wife won't let me drive anymore." He waited for the laughter to subside. "But I remember when it was nineteen-nine a gallon in my hometown. I hope you like the color. It's supposed to be silver, but I can't tell for sure." He squinted at one of the screens.

The congregation stood to their feet and applauded their beloved pastor and his wife for several minutes. Emmy stood next to Chase at the side of the platform.

Chase nudged her. "Should we tell him Kenny donated the van and gas card?"

"No! Kenny told me he didn't want anyone to know," Emmy said as she nudged him back. "How did you find out?"

"I figured it was either you and Kenny, or maybe Tony. So, I took a chance and guessed you guys."

"You stinker! You didn't know, and I just gave away the secret. You are devious sometimes, Chase."

"I'm sorry. Maybe you should pray for me," Chase said as he laughed.

"Please don't tell anyone, okay? Kenny doesn't want anyone to think he did this to get attention, or just as a tax write-off."

"I won't say anything, but I'm sure there are people who already know—other than the people on the board who probably all know. I'm sure they won't say anything."

"I hope they like it. Kenny's father has always driven Hondas because of their reliability," Emmy said.

"I'm sure they will love having a reliable vehicle."

A few minutes later, Kenny held Emmy's hand as they walked toward the large gym. "You sounded great today, Em."

"Thank you, Kenny. I thought for sure I would start bawling. Maybe I'm getting better at not showing my emotions."

Kenny lifted their hands, and Emmy grinned as several young kids dashed in between them.

One of the kids stopped and turned around. "Sorry, Miss Emmy. I know we're not supposed to run in church. I forget sometimes."

"Just be careful, Noah." Emmy grinned at him. Then she looked up at Kenny and bit her lip. "I kinda let it slip to Chase that you bought the new van. I'm sorry, but he promised not to tell anyone else."

"Did he trick you?"

"Yes. I told him I would pray for him."

"He tried that same ploy on Tony and me, but we didn't cave."

"I'm not as smart as you."

"You're smarter, but you're too trusting sometimes."

They stepped into the gym and Emmy gasped. "Look at how many people decided to stay for the potluck. It will take hours to go through the line. I'll starve to death."

"You could sneak over to the dessert table, Em."

"What would you like if I do?"

"See if Mrs. Haggerty made one of her homemade pies," Kenny said.

Emmy pointed to the line for the senior guests. "Hey! Your mom and dad are in line with Mama. How did they get in here so quick?"

Kristen walked up behind Emmy and Kenny. "I brought them in here right after the service. I knew there would be long lines."

"There's a table with more gifts." Kenny pointed. "Everyone must really love the Auslands."

"Ya think," Emmy said. "I'm going to grab some dessert. Krissy, would you find a place for us to sit, please?"

"I'll try, but it won't be easy. We may have to wait."

Emmy filled a plate with desserts and then sat by Chase, Yvonne and their daughters for a moment.

"Hey, Dad, look! Emmy's eating her dessert first," Jada said.

"Way to set a great example, Emmy." Chase tried to steal one of the brownies from Emmy's plate.

"Stop that!" She smacked his hand. "You're a real stinker for tricking me like that. Kenny told me how you asked him and Tony."

"It wasn't that difficult to guess, Emmy. There are only a handful of people in the church with the resources to purchase a minivan on short notice. For most people it would take a lifetime of saving to be able to buy a new Odyssey, but for Kenny it's kinda like buying the weekly groceries."

"I suppose, but you'd never know it from the way he lives.

He is just as... just as..." Emmy waved a hand in the air.

"Cheap? Tight-fisted? Parsimonious? Penurious?" Chase teased. "Oh, wait. Those are your characteristics."

Emmy poked him in the arm. "You are so funny. I was thinking of frugal."

Yvonne laughed and said, "You are both very prudent about your earnings."

"I had to learn how to make due with little in the way of material possessions," Emmy said as she grinned at Jada and Anna. "I'll talk to you guys later. I need to find Kenny, so we can eat. I'll get back in line and fill a plate with vegetables and other healthy food."

"Yeah, right," Chase said.

Jada and Anna giggled.

She located Kenny and his parents, but didn't see Kristen or Mama. She told him about her conversation with Chase and Yvonne.

Kenny smiled. *I'm not supposed to tell you, Em, but there is one more gift that would really surprise you and Chase and even the church board. Mr. Robertson paid off the mortgage on the new home the Auslands recently purchased.*

"Why are you grinning at me?" Emmy asked.

"No particular reason other than I love to look at you."

"You've got something up your sleeve. I know that look."

Chapter Twenty-Eight

The trip to New Orleans the next weekend left a bitter taste in the Chicago Bears' mouths. They lost a close game that could have easily gone their way. Three turnovers and a few costly mental mistakes changed the outcome of a close game.

Tony sat next to John on the flight home. "That's three losses in a row. We should have won this game and last week against the Raiders. We can't keep beating ourselves with stupid mistakes."

John shrugged. "I'm not making excuses for the way the offense played today, but we are missing two key players."

"Everyone has to step up. We are supposed to be professionals. This is our job, and injuries are a part of it." Tony smacked the arm of his seat. "We have to stop accepting excuses. We need results."

Nothing improved over the next two weeks. They lost at Seattle in a game that was not as close as the final score indicated. Then the Detroit Lions came to Chicago. Even without their starting quarterback and best running back, the Bears had hoped they could beat the lowly Lions. The Lions did not see it that way. They came to Chicago expecting to win and they did—easily. Emmy, Kenny, Kristen and Sloane were at the game with Barry Newton and his neighbor, Seth Lewis.

After the game, Barry stuck his hands in his pockets as he shuffled along through the parking lot beside Emmy, "Maybe I shouldn't come to any more games. Every time I do, the Bears lose. I'm starting to think I'm a jinx."

"I'm beginning to think the same thing, Barry," Emmy teased as the wind jostled her and she bumped into him. "You've been to what? Three games, and they've lost them all. Coincidence? I think not. You must be a jinx. It's the Barry Newton curse just like in grade school."

"What did I do in grade school, Em?" Barry asked.

"You substituted for the basketball team manager, and we lost three games in a row."

"How on earth can you remember that?" Barry bumped into Emmy and put an arm around her shoulder.

"Not sure, but I do," Emmy answered.

"I've got an idea," Kristen said. "Maybe we should bring Linda to a game instead of you, Barry. How about that?"

"You know she won't come to a game. She didn't like to watch football in high school because of the violence. She would never be able to watch the pros play."

Tony and John barely spoke as they made their way back to SoHam after the game. Kristen, Sloane, Emmy and Kenny waited with Mama Bertucci for the guys to return. Emmy and Kenny agreed to stay until the guys returned despite being anxious to get home because he was leaving in the morning.

"What should we say to them?" Kristen asked. "I'm sure they are going to be upset and disappointed. Just a few key plays made all the difference in the game."

Emmy thought for a moment. "Maybe we can blame it on Barry. Yeah! Let's tell the guys it was our fault because we brought Barry to the game. We can make a big deal about the so-called Barry Newton curse and that might brighten their mood."

"It might," Sloane said. "Or else they might get more upset because we are making fun of their careers."

"I can think of another way to take their mind off football," Kristen suggested.

Emmy looked at Kristen and sensed Kristen was looking for approval. "Krissy, are you suggesting what I think you are?"

"I know it is supposed to be wrong, but sometimes I have a difficult time resisting the temptation."

"I guess I can understand. I don't think it would be the end of the world, but if you give in this time, you might think it's all right to do it again and then again."

"Okay, Em, I see what you're trying to say."

"I think it is in Matthew twenty-six where Jesus said something about watching and praying so you will not fall into temptation because the spirit is willing, but the flesh is weak..."

"Oh, Emmy, I know this flesh is certainly weak. Especially when he starts kissing me."

"Believe me. I know what that's like."

"What? Have you been kissing John, too?" Kristen asked. "You aren't supposed to kiss him."

Emmy blushed. "No, I meant Kenny. I've never kissed John."

Sloane and Mama laughed at Emmy's embarrassment.

"You guys are creeps!" Emmy stuck out her tongue and put her arms over her chest.

When the guys pulled in the driveway, Emmy and Kristen ran outside to greet them.

"We're sorry, guys. It's all our fault," Emmy shouted as she waved her hands around frantically. "Linda won't go to the games. Please don't hate us for causing you to lose the game."

"She's right, John. I'm sorry. Will you forgive us?" Kristen looked up at him.

"What are you talking about, Emmy? What's all your fault? Did something happen? Did you have an accident? Are you okay?" Tony was concerned about Emmy and Kristen. "Where's Sloane? Is she all right?"

Emmy spoke even faster than normal. "Nothing like that. Sloane's inside. It's our fault you guys lost the game."

"Sorry, but you've lost me." Tony shrugged. "Slow down and tell us what happened, Em."

John put an arm around Kristen and then kissed her.

"We took Barry Newton to the game with us. We're sorry. We forgot about the curse."

Tony tilted his head. "What on earth are you babbling about, Em? Kristen, do you know what she means?"

Kristen looked at the guys and told the story with a straight face. "Every time Barry Newton is at the game, you guys lose. He has been to three games. Each game was against a weaker team that you should have beaten easily. In each game there was a strange play that turned the momentum against you. Like today in the first quarter. There was that play when one of the guys blocked the pass at the line of scrimmage and one their linemen caught it. He was running, and he fumbled it into the air and Aron Pelfrey tipped it and another Lion grabbed it and ran it in for the score. Do

290

you remember that play?"

"Yeah, how could I forget that play?" John said.

"That turned the whole game around," Tony added.

Emmy explained, "Last year against the Vikings, Barry was there and there was that play."

Tony looked at John. They both remembered the play in question. Tony looked at Emmy and Kristen, shook his head and pretended to be angry. "You mean to tell me you intentionally took Barry Newton to the game so we would lose? How can you call yourself a Bear fan? Wait till I see him. I'm going to make sure he starts going to all the Packer games so they will lose. I am so disappointed in you, Emmy."

Emmy and Kristen were glad to see that the guys still had a sense of humor. They went inside, sat in the living room and talked for close to an hour.

"I need to head home. I have school in the morning," Sloane said.

"I should get going, too," John said as he looked at Mama.

"Hang on a second, John." Mama got up and headed for the kitchen. "I have a care package for you. I made some of your favorites. Lasagna, country-style rigatoni, some mostaccioli."

John grinned and followed her.

"Mama, you are spoiling him," Kristen hollered. "He needs to learn to eat my cooking if he wants to marry me."

"No! Not that," Tony said as he grinned. "You will poison him, and the team needs him."

"I'll poison you first." Kristen poked him in the chest. "The defense hasn't been performing up to par either."

John got ready to take Kristen home and as they were leaving, she looked at Emmy and whispered, "Please don't be mad at me, Em."

Kenny and Emmy headed home. Emmy was worried about Kristen because of what she said. She prayed for her as they headed home. She didn't say anything to Kenny about what she thought Kristen might be doing. When they got home, Kenny went in the house first. Emmy stayed outside for a moment before walking in the back door and into the kitchen. She looked around and saw flowers and potted plants everywhere.

"Where did all these come from? Why on earth did you buy me all these flowers?"

"Kristen came up with the idea. She wanted you to have something to remind you of our last night together for a while. You are supposed to plant a different plant, or bush, every day until I get back, or until they die, I guess, or you run out."

Emmy started to cry. "She said something about not getting mad at her, and I thought she meant she was going to stay over at John's apartment and... you know."

Kenny understood. "I don't think she's going to do that, Em. I think she meant not to be mad at her for the mess in the kitchen."

"When did you guys have time to do this?" Emmy sniffed one of the plants. "This smells good. What is it?"

"Her parents came over after we left," Kenny said. "There should be a plastic thing that tells you the name of the plant and how to take care of it."

"Oh, I see. It's a lavender plant. I have to call her and apologize."

"You should," Kenny suggested while sniffing one of the other plants. He shuddered. "Plant this thing far away from the house. It stinks."

Emmy called Kristen. "I'm sorry about my lack of faith in you. I assumed you were going to be sleeping with John."

"I forgive you, Em. I'll come over after work tomorrow and help you clean up the kitchen."

Emmy and Kenny didn't fall asleep until after midnight. They had done all they could to prepare her for his two-month-long absence.

They were up early the next morning and ate breakfast.

Emmy grabbed her backpack, keys and kissed Kenny. "I'm sorry I have to get to class before the limo arrives."

"That's okay, sweetie. At least Andy chartered a jet to fly us out to Boston. If he hadn't, we might not have been together last night." Kenny grinned.

She giggled and said, "I'll send him a thank-you note."

Chapter Twenty-Nine

"Hi, Lynette. What's up?" Emmy answered her landline and tossed her backpack on the kitchen table. "I just got in the door."

"Should I call back later?"

"No need." Emmy opened the fridge, grabbed a bottle of water, walked into the TV room and plopped down on the couch.

"Have you heard the news?"

"What news?" Emmy took a sip of water and kicked off her sneakers.

"A few weeks ago the board voted to hire Dave Behren as the new senior pastor. Did you know that already?"

"Not really. Is that the same guy Kenny knows from California?"

"Yes, and he and his wife Cathy bought a house already. They found an older home about a mile from the church. He is going to preach this Sunday."

"Do you guys know him?" Emmy lay on her back and put her feet on top of the back of the couch.

"We met him about ten years ago. He spoke one weekend for some special services. They've been here a couple of other times. He preached the week Pastor Herb took a vacation. You were still on tour with Kenny."

"Doesn't the church get to vote on whether they want him or not?"

"They already voted, Em."

"I didn't."

"You need to be an official member to vote. You guys should take care of that."

"Did anyone vote against him?"

"I'm not supposed to know, but eight people voted no."

"Probably Mrs. Thompkins and her clique. She's so negative about everything," Emmy said and then giggled.

She talked to Lynette for a few more minutes.

"Talk to you later, Em. I have to fix dinner."

Emmy called Yvonne Hillman. "I just heard something, and I want to know if it's true."

"What did you hear, Emmy? Not gossip, I hope."

"Does the whole staff have to resign because Pastor Herb did?" Emmy asked in an agitated manner.

"That's customary."

"That sucks! I don't want you guys to leave," Emmy said as her voice cracked.

"Oh, sweetie, we're not leaving. Dr. Behren interviewed everyone and asked us all to stay."

"So, you guys aren't going anywhere?"

"No. We will be there on Wednesday and on Thursday for practice."

"And on Sunday and the Sunday after that?"

"Yes, Emmy."

"Good!" Emmy paused and then added, "Will you do me a favor and not tell Chase? I don't want him to know I would have missed him."

Yvonne laughed and said, "It will be our secret, Emmy."

Dr. Behren stopped by the music room to listen to the worship team practice. He heard the team a few weeks ago and was very impressed by their talent and spirit, but this was the first time he had heard Emmy in person. The team took a break and Chase introduced everyone again. Pastor Dave shook everyone's hand. Emmy greeted him last.

"Hi, Dr. Behren. I'm Emmy," she said quietly.

He chuckled and said, "The people in my last church called me Pastor Dave, not Dr. Behren, so please, feel free to call me Pastor Dave."

"All right, Pastor Dave."

He glanced around the room. "It will take Cathy and me a little while to learn everyone's name, so please be patient."

Emmy stood beside Kristen and listened for a moment as she checked out Pastor Dave. *I like your goatee even if it is mostly gray, and your gray hair kinda makes you look more distinguished.* Then Emmy boldly asked, "How old are you, Pastor Dave?"

"Geez! Emmy! How can you ask such a question?" Kristen poked Emmy in the side. "Please forgive her, Pastor Dave.

Sometimes she doesn't think before she opens her mouth."

"It's quite all right. I am forty-seven, and my birthday is on July twenty-fourth. Are you going to buy me a present? If you are, I would like a new motorcycle helmet."

"I'll buy you a purple helmet," Emmy said and then giggled. "My birthday is on July eighth, and I'll be twenty-four."

"Yeah, and you act and sound like you're fourteen," Kristen said and Chase and Pastor Dave doubled up with laughter.

Emmy stuck out her tongue at Kristen as if to prove her point.

Chase pointed out something about Emmy to Pastor Dave. "You may find this difficult to believe, I know I do, but Emmy is actually married. She usually acts like a teenager—a young, immature teenager, I might add—but she is married to Kenny Colwell."

Dave looked at Emmy and then grinned as he turned to Chase. "I don't believe that for a second. I know fourteen-year-old girls are not allowed to marry in this state." He turned back to Emmy and she held up her hand to show him her ring.

"I'm not really fourteen," Emmy told him as she giggled, "but I will be in a couple months."

Pastor Dave again nearly doubled over as he laughed so hard. Emmy poked Chase in the ribs for teasing her.

When Pastor Dave stopped laughing, he told Emmy, "I know Kenny. He came to our church a few times with Becky Morrison and, I guess it's been over two years ago now, one morning he re-dedicated his life to Christ. I remember that day very well. Will he be home soon?"

"He won't be back until the twenty-second of December." Emmy lowered her face and bit her lip.

Kristen added, "Pastor Dave, Emmy is still a newlywed, and, when Kenny is gone, she gets really..."

Emmy's eyes opened wide. "Kristen Lynn Keasling, don't you dare mention anything about me getting horny."

"I wasn't, Em, I was going to say you get very quiet and shy, even more than normal."

"Oh crap!" Emmy put a hand to her mouth. "Oops! Sorry

for swearing, Pastor Dave." She poked Kristen in the side and said, "I thought you were going to embarrass me."

"No need, Em," Chase said. "You do a good enough job of that without our help."

Pastor Dave laughed and gave Emmy a hug," You don't need to apologize for being who God made you. I've heard much worse swearing in my life."

"You'll probably hear it again from Emmy. She's been known to use some colorful language at times."

Emmy frowned at him. "Thanks a lot, Chase."

"I won't hold it against her," Pastor Dave said.

Emmy quickly realized she was going to love her new pastor just as much as she did Pastor Herb.

The ladies of the hospitality committee organized a potluck dinner to celebrate Pastor Dave's first Sunday service as senior pastor. This allowed the congregation a chance to talk to Dave and Cathy and get to know them a little better in a casual setting. It was a big change for the church. For many of them, Dr. Ausland had been their only pastor. Dave and Cathy settled in, and it didn't take them long to learn most everyone's name.

On Monday, Dr. Behren was given a full tour of all the facilities by Reed Shafer, the manager of the building and grounds maintenance team.

"We have identified several concerns and prioritized them. For instance, the carpeting in this classroom is going to be replaced next week." Reed pointed to the old carpeting.

"I can see a few water stains. Is there an issue with the roof?"

"This part of the building has a flat roof. We had it replaced three months ago, and there hasn't been a recurrence of the leaking."

They continued the tour.

"Are you here forty hours a week?" Dr. Behren asked as he noticed a few opportunities.

"I'm usually here more than forty hours. I can email you a

copy of the plans we have for the upcoming year. We also have a master plan for the next five and ten years. The financial committee has a fund raising plan."

"I'd love to see that. I might have asked before, but how old is this sanctuary?" Dr. Behren glanced up at the lights as he and Reed stood at the back.

"The sanctuary is thirty years old, and the educational unit was completed two years later. No, I take that back. I think it was three years later."

"I would not have thought it to be that old. It looks amazing."

"We have been fortunate in the faithful giving of our people. That has allowed us to keep up with the maintenance over the years." Reed pointed out a number of improvements. "We painted the walls two years ago, and replaced the carpeting five years ago."

Dr. Behren took a seat and stretched his arms along the top of the two chairs next to him. "I like the fact we are using chairs instead of wooden pews."

Reed grinned. "That was a wise decision made at the very beginning. I'm rather proud of the fact my father was a member of the building committee way back then. They didn't necessarily do things just because the church had always done things a certain way. Does that make any sense?"

"It does. Where is your father now?"

"In heaven. He passed away before the building was finished."

"I'm sorry to hear that. I'm sure he would have felt quite a sense of accomplishment. This is a beautiful facility."

Dr. Behren had a background in economics and was also very handy with a hammer. He and Cathy had purchased their home knowing they would do some updating. There was one other very special reason for Dave and Cathy to move to South Hampshire. Actually, six reasons. Grandchildren! Their two daughters and their families lived about forty miles away in the town of Herscher Park. Both of his sons-in-law worked for Olivet Nazarene University.

Chapter Thirty

Bobby McMullen and Clinton Bishop recovered from their injuries in time for the game at home against the San Diego Chargers. Their return had an immediate impact on the team. On the third play of the game, Bobby threw a a short pass in the flat to the right.

"Come on, Bishop!" Emmy yelled as she jumped to her feet. "Krissy, look! He's gonna score."

"I can't see because of the guy in front of me."

Bishop broke one tackle and made a move to make the second defender miss before racing the final seventy yards untouched into the end zone.

"John took out the safety with a cool block," Emmy said.

"I missed it," Kristen complained.

"I knew getting those guys back would make a big difference."

"You are so smart, Em. You should be the offensive coordinator."

"Ha! Ha! You're a real riot."

The offense scored a touchdown on each of its first four possessions. The defense stymied the Chargers passing attack all day long by putting pressure on quarterback Darren Bretz. They sacked him four times and knocked down three passes at the line of scrimmage.

The Bears made up for the loss at home to the Lions by stomping them the next week in Detroit. The Bears won by twenty-eight points and totally outplayed the Lions in every phase of the game. They upset the St. Louis Rams at home on a late pass interception. Emmy and Kristen were in the stands with Fernando Ramos and Ethan Hanks when Tony picked off a pass and ran it back fifty-three yards for the winning score. Emmy high-fived both guys as she went totally nuts when Tony scored. She whistled as she jumped up and down. Kristen was more sedate in her celebration. She smiled.

"I think we will bring you guys to all the games," Emmy

told the the guys on the way home. "You must be good luck charms or something."

"We've been to two games, and the Bears have won both of them so I guess it must be true," Fernando said.

Ethan added, "I came to a game ten years ago and they lost."

"That doesn't count because Tony and John weren't on the team," Emmy said.

The Bears traveled to Denver for the next game. Emmy and Kristen watched in the TV room.

"The weather is really gonna favor the Broncos," Emmy said as she stared at the TV. "It's like a blizzard, and the wind makes it almost impossible to get a passing game going."

"How can you even tell who has the ball? I can't see a thing. Are you sure you turned on the TV, Em?" Kristen asked.

"I think so. Maybe we should call the power company," Emmy teased. "Maybe they can stop the blizzard."

"I'm going home." Kristen tried to get up, but Emmy wrapped her arms around Kristen's waist and held onto her.

"I won't tease you anymore." Emmy tackled Kristen and ended up on top of her.

"Let go of me! I'm not playing football with you. We are just watching the game." Kristen squirmed out from under Emmy and rubbed her side. "Just because Kenny isn't here, does not mean you can goof around with me."

"I don't want you to go home. I didn't mean to tackle you so hard."

"It's all right. I don't think you broke my ribs."

The Bears defense shut down the Broncos offense for most of the game. Neither team could generate many points, but the Bear's offense did manage to score one touchdown. That along with four field goals by Brad Ellington allowed the Bears to escape with a 19-10 win.

"Did you see how far Tony slid on that one play?" Emmy asked and then giggled. "I bet the guys loved playing in the snow."

"They're grown men, Em," Kristen said.

299

Emmy thought about her second date with Tony. He took her to Windsor Park and they played for hours in the snow. She put a finger to her mouth as she remembered kissing him.

"It's still fun to play in the snow, Krissy," she said.

Despite all the momentum and confidence generated by their four game winning streak, the Bears lost on the last Sunday in November at home to the Arizona Cardinals. It rained heavily the entire game and the playing conditions were miserable. The footing for the players was treacherous at the start and continued to worsen throughout the game. They should have won, but four costly turnovers in the second half allowed the Cardinals to escape with the victory. The Bears record slipped to five wins and seven losses ending any realistic hope they had for making the playoffs.

When Tony and John got back to SoHam after the game, Tony called Emmy. "Did you guys take Barry Newton to the game?"

"We're sorry, Tony. We were going to bring Paul and Lynette, but the girls were sick so they had to cancel. It's a good thing they did or else they would have gotten sick, too. It was miserable in the stands. I think I caught pneumonia." She coughed several times to prove her point.

"That sounded fake. You could have stayed home, Em," he mentioned as he tossed a football from hand to hand.

"Why? You guys had to play in the rain. We're not fair-weather fans."

"We would have understood if you stayed home," Tony said. "I could see empty seats all around the place."

"We called around but couldn't find anyone who could go on such short notice. Probably because they were smarter than us and didn't want to sit in the rain all day. We took Barry and his friend Seth again. Neither one of them has a lick of sense."

"I'll tell Barry you said that when I see him again."

"We're really sorry. We didn't really believe Barry was cursed, but I guess it's true. We'll never take him to another game, honest. Will you forgive us?"

"I suppose so, but just to be sure, maybe you shouldn't

300

bring Barry or Seth to any more games this year."

Tony looked at John after hanging up the phone. "Did you hear who the girls brought to the game?"

John said, "I knew it wasn't our fault. How else could you explain losing four fumbles on our end of the field?"

"I'm sure the wet ball had nothing to do with the fumbles. It was Barry's fault entirely." Tony dropped the football. "We aren't mathematically eliminated yet. Granted, other teams will have to lose key games for us to make the playoffs."

"It could happen," John said as he picked up the football, and Tony smacked it out of his hands.

Though the odds were against them, Tony and John didn't give up hope.

The next week they played the Packers in Green Bay. The Packers led the division, but the Bears played an almost perfect game and left town with a three point victory. This gave them momentum for their next two games at Soldier Field. They beat the Minnesota Vikings in a close game and then soundly defeated the Washington Redskins to move their record to 8-7. They still had a chance to make the playoffs. The final regular season game was against the Kansas City Chiefs in Kansas City—three days after Christmas.

Chapter Thirty-One

Dr. Behren started making changes in the morning service his second Sunday, and Emmy heard several older people make comments.

"Can you believe it? He stood in one spot the whole time."

"I noticed," one older lady said. "Pastor Herb would often start on the platform, but then he would speak from the floor of the sanctuary. I like that better."

There was one other difference between the two men.

"He actually uses notes as he preaches," another person said. "I saw him turning the pages."

"I know. You'd think by now he would be able to memorize a simple sermon."

"He had to look at his Bible as he quoted scripture. Pastor Herb never had to do that," Lois Hobbs added as she leaned on her cane.

Emmy smiled as she listened to the comments.

"Is he going to make us sing hymns every week? I sure hope not. Hymns are too old-fashioned. None of the kids like them." Emmy overheard one teenager complain to another.

"Oh, God! I sure hope not. We will have to talk to Emmy if he does. We'll lose all of the new teens who come strictly for the music."

Emmy heard one middle-age woman complain to her friend, "I've been attending this church for twenty-five years, and he thanked me for coming. Can you believe the nerve? He even called me Mrs. Thompkins."

Her friend reminded her, "That *is* your name, you know."

"Well, yes, but that doesn't mean... oh, never mind. I guess we will have to learn to make allowances for him."

"Cut him some slack. I bet you were one of the members who voted against him."

Mrs. Thompkins replied indignantly, "I thought we needed an older man. I bet he's not even fifty. We need a senior pastor with more experience. That's all I meant."

"You're really something," her friend said.

Emmy walked along behind them and eavesdropped.

"I even heard from one of the board members that his wife doesn't know how to play the piano. That certainly wouldn't have happened before Pastor Herb arrived." Mrs. Thompkins shook her head vehemently.

"In case you haven't noticed, the pastor's wife hasn't played the piano for the morning service for the last twenty years."

"I believe she should still know how in case she has to play because no one else is around," Mrs. Thompkins said.

"There are probably a dozen people I can think of just off the top of my head who can play the piano."

"Well, I'm just saying that when I was a teenager the pastor's wife always played the piano." Mrs. Thompkins stopped suddenly and Emmy nearly ran into her.

"Excuse me," Emmy apologized. "I didn't know you were going to stop so abruptly."

"Please watch where you're going, child." Mrs. Thompkins frowned. "I might have fallen and broken my hip."

The friend laughed. "That was a hundred years ago, and there were twenty people in the little church you attended."

Emmy covered her mouth trying to stifle her laughter, but she couldn't. She turned and walked quickly in the opposite direction. *Mrs. Thompkins is exactly the kind of lady Kristen thought would go to church. She is always complaining about something.*

Pastor Dave and Cathy talked to as many people as they could after the service. He tried to call as many as he could by name. This Sunday Emmy hung around even though it meant she would miss part of the game. She waited patiently for a chance to talk to him.

"I thought that was a very good message, Pastor Dave," she said as they shook hands. *And it doesn't matter to me if you refer to your notes.*

"Thank you, Emmy. I thought you sounded very good today, too."

"I hope it doesn't bother you that I sometimes get excited and dance around a little. I grew up listening to rock music, and

303

I've always loved to dance."

Cathy Behren listened quietly as she observed. *You really don't look your age.*

Pastor Dave shook his head. "It certainly doesn't bother me, and I think even the older crowd loves to watch you. I hope you didn't mind that I asked Chase to include an older hymn once in a while. It doesn't have to be every Sunday, but just once in a while. I need to please the older crowd."

Emmy grinned and confessed, "I didn't know 'Victory In Jesus' was an old song. I didn't grow up in the church, so a lot of those *old songs* are new to me."

"I enjoyed the arrangement the band used. It made an old song sound new and fresh," Cathy commented. "Would you excuse me, please? I need to talk to Mrs. Gerl."

"Are your grandkids going to come to church soon?" Emmy asked before Mrs. Behren walked away.

"I believe they might be here next Sunday," she answered.

"I can't wait to meet them." Emmy grinned and then turned back to Pastor Dave. "Maybe someone can play the original arrangement for me sometime?"

"I'm sure my wife could play it for you if you twist her arm enough."

"So, your wife knows how to play the piano, huh?" Emmy put a finger to her mouth and then grinned.

"She does, but she doesn't play very often and never volunteers. She will play in a pinch if there's no other option." Dave paused and chuckled before continuing, "When we were being interviewed for this position, Cathy and I talked a little about our life, and we both got a little emotional. After we finished, Dr. Wilson asked the board if they had any questions. One of the older board members asked Cathy if she could play the piano and everyone kinda laughed. I eventually figured out that board member is known for his 'sense of humor' if you want to call it that."

"Chase said you have a good voice and like to sing. Are you going to sing sometime for us?" Emmy asked as Dr. Behren shook hands with one of the board members.

"Oh, I might someday, but we have such a talented worship band and a fantastic singer..."

"I suppose you mean Kristen." Emmy put her hands on her hips and made a face.

"Of course. She sounds fantastic," Pastor Dave teased. "Seriously though, I have listened to your CD a thousand times, I bet. Have you guys talked about recording another one?"

"Chase has mentioned it, but he wants to have Kenny produce it again, so we have to set up a time when he's home and available."

Pastor Dave rubbed his gray goatee. "I thought Chase mentioned something about a new CD coming out next year. Am I mistaken?"

"Oh, that," Emmy said and then bit her lip. "That one is kinda a solo project thing. I thought you meant the worship band."

Dave shook more hands. "I would certainly like to hear your solo CD, and I think the worship band should record again, too."

"We will," Emmy said as she smiled at an older couple.

"It must be difficult for you when he has to leave, and I'm not thinking about what you said before." He grinned as Emmy blushed.

"I went on tour in the summer, but now I'm back in school—college. I'm not in high school. After I finish and have my degree, I might join the organization and travel with him. It's not as easy as people might think. He works hard and doesn't have much private time."

"I have an idea of what it's like. We talked quite a lot when he was in California."

"So, you know he and Becky were dating?"

"Yes, it was common knowledge. I've known Becky and her family for many years." Dr. Behren wondered, *Where are you going with this, Emmy? I certainly hope you know I can not divulge anything they talked about.*

"I've met Becky, and we're friends, but I would be lying if I said I was sorry they broke up."

"God has everything under control."

305

Emmy bit her lip, but then slowly grinned. "I'm sure happy about that."

Emmy and Kenny called each other every day, and she kept him up-to-date about news concerning the church.

"How are the people accepting Pastor Dave?" Kenny asked. "Some of them are dead set against change of any kind."

"There's been a few comments over the weeks, but I guess that's to be expected. Some people don't deal with change very well," she said. "He read a letter from Pastor Herb and became emotional. They're still in the Philippines. I think that helped the whole congregation accept him completely. Even Mrs. Thompkins voiced her approval."

"I know there is a big difference in their preaching styles if you want to call it that. For one thing Pastor Herb was very soft-spoken, and he was even hard to hear at times. People won't have any trouble hearing Pastor Dave. He has a bigger voice."

"He seems more outgoing to me. Pastor Herb was very nice, too, but more reserved at times. I think both guys have a real love for people. Pastor Dave teases me more than Pastor Herb."

"No! Is he really teasing you?" Kenny grinned. *I can picture him teasing you. You're so easy to tease.*

"Yes, he told me I was fourteen years old."

"And I imagine you teased him right back."

"Yep, I told him I would be fourteen on my next birthday," Emmy said and then giggled.

"Do you still miss me when I'm gone, or do you like it better when I'm on tour?"

"I still miss you. I get lonely and cold when you aren't in bed with me."

"Has Kristen been staying with you?" Kenny asked. "I can hear you begging her to stay."

Emmy quietly answered, "She's been staying with me most nights."

"Do you want her to move back in so she can be there even when I'm home?"

Emmy giggled and then said, "No way! I want to be free to

attack you without her here."

"That's good news."

Emmy finished final exams on Friday the nineteenth. She started her Christmas break and spent much of the weekend anxiously waiting for Kenny to get home.

"For crying out loud, Em. Will you stop pacing around? He's not going to get home until Monday, and no amount of pacing and worrying is going to get him here any sooner," Kristen said on Saturday evening.

"I know, but they're flying home. I can't help but worry."

Kristen hugged her and whispered, "He will be okay. God will watch over him. God certainly doesn't want you to get mad at Him."

"You're so funny. Are you gonna stay all weekend?"

"I'll stay Sunday night, but I'm going home after that. I don't want to be around when he gets home," Kristen said.

"I'll make sure we're alone in the house before I attack him, this time."

Kristen raised her eyebrows. *What do you mean by that? I would ask, but maybe I don't really want to know.*

Emmy woke up early Monday morning. She looked at the clock. "Crap! It's only six-thirty. I might as well get up because I'm not going to get any more sleep."

She got out of bed and tiptoed into Kristen's room. Emmy sat on the edge of the bed and listened to Kristen breathing for a moment before gently nudging her.

"It better be almost time for my alarm to go off, or else I'm gonna smack you, Em." Kristen sounded annoyed.

"It's just after six-thirty. You have to get up in a few minutes anyway."

Kristen groaned and hid her head under the pillow.

"Do you know who's coming home today?" Emmy asked.

"I hope he has a headache when he gets home."

"I've never used that excuse!" Emmy proclaimed.

"Everyone knows that," Kristen mumbled from under the

pillow. "You've never used any excuse."

"I'm so excited. I can't wait 'til he arrives."

Kristen threw the pillow at Emmy. "Please try, okay?"

Kristen reluctantly rolled out of bed, got dressed, ate breakfast with Emmy, before heading off to work. Emmy cleaned up the kitchen and then checked the rest of the house. She decided the house was clean enough, so she got her devotional book and began to read. She spent time in prayer and was surprisingly relaxed as she waited for Kenny to get home. She called and talked to Mrs. Colwell and Mama Bertucci. She even called home and talked to her mother. Finally she heard a car pull into the driveway. Even though the temperature was in the low thirties, she ran outside without a coat. She ran over to Kenny and hugged him. They kissed for a moment.

"Emmy, it's freezing out here. Where's your coat?"

"It's not that cold, and I just needed to hug you. We can go inside now. I'll help you with your bags."

"I can get them. You get back in the house. I don't want you to catch pneumonia."

"I'll carry this one and wait for you inside."

Kenny carried the rest of his bags into the house and dropped them in the kitchen where Emmy was waiting. He kissed her again and she jumped onto the counter. They hugged and then hungrily kissed each other.

"I'm so happy to be home. Did you miss me, Em?"

"Oh, where you gone?" Emmy teased.

Chapter Thirty-Two

"Kenny, I think this is the first time in my life I haven't had to worry about having enough money for Christmas," Emmy said one morning.

"That's why we set money aside throughout the year," Kenny said with a smile.

"I still don't know what to get my parents. They won't ever tell me what they want." She stood behind him as he worked on the computer. "All they say is we've got everything we need, and we don't want you to spend anything on us."

"Maybe you shouldn't think about finding more things to buy for them. They are used to living simply, and they don't buy things they don't need. We need to think about what they like to do and be smart."

"Like how?" She ran her fingers through his hair. "You either need a haircut, or at least get it styled."

"Andy and I are going to the barber this week. Now, about your parents, they like to take little trips with their friends. Maybe we could buy them tickets to go somewhere they have always wanted to go, but just never have."

"Yeah, they've always wanted to see some of the historical sights back East."

"Let's try to find them a vacation package where they don't have to drive. You know one of those senior citizens tour bus trips," Kenny said. "Do you think your father would be able to handle the travel and the walking around?"

"I think so. He's getting better. He's not using his cane as much."

They searched online for an hour.

One of the packages caught Emmy's attention. "This one looks perfect. It starts in D.C. Then it goes to Baltimore and Philadelphia."

"I bet my parents would like to go, too," Kenny added.

"Maybe we can even buy a ticket for Mama Bertucci. She could see Marco and his family."

Emmy knew Kenny wanted a new TV and bought one with

help from Andy. Kenny found a necklace for Emmy and bought her a couple of new games for the PlayStation. He chuckled as he thought. *I bet she'll be more excited about the PS2 games than this necklace.*

On Christmas Day, Emmy and Kenny squeezed in visits with both sets of parents, the Keaslings and even stopped at the Bertucci home. Emmy wanted to get her share of the cookies Mama made every Christmas. Only after they had returned home did they sit down and open the presents they bought for each other. Emmy didn't bother to wrap the box the new TV came in because it was too big. She didn't even try to hide it.

"Andy helped me pick this out. He told me about all the technical stuff. I knew you wanted a bigger screen."

"I'm sure it will be great. Andy keeps up on all the latest tech stuff." He kissed her. "I have a couple of small gifts for you, Em. Which one would you like to open first?"

She opened the necklace first. "Oh, Kenny, this is lovely. Thank you so much." She kissed him and then opened the PS2 games and screamed. "Can we play this now?"

Kenny shook his head as he grinned.

"Why are you grinning at me like that?"

"Because I knew you would like the games better than the necklace."

"I do not!" Emmy took the necklace out of the small case and put it on. "It's just that I don't have anywhere to wear it right now."

"And we can play the games at home, huh?"

"I could wear the necklace while we play," she said.

"No, you should put it back because I know how excited you get. You might break it."

Kenny and Emmy headed back to the Steward Music Group complex the day after Christmas.

"We need to listen to a couple of the tracks, Em," Kenny mentioned as they parked the car. "I think everything else sounds perfect."

310

"I bet I know which tracks you mean. I still don't like the way 'One More Mountain' sounds. What's the other track?"

"The studio version of 'Yolanda's Song.'"

"I was afraid of that. Do I have to redo the vocal?"

"Just a couple of lines. I know you can do it, Emmy."

"You know how emotional I still get when I sing that song."

Four hours later, they were satisfied.

"That does it, Em. Everything is ready to go. All the artwork and other stuff just has to be approved by the boss and we're good to go. I'm sorry I couldn't get it ready before the holiday."

"That's all right. It is kinda exciting, Kenny. I never thought I would have my very own CD released," Emmy said and then kissed him.

Mr. Kesson listened to the finished project and gave the go ahead. A production run of fifty thousand was ordered and the CD would be shipped to stores for release on January thirteenth if all went according to plan.

December twenty-eighth was the Bears final game of the season. They were in Arrowhead Stadium to play the Chiefs. The Chiefs were 13-2 and already assured a spot in the playoffs, but they were still fighting for home field advantage with the New England Patriots. The Bears, however, were fighting for their playoff lives. The Bears started off quickly and by the end of the first quarter had a seventeen point lead. The Chiefs came back in the second half to take the lead at 24-23.

"I'm not sure I can watch this, Emmy. The guys will be so disappointed if they lose." Kristen alternated between watching the game and hiding her head in a pillow as they sat on the couch in the TV room.

"They're gonna win, Krissy. I just know it." Emmy groaned as the Chiefs made another first down. "Come on, Tony. You have to stop them."

The Bears recovered a fumble in the fourth quarter and moved the ball into position for Brad Ellington to attempt his fourth field goal of the game.

Emmy held her breath as the football soared through the air. "It's good!" She raised her hands in the air making the same signal as the officials.

The Bears had a two point lead late in the fourth quarter. Kansas City had one last chance to move down the field for a game winning field goal attempt.

"Shoot! They only need about fifteen more yards for their kicker to have a legit shot," Emmy whined.

Kristen covered her face with the pillow. "I can't watch. Tell me when it's over."

"Don't be a baby. You have to watch." Emmy held onto Kristen's hand as she set the pillow down.

The Bears were in a zone coverage and Tony was responsible for the short middle of the field. He was watching the quarterback's eyes and sensed the tight end moving toward him from the left. He moved to his left, stretched out and got enough of his hand on the ball to tip it into the air. Von Mitchell picked it off.

Emmy jumped off the couch and screamed, "They're gonna win!"

"Does that mean they're in the playoffs?" Kristen managed a smile now.

The Bears ran out the clock to win 26-24.

"Now they have to hope for a Seattle loss. If the Seahawks lose, the Bears will win the tiebreaker."

The Seattle Seahawks lost their final game in San Francisco against the 49ers, and, despite the near disastrous start to the season, the Bears made the playoffs.

On New Year's Eve, Emmy and her friends gathered at the Keasling house for Derrick's annual party. Once again Daniel and Karla took Mama with them to their cabin in Wisconsin.

"Derrick, are you gonna open a bottle of wine, or do we have to wait for the champagne?" Emmy asked.

"I could open a bottle, Em," Derrick answered.

"I never get to drink wine anymore. We used to have it for dinner at our house all the time. This party is now my only chance to have a glass of wine the entire year," Emmy said.

"Do you want me to open a bottle of wine, Em?" Derrick asked. "It might be up to John, you and me to drink it all. Unless we can convince Kenny or Kristen to have some."

"No, I guess I'll live without it. I wouldn't want to create a temptation for anyone to do something they feel is wrong."

"I certainly don't want to start a debate, but there are numerous instances in the Bible of wine being consumed," Chase said.

"Isn't there a story about Jesus turning water into wine?" Amber asked.

Tony nodded and said, "Yeah! It was these huge casks or whatever they were called."

For the next ten minutes they discussed whether or not drinking wine was wrong. Most of them believed an occasional glass of wine was neither harmful nor sinful. When countdown to midnight began, everyone held hands as Chase led the group in prayer.

Afterward Emmy teased, "What a bunch of party poopers. No one is even close to being inebriated and instead of kissing and carrying on like other people, we say a prayer."

"What are you suggesting we do, Emmy?" Derrick asked.

"Can we turn the music up and dance at least?"

"I don't see why not."

Derrick turned on some dance music and they had a *real* party for the next hour. Emmy danced with all the guys—including Chase.

"You're not a terrible dancer," Emmy said with a straight face.

"For?" Chase waited for the punch line.

"For a preacher with no sense of rhythm in your body."

"I haven't had as much practice as you, Emmy."

"Haven't you ever danced with Yvonne?"

"Sure, but we mostly slow dance."

"I'll see if Derrick has some slow tunes, so you and Yvonne can dance. I would love to see you guys dancing." *I love to slow dance with Kenny, but we probably shouldn't tonight. Not in front*

313

of everyone. I might get turned on.

Sloane had a chance to talk to Cam and Lindsey. "How was your trip back home?"

"It was good to get back to Ohio," Cam answered. "The weather cooperated. The roads were fine."

Lindsey mentioned, "I brought him over to meet Mom and Dad."

"What about your sisters?" Sloane asked.

"They met Cam, and voiced their approval."

"We spent a day in Sidney to visit my parents, and Lins got to meet my brother Zack," Cam said.

Sloane grinned. "Oooh, it must mean something if you guys are meeting the parents."

"Maybe it does," Lindsey said as she smiled at Cam.

After making it into the playoffs on the last weekend of the year, the Bears traveled to Green Bay to play the Packers again. They knew the Packers would be seeking revenge for their last loss to the Bears. They certainly didn't want to lose two home games to their bitter rivals from Chicago. An hour before kickoff, it started to snow, and it didn't let up. The game was played in near blizzard conditions, but the Bears didn't mind.

"This is gonna be like the game in Denver," Emmy told Kristen.

"They won that game, right?" Kristen asked.

"Yes, don't you remember?"

"I don't remember all the details of every game like you do, Em."

The conditions made it difficult for both offenses and the Bears escaped with a one point victory. After the game Tony had a chance to shake hands with the Packers legendary quarterback, Bart Farber.

"Good game, Mr. Farber," Tony said.

"I suppose so if you are a polar bear or something. We never had to play in a blizzard in Mississippi. Good luck next week, kid. It's young guys like you who are starting to make me feel old."

The Bears unbelievable season came to an end the next Sunday with a loss to the Philadelphia Eagles. The Bears didn't make it to the Super Bowl, which was Tony's goal, but it was a successful season anyway. John Randolph became an important part of the starting team and led the team in receptions. Tony led the team in tackles again.

Emmy's classes began again at North Park on January twelfth. She was taking eighteen hours again this semester. She knew it would be difficult, but she was determined to get her degree as quickly as possible.

After her last class on Tuesday, Emmy drove to the Mole's Den. She ran into the store and checked the new releases section in the first aisle. She let out a holler as she saw *The Only Hope*, her second release. "Oh my! It's really here."

Michael Dunewillis, the owner of the store heard Emmy and waved. "Hey, Emmy, are you here to buy a copy?"

"I would buy all the copies, but that wouldn't be fair to my fans." She blushed and put a hand to her mouth. "I mean if I had any fans."

"You are too modest. You have fans."

Emmy shook her head. "Kenny has fans, not me."

"Then why have we had to fill this rack three times already today, huh?" Michael emptied another box of the CD as he refilled the rack.

"Have you really?"

"Yes, and it won't surprise me if I sell out of your CD by the end of the day, or at least by tomorrow."

"I guess that will please Mr. Kesson."

"Did I mention that I bought five CDs myself to give to my daughters and a couple of friends? Would you mind autographing them for me, Emmy? I'm sure the girls would get a thrill if you did."

Emmy giggled as she signed the CDs.

Chapter Thirty-Three

"Hey, Emmy, what would you think about inviting some friends over on Saturday? We could have hot chocolate, play games, make a night of it," Kenny asked as they were doing the dishes after dinner on Wednesday night.

"That's the seventeenth, right? Emmy looked at the calendar on the kitchen wall. "There's nothing listed. Sounds all right to me."

"All right. Let's do it." Kenny high-fived her.

Tony and Sloane were the first to arrive on Saturday. "Hey guys, did you know it's like a blizzard out there?" Tony asked as they entered through the back door. He helped Sloane remove her coat and hung both coats on the hooks by the entryway.

"No, really, is that what all that white stuff is? I wasn't sure," Emmy said from in the kitchen.

Tony entered the kitchen, grabbed Emmy and carried her into the living room as Kenny and Sloane watched.

"Why does she put up with him doing that?" Sloane asked as she put her hands on her hips.

"She loves it," Kenny answered.

Tony dropped her on the couch and tickled her for a few seconds. She began to squirm and giggle.

"What if I hold you with one hand and use the other one to tickle you—like this!"

"No fair! You're not supposed to tickle me anymore because I'm married now."

Tony sat on her, and she squirmed all over the couch.

"Stop it! I'm gonna tell Mama you were tickling me in inappropriate places."

"I was not. I only tickled you behind your knees, and when you start acting like a mature married lady, I will stop treating you like my immature kid sister."

She stuck out her tongue and made a face at him.

"All right. If that's the way you're gonna behave." He shook his head and tickled her some more.

"All right. I give up. I'll act like a grownup now."

The doorbell rang. Kenny smiled as he opened the door. "Hi, Lindsey. Hi, Cam. Come on in. Tony and Emmy are fighting like brother and sister as you can tell."

Tony stopped tickling Emmy and let her up. She immediately jumped on his back.

"I lied. I'm gonna act like a kid all night," Emmy said as she covered Tony's eyes with her hands.

Cam and Lindsey saw Tony and Emmy goofing around and laughed.

"Do they always act like kids?" Lindsey asked.

"Stop it, Em." Tony grabbed her hands.

"Yes, they do," Kenny answered. "I'm glad to see you guys made it safely. Is it getting worse out there?"

"We didn't drive. We rode with Tony and Sloane."

"Then why are you just now ringing the bell?" Kenny asked.

Emmy moved her hands so Tony could see.

"We were in the backyard making a snowman," Cam said. "You should come out and see it."

Emmy and Tony stopped goofing around.

"I want to see the snowman," Emmy hollered as she poked Tony in the ribs. "Let me down, you big dork."

"With pleasure!" Tony dumped Emmy onto the couch.

"You're a creep!" Emmy shouted, but then laughed.

"You're a brat."

Kenny shrugged as he looked at Emmy and Tony. *I really should film this sometime. Thirty years from now we can all laugh at how you guys used to behave.*

Everyone went outside to admire the snowman. As they were walking out the back door, John pulled into the driveway and parked behind Tony's GMC.

He and Kristen got out and Emmy hollered, "Come on! We're going to look at the snowman Cam and Lindsey built."

John and Kristen held hands as they followed everyone to the backyard.

"Wow! You guys built this in just a few minutes? That's

317

amazing," Kenny said.

"The snow is wet and it packs real easy," Cam said. "It's coming down so hard. I think we're supposed to get over six inches tonight."

"And it makes great snowballs," Emmy hollered as she made one and threw it point blank at Tony.

He took it in the chest and bent down to make one to throw at Emmy. She knew he was going to try and get her back so she screamed and ran away.

"Kenny! Protect me. Tony is going to hit me with a snowball."

Kenny laughed and told her, "You started it, Em."

Tony hit her with a snowball right in the chest. She laughed and made another one to throw at Tony. Soon everyone joined in. At first the girls ganged up on one guy at a time and were able to hit their target most of the time. Then the guys started to retaliate. They aimed for their own girl until Tony suggested, "Let's get Emmy since she started this fight."

"No fair!" Emmy screamed as she got nailed by seven snowballs at once. "You can't all gang up on me."

She started running in circles as she tried to escape.

"Em, will you stop. You're making me laugh," Kristen said.

Sloane added, "You're making me cry."

Emmy ran out of breath and collapsed to the ground. She lay on her back and didn't move. Tony, John and Kenny walked over and stood next to her.

"What should we do with her?" Tony asked. "I don't think she's breathing."

"I am so," Emmy yelled as she tried to kick Tony.

"What do you say?" John asked as he smiled at Kenny. "She's your wife, after all."

Kenny rubbed his jaw for a moment before saying, "I think we should bury her in the snow."

"No! Don't you dare," Emmy yelled, but the guys knew she didn't mean it.

Just then Chase and Yvonne Hillman walked into the backyard.

"We've been ringing the bell, but no one answered. Then we heard the commotion and figured you were out here."

"I'm sorry, guys. We came out here to see the snowman and then Emmy started a snowball fight. We've been teaching her a lesson."

Emmy tried to get up, but Tony leaned down and put a hand on her chest to hold her on the ground.

"Are you gonna behave now, Em, or do we have to bury you in the snow?"

"I'll behave," she told Tony, but he knew she was lying. He let her up, and she immediately threw some snow at him. He grabbed her before she could run away and tackled her to the ground. He put a hand on her back and wouldn't let her up. She kicked her legs and tried to get away, but couldn't.

"Are you gonna stop?"

She was finally tired and stopped fighting against Tony. He stood up and pulled her up with him.

"Hi, Yvonne, did you see what these mean guys were doing to me?"

"Emmy, I know you well enough to know you undoubtedly started the whole thing and loved every minute of it."

Kenny told everyone, "Come on, let's go inside. We've got hot chocolate and cookies and even some brownies. We can eat and drink..."

"And be merry," Sloane finished.

They headed inside. Kenny and Emmy took everyone's coats, hats and gloves and put them in the TV room.

Emmy got back to the the living room and looked at Kristen. "Why do you have such a silly grin on your face? You look like the cat that swallowed the parakeet."

"Canary, Emmy, the cat that swallowed the canary."

"Whatever. Why do you have such a silly look?"

Kristen stuck out her hand and showed Emmy her brand new engagement ring.

Emmy saw it and screamed, "Is it true? For real?"

"He proposed last night."

Emmy hugged Kristen, and they danced around while

hollering like a couple of kids. Tony smiled at Emmy. She realized he knew this was going to happen but didn't tell her.

"How long have you known?" Emmy glared at him.

Tony raised his hands and backed away. "John told me he was going to propose two weeks ago."

Emmy looked around the room and everyone was smiling. Emmy smacked Tony's arm. "Am I the last one to know?"

"I'm afraid so, sweetie," Kenny replied. "I've known for almost as long."

"Is this why you wanted to invite everyone over tonight?" Emmy asked.

"I guess that is the main reason. But we can still play games and stuff."

"You better not keep any more secrets from me if you want me to kiss you anymore. Hey, why is it no one ever tells me about these things? Kristen knew you were going to propose to me two weeks before you did, and now you, and all our friends, knew John was going to propose to Kristen before I did. Is there some kind of secret conspiracy against me that I don't know about?"

"If you knew about it, it wouldn't be a *secret* conspiracy," Kenny teased.

Emmy gave John a big hug and he whispered in her ear, "I followed your advice, Emmy. It took me a little longer than you hoped maybe, but I finally did it."

She kissed him on the cheek. "You better be very good to Kristen, or else I will get her mafia cousins after you."

Tony and John looked at Emmy like she had lost her mind, but didn't say anything. Kristen showed Kenny her ring, and he gave her a hug. Tony was so happy for Kristen that he almost cried as he hugged her tightly. Kenny made the hot chocolate, and, when everyone had a cup, he proposed a toast to John and Kristen.

"May you be as happy as Emmy and me."

"But I hope you act more maturely than Emmy," Tony said.

Everyone sat in the living room and talked. Later, Emmy and Tony were in the kitchen together. She looked at him and grinned.

"Okay, Em, what's going on in your devious mind?"

320

"I was thinking since John and Kristen are going to get married, have you and Sloane given any thought to announcing your engagement?"

Tony grabbed her around the waist and set her on the counter.

"Maybe we have discussed it, and maybe we haven't. Does that answer your question, little sister?"

Emmy looked into his eyes and could see the love he had for her. "Am I always gonna be your little sister?"

"Yes, you will always be very special to me, Em. No matter how much you misbehave or mistreat me, I will always be your adopted big brother."

"I hope you will be as happy as I am when you get married. It doesn't matter if it's with Sloane or someone else..."

"What about Nikki or Brenda?" Tony pushed Emmy's buttons to get a response.

"Anybody but Brenda. If I never see her again, it will be too soon. Nikki, I could tolerate, but does she go to church?"

"I don't think so."

"I think you need to limit your choices to girls from church. I really like Sloane, though," Emmy said.

"I know you do and so does Mama. You know Mama will always compare any girl I date with you."

"I'm nothing special," Emmy said and then sighed.

"Ya think? I know that, but Mama thinks otherwise for some strange, unknown reason," Tony teased.

Kenny walked into the kitchen after listening to the conversation in the doorway. "Em, are you trying to pester Tony into proposing to Sloane?"

"Sorta, but he won't. Don't you think Sloane is the perfect girl for him?"

"I think she would be an excellent wife, but what do I know?" He shrugged. "Look who I ended up marrying."

Tony moved out of the way and Kenny moved up close to Emmy and kissed her.

"Would you rather have someone else in your bed tonight, m'lord?" Emmy made a face as she asked.

321

"No, m'lady, you're the only one I want in my bed."

"Just remember you have guests," Tony said as he headed back to the living room.

Emmy wanted to help Kristen and John with their wedding plans, and they started later that night after everyone else had gone home.

"Anyone need anything to drink?" Kenny asked as they sat at the dining room table.

No one was thirsty.

"Do you have any ideas for the wedding?" Emmy asked as she smoothed out the white tablecloth.

Kristen answered, "I want to have an outdoor wedding at my parents house in June."

"Wow! That's quick. That's a great idea, and you could have the reception there, too. The yard and grounds are big enough, and you wouldn't have to worry about if it's available or not."

"That sounds perfect to me," John said.

"Are you pregnant?" Emmy asked bluntly.

"No! We want to get married before football season starts. That's the only reason."

"I just had to ask, Krissy. I'm sorry."

"It's all right, Em." *I asked you that question plenty of times, so I deserve to have it thrown back in my face.*

"Well, we better get to work. We've only got five months to plan this wedding. We have to call Paula and make sure she's available. You can't plan a wedding without her. We need to find a dress and pick out invitations and find a caterer..." Emmy rattled off a ton of things to accomplish over the next few months.

Chapter Thirty-Four

"Where can we have your birthday party?" Emmy asked as she lay next to Kenny in bed. She wanted to throw a party for him—he would turn twenty-seven on January thirty-first. "I want to invite all the guys in the band and the crew. I know some of them will want to have beer at the party, but I want to invite our friends from church, too. I first thought of having the party at church, but that won't work. They won't allow any alcohol. I don't think the Keasling house, as big as it is, would be big enough for everyone."

"We could use that big room at the Steward Music Group office. I'm pretty sure Mr. Kesson would allow it. We could have beer there if you really think we should."

"I don't know. I'm torn. I know some of our friends like to have a beer or some wine once in a while, but I know some of the people from church will not come if alcohol is being served. What should we do, Kenny?"

"We should pray about it before we make a decision," Kenny responded and then kissed her. "What do you think?"

"I don't think this is the way to pray," she said and then giggled.

They did pray and the answer quickly arrived.

"You know there are only a few of the people from your office staff who would want beer or wine and so many more from church who don't drink. Why don't we see if we can use the big gym at church on Saturday night? We could invite the whole church. We could make it a family night and have games and play basketball. It doesn't even have to be at night. We could do it in the afternoon so families wouldn't have to stay out late. Then we could invite the other people over to the house Sunday afternoon."

"I think that's a great idea, Em, except that we should do it on Friday night at the office. I want to be able to spend Sunday with just you and family," Kenny said as he rubbed her back.

"We will have to ask this morning to see if we can use the church because we will only have one Sunday besides today to invite people."

"Who do we need to ask?" Kenny needed to know.

"I'll ask Chase. He'll know."

"Should we get out of bed now?"

"We have a few minutes." Emmy grinned as she pulled him on top of her.

As soon as she got to the music room and saw Chase, Emmy told him about her idea. "Who do I need to ask about using the gym?"

"I was just heading to the main office, so follow me." Emmy followed Chase along the back hallway. "There is a big calendar in the office and all the events at the church are listed. I'm not sure if there's anything scheduled for that Saturday afternoon. There might be in the morning."

They checked the calendar and the gym was free that afternoon.

"Who do I have to ask to reserve it?"

Just then Paul Jefferson walked into the room. "What do you need to reserve, Emmy?"

She explained everything, and Paul approved it for her.

"That was easy. How much do I have to pay?"

"Nothing, since you are kinda part of the team, but if you would care to make a donation, we won't decline it," Paul said.

"I'll take it. I want to invite the whole church. I want to make it a family day. I know it's really late notice, but can we put it with the other video announcements?"

"Sure, Em. Come with me," Chase said.

"I'm following you everywhere this morning, Chase."

Chase took her to the music suite where one room was set up to produce the video announcements. In five minutes, he added the *family day* to the rest of that week's announcements.

"Can we play it again next Sunday?" Emmy asked. "Some people might not see it today."

"We can make a better video during the week."

"Cool. Can I be the director?"

"No, you have to make the announcement. I'm the director," Chase teased.

324

On Thursday night before worship band rehearsal Chase and Emmy took the time to make a more professional thirty second promo for the party. At Kenny's suggestion, they didn't say anything about it being a birthday party, but simply an afternoon for families to have a fun time at the church.

"Kenny, are you ready to go? We're supposed to be there at six to get everything set up. The caterers will be there at six thirty," Emmy asked as she stood in the doorway of their bedroom.

"I'm putting on my shoes. I'll re right there."

On Friday, the day before his birthday, Kenny and Emmy were hosting a party for the guys from the band, crew and office, and their spouses.

"We didn't leave anyone out, did we?" Emmy asked as Kenny pulled into the main parking lot of Steward Music Group.

"I don't think we invited everyone who lives in SoHam, but most of them," Kenny said.

"I'd hate to slight anyone."

"You didn't, Em. I'm sure not everyone will be able to be here, but they were invited."

The caterers arrived on time. By seven everything was ready. The guests started arriving immediately.

"I'm glad we're just having beer and wine," Emmy mentioned to Kenny later, as she kept an eye on the dwindling supply of both.

"It's too bad Mr. Kesson and his wife couldn't be here."

"Where are they?" Emmy asked as she opened a bottle of Ice Mountain water. "I know you told me, but I forgot,"

"They're in the Caribbean somewhere. He's island hopping with his sailboat."

"Must be nice. He's made a lot of money off you guys."

"He's earned it, and he's been very generous with us." Kenny spied someone walking in the door. "I gotta go talk to someone, I'll be right back."

Emmy saw Frances Rawlings, waved and raced to her side. "How is baby Frank doing? Do you call him Frank or Frankie?" Emmy asked as she took the sleeping baby from Frances.

"For now, we call him Frankie," Frances said as she adjusted the blanket. "This is quite a party, Emmy. Do all of these people work here?"

"I'm pretty sure they do." Emmy looked around the room. "There are a few people I don't recognize. Maybe they're party crashers."

Kenny shook hands with Dale Wirth whose company handled security for Fridays At Five. "Good to see you again, sir."

"Thanks for inviting me. Happy birthday, by the way."

"Thanks. Would you like something to eat or drink?"

"No, but thank you. Is there somewhere we can talk privately?"

"Let's go upstairs." Kenny ushered him to the office used by Fridays At Five on the second floor. "Please, have a seat."

Mr. Wirth noticed the five platinum records on the wall as he settled into a recliner opposite Kenny, who sat on the leather couch. "I know you have been opposed to having a lot of security around in the past."

Kenny nodded in agreement.

"Because of the incident in Dallas, Andy has suggested we double the security."

Kenny remembered the incident where a man managed to get backstage with a gun.

"In addition to the regular crew, for this tour there will two men assigned to each of the band members. They will be with you every time you leave the bus or your dressing room. I'm afraid you won't have as much privacy, but..."

"As much as I hate to, I feel I need to agree with you and Andy."

They talked for several minutes and then Mr. Wirth stood up to leave. "I'll introduce you to the men on Monday."

"I hope Emmy doesn't hear about this," Kenny said.

On Saturday afternoon Emmy smiled as she listened to the echoes bouncing off the walls of the kids screaming and yelling as they ran around like maniacs. They rented two bouncy houses and had games for the younger kids in the small gym. The teens and

326

young adults played basketball and volleyball in the larger gym.

"It looks like everyone is having a good time," Pastor Dave mentioned to Emmy and Kenny.

"I'm glad we were able to pull everything together on short notice," Emmy replied as she caught a tennis ball thrown by one of the kids. "Thanks for letting us use the gyms."

"You're welcome and thank you for the donation. I see that some people brought cards and a few gifts."

"We tried not to turn it into a birthday party," Emmy said.

They ordered pizzas and had soft drinks and water. People brought in various dishes and desserts. Emmy ordered a birthday cake for Kenny, and he even let her smear some frosting on his face.

"Are you going to pay me back for this, Kenny?" Emmy asked and then giggled.

"You better believe it."

"Oooh! We could have some fun"

After the morning service on Sunday, Kenny and Emmy visited her parents and invited them over to the Colwells for lunch.

"Kenny, can you pull the car into the alley, please?" Emmy asked. "It's closer than going out the front door."

"Whatever you wish, m'lady." Kenny grinned.

"Nonsense! We can walk. It's only a couple of houses away," Raymond said as he grabbed his good coat from the closet in the living room.

"I can help you get up and down the stairs, Daddy," Emmy said as she waited outside the front door of her parents' house.

"Thank you, Emmy, but I can manage by myself." He still occasionally used a cane, but managed to get around better now.

Emmy waited at the bottom of the stairs and then took her father's arm as they walked over to the Colwell's home.

"Does your hip still bother you?"

"Once in a while, but it's not nearly as painful as before. I actually feel better than I have for years."

"Maybe staying sober is part of the reason, Daddy."

Kenny escorted her mother a few steps ahead.

327

"Are you and Emily thinking about starting a family soon?" Patricia asked.

Kenny knew Emmy kept her medical condition private. Emmy's doctor did not believe she would ever conceive a child.

"We aren't thinking about a family just yet. Em wants to finish college first." He figured that would be a good enough excuse.

"Raymond and I aren't getting any younger, and Diane lives so far away."

"I understand that, Mrs. Colasanti," Kenny said.

They ate lunch and then spent an hour sitting in the living room. Emmy listened with pride as her parents talked to the Colwells about a variety of subjects. Not once did they raise their voices.

"Should I get the car?" Kenny asked. "It's getting colder. There might be some ice on the sidewalk."

"That won't be necessary."

Kenny didn't want to insult his father-in-law's pride, so they walked back to the house.

"Are you coming in, Emmy?" Mom Colasanti asked from the top of the stairs.

"I think we'll just go home, Mom. Kenny is leaving tomorrow."

Mom smiled. "I understand, dear. You can work on starting that family."

As Kenny pulled away from the curb a few minutes later, Emmy poked his arm, "What was that about, huh?"

"Your mother asked me if we are going to start a family soon. Haven't you ever told her about..."

"No, and don't you tell her either. It will just make matters worse."

Kenny and Emmy were in bed by ten.

"I really need to get some sleep, Em," Kenny said just before one o'clock.

"If you must," Emmy said, kissed him and then giggled.

"Em, are you almost through in the shower? I've gotta get

328

going. Frances and Jeff will be here any second."

"Give me a minute," Emmy answered as she turned off the water. She wrapped a towel around her as Kenny watched from the doorway.

"You know you're dripping all over the floor, right?"

Emmy looked down and wiggled her toes.

The front doorbell rang.

"That's them. I gotta run."

"I'll come downstairs with you."

"You're in a towel!" Kenny exclaimed.

"Oh, right, sorry." She let the towel fall to the floor. "Is this better?"

He thought about the time they spent in bed just ten minutes prior.

"I'll let them in and stall them for two minutes. You can throw something on and come downstairs." He turned to leave.

Emmy hollered, "I have a negligee I could wear."

"Emmy!"

"All right. I'll be there in a minute."

Kenny let Jeff and Frances in and a minute later Emmy ran into the living room. Kenny glanced at her. She wore shorts and a sweatshirt.

"Hi, guys. I just got out of the shower," she explained as her wet hair dripped all over the carpeting.

Jeff helped Kenny carry his luggage to the car as Emmy and Frances talked. Kenny came back inside and Frances joined Jeff in the car.

"I'll call you later, Em." Kenny hugged her and slipped a hand to her bottom. "You're not wearing anything under this, are you?"

"I didn't have time. At least I didn't put on that negligee."

"You're so bad. I love you." He kissed her and slipped out the door.

Chapter Thirty-Five

The skies were clear and sunny in SoHam on Monday morning, March first, but not so in western Iowa. A narrow-bodied airliner crashed shortly after takeoff. The plane crash ended the lives of ninety-seven people, but changed forever the lives of many hundreds more. Including Emmy Colasanti Colwell. Four men from Robertson Industries perished in the fiery crash. Richard Demarco among them. When Emmy saw the news on TV about a plane crashing into a field, she didn't pay much attention at first. Only later when Kristen called did Emmy fully realized what had happened. She fell to her knees and began weeping. Later that night she called Kenny, and they talked about the crash.

"Do you want me to come home? We could cancel a few shows if you need me to be with you. Otherwise, I'll be home in a couple of weeks."

"No, I can't ask you to do that." Emmy's voice raised in pitch as she sounded frantic.

"Do you want to join me? I know you said you couldn't before because of church, but maybe you should."

"No, I can't. I'm on spring break, so I'll be all right. It's just been a real shock. Kristen can stay with me and Tony and John are around."

"Okay, but call me if you want me to come home and I will," Kenny said.

"It's just so sad," Emmy said as she sniffled. "I had been talking to Richard occasionally over the last several months about giving his life to Jesus, and I think he was close to making that decision. He had gone to church a few times, and he told Krissy just a month ago that he was reading the Bible."

"I hate to trivialize his death, or turn it into a cliche, but we never know how long we have on this earth."

"I guess I don't think about that since we're still young."

The families of the men from Robertson Industries arranged for their funerals. Kristen called Emmy after all the details were finalized. "I don't know if you've heard, but all the funerals are out of state. Two of the men were from California. Mr. Schneider was from Germany. His family is holding a service for him in Berlin. Did you know any of them?"

"I didn't recognize the names. What about Richard? He doesn't really have any family. His parents are gone. I never heard him talk about any brothers or sisters."

"Apparently, he has a sister who lives somewhere in Idaho," Kristen said and then explained the details to Emmy. "I saw him two weeks ago, but I didn't have a chance to talk to him."

"It's just as well. I don't like funerals. It was difficult enough to go to your Grandpa's. I will keep busy."

"Mr. Robertson scheduled a memorial service for ten o'clock tomorrow morning. After that, the whole company is closed for the rest of the week. We had to take care of anything really urgent today."

"Should I come to the service?" Emmy asked.

"I think you should. It will be one way of showing respect for Richard."

Kristen brought Emmy to the service the next morning. Kristen expected Emmy to cry during the service, but she didn't. Emmy sat still and didn't seem to be paying any attention.

"Are you all right, Em?" Kristen whispered.

"Sure, I'm okay."

You're not okay, Em. Something is really bothering you. It's almost like you're denying this whole thing happened. Kristen put an arm around Emmy's shoulder.

Tony and John attended and also noticed Emmy's strange behavior.

When Mr. Robertson embraced Emmy after the service, she broke down totally. She cried in his arms until she was drained emotionally and physically.

"It's all right, Emmy," he whispered as tears filled his eyes.

Mr. Robertson knew why Emmy was so distraught and he told Kristen, "I am assigning you to a new department effective immediately. You are to look after Emmy and take good care of her until I tell you differently. It's a twenty-four hour a day job, but I'm

331

sure you can handle it."

Kristen didn't know what to say at first. "Yes, Mr. Robertson, I can handle it. Thank you, sir." She hugged him and was not alone in thinking Mr. Robertson must be the greatest boss in the whole world.

Kristen took Emmy home, and Emmy went right to her room and lay on the bed.

"Are you going to be okay, Em? I know this is upsetting to everyone, but it's really knocked you for a loop. You've been acting like it's no big deal, but then today you totally lost it. Do you want to talk about it?"

"I can't talk about it now, Krissy. I just want to sleep. I want to sleep forever."

"I'll make you some soup," Kristen said. "I can warm up a can of soup."

"No, I can't eat anything. I'll just throw up."

"Then I'll make you some tea with honey. You have to put something in your stomach to help settle it."

"I'll try to drink some tea."

Emmy drank some tea and then slept for three hours. She woke up and came downstairs.

"Kristen, where are you? I need to tell you something."

"I'm in the living room, Em."

Emmy walked into the living room and sat next to Kristen on the couch.

"What do you need to tell me, Em?" Kristen put an arm around Emmy as she began to cry. Kristen rubbed Emmy's back and whispered, "You can tell me anything. It will be all right."

After she regained her composure, Emmy explained why the plane crash had devastated her so.

When Mr. Robertson walked into his office Wednesday morning, Mrs. Moneywell was waiting with a smile and a cup of coffee.

He accepted the coffee. "Why are you here, Mona? Everything is closed for the week."

"I know you need to make some travel arrangements, so I

thought I would help."

"You don't have to do that, but I appreciate the thoughtfulness."

Mrs. Moneywell smiled and said, "I know a secret."

"Not a word, Mrs. Moneywell, not a word." Mr. Robertson pointed a finger at her.

"I'm afraid it's too late, sir. The whole company knows what you have done for the families of the men who lost their lives and for Emily and Kristen, too. Am I fired?"

"You know as well as I do, Mrs. Moneywell, that this company would collapse if you weren't here."

Mrs. Moneywell smiled and whispered, "Yes, sir. You old softy," as Mr. Robertson walked into his office.

"I heard that Mrs Moneywell!"

Emmy called Kristen's cell phone later that morning. "Kristen, can you stay with me? I'm on spring break, and I don't want to be here by myself."

"Sure, baby." Kristen laughed softly. "Don't you remember that Mr. Robertson ordered me to take care of you?"

"When did he do that?" Emmy asked.

Kristen walked up the stairs and into Emmy's bedroom. "At the memorial service."

They looked at each other and ended the call.

"I didn't know you were here."

"I spent the night in my old room. You were too exhausted to realize it."

"Did I tell you what happened?" Emmy bit her lip.

"Yes, sweetie, you did." Kristen sat on the edge of the bed. "Tony and John aren't doing anything except off-season workouts. They can be here during the day. That will allow me to do some work from home. Here, I mean. We won't leave you by yourself."

"Thank you, Krissy. You're the best friend in the world." Emmy forced a smile. "Did you tell anyone?"

"No, I haven't mentioned it to anyone, but you have to tell Kenny the truth, Em. He needs to know."

Emmy shook her head.

"I heard you talking to him on Monday."

333

"You were eavesdropping on us?"

"I didn't mean to, but I heard most of the conversation. You led him to believe that everything is hunky dory when it isn't. It's far from it."

"I don't want him to worry about me. He's got enough on his mind right now."

"You're his wife, and he needs to know how upset you are. You have to tell him," Kristen insisted.

"I don't know if I can." Emmy closed her eyes.

"You can do anything with God's help. It says so in the Bible."

John and Tony came over that afternoon. John came mainly to see Kristen. He treated Emmy sympathetically, and he and Tony didn't tease her at all. Kristen ordered Chinese for dinner, but Emmy couldn't eat a thing. She stayed in her bedroom and tried to sleep. Instead of sleeping though, she tossed and turned. She came downstairs and joined everyone in the TV room.

"Are you hungry, Em?" Kristen asked.

"No, I can't eat. I couldn't fall asleep either. Can I just sit here with you guys?"

Kristen scooted over and made a spot for Emmy.

"Are you cold?" Tony asked as he noticed her hugging herself.

"Sorta." She bit her lip as she looked up at him.

Tony got a blanket from the hall closet. He wrapped it around Emmy and sat next to her. She moved close, and he put an arm around her.

"Thanks for coming over, Tony."

"Hey, it's okay. You're going through a hard time." He pulled on her hair and grinned. "What are big brothers for, anyway?"

Lynette Jefferson came to the house on Thursday morning.

"Thanks for coming over," Kristen said as they sat down on the living room couch. "I need to run home this morning and the guys are at the gym. I didn't want Emmy to be alone."

"I can understand that. I'm glad I can help." Lynette looked around. "Where is she?"

"She's still in bed. She didn't get much sleep last night. I heard her crying, so I stayed with her for most of the night. She finally fell asleep around three. I thought I would let her sleep all morning."

"I won't bother her," Lynette said.

"She hasn't been eating."

"I'll make her some soup and some tea. That helps me."

"Thanks Lynette. I will be back by two. I really appreciate this."

Emmy woke up just before noon and came downstairs. She saw Lynette reading a book in the living room.

"Hi, I didn't know you were here. Where's Krissy?"

"She had to run home for a while. Are you hungry, Emmy? I can make some soup."

"I'm not hungry, but thanks."

Lynette noticed a tear escape and slowly fall down Emmy's cheek. "Would you like for me to pray with you?"

Emmy nodded.

Lynette prayed with Emmy on the couch.

"You can always talk to me about anything, Em."

"I know. Thank you for that." Emmy hugged Lynette. *But you can't help with this. No one can understand how I feel.*

Emmy felt as if her heart had been shattered into a million pieces. In her music box, under all her other keepsakes, Emmy had placed an unused plane ticket. She was scheduled to be on that flight.

"Aren't you going to practice tonight?" Kristen asked when she came home and found Emmy still in her pajamas.

"No, I called Chase and told him I wouldn't be there on Sunday."

"Did she eat anything for lunch?" Kristen asked Lynette.

"I made some tea, but she didn't eat. I should get back to my girls."

"Thank you so much for coming over," Kristen said as Lynette left.

"Call me if you need anything. I know she's hurting, but

335

she wouldn't talk about it."

Kristen looked in the pantry and found a can of chicken noodle soup. "I'm going to make this and you have to eat some of it. Do you want to get dressed?"

"No, I'm not going anywhere, so I'll just stay in my pajamas."

Emmy ate a bowl of soup and an hour later Kristen asked her, "Have you talked to Kenny? You promised you would tell him what happened."

"I can't." Emmy bit her lip.

"You've been putting it off all week. You have to call him now."

Kristen saw Emmy's cell phone on the dining room table and handed it to Emmy.

"Do you want me to dial his number or will you?"

Emmy shook her head and then ran to the bathroom. She lost the soup and went back to bed.

Kristen went out to do some grocery shopping on Friday. She came home at noon and discovered Emmy in bed still in her pajamas.

"All right! That's it!" Kristen pulled her out of the bed. "Shower! Right now!"

Emmy bit her lip but did as Kristen ordered. Kristen grabbed some clothes and laid them on the vanity in the bathroom.

"After you get dressed, you are calling Kenny," Kristen shouted above the sound of the water. "If you don't then I will, and I'll tell him everything myself."

Fifteen minutes later, Kristen handed Emmy her cell phone. "Call! Now!"

Kristen stood in front of Emmy with her hands on her hips until Emmy made the call.

Emmy confessed to Kenny on the phone.

"I hadn't seen him for over a year. Not since we were in San Diego, but I did talk to him on the phone once a month or so. I would talk to him about God and he responded a little, but he would never make the commitment. Kristen would see him in the cafeteria once in a while, and they would talk briefly."

Neither one spoke for ten seconds though it seemed like a much longer time.

"Is there more that you need to tell me, Em?"

"Yes, and I'm afraid you will hate me."

"I will never hate you. You can tell me anything."

"Richard asked me to go with him on that trip. He knew I was on break from school. I had thought about it and was planning to go up until the very last day. I didn't tell you because I was afraid to. I was going to tell you at the last minute, so you wouldn't have time to stop me. If Mr. Robertson had not called, I would have been on that plane, Kenny. Mr. Robertson called the morning I was supposed to leave. He found out I was going, not as a member of the team, but just kinda like a vacation. He knew of my brief relationship with Richard, and he did not feel it wise of me to be with him and away from home. Mr. Robertson told me it was my decision to make, but he strongly suggested I not go."

His own past indiscretions had given Mr. Robertson invaluable insights to human behavior. He knew Richard might want to resume a relationship with Emmy.

"I told myself I just wanted to go on the trip so I could talk to him more about Jesus. I thought I would invite him to our church and be friends with him, but that wasn't totally true. I think I was also going on this trip to prove to myself that I could resist his charms. I was such a fool. Can you ever forgive me?"

"You didn't do anything, Emmy."

"I might have, and that is just as bad. We need to talk to Dr. Behren. I hate to think of what would have happened if I had gone. You would not have a wife anymore, and I would probably be in hell."

"I've gotta go, Em. I'll talk to you later." He hung up abruptly. *Oh, Em, you wouldn't be in hell, but what would I have done? I can't imagine my life without you. Why didn't you tell me?* Kenny thought as he wept.

Now Kenny understood why Emmy felt so devastated by the crash.

Kristen made sure Emmy got out of bed early Monday morning.

"Your classes start today and you have to be there."

"I'm not sure I can go," Emmy said and then bit her lip.

"You can't mope around here forever. You need to get back to real life. I know you still feel upset, but maybe going back to class will help."

"Do I have to?" Emmy whined.

"Yes," Kristen insisted. "I'm going back to work today. If you want me to stay in the evening, I will. But I'm going back home to sleep. You should call Kenny tonight."

Emmy struggled at times, but she made it through the week by taking it a day at a time. She went to church on Wednesday and to practice on Thursday. But she didn't call Kenny.

Andy and Kenny were in the back of the SUV taking them to the hotel after a show in Tampa, Florida, when Andy asked, "Have you talked to Emmy at all this week? I know you were upset with her last Friday."

"No, I've been too busy to call."

"Bull!" Andy yelled as he punched the seat between them. "That's a load of crap. You haven't been any busier than normal, and you always make time to call her."

Are you going to get on my case, too, Andy? Kenny wondered. *I'm getting enough of that from my mother.* He tried to ignore Andy by staring out the tinted window.

"Are you going to call her?"

"Yeah, I'll call her."

"There's no better time than the present," Andy said as his voice returned to normal. "I know you have your phone with you."

"Fine. I'll call." Kenny dialed her number, but the call went right to voicemail. He ended the call without leaving a message.

Andy glared at him.

"What? I called. Her phone must be turned off. It went right to voicemail."

Andy shook his head. *All right, be that way. I try not to meddle in you guys' private lives, but you need to talk to Emmy.*

338

"I'll try again in the morning," Kenny said.

Andy let the matter drop and didn't mention it again.

Two weeks later, Andy Walker chartered a flight to get the band back to SoHam for two days after the Saturday night show in Indianapolis. They arrived at the SoHam Regional Airport and Jeff, Jeremy and Dave headed home.

"Andy, would it be all right if I crashed at your place tonight?"

Andy cocked his eyebrows. "Is there anything wrong between you and Emmy? I thought you talked to her yesterday. Should I be concerned?"

"No, I just want to surprise her at church."

"Uh-huh," Andy glared because Kenny had told him about Emmy's trip.

"All right. I'm still upset she didn't tell me about the trip. How could she have ever thought about going? And the fact she withheld the information just totally infuriates me. I would never do that to her."

Andy scowled at Kenny. "I can think of at least two instances where something very serious happened, and both times you withheld the info from her."

"That's different!"

"You care to explain how those events are different?" Andy asked calmly.

"Nothing happened to me or the band."

"Did anything happen to Emmy?"

Kenny stared at the asphalt. "Not really."

"Get over it! The way I see it is that God intervened and wouldn't let her on the plane." Andy placed his hands on Kenny's shoulders as Kenny stared at the ground. "You're welcome to stay, but I think you should go home."

"I know you do, but I just can't face her tonight."

Kenny spent the night with Andy in his townhouse.

Andy was in the kitchen when Kenny came downstairs the next morning.

"You look like crap. Did you get any sleep at all?" Andy asked as he sipped his coffee. He pointed to the wooden caddy on the counter. "There's cups if you want some."

"I might have slept for an hour. You got anything to eat?"

Andy and Kenny grabbed some breakfast and headed over to Crest Ridge United Nazarene for the morning service. Kenny had emailed Chase to let him know he would be there. Chase had the guys set up an extra electric guitar. Kenny and Andy timed their arrival perfectly. Andy grabbed a seat in the sanctuary just before the worship band started to play. Emmy and Kristen walked out onto the platform and started to sing. Kristen was the first to see Andy sitting in the second row off to their right. He placed his finger to his mouth and Kristen nodded—Emmy didn't see him. After the first song, Chase took a moment to pray and this allowed Kenny to move onto the platform unnoticed. After Chase finished, Emmy introduced the next song.

"This is a new song Kenny and I wrote a couple months ago. It's about choices we need to make in our life, and it's called 'The Narrow Road.'"

Chase had been playing as Emmy was introducing the song, and he kicked the band off as soon as she finished. Right away Emmy could hear an extra guitar playing. She looked to her right where Steve Van Zant stood on a riser. She shook her head as she saw Kenny almost hiding to Steve's right. He smiled at her, and she kept singing. She was getting better at not being surprised by him.

After the worship band finished their set, Emmy and Kenny headed back to the music suite. The rest of the group followed. Kenny opened the door for Emmy and they walked into the suite. Before anyone else could enter, Chase stopped them and closed the door.

"I can't tell you why, but we need to let Emmy and Kenny have some privacy," Chase said.

Everyone glanced at Chase and then at each other.

"Sure. Is there anything we can do?" Hank asked.

"You could say a prayer for them."

The guys knew about the plane crash, and that Emmy knew

at least one of the men who perished. They did not know any of the other details.

"Come on, guys. Let's use the restroom and pray for them." Steve led the way.

"Hey! I can't go in there," Kristen said.

"Oh, sorry, Kristen. We forgot you're a girl," Hank said as he slapped his forehead.

Skip Mason smiled. "I didn't forget, Kristen."

"Not now," Steve poked him in the ribs. *I know you have a crush on Kristen, but get over it.*

"We can use the library to pray," Chase suggested.

Kenny noticed that no one had followed them into the music suite. He and Emmy stood five feet apart and looked at each other for a moment, but then averted their gaze. Kenny glanced at the piano in the corner. Emmy found something interesting about the carpet. They looked at each other again for a split second before turning away once more. Emmy bit her lip. Kenny ran a hand through his hair, tugged at his collar and loosened his tie. Thirty seconds passed before they made eye contact again.

Kenny coughed to clear his throat. "Emmy, you didn't look very surprised to see me."

She twisted part of her hair into a braid. "I think I'm getting used to you showing up on the stage unannounced."

She shifted her eyes to the drum kit. Kenny stared at the ceiling.

"Are you aware that tomorrow is our first anniversary?" he whispered after a moment.

"Is it really? I had no idea."

Their eyes met.

"Oh, Emmy, I'm so sorry,"

He opened his arms, and they each took a step forward.

"I should have told you. I'm so sorry."

They took another step and Kenny closed his arms around her. They didn't have to say anything more as the tears escaped. They held each other for several minutes before he let her go.

"I really didn't forget about our anniversary," Emmy whispered.

"I thought maybe we could celebrate somehow. Is there anything special you would like to do?" Kenny asked with a wicked grin.

"Let's go sit with Cousin Andy, and we'll discuss this after church."

Andy patted Emmy's hand a few minutes later as she sat next to him with Kenny next to her. "Is everything okay now?" he asked tenderly.

"Yes. I guess we had our first fight, but we made up."

It wouldn't have happened if I made him go home. I should have canceled a couple of shows, Andy thought. *I will know better if something like this ever happens again.*

That evening, Andy, the guys from the band and their wives gathered at Jeff's house for a celebration for Kenny and Emmy.

"We know this isn't your anniversary, but we thought you might be too busy to get together tomorrow... if you know what I mean," Andy teased.

"Andy, you are so bad. We don't have anything special planned for tomorrow since I didn't know you would be home. We'll probably just stay in..." Emmy paused as the guys started laughing.

"Do you want me to finish that thought for you, Em?" Andy asked.

"No, I think everyone knows what I meant to say."

Even though the guys in the band saw each other all the time on the road, they still enjoyed getting together. In addition to being partners in one of the most popular bands in the world, they remained good friends. They hung out at Jeff and Frances' house until close to ten.

"I want to remind everyone we will be leaving at eleven sharp on Tuesday morning. We need to be at the venue in Memphis by three. I'll see everyone then." Andy looked at Emmy and smiled. "Will that give you enough time?"

Emmy grinned, nodded and said, "Thank you for letting him come home, Andy."

"You're welcome, cuz."

The next morning Emmy woke up before Kenny. She looked at him and decided to let him sleep. She quietly headed downstairs and started the coffee. She looked in the fridge to see what she could make for breakfast. She pulled out the eggs and checked to see how many were left. Just then Kenny walked into the kitchen.

"Morning, sweetie. Happy anniversary!" Kenny said as he kissed her.

"I started the coffee. What should we have for breakfast? I can make eggs and we have bacon."

"Sounds good to me. What do you want to do today?"

"I have classes until three. Would we have time to make a quick stop to see our parents tomorrow before you have to leave, or should we go see them today?"

"I'd rather wait. I want to spend today with you. Maybe do Ciao Bella for dinner."

"That sounds good. I would like that."

"Maybe after you get home this afternoon we can turn off all the phones and computers and just hang out here."

"That sounds even better to me."

They were sitting on the back deck in the afternoon and Emmy sighed.

"What are you thinking about, Em?" Kenny asked.

"I was thinking about Richard Demarco and those guys from work."

"Did you know any of the other guys?"

"Not really. I might have seen them, but I didn't know them."

"Are you still feeling guilty about the crash and all?"

"I don't think I will ever forget about that. I realize now that God was looking out for me. It wasn't His will that I was on that plane, and I didn't realize it. I was doing my own thing and lost sight of what He wanted. It makes me realize that I need to pray more often."

"You were trying to lead Richard to Christ..."

"Yeah, but I was doing it all wrong. I was trying to lead him to Jesus through my own strength. I know now that I need to

343

let the Holy Spirit work, and I have to follow His leading."

"It's not always easy to know just what to do."

"Do you think it will get easier as we get older?"

"I sure hope so, Em."

That evening they had dinner at Ciao Bella and went to bed early. They wanted to visit their parents in the morning before Kenny had to leave.

They woke up early and arrived at the Colwell home a few minutes before seven o'clock.

"It's good to see you, son. I wasn't sure if you would have time to stop by."

"We can't stay too long because we need to see Emmy's parents. Then she has to get to class."

"Have you had breakfast yet?" Mom asked.

"No, we didn't have time." Emmy blushed and Mrs. Colwell understood why.

"Would you like some pancakes?"

"Do you have any blueberries?" Emmy asked.

"Yes, dear, I know you like blueberries in your pancakes."

After visiting with the Colwells, they walked over to visit with her parents. Her mother let them in.

"Good morning. Your father is trying to fix a leak in the basement. During that last storm we got a foot of water in the basement. Lately, we are having to fix something every month. First the furnace. Then the water heater. The roof needs to be replaced, and the windows are so drafty. Sometimes I just don't know what to do."

"Mom, have you guys ever thought about moving to a newer home?" Emmy asked as she sat on the couch with Kenny.

"We've thought about it, but we can't afford it." Mom removed the newspaper from her recliner and then sat down.

"We could help you out," Emmy offered just as her father entered the room.

"No, I'm not going to take money from my daughter."

"Why not? We could help you out. Grandma Isabel has helped us out before. Why won't you let us help you?"

344

"Because he's too stubborn," Mom answered.

"I'm not going to take charity from anyone." Dad wiped his hands on a rag, then slumped in his recliner.

"Oh, Daddy. Don't be that way. We can help you out. You are getting too old to take care of this place. If you had a newer house, it would be easier. You could move into one of those senior developments and not have to worry about outside maintenance at all."

"I like to work on my house."

"Hmmmph!" Mom guffawed. "No you don't. You used to, but not now. It's getting too hard for you to even mow the yard. We should think about it and maybe take a look at some of those places."

Raymond pointed a finger at Patricia. "Maybe we can look, but that's all."

Emmy was thrilled her father had even agreed to look at a place. To her that was progress.

"If you want me to take you around this week, I will."

"We need to get over to the airport, Em. We're supposed to leave at eleven."

"Okay, we need to run. Please think about what we talked about. I will take you to see a couple places."

"Goodbye, dear, we'll think about it. Have a safe trip, Kenny."

"Happy anniversary. I know it was yesterday, but we didn't see you."

"Thanks, Daddy. I'll talk to you guys later."

Chapter Thirty-Six

Emmy gazed into the TV room from the doorway. She recalled the last time Richard Demarco had been in that room. Only the timely phone call from Mama Bertucci had stopped his unwelcome advances toward her. She shuddered and felt goosebumps up and down her arms. *Maybe I should tell Kenny we need to move. I don't like to be in here by myself.*

She jumped as the phone rang—interrupting her thoughts. *God! That was spooky.* She checked the caller ID. "Hey, Kristen. What's up?"

"It's such a gorgeous day. John and I want to go for a drive. Tony and Sloane are coming, too. Would you like to go?"

"Sure. When are you leaving?"

"We'll pick you up in an hour. Tony's driving."

"Good. That'll give me time to get in touch with Kenny."

"The guys want to check out some neighborhoods. John wants to buy a house, and I think Tony is even thinking about moving out."

"No way! Tony is actually considering moving out? What will Mama think about that?" Emmy asked and then giggled.

Emmy shared her thoughts and desires with Kenny in an email. He replied back and suggested an area they might want to consider—Bristol Ridge.

After driving through several parts of SoHam, and not finding anything that rocked their boat, Tony drove into an area on the northern edge of the city.

"This is the area Kenny suggested, and it would be the perfect place to build a home," Emmy mentioned excitedly as they rode through the development of Bristol Ridge.

"It's brand new," Tony said as he looked at the largely undeveloped area. "The streets aren't finished. There's not even a model home or a sales office."

Kristen asked Emmy, "Are you guys thinking about moving?"

"I have been thinking about it for a while, but we would have to get out of our lease. I almost hate to do that because our

346

rent is so cheap."

"Kenny told me you need to start investing your money better. He said a house is always a sound investment."

"Then why don't you own one, Tony?" Emmy asked. "Is it because Mama won't let you move out?"

"Ha! Ha! Aren't you just too funny?" Tony frowned at her. "I've been thinking about buying one or maybe building a new one. Why are you guys still in that house?"

"Kenny bought some land out West before we got married, and he claims he owns property somewhere close to SoHam, but isn't ready to build a house yet." Emmy spotted a small sign, nearly hidden by weeds, partway up a small hill. "Tony, stop the car."

He stopped in the middle of the road and turned to look at Emmy. "What is it, Em?"

"I thought I saw a for sale sign." Emmy jumped out of the back of Tony's Envoy and ran back up the road. "Come here, you guys. I see the sign. Let's check it out."

Tony parked on the edge of the unpaved road.

"We should at least check it out, John," Kristen suggested.

After some investigation, they discovered two lots for sale.

"If there aren't any other lots between these two, they are huge lots," Sloane said. "These lots could easily be several acres."

Kristen grinned and said, "Maybe we could buy one, and you could buy the other one, Tony."

"And end up as neighbors? I don't know if I want to live that close to you, Kristen," Tony teased. Actually, he thought it would be almost perfect to live next door to her and John.

They drove around, but didn't see any other for sale signs.

As soon as they got home, Emmy called Kenny. After a few minutes, she brought up the property they saw. Everyone else sat in the living room to talk about the properties.

"We were out for a drive and found the Bristol Ridge area. It looks nice. It's mostly hills and woods, but we did see two properties for sale. Maybe we should look into it. There might be more lots for sale."

"What did Tony and John think about the area?" Kenny asked.

347

"They both liked it. We were badgering Tony about buying a house, or at least some property. He needs to move out of Mama's house if he ever wants to marry Sloane."

"Maybe Tony or John should look into buying the property."

"What about us? Do you think we could afford it?" Emmy asked while twisting her hair into a braid.

"How much was it?"

"We're not sure. We would have to call the Realtor."

"If you like it, go ahead and call, Em."

"Okay! I'll call tomorrow."

Emmy called the attorney who represented her landlord before she left for North Park the next morning. He just happened to be in his office. Emmy explained who she was and where she lived.

"We want to purchase some acreage and build a new home. We might want to end our lease early. Would that be possible?" Emmy asked.

"I will have to call you back, Mrs. Colwell."

The attorney called Mr. Robertson. "Yes, Bill, she just called, and I thought I should let you know right away."

Mr. Robertson had anticipated this would happen someday and told the attorney, "I will handle the matter from here on. Thanks for calling me so quickly."

As soon as Mr. Robertson got off the phone, it rang again.

"Hello, Kenny. I think I know why you are calling..."

Mr. Robertson talked to Kenny for fifteen minutes. Then he leaned back in his large black leather chair in his home office. He put his hands on the back of his head and thought about the matter. He reached a decision and called Gordon Carter. Gordon managed the Aberdeen Holding Company. A company owned by Mr. Robertson.

"Gordon, it's Bill." After taking care of some other business, Mr. Robertson brought up why he had really called. "I need you to take care of something for me..." He explained everything.

348

"I will take care of it, but I'm sure you realize you will be taking quite a loss on those properties. Not a loss exactly, but you could sell them for twice the amount you mentioned."

"I know, but I don't think it will matter. I'm willing to sacrifice any profit I might have made. This is far more important to me than money."

Later that day, Tony and John checked more thoroughly about the property they found.

"John, this can't be right. That property is probably worth a lot more."

"Let's call the number. What can it hurt? We'll find out the price was listed wrong and that will be that."

Tony called the number. After talking to a Mr. Carter, Tony hung up, looked at John and smiled. They called Mr. Robertson's office and talked to Mrs. Moneywell.

Tony explained the situation. "We are thinking about buying some property, and Mr. Robertson is the only person I know who I trust to advise us. I hate to bother him, but it's a lot of money."

She listened patiently and then told them, "I will pass your message along, and Mr. Robertson will look into this for you. It sounds like you guys are getting a really good deal though."

Mrs. Moneywell knew very well why they were getting a bargain. It was because the properties, and all of Bristol Ridge, were owned by the Aberdeen Holding Company and the owner of that company made them a special offer.

Tony and John were waiting on the back deck for Emmy when she got home from school.

"Hey, guys. What's up? Did you call about the property?"

"We sure did!"

"Why are you grinning like that, and why didn't you let yourself in?" Emmy asked as she unlocked the back door.

"We didn't think we should go inside."

"You know Kenny's not home, right? You wouldn't have walked in on us doing anything."

"See! I told you she wouldn't mind." Tony poked John in the arm.

The next afternoon Tony and John each placed an offer for the properties. They headed to Emmy's to eat dinner. Kristen came straight to Emmy's after work because John told her he had some important news that concerned all of them. Emmy rushed home after her last class because she received the same message.

Emmy's home phone rang while she was upstairs changing clothes.

"Emmy, the phone's ringing. Should I pick it up?" Tony asked because he knew she was busy. When she didn't answer, he picked it up. At the same moment Emmy picked it up in the bedroom. Tony heard Emmy answer and started to hang up, but he didn't for some reason. He listened quietly.

"Hello, Emmy, it's Mr. Robertson. How are you doing?"

"I'm fine, sir. How are you?"

"I'm doing great. Mrs. Moneywell told me of some plans you and Tony and John have. I'm sorry I didn't call you back earlier, but I've been busy with some business. Is Tony there now? I tried his house, and his mother told me he might be at your place."

"Yes, would you like to talk to him?"

"If I may."

"I picked up the other phone, Emmy. I'm sorry," Tony said.

"That's all right. I'll hang up and let you talk to Mr. Robertson."

Emmy hung up, flew down the stairs and sat on the living room couch next to Kristen while Mr. Robertson talked to Tony.

"Can you talk without Emmy hearing you?" Mr. Robertson asked.

"I'm not sure. She's in the living room. I could go outside."

"Why don't you do that? I don't want her to overhear our conversation."

"Okay," Tony answered even though he didn't understand why. Ten minutes later he did.

"Now about the properties you and John are interested in, just how soon do you plan on building and moving?"

"We don't know for sure. John will be ready to build first since he's already engaged. We each made an offer on a piece of property and want you to take a look at the contract for us, if you could. We haven't signed the contract yet. We had it faxed to your office, I hope you don't mind. I hate to bother you because I know how busy you are."

"I don't mind at all, Tony. I passed the contracts along to a man I know. He's an expert in real estate law, and he assured me everything looked great."

"We are concerned there might have been a mistake on the price, and the deal will fall through."

"No, I don't think you need to worry about that," Mr Robertson said and then grinned. "Are you sure about what you want to do, Tony?"

"Yes, I've been wanting to find a place of my own."

Mr. Robertson was quiet for a moment until he reached a decision. "I need to tell you something."

"What is it, Mr. Robertson?" Tony asked wondering what it could possibly be.

"The properties you and John are buying belong to me. I am the Aberdeen Holding Company."

"What do you mean? I don't understand, Mr. Robertson."

"Aberdeen is owned by me. It's an umbrella company."

Tony knew what Mr. Robertson meant, but he stifled a laugh because he could picture Emmy thinking about umbrellas.

"I bought the entire area a few years ago, and now we're ready to develop it. The city finally approved the plan. I'm going to build a new house close to where your properties are located and Kenny owns the property across the road from yours."

"So, Emmy and Kenny will live across the road from us?"

"Yes, but you can't tell her. She doesn't know. Kenny wanted to keep it a secret."

"Right. She is going to be so surprised. Do you want to talk to her now?"

"Yes, I need to explain some things to her. Maybe you should stay close by in case she needs someone's shoulder to cry on."

"You and Kenny have certainly been rather devious, sir."

You don't know the whole story, yet. Mr. Robertson thought.

351

Tony went back inside. "Emmy, can you come in here, please? Mr. Robertson needs to talk to you."

"Okay, is there anything wrong?"

"You had better let him explain it, Em." Tony pulled out a kitchen chair and Emmy sat down. Tony stood behind her.

"Hello, Mr. Robertson, is everything all right?"

"Yes, everything is okay, but I need to explain a few things to you. First of all, the house you are living in belongs to you and Diane."

"You must be mistaken, Mr. Robertson. Kenny and I are just renting this place. It's owned by the Aberdeen Holding Company. Whoever, or whatever, that is. At least that's who we make out the rent check to every month."

After a pause, Mr. Robertson told her, "Emmy, I own the Aberdeen Holding Company."

"No you don't," she said and then tried to laugh. "You own Robertson Industries."

"True, but I also own some other companies now."

He explained some of the technical and financial details about Aberdeen to her, but she still didn't understand.

"Emmy, do you remember the dinner party at the Santiago's home when I was telling you about a man that helped me get started many years ago?"

"I think I remember something like that, but you never mentioned his name." Emmy bit her lip and glanced over her shoulder at Tony.

Mr. Robertson paused for a moment to gather his thoughts. "Emmy, that man was your grandfather—Joseph Colasanti. Before he died he asked me to do something for him. I was indebted to him for his generosity, and I wanted to repay him somehow. He asked me to promise him that if I was ever in a position to help his granddaughters I would and he would be so grateful. He knew he wouldn't be here to help you or Diane himself. I promised him I would."

Emmy couldn't speak. She choked up as she thought about her grandfather, who passed away many years ago. Emmy remembered sitting on his lap as a little girl. She vaguely remembered her grandfather telling her father about a new business partner he was helping start a new company. She recalled how her father and grandfather argued about it.

Mr. Robertson continued, "Emmy, I remember seeing you when you were only a few days old. Your grandfather was so proud of you. When you were about two months old, I held you on my chest while you took a nap. Then a few months later, I remember how upset your grandfather was when you were in the hospital. He was afraid you were going to die, and it tore him apart. That was the only time I ever saw him cry. I remember watching you as you learned how to swim along with Diane. I wasn't a real part of your life, Emmy, but I kept track of you and Diane throughout the years waiting for any chance I could to help you."

"Grandpa knew he was going to die. I didn't realize it back then, but I do now," Emmy said.

"He faced his illness with bravery, but after your grandmother passed away, he lost some of the will to fight. Emmy, your grandfather was one of the biggest reasons I am successful today. He helped me get started and saw the potential in my company. Back in 2001, I purchased the property you are living in. You and Diane are free to do whatever you want with the house. You can sell it if you want, or maybe now that you know it is yours, you and Kenny could stay. Whatever you decide to do, I will help in any way I can."

Mr. Robertson didn't mention how her rent money had been invested and that money belonged to her, also. He also didn't tell her about the property Kenny owned.

Emmy was stunned, and now she began to understand why she was chosen for her job. After she regained her composure, Emmy asked Mr. Robertson, "Did you know who I was when I applied for the job with your company? You did, didn't you?"

"Yes. Please don't be upset with me for making sure you had a good job, Emmy. You worked very hard and earned the respect of all the team members who worked with you. When I hired you, or should I say, when I made sure you found out about the opening in my company, I knew you had great potential. I was impressed by your determination to put yourself through college on your own even after you were offered financial help. I would have gladly paid for you to go to college, but I knew you wouldn't have accepted my help. Your grandfather could be a very stubborn man, and I guess you inherited that trait from him."

"So I've been told," she said. "I remember telling Diane when I got the job that I must have had a guardian angel looking out for me, and I really did. I loved my grandfather very much, Mr. Robertson, and he would be so grateful for what you have done for Diane and me."

"I'm happy and grateful that I am in a position to have been a small help to you, Emmy."

"Would you be upset if we gave the house back to you?"

"Yes, I would be upset because I want you to keep the money after you and Diane sell the house, if that's what you choose to do."

"Wait a minute!" Emmy finally realized something and stood up. "Wait a second!"

"Yes, Emmy. What is it?"

"The property Tony and John made offers on is owned by the Aberdeen Holding Company. That means it's really owned by you, right?"

"Yes, it is, Emmy."

Emmy broke down in tears, sat back down and couldn't continue as she fully understood the generosity of Mr. Robertson.

"Mr. Robertson."

"Tony, is that you?"

"Yes, sir, I don't think Emmy can talk right now. She's crying just like you thought she would."

"Please don't mention the property Kenny owns just yet. He wants to tell her himself when he gets home. He's just been waiting for the right time."

"I understand. I don't know what to say. I don't know how John and I can ever repay you."

"Tony, you guys don't owe me anything." *There's more to the story, but I have to talk to Kenny first.* "I need to let you go because I have to take another call."

"Thanks again, Mr. Robertson. I'll talk to you soon."

Mr. Robertson hung up with Tony and took the other call. Tony stood behind Emmy as she cried at the kitchen table. He held her shoulders, rubbed her back to comfort her and then sat next to her.

She looked at him and sighed, "Oh, Tony. What should I do? Mr. Robertson bought this house for me and Diane. If we decide to sell it, would we come across as being ungrateful?"

"I don't know, Em. You and Kenny need to take some time and pray about this. You don't need to make a decision right away."

"Hello, Kenny, it's good to hear from you," Mr. Robertson said as he leaned back in his chair.

"You, too. Mrs. Moneywell told me I needed to call you ASAP. Is this about the property?"

"Not really. Do you have a few minutes to talk?" Mr. Robertson asked.

"I've got a free hour. What is it?"

Mr. Robertson gathered his thoughts. "I'll go over this quickly, and if you have any questions, I'll answer them at the end."

"Okay," Kenny wondered what could be so important.

"Has Emmy ever mentioned a trust fund, or stock in my company?" Mr. Robertson asked.

Kenny thought about it for a few seconds. "Not that I can recall."

"Let me explain. Emmy's grandfather bought stock in Robertson Industries and put it into a trust for Diane and Emmy until they turned twenty-five. In his will he named me as the trustee of the trust fund. I'm not sure how much you know about Robertson Industries, but the stock is held privately. Diane has turned twenty-five and is starting to use some of the money. When Emmy turns twenty-five, she can do the same."

"I don't think she knows, Mr. Robertson. She has never said a word about stocks or a trust or anything like that to me. Kristen has never said anything about a trust. I think if Emmy knew, she would have told Kristen or me."

"When she has her twenty-fifth birthday, you guys should make an appointment to see me. I will go over all the details at that time. I can't reveal anything until then."

"Okay. We'll do that. It was good to talk to you again, sir."

Later that evening, Emmy talked to Kenny about the property.

"Tony and John made offers because it was just too good an opportunity to pass up. What do you think we should do?"

"I think we should wait until I get home before we do anything. We have time to decide what we want to do."

"Are we ever going to build a house on that property you own?" Emmy asked.

"We might one of these days, but not yet." Kenny wanted to change the subject so he told Emmy, "Oh, did I tell you Becky is getting married on May twenty-ninth?"

"You told me she was engaged, but not when the wedding was. What is her fiancee's name again?"

"Taylor Claussen. He's a staff minister at Living Water Bible church where Dr. Behren was the senior pastor. It's a Nazarene church, but with a different name."

"Oh, that's right. We met him once. Taylor, I mean. Are you disappointed you can't go to the wedding?" Emmy asked. *You can't go to the wedding even if you could.*

"No, I didn't think it would be a good idea even if we weren't playing that night."

"Becky will make a great pastor's wife."

"I think you're right. I think God always knew we weren't meant to be together, so that's why we broke up, and she met Taylor."

Chapter Thirty-Seven

Derrick Keasling graduated from the James E. Rogers College of Law. On Thursday afternoon his parents and Kristen flew to Tucson to attend the ceremony to be held the next day.

"I see them now," Derrick told Amber. They had been waiting at the baggage claim carousel in Tucson International Airport for thirty minutes.

Kristen spotted her brother and waved as she walked toward him. "We're finally here. I think the pilot got lost and took us to California or something."

"Hi, Mom. Hi, Dad. I'm glad you made it. Did you guys have a good flight, other than getting lost, I mean?" Derrick teased as he hugged them and then his sister.

"It was bearable. Hello, Amber, how have you been?" Mrs. Keasling did not enjoy flying in coach.

"I've been rather busy finishing up this semester, but now that's it's over, I will have some time to relax." Amber was working on her PHD. She turned to Kristen and smiled. "Are you getting anxious for the wedding? It's only three weeks away."

"Exactly. It feels like it's taking forever to get here."

Amber and Kristen walked along talking about the wedding. Derrick took his parents' luggage, loaded it onto a cart and they followed behind. Twenty minutes later they arrived at the rented townhouse Derrick and Amber shared.

"This is a lot bigger than that apartment you had," Karla Keasling told her son. "Are you sure you don't mind us staying here? We could always get a room at a hotel."

"We don't mind, Mom. There are three bedrooms upstairs although one of them is set up as a study room. There is a day bed in there."

"Is that where I have to sleep?" Kristen asked as she picked up a colorful piece of pottery.

"It's either in there or on the couch down here—your choice." Derrick took the pottery from Kristen and set it back on the glass table. "You might drop it."

"I need to call John to let him know we arrived safely."

"I'll take your luggage up to the guest room and you and Amber can decide where we are going for dinner."

"Thank you, son." Mr. Keasling made himself comfortable on the large leather couch.

"The remote's on the end table, Dad. That's a new plasma TV."

They ended up eating at O'Sullivan's Steakhouse, only five minutes away.

After the meal Mr. Keasling mentioned, "That was a mighty good piece of beef."

"We like to come here once a week. Amber usually has chicken or salmon, but I need a steak..."

"I noticed you scarfed that one down pretty fast," Kristen said. "You and Tony and John will have to see who can eat the biggest steak when you're home."

"Tony will win, unless John is a big eater, too."

"He can keep up with Tony."

After the graduation ceremony the next day, Derrick allowed Kristen to take hundreds of pictures.

"Are you finished already?"

"Hey! How often is my big brother going to graduate from law school? Just hold your horses. I'm about through."

"Would you like to go out for Mexican tonight?" Amber asked the Keaslings.

"Sounds good to me."

"I could use a large margarita," Mrs. Keasling said with a smile as she hugged Derrick one more time.

After dinner at the El Dorado Grill, Mr. Keasling suggested, "I think your mother and I would like to go back to the townhouse and relax. Why don't you take Kristen out and show her the town?"

"Sounds okay to me. We'll drop you and Mom off and take Kristen out. I know the perfect place. We might even bring her back with us." He teased her, and she made a face at him.

"Maybe Amber and I will drop *you* off somewhere and have some fun on our own."

358

Derrick took his parents to the townhouse and asked Kristen, "What would you like to do? We could go to a show or go dancing."

"I can see a movie back in SoHam. Let's do something different."

"We like to go dancing at this club called Maloney's Blue Moon. They have live music on the weekends."

"That sounds like fun."

They headed to the club. They could hear the throb of the music as soon as they got out of the car.

As they found an empty table, Kristen noticed the wall. "Everything is so colorful here. I like this tapestry."

"We usually don't spend more than a couple of hours here because the lights can get a bit annoying. Plus the fact Amber's head begins to throb in time with the bass."

Kristen looked at the gyrating mass of humanity on the dance floor. "The place is packed, and I don't see anyone who looks over thirty."

"I think it's the reverse carding they do at the door," Derrick said and then grinned.

"What do you mean?" Kristen asked as she swayed her hips in time with the driving rhythm.

"They check IDs at the door."

"Yeah. I was surprised they didn't card me."

"They will check your age when you order something to drink. Even if it's just bottled water."

"Then why do they check IDs to get in?" Kristen asked.

"To make sure no one over thirty gets in," Derrick said and then laughed.

Kristen poked him in the arm. "You're teasing."

On the way home ninety minutes later, Kristen admitted, "I know I'm getting married in three weeks, but I had a blast dancing with all those guys."

"I'm sure John would understand," Amber said. *I've never seen you acting so uninhibited with strangers.*

"I had fun dancing with you, too, Derrick."

"It was better than dancing with Mom," Derrick teased.

"You guys looked so good together. I'm not very close to my brother. In fact I haven't seen him for over a year," Amber mentioned.

"He lives in South Africa and doesn't get back to the states very often," Derrick informed Kristen.

"I wouldn't like that at all. Although he is a dork at times, I love my brother."

"How many drinks did you have, Krissy?" Amber asked. *That might explain your behavior tonight.*

"I just had one." Kristen held up a finger. "I'm not saying that because I had too much to drink. I really mean it."

"I know. I'm just teasing. I'm envious of the relationship you have with Derrick."

"If you guys keep this up, I am going to be sick to my stomach." Derrick pretended to be annoyed.

Derrick took his parents and Kristen back to the airport on Saturday afternoon. Kristen needed to get back in time for church on Sunday morning.

"How's Emmy doing?" Derrick asked. "I know she had trouble dealing with that plane crash."

"She seems to be over it now. Her semester is over, and she took her last final yesterday."

"Tell her I said hi."

"We will see you in three weeks, son," Mom said as she hugged Derrick.

"What's going on in three weeks?" Derrick asked with a straight face. "I wasn't planning to come home for a couple of months."

Kristen smacked his arm. "You better be home for my wedding."

"I forgot all about that. Do I really have to show up for your wedding?" Derrick asked. "Can't we just send a cheap card?"

Kristen made a face. "Yeah, sure. I'll just tell Mama that you weren't interested."

"Point taken. We will be there." Derrick laughed as he hugged his sister.

360

By the end of May, Tony and John made their decision about the properties. They prayed and talked to Dr. Behren and their financial advisor. Tony, John, Kristen and Emmy made an appointment to see Mr. Robertson in his office. When they arrived, Mrs. Moneywell fussed over them like a mother hen. Mr. Robertson came out of his office to greet them.

"Emmy and Kristen, you are becoming more beautiful every time I see you." He chuckled because, though Kristen wore a skirt and top, Emmy wore faded jeans and a sweatshirt. "Tony, John, it's good to see you, too."

"It's good to see you, Mr. Robertson." Both guys wore sport coats, ties and black jeans.

"Come on in and have a seat. I'll be right there. I just need to tell Mrs. Moneywell something."

They went into his office. Everyone sat down except Emmy. She inspected some photographs on the wall and noticed one she had never seen before.

"Mrs. Moneywell, I need you to..."

"Your appointments have been canceled for the rest of the day and rescheduled. Your car will be waiting downstairs, and I ordered a small lunch to be sent up."

"You are the most amazing woman I know, Mrs. Moneywell."

"Why, thank you, Mr. Robertson."

He smiled at her, and she smiled back. He re-entered his office to talk to everyone. "I have been informed you have reached a decision."

"After much prayer and on the advice of our financial guru, we have decided to purchase the properties," Tony said.

John looked at Kristen and added, "We want to build a house as soon as possible."

"I think that is a very wise decision. The chance to purchase the property in Bristol Ridge is too good to pass up."

"We know you are practically giving the property away," Tony added. "If you sold it to someone else, you would make five or ten times the money."

"There are some things more important in this life than

361

money. This is one of them. Do you guys have time to run out to Bristol Ridge? I want to show you around the place myself."

"We've got time." Emmy turned around and grinned. *You have a picture of Grandpa.*

"Good. My car is waiting downstairs. We'll go as soon as we finish the lunch Mrs. Moneywell is sending up."

"Did I mention I finished another semester at North Park?" Emmy asked.

"No, you didn't. How did you do on your finals?" Mr Robertson asked.

"I'm sure I passed them."

Kristen rolled her eyes. "She's trying to be modest. She never gets anything lower than an A. She is such a brainiac."

I know she is. Her grandfather would be so proud of her. Mr. Robertson smiled. "How many more semesters do you have left?"

"I still need eighteen hours to earn my degree, and I plan to finish them in the fall semester." Emmy added proudly, "And I won't owe a dime in student loans."

After eating lunch, they were driven to Bristol Ridge in a large, black SUV. Emmy and Tony sat in the third row.

"Hey, Em, does this SUV remind you of anything?" Tony asked.

"Not really," she answered with a puzzled expression. "It's a lot fancier than your Envoy."

"I think it looks like it belongs to the Secret Service, and Mr. Robertson's driver is his bodyguard."

"You're goofy. Did you forget to wear your helmet again?" Emmy teased.

Tony poked her in the side.

Mr. Robertson had his driver stop first at the property Tony had purchased.

"There are ten acres and most of it is hills and trees." Mr. Robertson waved a hand. "Have you given any thought as to where you would build your house?"

"I thought it would be best to build right on top of that hill." Tony pointed to the place. "I'm guessing there are a couple acres of flat land up there."

"That is where I would build," Mr. Robertson said.

"What are you gonna do with all this land?" Emmy climbed on top of a three-feet-high boulder and looked around.

"I might let you put up a small shack way back in the corner," Tony teased.

"No way! I'd never want to live so close to you," Emmy teased back. "I pity Kristen, but at least the lots are humongous."

Tony shook his head. *You are in for a big surprise, Em.*

They moved to the property John and Kristen had purchased.

"We kinda know what kind of house we want. We talked to an architect already," John mentioned to Mr. Robertson.

"If you need any help on that end, let me know," Mr. Robertson replied. "I have some experience with building homes."

Mr. Robertson pointed out the acreage across the road and told them it had been purchased, but didn't reveal the owner's name. He smiled at Tony and John. Emmy and Kristen still had no clue who owned the property. Mr. Robertson also showed them the area where he planned to build a new home.

"There are over a hundred acres all total in Bristol Ridge, and it's divided up into fifteen properties. I'm keeping two to give to my sons, but are still ten to be sold. It might take a while before you have neighbors."

He took them back to his office to retrieve their car.

"How can we ever repay your kindness to us, Mr. Robertson?" Emmy asked.

"I do not expect anything, Emmy—nothing like money or anything. To see you and Diane happy is all I ask."

Emmy hugged him for a moment. He patted her on the back as she rested her head on his chest—just as she did when she was a baby.

363

Chapter Thirty-Eight

The temperature climbed above seventy as the trucks started pulling into the area behind SoHam Memorial Stadium in the early morning hours of May twenty-ninth. An hour later four touring buses arrived—Fridays At Five had made it home. Emmy and the other wives waited to greet the guys. The door of Kenny's bus opened and he stepped out. Emmy ran over to greet him and almost knocked him over as she jumped into his arms.

"Does this mean you missed me?" Kenny teased.

"Maybe a little bit."

"Are you going to kiss me?"

Emmy grinned and said, "I don't know if I should with all these people around."

"It's never stopped you before."

Emmy kissed him and then he set her down.

"What time do you have to be back?"

"Soundcheck is at four, but I have to be here at least by three-thirty. We are supposed to go onstage at eight and we have to finish by eleven."

"No interviews or meet and greets today?" Emmy grinned.

"No, I am all yours."

"Oooh! I like that." She grinned and held his hand.

He kissed her again, and she noticed everyone watching them.

"Were you planning on coming to the show?" Kenny asked in jest.

"Probably not. I didn't get any tickets, and, anyway, I've seen you guys perform before. Same old songs, you know."

"We play some new songs now," Kenny said.

"I might be persuaded to come to the show if I can get in for free."

"Only very special guests get in for free," he said with a straight face. "Is there any reason I should consider you a *special* guest?"

"I could..." she whispered in his ear what she could do.

"That sounds like it could be very special. I might be able

364

to find a ticket and a backstage pass for you. Do you have any friends who might want to see us?"

"I've got a few friends, but they're busy doing important stuff today like dusting lightbulbs and folding underwear. You know... really important stuff."

Kenny shook his head and then smiled. "I've got a feeling this is going to be a very busy summer."

Emmy pulled into the driveway, and they walked in the back door. "Should we head upstairs right away?" she asked as they hugged in the kitchen.

"We can do that in a minute, but first I need to tell you something." He pulled out a chair for her and sat down to face her.

"Is it bad news?"

"No, no, it's nothing bad." He waved a hand. "Do you know anything about a trust fund?"

"What trust fund?"

He grinned. *So you don't know. I hope you don't cry too much.* "I talked to Mr. Robertson a while back. Apparently, your grandfather set up a trust for you and Diane."

"Really?" Emmy thought about it for a few seconds. "Oh, that. I kinda remember him telling Daddy about some money he set aside. It's nothing to get excited about. I think Grandpa bought some savings bonds or something. Daddy has probably forgotten all about it."

"I just thought I would mention it, Em." Kenny tilted his head. *I think there's more to this trust fund than a couple of savings bonds from the way Mr. Robertson talked.*

"Did you remember that Becky is getting married today?" Emmy asked.

"I did. We sent a card, right?"

"Yes, I took care of that." She stood up and pulled him over to the stairs.

After spending the rest of the morning and early afternoon at home, Emmy took Kenny back to the stadium. She had an all-access pass so she could wander around backstage.

"It looks like it's going to be a gorgeous day." Emmy shielded her eyes as she looked at the sun.

"I believe the forecast is for rain on Memorial Day," Kenny said as he waved to some of the crew.

"It's a good thing you guys are playing today."

She joined Kenny onstage as the guys did their soundcheck. Kenny wanted her to sing "I Will Be True To You" as a duet.

"Dan, could I have just a little more of Emmy in my monitor, please?" Kenny asked.

Dan Belanger handled the monitor mix for the band while his brother Noah kept all the wireless systems operating flawlessly.

"That's better, Dan. Thank you."

After the tech crew and the guys in the band were satisfied, they headed backstage. Kenny and Emmy meandered toward his bus. Emmy saw Andy Walker talking to Ralph Glissman and ran over to see him.

"Hi, Cousin Andy. Hi, Ralph. How are you guys doing? I'm sure you must be delighted that the tour is finally over."

"Hello there, cuz. How did you get in here? This is a restricted area."

Emmy looked at Ralph and bit her lip. She reached up and whispered in Andy's ear, "I had to sleep with one of the guys in the band."

Andy teased her by pretending to be shocked and said, "You slept with one of the guys in the band. Which one? You know they are all married, don't you?"

Emmy poked him in his ribs for embarrassing her in front of Ralph.

"You know who I mean."

"He will be home for over four months before I take him away again," Andy said.

Emmy grinned and responded, "And I am ever so grateful for that."

"You know they will be rather busy finishing up the CD," Andy reminded her. "They will be in the studio for days at a time."

"I know, but we might be able to squeeze in a small vacation after that's done. I'd like to go out west for a couple of weeks."

Ralph said, "Alice and I took the boys out to Utah and

366

Arizona several years ago. We loved it."

"I want to go hiking and maybe climb some mountains."

"There's plenty of that available," Ralph added.

Kenny walked up behind Emmy, squeezed her shoulders and asked, "Is she bothering you guys? I gave her a pass, but if you want to toss her out, that's okay."

Emmy looked at Andy because she knew what Andy was going to say because he had a big grin on his face.

"Don't you dare!" she threatened, but to no avail.

Andy kept a straight face. "She told us she got the pass by sleeping with one of the guys in the band. Did you know that?"

"No, I didn't. She must mean one of the guys in the opening act because I know none of us would do something so despicable."

"I hate you all," Emmy said, but without much conviction.

"Are you hungry, Em? Wanna grab something to eat?"

"Maybe in a little while. I'm supposed to meet Kristen and everybody at six. What time is it now?"

"It is exactly... five forty-two," Andy announced.

"You are the only guy I know who still wears a big watch like that," Emmy teased Andy. "Everyone else looks at their cell phone to tell time."

"I happen to like this watch."

"If you want to meet Kristen, we should walk over to the gate and make sure they can get in." Kenny took her hand and walked with Emmy to the security gate in the back.

"There they are!" Emmy shouted as she waved at Kristen.

Kenny talked to Brent Luckey, and Brent made sure everyone had an all-access pass. John, Kristen, Tony, Sloane, Cam and Lindsey joined Kenny and Emmy.

"Are you glad to be home?" Tony asked while shaking hands with Kenny.

Emmy hit his arm.

"What was that for, Em?"

"Because you are trying to embarrass me."

"How did that embarrass you?" Tony asked as he shrugged. "I just asked a simple question."

"You asked because... because now we... oh, never mind."

The guys laughed because they understood Emmy so well.

Emmy frowned at Tony and said, "You're a creep."

Kenny had an arm around Emmy's waist as he asked, "Do you guys want to wander around, or are you hungry?"

"Kenny, don't ask Tony and John such a silly question. You know they will eat everything in sight."

Emmy stuck out her tongue at Tony and he grabbed her and held her over his shoulder.

"Since we're outside I can't hang you from the ceiling, but I can carry you around like a sack of potatoes."

"Put me down, you big ox."

Tony set Emmy down, and she stood next to him. He put an arm around her shoulder and hugged her.

"How many tickets did you give away at church?" Tony inquired.

"I had a hundred tickets. Most of them went to the teens, but I had about twenty for the adults."

"Are all the guys in the worship band gonna be here?" Cam asked.

"Yes, and by the way, I heard that you can sing. Is that true?" Emmy wanted to know as she looked up at Cam. "How tall are you, anyway?"

"He's six three and has a very good voice, and he told me he used to lead worship back home while he was in high school," Lindsey answered for him.

Cam added, "It's a much smaller church."

"Have I ever mentioned that you look like Buddy Holly? He played guitar. Can you play an instrument?"

"I play the piano..."

"Great! Chase wants to add another keyboard player. You should tryout for him."

"Emmy! Maybe you should ask if Cam is interested before you add him to the band," Kenny said.

"Yeah, I suppose I should. Are you interested, Cam?"

"I might like to give it a shot," he answered.

"Why don't you talk to Chase in the morning and maybe stop by Thursday for practice?"

368

Some members of the crew spotted Tony and John.

"Hey, guys, can we get a couple of pictures?" someone yelled.

Tony and John patiently posed for photographs with the crew.

"Sloane, does it seem funny to you that these guys get excited about a couple of jocks when they travel all over with one of the biggest rock bands on the planet?" Kristen asked as they stood close by.

"You wouldn't think they would be impressed by those goofballs. They probably meet all kinds of celebrities."

Tony and John returned to the girls.

"What's so funny, Kristen?" Tony asked.

"Those guys think you're celebrities for some reason."

"They like football."

"Yeah, whatever."

"I heard your parents are coming today, Em. Is that true?" Sloane asked.

"Yes, they're coming later with Mom and Dad Colwell, and Mama is coming and so are Kristen's parents. Andy arranged for two limos to pick them up. They are all going to sit in a special section off to the right about twenty rows back. They didn't want to be too close to the stage."

"I told them to wear cotton in their ears," Kristen said. "Oh, not because the band isn't very good, but because of the noise level." *Shoot! I should have kept my mouth shut.*

Everyone wandered around, and they listened to the opening act for a few minutes. Emmy introduced as many of the crew members as she could.

Two hours later Larry Polmonari introduced Fridays At Five and the show started.

"Have you ever seen a rock show from the stage?" Emmy asked Cam and Lindsey. "It's really different from here."

"No, I haven't actually been to many concerts," Cam admitted. "And nothing with a light show anything close to this."

Emmy grinned as Lindsey was startled by the pyrotechnics.

"The only ones I've been to are the ones at Olivet. But

those weren't really rock concerts," Lindsey yelled in Emmy's ear.

Emmy danced along with the music until Kenny motioned for her to join him at center stage.

"I have to go sing," she told her friends.

Sloane stood on her tip toes to reach Tony's ear. "She acts like it's nothing special to go out there and sing with the band. Doesn't she realize the world sees Kenny and the other guys as famous rock stars?"

"I don't think she does. She still thinks of him as her lifelong friend," Tony answered. "She is still a little naive."

Emmy stayed on stage for the rest of the show. She danced around and sang harmony and background. She even played a keyboard on one of the songs.

At ten forty-five the band walked off the stage soaked with sweat and nearly exhausted. They always gave everything they had for their hometown crowd and tonight was no exception. The guys hugged each other, and kissed their wives, who had been so supportive through the years. They would soon return to work in the studio to finish the *Common Experience* CD.

Chapter Thirty-Nine

"Hey, look who's first in line for the food?" Tony nudged John in the back.

John turned, grinned and replied, "Just like at her rehearsal dinner."

John and Kristen chose Kerry Lynn's Pizza and Pasta for the wedding rehearsal dinner just as Kenny and Emmy had chosen. They even used the same room for the party.

Kristen led Emmy to a table in the corner of the room. "Em, will you stay with me tonight? I'm kinda nervous, and I don't know if I'll be able to sleep."

"Uh, duh! You do know Kenny is home, right?" Emmy said before taking a bite of pizza.

Kristen's eyes pleaded. "I know, and I realize what a sacrifice it will be if you don't get to sleep with him tonight."

Emmy chewed her pizza carefully for a moment.

"Please, Em?"

Emmy swallowed her pizza, rolled her eyes and then sighed. "Oh, all right. You're gonna owe me, but since you're my best friend, I'll do you a favor."

"That was way too easy." Kristen tilted her head and stared at Emmy. "You've got your period. Otherwise you'd never agree to leave his bed."

Emmy nodded as she took another bite of pizza. *Yeah, what lousy timing.*

Months earlier, Kristen had chosen Emmy to be her matron of honor, and John had picked Tony as his best man. Kristen had a difficult time deciding who she wanted to be her bridesmaids, but finally decided on Lynette Jefferson from church and two friends from school, Tess Easterly and Jenna Lowe. John's brothers Kirk and Keith along with Derrick Keasling were groomsmen. The wedding and reception were taking place at the Keasling home.

Emmy spent the night with Kristen, and they stayed up later than planned because Kristen was just too wound up to fall asleep.

"Kristen, I don't mean to be nosy but have you and John..."

"No, Emmy, but believe me I have wanted to so many times, and I know John was willing to oblige me, but I just thought about you and Kenny and how you were so strong and resisted when the easy way would have been to give in to your sexual desires. I know we did some stuff that you and Kenny probably didn't, but we didn't do everything."

Emmy grinned and said, "Kristen, that's really nice, but I was going to ask if you and John have thought any more about where you were going to live when his lease is up."

Kristen put a hand to her mouth. "Oh, Emmy. I'm so embarrassed. I thought you were thinking about sex."

"Me?! Thinking about sex?!" Emmy said and then giggled. "I can see where your mind is, Krissy. Just wait until tomorrow night, okay? Believe me it will be worth it."

"I know you guys are making love in every room in the house."

"We are not!" Emmy responded indignantly.

Kristen laughed. "Name one room where you haven't."

"We haven't done it... I'm not telling you. You just want to embarrass me later in front of everyone."

"I don't know if I ever told you or not, but when I was fifteen years old I had a big crush on Tony, even though we are cousins. He treated me better than any of my other cousins and probably was nicer to me than Derrick."

"What's your point?" Emmy asked.

"Nothing, I'm just glad that Kenny took pity on you and decided to marry you even though you are rather plain looking and not at all attractive."

Emmy looked at Kristen with such a sad expression on her face that Kristen couldn't keep a straight face and began laughing. Emmy knew Kristen was teasing her as they were both laughing uncontrollably. They finally fell asleep in Kristen's king-sized bed.

Kristen woke up as soon as the sun rose. She looked at Emmy who was sprawled out and taking up two-thirds of the bed. Kristen couldn't stay in bed any longer so she nudged her best friend and said, "Wake up, Emmy. Let's go downstairs and make ourselves some breakfast."

Emmy groaned, but didn't open her eyes. "Do we have to? Can't we just stay in bed? I'm still sleepy."

"Come on, Emmy. This is my special day, so you have to do what I say."

Kristen pulled the covers off of Emmy, and she reluctantly got out of bed. They went downstairs in their pajamas and Kristen opened the fridge.

"What do you want to eat, Em? We've got everything imaginable in here," Kristen said as she grabbed a carton of eggs.

"I'm not eating your eggs."

"I can make eggs," Kristen raised her voice.

Kristen's parents had a new cook, Cecile from Aspen, working for them now. Cecile heard them from her bedroom close to the kitchen.

"Do you girls need help with anything?"

Emmy jumped.

Kristen saw Cecile and said, "I'm sorry for waking you up. I didn't mean to."

"It's all right." Cecile tightened her robe and then smiled. "I planned to get up early today, anyway. I hear it's a special day for someone."

Emmy asked, "Could you please fix us something to eat? Kristen can't make instant oatmeal without burning it."

"I can so make breakfast."

"Kristen, I've had some of your *breakfasts* when we were living together and trust me, dear, you can't cook."

Kristen pretended to be deeply hurt and started to whimper.

"I'm so sorry, Kristen, I didn't mean to hurt your feelings," Emmy said as she gave Kristen a hug.

Kristen smiled. "I know I can't cook, but God has given me other talents. I just pretended to be hurt so somebody would make me something to eat. I am such a good actress. I'm starving, and it is *my day* remember."

"Yes, your highness. I remember."

Cecile looked at the two girls as if they were loco. "How

373

would you like some breakfast burritos and fresh orange juice?"

"That would be delightful, Cecile. Thank you." Kristen smiled and then made a face at Emmy.

Emmy yawned as she rolled her eyes.

Paula Kratzsky left specific instructions for Kristen and Emmy to be upstairs at ten thirty so Kristen could get ready. The wedding didn't start until one so they had plenty of time to kill.

Kristen drained her second glass of orange juice and jumped up from the barstool by the breakfast counter. "Let's wake up my lazy brother and see if he wants to go for a hike. No, wait, let's wake him up and *tell* him he's going on a hike. We won't give him the option of going, he's just going."

"I know, it's your day," Emmy said.

"Don't you forget it, Mrs. Colwell."

"I haven't seen Derrick since the New Year's Eve party," Emmy said.

"You know he graduated from law school just three weeks ago."

"Duh, I know. I gave you a card to give him. You did give it to him, right?" Emmy asked.

"I'm sure I did." Kristen hoped. "He and Amber flew in late yesterday afternoon."

Emmy poked Kristen in the arm. "You forgot to give it to him, didn't you?"

"Maybe. It might be in my room."

Kristen and Emmy finished breakfast and thanked Cecile. "Go back to bed, Cecile. I don't think anyone else is going to get up for awhile."

Cecile hugged Kristen and said, "Don't go too far away on your hike."

Kristen and Emmy ran upstairs and into Derrick's room and jumped on his bed. Derrick had been up late studying and had wanted to sleep as late as possible today. Although Kristen was twenty-four years old, and Emmy would be in another month, they acted like teenagers as they jumped on Derrick's bed and woke him up.

Kristen whispered in his ear, "Wake up, lazybones. You're going for a hike."

"No, I'm not." Derrick looked at them both as they sat on either side of him. "Stop poking me before I hurt you." Derrick frowned at Kristen and groaned. "Not you, Em. I just meant Kristen." He hid his head under his pillow.

Kristen told him, "Get your butt out of bed. You're coming with us. Where is Amber? What have you done with her?"

"Where are you going?" He tried to focus on the clock on the nightstand. "It's six thirty in the morning? Amber is in the guest room—sleeping. Like we should be."

"Did Daddy tell you that you couldn't share a room?" Kristen asked. "He can be a bit old-fashioned about sleeping arrangements."

Emmy whispered, "Why would he do that? I'm sure he knows you guys live together?"

"It was Amber's choice," Derrick said.

"It must be that time for her, too," Kristen said as she and Emmy giggled. "It doesn't matter. We, I said we, are going for a hike and do not question me on my day."

Emmy explained, "She wants to be called 'Your Highness' today, Derrick. If I were you I wouldn't cross her. You're liable to be disinherited or something."

Kristen poked him in the side. "Meet us downstairs in ten minutes or else."

"Or else what?"

"Or else I'll tell Dad what you and Tony did to me..." Kristen whispered the rest into Derrick's ear.

"I'll be down in ten minutes. You would make a hell of a negotiator, Kristen."

"See, Emmy, I told you God gave me other talents." She got off of the bed. "Plus, Daddy loves me more. I'm his only daughter."

"Kristen, sometimes I think I better be praying for you more than I do." Emmy waved at Derrick and followed Kristen back to her bedroom.

Emmy and Kristen put on t-shirts and running shorts and

ran back to Derrick's room to make sure he got out of bed. Derrick came out of his bathroom. "For Christ's sake, give me a chance to get dressed, will ya? I"ll be right down."

The girls ran downstairs to wait.

"Kristen, what did you say to Derrick? What did he do to you?"

"Don't tell me Tony has never told you about the time at the lake in Wisconsin when..." Kristen whispered the rest in her ear.

"Kristen! Tony has never said a word about that. Wait till I see him later."

"Emmy, he has probably forgotten it ever happened. Don't bring it up now. It will embarrass him and then I will be embarrassed."

"All right, I won't say anything," Emmy agreed.

Derrick came down to the kitchen and poured himself a glass of OJ.

Kristen grabbed a loaf of bread. "Hurry up, let's go."

"Where are we going?" Derrick asked as he chose a bagel from the fridge.

"Just follow us and make sure you keep up."

Derrick shrugged and kept quiet. They headed for the wooded and hilly hiking trails that wound their way through the Barclay Estates. The birds sang their morning songs, and the wet morning dew still covered the grass as they headed up the large hill behind the house. Kristen and Emmy were full of nervous energy and constantly had to tell Derrick, "Keep up, or else you will get lost in the scary woods."

Kristen looked around and whispered to Emmy, "When we first moved here, I was afraid to walk in these woods by myself, so I always made Derrick come with me."

"I can understand why. They are still a little spooky even now," Emmy said and then started singing, "Lions, tigers and bears. Oh my! Lions, tigers and bears. Oh my!"

Derrick heard them singing and shook his head. *There's no way those two are old enough to be married. Emmy still doesn't look any older than the night I met her at Roosevelt High.* He chuckled. *She doesn't act any more mature, either.*

"Follow the black asphalt road. Follow the black asphalt road," Emmy sang as she and Kristen skipped ahead of Derrick.

They reached one of Kristen's favorite spots on the trail. A small lake where ducks and geese gathered. The birds had grown accustomed to being fed by people and soon a large group of them were waiting for food. Emmy and Kristen began feeding the ducks. Derrick watched as his sister threw the bread into the water. He had watched her do this since she was in junior high and now he pictured her as she was then. He saw the joy on Kristen's face as she happily fed the ducks.

Emmy moved close to Derrick and whispered, "A penny for your thoughts."

"I was picturing how Kristen looked the first time we came to this spot."

Emmy put her arm through Derrick's and held him close. Derrick moved his arm and placed it around her shoulder. He hugged Emmy tightly.

"I was just thinking about the future, and picturing Kristen bringing her daughter to feed the ducks and geese and how much fun they would have. You should bring Carson here someday, Auntie Em."

"I might just do that," Emmy said.

Kristen ran out of bread and turned to face them. Kristen smiled at Emmy and Derrick. "I wanted to do that once more before I became an *old married lady.*"

"It will be a long time before you become an old married lady, Krissy."

Kristen laughed and then said, "One time when I was a freshman in high school, Derrick and I came up here, and Derrick ended up throwing me in the lake for no reason at all."

Derrick offered a rebuttal. "She deserved it because of what she did."

"I did not," Kristen asserted.

Emmy asked, "What did she do?"

"She got mad at me and swore."

"Big deal. What did she say?"

Derrick whispered in her ear.

"You didn't deserve it," Emmy said as she looked at Kristen. "I've used that word before."

Derrick looked at Emmy with surprise.

"I grew up hearing it all the time. I didn't know it was a bad word until Kenny told me what it meant." Emmy bit her lip. "I try not to use it now, but I slip up once in a while."

Derrick warned Emmy, "Mama will swat you if she hears you use it, even though you are married."

"You shouldn't have thrown your sister in the lake for that."

Emmy grinned at Derrick and said the very same naughty thing Kristen did all those years ago and started to run away from Derrick. Derrick chased Emmy and quickly caught her. He grabbed her around her waist and picked her up. He carried her toward the lake.

"I hope you will enjoy going for an early morning swim, Mrs. Colwell. The water is sure to be cold."

Emmy squealed and told Derrick, "Put me down, or else I will tell Kenny."

"Kenny is not here to protect you. Just accept your punishment like a man."

Kristen yelled, "She's not a man."

"I was just using that as a figure of speech, not literally," Derrick said and then thought of something. "I wouldn't have kissed her if she was a man."

"Derrick!" Kristen shouted.

"That was a long time ago, and it only happened once. You said it was like kissing your sister," Emmy reminded him.

"I might not have been totally honest about that," Derrick admitted.

Derrick was close to the water now, and Kristen ran over to help Emmy. Derrick had no intention of throwing Emmy in the water, but, as Kristen ran into him, he slipped and began to lose his balance. Kristen tried to grab him, but she couldn't hold him up and all three of them fell into the lake making a big splash. Ducks and geese quacked and honked as they flew away. Derrick regained his balance first. The girls stood to their feet in the shallow lake and laughed until Kristen thought of the way her hair

378

would look for the wedding.

"My hair! My hair is ruined. Emmy, what will I do? John will never want to marry me if I look like this." Kristen grabbed her long hair and tried to wring the water out.

"We can hide it under the veil, and, if you're lucky, he won't see it until it's too late," Emmy teased.

Derrick scrambled out of the water and stood on the bank to help the girls out. He pulled Kristen out, then reached out his hand to Emmy. She took his hand and pulled hard to bring Derrick back into the lake. Derrick fell on her and they both went under the water again. Derrick regained his feet and helped Emmy stand up.

"You are so going to get it, Emmy."

Derrick grabbed her around her waist again and dragged her to the bank. "Why are we always having to pull you out of the water, Em? Remember the river in Colorado?"

"I'll never forget that. You guys were going to use mouth-to-mouth on me."

Kristen was on the bank laughing at them. "Derrick, look where your hand is. You better let her go."

Kristen reached out to help Emmy up the slippery bank and Derrick put his hands on her butt to boost her up. Derrick grabbed the girls outstretched hands as they offered to help him. He thought about pulling both of them back in the water but decided not to because it was Kristen's big day.

"I'm sorry I had my hand where it was, Emmy."

"You were just helping boost me up the bank, Derrick."

"No, Emmy, I mean before that."

"Derrick, I don't know for sure where your hand was, but you are like a brother to me. I know you love me, and I love you, too."

"I know, Emmy, Jesus loves me, too."

"That's right, Derrick. Jesus even loves lawyers—believe it or not."

They headed back to the house. Kristen and Emmy walked into the kitchen, dripping water everywhere. Derrick conveniently used the back stairs to disappear. Kristen's parents were eating breakfast. Mrs. Keasling had her back to the girls as she poured herself a cup of coffee.

Cecile looked at Kristen and Emmy and gasped audibly. "What have you girls been doing?"

"Derrick threw us in the lake," Kristen announced.

"Not again," Mr. Keasling said matter-of-factly without taking his eyes away from his morning paper.

Emmy told them, "It was an accident. Derrick did not intentionally throw anybody in the lake. He was pretending he was going to throw me in the lake, and Kristen tried to stop him, and we just lost our balance and fell in."

Mrs. Keasling added cream and sugar to her coffee, turned around, looked at Kristen, splashed her coffee and screamed. "Kristen Lynn! You look atrocious!"

That got Mr. Keasling's attention. He dropped his paper into his bowl of oatmeal, looked at Kristen and then Emmy. "It's a good thing the hairdresser is coming today." Then he wiped the oatmeal off of his paper and turned the page.

"Get upstairs immediately!" Mrs. Keasling pointed. "Daniel! How can you be so calm about this? Did you see her?"

"I saw her. What's the big deal? The hairdresser is coming to fix her hair."

Cecile wiped the spilled coffee and poured Karla another cup. "Everything will be all right, Ms. Karla."

"I'm already a nervous wreck, and the day is just beginning," Karla said. "How on earth will I ever make it through this wedding?"

Emmy and Kristen headed upstairs to Kristen's room to shower and change into dry clothes.

"I think your mother was kinda pissed," Emmy said as she grinned.

"Ya think?" Kristen sat on the edge of her bed and sighed. "Shoot! I'm getting the bed wet."

"I'll use the room across the hall to shower and change. My clothes are in there," Emmy said. Then she sat next to Kristen. "This is the second happiest day of my life."

"Really?" Kristen jumped up, grabbed Emmy and yanked her off of the bed. "You're getting my comforter wet."

"Ooops! Sorry, Krissy," Emmy said as she nodded.

"The happiest day must be when we first met," Kristen teased.

"That was the third happiest day, Kristen." Emmy looked at Kristen and they both laughed.

"What are you thinking about, Em?" Kristen tried to run her fingers through her hair.

"I was wondering if we should shave your head because your hair is such a mess."

"You're gonna get it, Emily Colasanti Colwell. I'm gonna get Derrick back for this."

"Maybe the hairdresser can salvage some of your hair." Emmy laughed and hugged Kristen. "If not, I can use the scissors and give you a little trim."

"You better look in the mirror. Your hair is wrecked, too."

Emmy looked over her shoulder into the mirror. "Doesn't matter. No one will be looking at me, and I've been thinking about cutting it all off." She made a snipping motion. "Where are your scissors?"

Chapter Forty

Workers labored all morning long setting up the humongous canvas tent and getting ready for the big day. Paula Kratzsky supervised everything for Kristen and John the same as she did for Emmy and Kenny's wedding. Paula decided to use the tent even though there wasn't a cloud in the sky. The weather was perfect. Sunny, but not too hot, with a gentle breeze blowing.

The guys gathered at Tony's house. They would get ready there so they would be out of the way.

"Tony!" Mama hollered out the back door.

He ran over to the steps. "Yes, Mama?"

"Don't you think it's time to stop playing football and get ready? Kristen will be very upset if John is late."

"All right. We'll start getting showered."

By eleven the ladies had taken over the upstairs at the Keasling house. The hairdressers worked their magic and produced a miracle.

"Your hair doesn't look too awful." Emmy grinned at Kristen as she inspected the final result.

"Gee thanks, Em. Yours looks all right considering how it looked this morning."

"I still think I'll get it cut much shorter. I'm getting tired of having to deal with it." Emmy looked in the mirror at her long, curly hair.

Paula checked her watch. "All right, ladies. It's time to get dressed."

The bridesmaids used the guest rooms while Emmy and Kristen used Kristen's room to get ready. Emmy and Paula helped Kristen into her dress.

"You look so beautiful, Krissy. Don't you agree, Paula?"

"You do look gorgeous, Kristen. I'll fix the veil later."

Emmy held her dress in front of her as she inspected it. "Krissy, do I have to wear this? Couldn't I just wear shorts and maybe a new t-shirt?"

"I thought you liked that dress. You helped pick it out."

"I know, but..."

"But what, Em?"

Emmy bit her lip. "Well, everyone else fills out the top better than I do. I look like a kid."

Tess and Jenna stood in the doorway and laughed at Emmy until Kristen glared at them. They fled back to one of the guest bedrooms.

"You look fine, Em," Lynette said. "Don't worry about anything."

"Maybe I should be the flower girl instead of the maid of honor."

By twelve-thirty the girls were all dressed and were being inspected by Karla and Mama. Karla was fussing over Kristen's dress to make sure it looked perfect.

Mama looked at Emmy and said, "You look so pretty."

"Thanks, Mama. Does this dress look all right?"

"It looks very pretty on you. Why?"

"The top is loose."

"It looks just fine. You don't need to worry, little one." Mama took a closer look. "Just don't bend over too much."

Emmy clasped her hands to her chest. "Kristen! I'm wearing a t-shirt."

Paula herded everyone downstairs to the kitchen, inspected them one final time and arranged the ladies in the proper order. "Okay, I want everyone except for Kristen and Emmy to head outside and wait at the back of the tent."

"Do I really look all right, Em?" Kristen asked.

"You look like an angel. John is such a lucky man."

Nobody would ever guess that only hours earlier they were both soaking wet in a lake. Five minutes later, Kristen glowed as her dad walked her down the aisle. Neither Emmy nor Tony cried during the ceremony, although he was very close to tears several times. Emmy smiled at Tony as they listened to John and Kristen say their vows. At last Dr. Behren pronounced them husband and wife and John took Kristen in his arms and kissed her passionately as the crowd cheered.

"He better not be using his tongue," Emmy whispered to Lynette.

"Emmy! You think of the weirdest stuff," Lynette said.

John and Kristen were almost running as they hurried back down the aisle. The bridal party filed back down the aisle and set up a reception line. Paula appeared everywhere as she kept everything organized and running smoothly. As Emmy and Tony were standing in the line, Emmy felt someone move behind her and then felt two hands on her bare shoulders. She turned her head and smiled.

"Sorry to cut in line, Emmy, but Kristen told me we have to sing 'I Will Be True To You' at the reception. Did you know about that?"

"She mentioned something about it a few days ago, but I wasn't sure she was serious. I was hoping she would forget."

"I think she was really serious. Are you willing to sing with me?" Kenny asked.

"If I have to. Can you sing on key this time?" Emmy turned to Tony and asked, "Should I sing with this amateur?"

"Well, I was hoping I could sing with him, but maybe it's better that you do. After all, you're the professional."

After the crowd made it through the reception line, Paula organized the wedding party. The photographers earned their money for the next two hours.

Most of the guests were staying at the house until the reception. Daniel Keasling had spent a small fortune on champagne and wine, but at Kristen's request there was no beer or hard liquor available until after the dinner. Guests wandered all over the grounds and some of them even took a walk back to the lake. Eventually, the photographers were finished.

John kissed Kristen and checked the time. "We still have over two hours before the reception. What should we do?"

Emmy giggled and then said, "You could run upstairs and kill some time."

"Emmy!" Kristen barked.

"Well, you could." Emmy bit her lip.

"John and I are not going upstairs. Cecile has been busy in the kitchen and prepared a spread of food to tide us over until the dinner at the reception."

"Too bad, John." Tony laughed, slapped John on the back and then headed toward the kitchen.

"I can see Tony has his priorities in order," Emmy said.

Everybody in the wedding party grabbed some food and headed to the family room to watch TV.

Emmy told Kristen, "I'm going to take Kenny for a walk. We'll be back in a little while."

"Don't get lost and don't fall in the lake again." Kristen tilted her head and said, "You better behave."

"I have to, remember?"

Emmy ran upstairs, removed her dress shoes and put on her sneakers. She resisted the temptation to change out of her dress and wear shorts and a t-shirt. She took Kenny back to the lake and told him what happened earlier.

"I wish I could have seen that, Em. I can imagine the three of you in the water."

"We scared the poor ducks away."

After spending a few minutes at the lake, they headed back to the house. Emmy looked at Kenny, and he could tell she had something on her mind.

"I know you want to ask something, Em. Go ahead and ask."

"It's about these dresses."

"Yeah, what about them? They look nice. I like the color burgundy on you. All the girls look very elegant."

"All the other girls fill out their dress better than I do."

Kenny looked at her and laughed. "Are you worried or feeling self-conscious because of how you fill out the dress?"

Emmy crossed her arms over her chest. "You mean how I don't fill it out. I look like a kid who hasn't reached puberty."

"I think you're exaggerating just a bit, Em. You may not be as... busty... as the other girls."

"You mean Tess and Jenna. They have large..."

"... but you are still the prettiest girl at the wedding."

"You're lying, but I don't care. You always know just how to cheer me up. Thank you."

Emmy wrapped her arms around Kenny's neck as they

385

kissed. They didn't mind the stares of some of the guests who watched. They kept walking and soon were back at the house. Emmy kissed Kenny before she took off to find Kristen. She didn't bother changing out of her sneakers.

The reception started at six, but by five-thirty, the tent was packed. There were cars parked everywhere in the subdivision. Paula had given the okay to set up tables in the yard since the weather remained perfect. The caterers set up their own tent by the pool house.

Emmy wandered around the yard with Kristen and asked, "Do you have any idea how many people are here?"

"I'm not sure, Em. I gave my list to my mom and she added everybody in the world." Kristen looked down and noticed Emmy's sneakers. She rolled her eyes. "Well, at least you are still wearing your dress."

"Those other shoes were uncomfortable."

"I appreciate the sacrifice you made by wearing them, Em," Kristen said as she grinned.

Emmy and Kristen didn't know exactly how many people were there, but it was even more than at her and Kenny's reception. The DJ arrived early, set up and started the music. He introduced the wedding party as they entered the tent.

Emmy poked Tony in the side as they walked in together. "You better not try to embarrass me."

"How would I do that, brat?" Tony asked as he waved to some people.

"Not sure, but you better be nice to me tonight."

"I will, Em. Have I mentioned how pretty you look in that dress?"

"No, you haven't, and don't you..." She bit her lip.

"What?" Tony pulled out her chair for her.

"Never mind. Doesn't matter. Thank you for being a gentleman."

Tony understood.

Just before dinner was served, came the time for the toasts. Emmy bit her lip and wrung her hands as she listened to Tony's speech. Tony did a great job and entertained the crowd like a professional standup comic.

He ended his speech with these words, "I don't mean to brag, but, actually, I am the reason you are here today. Let me explain. I was in a car accident and ended up in the hospital. Kristen came to see me because she was concerned about her favorite cousin, and she happened to meet my roommate John at the hospital. For some strange reason John thought Kristen was someone he wanted to get to know better. Go figure!" He made a circle around his ears and the crowd roared. "I set them up, and so here we are today." Tony spread his arms out, then continued, "So I highly recommend to you single ladies out there, if you want to catch a husband, visit the local hospital."

Tony's speech got several laughs from the crowd and a big round of applause as he finished and handed the microphone to Emmy.

Shoot! How am I gonna follow that? Emmy looked at Kristen, bit her lip, and started talking. "I first met Kristen Keasling in a bathroom." The crowd laughed, and Emmy went on to explain where and how they met. "We became best friends right away. Now it seems that we have known each other forever. I can't imagine what life would be like without Kristen Keasling, I mean Kristen Randolph. Sorry, Krissy, it will take some time before I get used to your new name."

Emmy talked to Kristen as if she were the only person in the room about how much they had meant to each other over the years. She managed to get through without breaking down and Kristen gave her a long hug and a kiss on the cheek.

After the dinner, Kenny and Emmy sang the song Kristen requested as she and John had their first dance as husband and wife. Mr. Keasling danced with Kristen and almost managed not to cry. The Keaslings had rented an actual wooden dance floor for the reception.

Later, Emmy asked Sloane, "Do you mind if I borrow Tony for a few minutes?"

"Go ahead, Em. I'll keep Kenny company."

Emmy walked up to Tony and grabbed his hand. "You have to come with me."

"Where are we going?"

"You'll see."

Emmy took Tony over to the far side of the pool house, and they sat on the low brick wall. "This is where I saw your grandma and grandpa at Derrick's graduation party. It was," she thought about the years. "Oh, my God! It was over seven years ago. I can't believe it's been that long."

"I remember how Grandma took care of Grandpa after he started losing his sight," Tony said and then told her about some of his memories of his grandparents. "Both of my grandparents came to this country from Italy when they were just children. They left behind brothers and sisters who never came to this county, ever. I've probably got hundreds of relatives still over there."

"Maybe someday we can all take a trip to Italy and you can show us where they were born. That would be a great vacation since I probably have relatives in Italy, too."

They returned to the party, and Emmy wanted to dance with John. She danced with John and Tony danced with Kristen as the DJ played one of their favorite love songs. Emmy thought it was going to be perfect that Tony, John and Kristen would end up living next door to each other. Later, Emmy watched as Tony and Sloane danced and even kissed each other. Emmy managed to drag Kenny onto the dance floor and they danced for several songs.

"You look very fetching today," Kenny said. "It is a pleasure to dance with you, m'lady."

"Why, thank you, m'lord. Do you think Tony and Sloane are in love with each other?"

"Are you going to take credit for bringing them together?" Kenny asked.

"Not really, but I did pair them up for our wedding. They were dating before that, though."

"What about Lindsey and Cam? They are enamored with each other."

"They do enjoy each other's company," Emmy replied.

"Do you know where John and Kristen are going to live until they can build their new house?" Kenny asked.

"Kristen said they were going to stay in his apartment until

388

the lease is up, then rent a house until theirs is built. Do you think we should build a new house, or stay where we are?"

"We would have to pay Diane for her share if we stay there. That would be the fair thing to do."

"I saw the plans for John and Krissy's house. Maybe we could use the same architect if we ever build a house."

"I suppose so..."

"Are you ever going to tell me where your property is?" Emmy asked out of the blue. "I want to know."

Tony, Sloane, John and Kristen heard Emmy's question, stopped dancing and looked at Kenny.

"You should tell her," Tony recommended.

"Okay, I guess it's time."

Emmy looked at Kenny, and he smiled.

"Do you remember when Mr. Robertson was showing Tony and John around Bristol Ridge, and he pointed out the property across the road?"

Emmy nodded. "Yes, he said it was already... purchased... Kenny Colwell are you trying to tell me that we are going to live right across the street?"

"Yes, baby, is that okay with you?"

Emmy kissed him as she started to cry.

Tony grinned and said, "I guess that means she doesn't like her neighbors since she is crying."

Emmy poked Tony in his side and then hugged him. "I suppose I'll learn to put up with you, but I love the fact that Krissy... and John... will be right across the street."

Mr. Robertson and Mrs. Moneywell walked over. "We couldn't help but overhear your conversation. Are you pleased with Kenny's purchase? His property is a little over twelve acres."

"Thank you, Mr. Robertson. You are the most generous man in the entire world," Emmy said as she hugged him and kissed his cheek.

John and Kristen had not told anyone, except Tony and Emmy, where they were spending their wedding night. Emmy told Kenny, so he knew, also.

Tony, Sloane, Kenny and Emmy waited for John and Kristen at noon the next day at the Portillo's in Melrose Grove. They had already ordered the food and chose a table in the far corner.

"Are you gonna eat, Em?" Kenny asked.

"I'm waiting for Krissy to get here."

Emmy jumped up as soon as she saw Kristen walk in and pulled her aside.

Kenny shook his head. "Sorry, guys, but you know Em wants details."

"Who chose Portillo's for lunch?" Emmy asked after she returned to the table.

John raised a hand. "That would be me. Why?"

"No reason."

Tony took another bite of his cheeseburger and then asked Emmy, "Would you have rather gone to Darby's?"

Sloane rolled her eyes. "Do you have to talk with your mouth full?"

"I think Darby's is better, but this is closer to the airport."

An hour later, everyone walked outside.

"Remember to take lots of pictures, Krissy."

"I'll try." Kristen hugged Emmy.

"I can't believe your parents are paying for two weeks in Hawaii. Have a wonderful honeymoon."

Tony checked the time. "Em, I have to get them to O'Hare. Will you let go of Kristen?"

"See you when you get back," Emmy said. "Remember the pictures. It may be the only chance I ever get to see Hawaii."

Chapter Forty-One

"Good morning, Kenny. Are you enjoying your time at home?" Mr. Tomanek asked as he entered the reception area of his office on the fifth floor.

"It's great to be home for the summer, Mr. Tomanek. This is Emmy."

"It's a pleasure to finally meet you, Emmy." He shook her hand.

Emmy turned from the view of the Kinmundy River and looked up at him. *You are taller than anyone I have ever met. I wonder if you played basketball somewhere.*

On Monday the seventh of June, Kenny and Emmy had an appointment with Carl Tomanek—the architect who had drawn up the plans for their house. The only problem was that Emmy had not seen the plans. Kenny had the plans prepared before they were married. He was going to build his dream home, and now they needed to make sure it was Emmy's dream home as well.

"Can I get you guys anything to drink? Coffee? Tea? Perhaps some water?"

"I would like some water, please," Emmy answered. When Mr. Tomanek left the room, she asked Kenny, "Is he a basketball player?"

"He played in the NBA for the Lakers and the Celtics," Kenny said. "But it was a long time ago."

Mr. Tomanek returned with Emmy's water and, after making small-talk for ten minutes, escorted them into one of the other rooms. He brought out the plans for Kenny's house and placed them on a large table.

"Emmy, what would be the most important thing for you in your new home?" Mr. Tomanek asked, confident he knew the answer.

Emmy grinned and answered immediately, "I don't want to have to carry laundry from the bedrooms all the way to the basement."

The guys laughed and Kenny mentioned, "That was the number one priority, Em."

"It may not be a big deal now, but it will when I'm old."

"There is a laundry room on the main floor off of the mudroom, and another one upstairs," Kenny said.

Mr. Tomanek went over the basics of the plan with Emmy. "The total square footage, not counting the basement is just over seven thousand square feet."

"That sounds like a lot. How big is our house now, Kenny?" she asked.

"Twenty-five hundred square foot. Give or take. Plus the basement," Kenny answered.

"This place will be three times as big?" Emmy asked as her eyes widened.

"I guess so," Kenny said.

Mr. Tomanek spent ten minutes going over details with Emmy. She was pleased with every part of the design—except one.

"The master suite is on the first floor back behind the family room. If we have babies, we will be too far away."

Kenny knew this might come up so he showed Emmy his solution. "This area here on the north end can actually become an upstairs master suite, Em. That way if we do have kids, we will be right there with them. I was thinking the downstairs suite could be used for either of our parents, or maybe a nanny. Actually, we don't have to build it right away. It could be added later. Then thirty years down the road when we are older, we could use it as our master suite and not have to climb stairs."

"So, you have actually planned ahead and put a lot of thought into this, huh?"

"I tried to anticipate our needs." He kissed her forehead.

"You did a good job. I love it. I love how the kitchen and this pantry area are so close to the garage. I won't have to carry groceries all the way across the house. Which direction does the breakfast nook face?"

Kenny touched the blueprints. "This is the west side of the house."

"I like the living room idea. It might not get used as much as the family room, but it would be perfect for entertaining guests." She looked closer. "Oh, the dining room is between the kitchen and

392

family room. I like that. Where's the butler's pantry?"

Kenny looked surprised. "Do you want one?"

"No, I was kidding."

""There is a front entryway, but I don't see us using it that much. We would normally come into the house from the garage." Kenny showed her an enlargement of the garage.

"Is that a stairway?"

"Yes, it goes to the basement. I'll show you the basement in a bit."

"How big is this garage? It looks huge."

"There will be three garage doors and a service door. Double garage doors. We could fit six cars inside it."

"Get out! We'll never have six cars," she said. "You aren't going to start collecting cars like Mr. Robertson, are you?"

"Probably not, but I want to have room in case we buy an RV or something."

Emmy laughed.

"What?" Kenny asked.

"Were you watching that movie with Chevy Chase when you guys drew this up? You know the one where Cousin Eddie pulls up in that crappy RV."

Kenny and Mr. Tomanek laughed.

She traced the path from the kitchen to the dining room. "This will work. I like how the stairs are directly opposite each other in the hallway. Oooh! There's a fireplace in the family room. That's neat. Here is a den you could use as an office and a room... what is this room for?" She pointed at the room she meant.

"I thought it could be a media room or a library," Kenny answered.

"You mean like the TV room we've got now?"

"Sorta, except this one would be twice the size, Em."

"I like that. Our TV room now is too small."

"We would probably have a TV in the family room, too." Kenny flipped a page of the blueprints. "This area of the basement is where I want to put a recording studio. There will be an basement entrance from the garage and the guys could come and go and not have to disturb us in the main house."

Emmy grinned at Kenny, and he just knew she was going to say something to embarrass him, but she didn't—for once.

"So you can stay at home and do all your CDs right there?"

"Yes, won't that be nice? You could even record your next CD without leaving the house."

"What is this area behind the house?"

"That's for the pool. See this area?"

"Yeah," Emmy said.

"We can put in a pool and have a built in kitchen for grilling and stuff. This area off the back is where we could put a tennis court, or something like that."

"How many bedrooms are there?" Emmy asked. "I didn't count them."

Kenny looked at Mr. Tomanek. "Would you explain it to Em, please?"

Mr. Tomanek cleared his throat. "There are a minimum of five bedrooms upstairs with the possible expansion to seven. As far as bathrooms go." He rubbed his jaw for a few seconds. "These two bedrooms share a bathroom. Those two each have a bathroom, and the master would have two if you still want separate ones." He explained about the steel structure and load-bearing walls and other technical details Emmy didn't fully understand.

"It will be built to last past our lifetimes, Em," Kenny said.

After spending over an hour looking at the plans, Emmy gave her stamp of approval. She looked at Kenny, then at Mr. Tomanek. Kenny knew she was about to cry.

"Oh, Em, it's okay," he said as he put his arm around her.

"I could have never imagined living in a place like this, Mr. Tomanek. I grew up in a really small house, and we never had much in the way of material possessions. I almost feel guilty to even be thinking about building a house this big."

"I suppose you could live in the guest house," Mr. Tomanek said as he chuckled. "It's only fifteen hundred square feet."

"What guest house?" Emmy turned to face Kenny, who found a sudden interest in a magazine. "Kenny! What guest house?" Emmy asked slowly for emphasis.

Mr. Tomanek clenched his jaw. *I shouldn't have mentioned*

394

the guest house. I stuck my big ol' foot in my mouth again.

"I thought we would build a guest house on the property for when we have company who might stay for a while."

"I hope you don't mean my parents. Mom would drive me nuts if she lived that close to us."

"I was thinking about non-family guests."

"You mean your rock star friends?" Emmy asked.

"No, people like Tom and Sherry or Andy..."

"Andy is family. Why do we need a guest house?"

"We don't *need* it, but it's... well... it's almost finished."

"What are you talking about?" Emmy placed her hands on her hips as she frowned. "Tell me everything."

"Don't get mad, but after I bought the property, and knew I would want to build a *dream house*, I decided to build a ranch house where I... we... could live until the main house was ready."

"You are in such trouble. Keeping secrets from me. You will pay big-time, Kenneth Travis Robert Colwell."

After they left Mr. Tomanek's office, Kenny asked, "Do you want to take a drive out to Bristol Ridge? You can see the ranch house and we could walk around."

Emmy's eyes lit up as she thought about what else they could do.

"We could have some fun playing in the woods."

It took twenty minutes to get to the Bristol Ridge development from the architect's office.

"This isn't where Mr. Robertson brought us that day. Where are we?" Emmy wondered.

"This is the back entrance to our property. The construction guys use this entrance. There won't be a front entrance until the main house is almost finished."

"We will have a front driveway though, right?"

"Yes, you won't have to walk through the woods to get to Kristen's house, but it will take a few minutes to walk over there anyway. It's not like we are going to be right next to each other."

"It's a good thing we took my car today," Emmy said as the Envoy bounced through another pothole. "I don't think your Civic would be able to handle this *road* if you can call it that."

Kenny avoided another large pothole. "It's just a construction road, Em. It won't be here forever."

It took a couple of minutes to reach the site of the ranch house. Kenny stopped the car, and Emmy jumped out.

"I like the porch on the front. It makes it look rather rustic and almost like it's been here for years." Emmy climbed the three wooden steps to the porch.

"That was my intention, but you'll find the inside is very modern and up-to-date."

"You mean I won't have to fetch water from the well every morning, or do my cooking over a potbellied stove?"

"Well, yeah, you will have to do that," Kenny teased.

Kenny gave Emmy a tour of the nearly completed house.

"It's just a simple three-bedroom, two-bath house. No basement or anything too fancy."

She looked into the largest bedroom. "I could live here. This isn't as big as where we live now, but I like it."

"That's good because we will have to live here until the main house is built." Kenny held her hand as they entered the hall bathroom.

"Can't we stay where we live now?"

"Yeah, we could, but I thought you wanted to move as soon as possible. Have you changed your mind?"

"Not really. I love that old house, but this will be better."

They walked into the kitchen.

"You can choose the paint colors and we have to pick out the appliances for in here."

"What about furniture?"

"We will need to buy some new stuff. I know some of the stuff, like the dining room table, has to stay at the old house."

"I like the big kitchen and the fact there is room in there to eat." Emmy ran a hand along the Corian Sandalwood countertop and then opened a cabinet. *These look like really well-made cabinets.*

"It's called a country kitchen. We won't need a fancy dining room in the ranch house."

They walked back into the great room. Emmy looked up. "I

396

like the high ceiling and there's a fireplace. This is a perfect little house. It feels so cozy."

"I'm glad you like it, Em."

"Can I see where the main house will be?"

"Sure, you can't see it from here, but it's not far away."

It took a few minutes to walk to the site of the main house. The work had already been started, and the basement and foundation was in place.

"The front of the house will face east. Back there is where the deck will be."

"And the pool?" Emmy asked.

"Yes, we don't have to build the pool right away, but I'd like one soon."

"This is going to be huge!" Emmy exclaimed as she stood on top of the foundation. "How long will it take to finish it?"

"Mr. Tomanek said it will take at least six to eight months minimum. Longer if we make any changes to the plan."

"So, it will be next spring before we can move in?" Emmy asked.

"Yes, but we will be able to move into the ranch house in less than a month."

Emmy was quiet for a couple of minutes, and Kenny knew something was troubling her.

"What is it, Em? I know something is bothering you."

"I still have to finish school, so I can't work." She paused before asking, "Do you know how much our monthly payments are going to be?"

"Yes, I know exactly how much they will be," Kenny answered, but then didn't say anything more.

"Well, are you going to tell me? We will need to come up with a budget."

"Em, we aren't going to have a monthly payment. Except for insurance and real estate taxes."

Emmy looked at him and didn't know whether to be mad and hit him, or to start crying—so she did a little of both.

"Are you telling me that you paid cash for all this?"

"Not yet, but we will." Kenny held her in his arms. "I

couldn't see the point of making payments for ten or twenty years when I could just pay for it now."

"But what about our income taxes?"

"I talked to Mr. Robertson, and he had his tax expert look into it and his suggestion was to pay cash. That way it is ours."

"What if the band suddenly stops making money?" she asked as she walked along the foundation. "How will we be able to keep it up?"

"The house won't take all of our money, Em. Most of it is still invested and will provide us with income for the rest of our lives even if I never make another dime from the band. I can't see that happening, but we will still be able to earn a living. There is always your royalty money. You never remember that."

"Oh, right. I guess I don't even think about that money. Maybe I should write some more lyrics for you guys. I might need the extra cash down the road."

"There is always the little trust fund your grandpa set up," Kenny said. *I can't wait to see if it's just a savings bond or something more substantial. Of course, it if was something more, Diane would have told you since she's already over twenty-five.*

"Maybe we can buy a chair or something with Grandpa's trust money?"

"See, you don't need to worry about money, but I know you will."

Emmy turned and faced the road. "Will we be able to see Kristen's or Tony's house from ours when they are all finished?"

"Not unless we tear down all the woods." Kenny grinned. "The construction has started on their houses, too. They will be done about the same time as ours, or maybe even sooner."

"I don't want to do that. We can have fun playing hide and seek in the woods," Emmy told him as though they were both kids again.

Chapter Forty-Two

Tony called Emmy on Sunday evening and asked, "Are you busy in the morning? Wanna go with me to pick up John and Kristen?"

"Yeah, I'll go. What time do we have to be there?"

"Their flight arrives at eight-thirty, so we need to be there shortly after that. We should leave by seven-fifteen. Can you get out of bed that early?" Tony asked.

She laughed. "It won't be easy, but I'll manage it."

Kenny and Emmy were eating breakfast when Tony arrived the next morning.

"Good morning, guys. I see you made it up in time, Em."

"We've been up since six. What time did you get out of bed?" Emmy asked as she finished her pancakes.

"About twenty minutes ago. Are you ready to hit the road?"

"Give me a minute to make a pit stop, and I'll be ready."

Emmy kissed Kenny on her way out the door, and she and Tony headed up to the airport. The drive wasn't too bad—just the usual bumper-to-bumper traffic. They arrived at O'Hare just a few minutes late. Tony dropped Emmy off and parked his GMC Envoy. He rejoined Emmy and five minutes later she saw Kristen.

"Krissy! Krissy!" Emmy hollered as she ran to greet her friend. "How was your honeymoon, as if I have to ask? You even look like you have a tan."

"This is the best tan I've ever had." Kristen reached out to hug Emmy.

"You look fabulous," Emmy said and then asked, "How was the sex?"

John and Tony laughed.

Kristen blushed because the people nearby heard Emmy.

"I'll tell you in the car, Em. Not in front of all these strangers."

Tony shook hands with John and helped load all the luggage onto a cart. "I told you she would ask about sex."

"I should have known." John chuckled.

"You look like you got a good tan, too. Are you glad to be home?" Emmy asked John.

"It's kinda difficult to leave paradise, but I suppose it is good to be back."

Tony added, "I put all your mail on the kitchen table. Mama said she was making dinner tonight, and you guys have to be there. She said you and Kenny could come over, Em."

"Is Sloane gonna be there?"

"Of course."

"Then we'll be there," Emmy answered.

On the ride home Emmy and Kristen sat in the back and whispered low enough so the guys couldn't hear them. Tony and John both knew what they were talking about. The girls started giggling, and John looked back at them.

"Are you sharing all the details of the last two weeks?"

Emmy answered for Kristen, "Not all of them, just the best ones."

"If I ever get married are you gonna ask me about my honeymoon?" Tony asked Emmy.

"No way! I will be consoling Sloane because I'm sure it will be torture for her to have to put up with you," Emmy teased.

They arrived at John's apartment and Tony helped carry in the luggage.

"How are you going to survive, Krissy?" Emmy asked.

"What do you mean?" Kristen tilted her head.

Emmy waved her arms. "This apartment is so small. I don't think it's as big as your bedroom at home. It's nowhere near as big as Derrick's old room. You guys should live upstairs at your parents' house."

"Em, would you want to live at my house if we were married?" Tony asked.

"I'm not married to you," she said.

"I'm asking hypothetically."

Emmy thought about that for a moment. "Oh, I get it. Even though the Keasling house is huge, you have more privacy here."

"You are so smart, Emmy," Tony said.

After carrying all the luggage inside, Tony looked at Emmy

and asked, "Are you planning to spend the day here, Em?"

"No, why? Are you in a hurry to get home?"

"Not really, but I think maybe John and Kristen... you know."

"Oh, right. I'm sorry. I wasn't thinking about that..."

"Since when?" Tony teased her.

Emmy smacked his arm and asked Kristen, "Are you guys gonna be at Mama's tonight?"

"Yes, we will be there," Kristen reassured her and then asked, "When does school start again?"

"I'm not taking any summer classes. I'm not even sure at this point if I will go back in the fall," Emmy said.

"Why? You haven't given up your dream of a college education, have you? You're so close."

"No, but I might need to take time off because of the house," Emmy explained.

"Emmy, if you don't go back in the fall, it will be that much harder for you to go back in the future."

"I know." She bit her lip. "I'll see."

"Are you thinking you will go with Kenny on the fall tour?"

"I was thinking about it, but I haven't decided for sure yet. It's just going to be a short tour to support the new CD."

"We will talk about this tonight, young lady." Kristen sounded like Mama Bertucci. "You are gonna finish college. That is an order."

"Okay." Emmy twisted her hair. "I'm so glad you're home, Krissy."

Emmy and Kenny were the last to arrive at the Bertucci home that evening. They walked in the back door and saw Tony in the kitchen.

"About time you guys got here. We were just about to start eating without you. Where have you been, or do I even need to ask?"

Emmy smacked him and said, "Is that all you ever think we do? FYI, we were discussing our plans for the fall."

Kristen heard Emmy and rushed into the kitchen. "What

401

did you decide about school?"

"I'm going back to North Park in the fall."

Kristen hugged her and whispered, "Good for you, Em. It might seem like you guys are always apart, but it will be worth it in the long run."

"Can we eat now? I'm starving," Tony said as he rubbed his stomach.

Kenny and Emmy followed Tony and Kristen into the dining room. Emmy noticed Lindsey and Cam were here in addition to everyone else she expected. Everyone sat down and then Tony stood up and smiled at Sloane.

"Before we say grace, I have an announcement to make. Yesterday I asked Sloane to marry me, and she said yes!"

"What!?" Emmy screamed.

"She did?" Lindsey shouted. "Sloane, you didn't even tell me."

"I wanted to keep it a secret until tonight."

Emmy looked around. "Does this mean I'm not the last one to know this time?"

"Yes, Em. You are hearing about it at the same time as everyone else...except..."

Emmy looked at Kristen, who was smiling.

"Krissy!" Emmy said with a trace of exasperation in her voice.

"Well, I couldn't let him pick out a ring by himself." Kristen shrugged. "You should have seen the look on Ramon's face when we went into Watson's to buy another engagement ring. I still don't think he has recovered."

John, Kenny and Cam shook hands with Tony and offered their congratulations. Sloane held up her hand to let the girls see her ring.

"When are you getting married? Where are you gonna get married?" Emmy asked. "You have to get married at the church, and you can have the reception at..."

Tony put a finger on Emmy's mouth, and she stopped talking.

"Emmy, we are going to get married in Troy, Ohio, because

that's where Sloane's family lives. We haven't decided where to have the reception, but there are several places nearby. We might have to hold the reception in Dayton."

"You will invite me to the wedding, right?" Emmy asked in all seriousness.

"I don't know. You're such a brat," Tony teased.

"Of course we will." Sloane poked Tony in the ribs. "Stop teasing her. You and Kenny have to sing for us like you did for John and Kristen."

"Do you know when yet?"

Sloane answered, "We are thinking about early June of next year. We know it will have to be after football season and before training camp. We want the weather to be nice and that rules out winter and early spring. Since we are all here, I might as well ask. Lindsey, will you be my maid of honor?"

"Of course I will, but you have to be mine if I get married."

"You know I will. And I want my sister, Meghan, to be in the wedding and I want Hannah. I want to ask you guys, too. Will you both be in my wedding?"

"Yes!" Kristen and Emmy shouted.

Emmy asked Tony, "Do you know who you want already?"

"I want John to be my best man..."

"I accept," John answered.

"And I will probably ask Derrick and Kenny. How many do I need all together?"

Sloane answered, "It would be nice if there was a guy for each girl and since I want five girls... that would be..."

"I get it. I do have a college education from one of the finest universities in the world..."

"Yeah, but you been hit in the head a lot of times, too," Emmy teased.

"You better behave, little girl, or else I will hang you from the ceiling... permanently!"

Emmy stuck out her tongue at Tony and giggled.

"You need to find two more guys."

"I will have to give this some more thought. I would like to ask Marco."

403

"That would be a good choice," Mama said.

"I'm still good friends with Marcellus Bell. I'll ask him if that's all right."

"Why wouldn't it be all right?" Emmy asked. "So he plays for the Bengals. Big deal."

"I've met Marcellus, and he would be perfect," Sloane said and then kissed Tony.

"Who's that?" Lindsey asked.

"He played football at Notre Dame with Tony, and now he plays for the Cincinnati Bengals," Kristen answered.

Emmy looked at Mama and asked, "Did you know about this before tonight?"

"Of course, dear, I know everything," Mama said as she smoothed out her dress. She didn't sound convincing.

"You didn't know, did you?" Emmy shrieked. "For once we have managed to surprise Mama."

"Yes, I admit it. I was not prepared for the announcement, but I am so thrilled to be caught off-guard. Did you call your parents, Sloane?"

"Yes, we called them last night and told them."

They managed to eat and talk about the wedding and John and Kristen's honeymoon without too much discussion about Emmy's favorite topic.

"Everything is delicious, Mama," John said later. "I've missed your cooking."

"I can always make extra for you, John."

Kristen froze with a fork full of spaghetti in midair. "That's not fair. You need to eat what I make."

"No! No! No!" Emmy waved her hands and grinned. "Krissy, he needs to maintain his weight. He might get too skinny and get cut from the team. Then he would have to get a real job, and what's even worse... You might have to go back to work, too."

"You are so funny, Em. I do know how to boil water now, and Sainsbury's has an excellent selection of ready-to-eat meals," Kristen said.

"I will be happy to give you some lessons, dear," Mama said as she patted Kristen's hand. "Emmy didn't know how to cook when she met Tony and now she's an excellent cook."

"Thank you, Mama." Kristen set her fork on her plate. "FYI, I checked my email this afternoon and saw one from Diana Barclay."

"Did she have a baby?" Emmy asked.

"Baby boy and they named him Davis Henry Barclay."

"That sounds like a rather formal name," Lindsey said.

Kristen explained some of the history of the Barclay family.

"So their ancestors really knew George Washington, huh?" Cam pushed his glasses into place.

"I'm not sure, but I think the Barclays owned a plantation even bigger than Mount Vernon," Kristen said.

After dinner, the conversation turned to the band's new CD.

"What is it going to be called?" John asked.

"*Common Experience* and the release date is set for October fifth as of now. We are nearly finished, so I don't think we will have any trouble with getting it ready by then."

"Are you guys gonna tour in the fall?" Mama asked.

"Yes, but not for very long. It will be a short tour, but we might go out again in the summer of 2005. We just have to see how everyone feels."

Emmy held up her hand and grinned. "We have more news..."

"Emmy, are you pregnant?" Kristen shouted.

Kenny's jaw dropped as Emmy smiled.